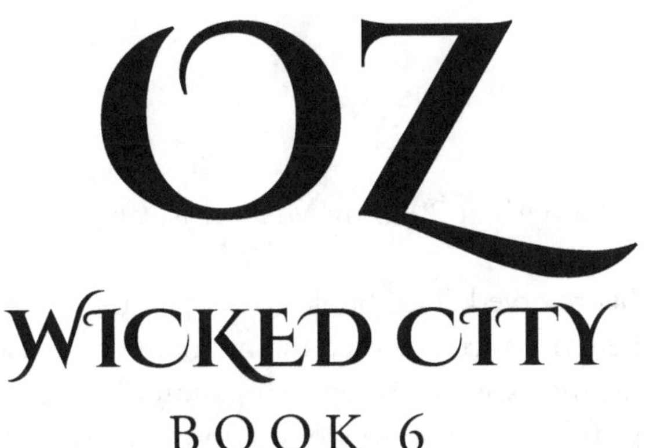

OZ
WICKED CITY

BOOK 6

MICHAEL R. OSBORNE

ISBN 978-1-961017-20-7 (Paperback)
ISBN 978-1-961017-21-4 (Ebook)

Inquiries and Book Orders should be addressed to:

Leavitt Peak Press
17901 Pioneer Blvd Ste L #298, Artesia, California 90701
Phone #: 2092191548

Michael R Osborne
31 Pine Dr.
Byron, Ga. 31008
Phone 1 478 956 4839

Sir,

Please read this humble fifth novel I am sending you for your fair
deliberation on the viability if it is worth the effort for me to have
published. I have written several other books and upon my personal
review decided not to peruse. With encouragement from wife and
friends who have taken the time to read this novel, they have offered
a very persuasive argument for the publishing of this story. I am cur-
rently writing a sequel to this story whether it is published or not.
This is one of my personal goals to achieve. As a retired teacher I
endeavored to teach my students to set goals and then go and achieve
them. I look forward to every one of those students to finally see the
one of many goals I have spoken to them, I planned on attaining.

If it is not too much trouble, please send the disc back if you do not
see the merit in it to publish. I will continue to find someone who
will. I do thank you for reading this story.

ABOUT THE AUTHOR

Michael Osborne a son of a Robert F Osborne Navy Chief Torpedoman and a southern belle Evelyn Spivey both deceased. One of three siblings and a twin to one. The only sibling to graduate High School and College. He graduated with a BS in Geology from Ga. Southwestern College and later received a MS in Educational Science from Ft. Valley State College. Created his own business doing clock repair which he learned from a local jeweler. He entered the U.S. Navy and deplored on a WESPAC, then completed twenty-one years total active and reserves, attaining the same rank of his father Chief Instrument man. Michael went on to earn several black belts in many Martial Arts disciplines as well as certification in sport diving. He set many goals for himself and strived to achieve each one. He refers himself to people as an over educated fool. He trained on various office machines, postal machines, copiers, engraving, jeweler repair, projectionist. When he is not busy, he builds scaled hand-crafted wooden ships, winning many firsts at State Fair. One of my greatest achievements was being a grade school teacher. The other was marrying his wife Dorothy, his partner and friend for life, so far thirty-eight years. He has written two unpublished books. This book was his first attempt in having published a book. In this book I hope the many adventures and some of my life lessons can inspires others to take the bull by the horns and do it.

ACKNOWLEDGEMENTS

This story is partly true. A whole lot of other unmentionables items were inspired and supported by my loving wife, Dorothy of 38 years, without her encouragements may not have been possible. Many of the stories I share have characters I meet in this adventure come from my many studies and encounters with people. Some of these stories were taught to my students. I used many of these stories as a teacher to provide lessons in life. I hope you who read this book enjoy my way of telling a story.

PROLOGUE

Mike had been captured by a CIA agent on a mission to make contact with a known Muslim terrorist. On board the plane was the one man, Mike sought to kill but could not deliver the lethal blow. The plane was shot down over the desert. After weeks of fighting the terrorist in the desert, a legend begun. OZ, known to the terrorist as the red glowing face demon and OZ to the Americans. He crossed the desert waging a battle to prevent the innocent peoples killed by the terrorist while seeking to locate his companions on the downed cargo plane. He learned they were held captive in a prison city many miles from where he was advancing. It was a chance encounter with two American snipers on a roof-top in the same city he went into to end the terrorist he been tracking. Terminating all the terrorist he surprised the two snipers. After discovering the unknown person was a young man that took out all the terrorist in the town single handedly, they fed him and gave him directions to the prison city. Unknown to Mike as he journeyed across the scorching desert, his father was coming for him. Cho followed after his lost son. Finally, both met at Twin Mountains and the cave people's haven. Together, Cho and Mike fought an epic battle.

Now, Cho and Mike travel to a remote island to be with their love ones. A party was given for Mike. The happiness ended shortly. Cheryl stormed out of the hotel. Bad people found her. Now, Mike and Cho and all the leadership must find her before Cheryl will be lost to them forever. Two new battles begin, one, Mike may not win. The other, Cho and Mike will fight changing the direction of their lives.

CONTENTS

1. An Island Resort...1

2. Mouth Blisters...12

3. Gone Missing...32

4. Second Time at the Same Bar.................................45

5. A Third Time Again...52

6. No Good to Run and Hide.................................59

7. The Split Up...71

8. The Night Went All Wrong.................................77

9. To Many on the Beach...98

10. Cheryl's Dilemma...111

11. The Blast...121

12. An Explanation...127

13. Gathering Storm...134

14. E R Stat...153

15. Two are Better than One.................................160

16. The Next Day...185

17. Room 311 on Third Street.................................193

18. A One Eye Mama...206

19. Trouble Back Home...212

20. Leaving is Hard...220

21. Homeward...236

22. Unexpected Shot...252

23. Wedding Bells...262

24. The Appointment...273

25. The Trial...278

26. The Punishment...297

27. War Comes...305

28. To Many Red Glowing Faces.................................323

29. Mainland 346
30. A Hole in the Escape Plan 363
31. Forest Screams...378
32. The Deal 385
33. Lost At Sea 394

AN ISLAND RESORT

The night was young. Dinner was served and the band played while everyone enjoyed their meal. After the meal, drinks were ordered all around by Chopper. Cheryl and Judy were permitted to drink. Judy was eighteen and hadn't need to get permission from her parents. Cheryl, on the other hand, looked at her mom nodding her approval. Mike never drank much. He decided to join in on the festive occasion and ordered a beer.

Everyone man finished with the first swallow, of their drinks, then a signal was sent to each man at the table by their wives. It was more of a look, than an asking. The meaning was clear. Every man ignored the silent request and guzzled the contents of their glass and asked for a second, then a third drink. Each man figured wearing their monkey suits was worth the scorn of nasty stares from their wives.

All the men stood taking each wife in hand to the dance floor. Pretty escorted Judy only after Jack escorted Rhoda to the dance floor. The only persons at the table not dancing, were Susan, Cheryl, and Mike. Mike looked at Cheryl and stood by her chair. Cheryl asked if she could decline. Her excuse was the foot shot at the gates exiting the Valley of the Pyramids by one of the gate guards was still bothering her. She drive through the gates as Mike kept the soldiers rushing to the gates occupied. All went well until she was shot. The truck, out of control went running up the side of the hill, turning over. She was trapped inside. The truck caught fire. Pretty ran from his sniping position to free her from the truck just as the other bikers crashed through the gates entering into the on-going battle Mike and Master Cho were engaging in. Cheryl grew strong venturing through the deep jungle after Mike rescued her from the pirates. She was a warrior and no longer a teenage girl.

Mike stood by her chair with a somewhat, "what should I do expression," on his face. Susan readily solved his problem standing to accept a dance in Cheryl's stead.

Both Susan and Mike walked to the center of the floor. Mike was a bit timid about putting his arm around her. She stood there in front of Mike with a beautiful smile accompanied with both arms held out to receive his embrace. Cheryl sat at her table and called for the waiter. She never looked at her mom with Mike on the dance floor. The waiter arrived.

"Please bring me another one of these."

"Yes madame."

Before the first steps with Susan, the waiter returned with another glass of red wine. Cheryl immediately gulped the glass down, then ordered another.

Neither Susan nor Mike saw her get her second drink nor her third and fourth glass of wine. Each of them felt the warmth of the other's body touching swaying to the music. Mike held Susan tight against him. Susan offered no resistance.

To Mike, he lacked formal training and was awkward in his dancing. Holding Susan was for security and to keep from stepping on her toes. That, he done the first step within the first minute. Susan excepted each apology with a smile. Mike sensed Susan seemingly prefer Mike holding her closer.

Everyone turned to look at the two dancing together. Susan wearing her long flowing blue chiffon evening gown and Mike in his tuxedo. Both looked like the king and queen of the ball. As if by some magical command, everyone halted dancing, stepping to the edge of the dance floor to watch the two dances.

Bell watched with tears in her eyes. Laura was beaming with happiness, and Cheryl, finally looked at her mom and Mike dancing. Bell had tears seeing her young man happy. Laura saw his love for Susan shine brightly and glad he was not alone. Cheryl saw Mike torn from her by her mom and rage filled her heart.

Bell recalled the time back home, "she worried about Mike's flying off on the plane chasing One Eye from the Valley of the Pyramids. When she was told, the plane was heading to the Mid-East, she and all the women went into hysteria. News came trickling back from Cho reports. Days would go by with not a word."

Bell sighed a relief hearing Cho located his son in the desert. She had not heard about their adventures at that time. Chopper kept that news private, so as to not worry the women.

The first report came to the club while still in Texas, "he was presumed dead. The plane crashed, sand pirates attacked, the crew escaped into the desert, Mike went off to look for help, a sand storm lasted for days. The crew was found and Mike was missing."

The second report was just as horrible. "Mike was alive, attacked some Black Muslim terrorist group, then a fortress filled with soldiers, a red glowing eyed demon was discovered. More attacks, and Cho reported, he learned Mike was walking across a desert to a prison city, to save some members of the plane's crew."

The last report was wonderful news. "Mike was alive. A great battle at the Twin Mountains, many soldiers killed, people rescued and a battle ensued to help some cave people, and the Army is flying them home."

After the first dance ended, Mike and Susan remained on the dance floor. All the other men had done the same. When the second dance ended, all the married men took their wives back to the table. Cheryl was still sitting and ordered her fifth drink.

Cheryl began to take notice of her mom and Mike when she did not return to the table with the others. The only persons on the dance floor was Pretty with Judy and Mike with Susan.

Few words were spoken by any of the riders returning to their tables. No one wanted to break the spell the two couples were enjoying. No one spoke, except Jimmie and Jamie drunk at the table. Before either had the opportunity to make a silly comment, both were given a drink with a strong insistence to drink it. Master Cho sensing no good was going to be said by either man he walked across the desert with. Their drunken comments would break the spell of the moment. Mike deserved this one moment and he made sure his son would have it, uninterrupted.

No one knew that Cheryl had taken some pain medicine for her foot. She continued to receive pain medicine coming home. After several weeks had past, the wound was nearly healed, the doctor wanted to take her off the medicine. He gave her a prescription for the last time.

"Cheryl, you shouldn't have much pain by now," the doctor told her.

"Doc, it still hurts so much, when I walk on it."

"The more you walk on your foot, there will be pain. That pain will quickly go away with exercise, Cheryl," replied the doctor.

Cheryl told the doctor, "I am trying to walk every day as required."

Unbeknownst to Cheryl, Susan conveyed to the doctor, she mainly laid around the house, watching TV.

It came to little surprise to Cheryl, when Bell made a comment about how many glasses of wine, she had ordered. She saw two drinks polished off and a third drink arriving. It was the fifth drink the waiter was returning with.

Bell stared at Cheryl lending across the table. It was a very familiar sight she knew all to-well with men and women, drunk. Cheryl was nearly at the onset of passing out. Bell assumed, "she could not hold her liquor."

Bell was unaware of the pain medicine Cheryl had taken before coming down to dinner. Also, she and others were unaware of her afternoon purchases the day before, the men returned to the isle. She met with a man on the streets going to the beach with Judy. To make Bell's ignorance even more profane, she assumed Cheryl only had two drinks.

Cheryl stood by her chair nearly topping the chair over and her with it. If not for Bell's quick response grabbing her, she would be lying on the floor. One wine glass Cheryl was holding spilt on the table and dripped down on Cheryl green gown. Watching her mom dance with her boyfriend evoked a horrible outburst. Cheryl jerked her arm from Bell's grasped then shouted to Mike and her mom engaged in a tightly held embrace.

"Mom, that is my boyfriend you are squeezing so tight against, in your arms. You get any closer to him, you to better get a room." Cheryl unloaded her glass in the direction of Mike. He ducked. The glass shattered against the wall.

Susan heard the outcry and pushed away from Mike. Mike turned to see Chery being propped up by Bell at the table while ducking the wine glass thrown at him. Susan quickly makes her way to her daughter. She immediately takes hold of Cheryl's arm. Cheryl reacted, pulling abruptly away from her grasp. With that yank from her mother's arms, Cheryl falls to the ground. Mike was quick to move to catch her before she splattered flat on the dance floor.

"Calm yourself down, Cheryl. I am with you. Let me help you back to the table."

Cheryl tried to resist Mike's hold on her. When that failed, she began a barrage of curse words directed at Susan and Mike.

"Get your stinking, cheating hands off me. You are a two-timing son-of-a-bitch. You and my mom, she couldn't get her own man, now she steals mine." Mike heard the accusation, stunning him.

"Cheryl, what are you screaming about. Susan, your mom, and I were just dancing. Nothing more."

"You look at my mom, I see you look at her. She does the same to you. You ain't fooling anybody."

"Your mom is a beautiful woman. Any man would look at her. I never told you, you were my girlfriend or me your boyfriend. I told you; I care a great deal for you. I told you before we ever saw each other, there could never be anything more than good friends. My path leads me in other directions. There is no time for me to expect anyone, to get close to. I cannot at this time, put you or anyone in danger. Not until my life is more stable."

Cheryl would not listen. Susan tried to keep Cheryl calm. Cheryl would have nothing of the kind. The wine opened her hidden feelings. Those feelings, she thought about, kept deep inside. They never came out. In the jungle, "she felt Mike and her were becoming more than friends. She thought, there was a growing love building between them."

In truth, Mike had strong feeling about her. The long trek in the desert allowed him to search his soul on many topics. The one thought that plagued him the most, "was not about her and him, but of Cho and Laura. He saw Cheryl placed in the same environment as Laura was in. How could he ever put someone he loved in that danger and fear of losing him forever on a mission. He saw the hurt in Susan's eyes every time he left to go on a mission. He was feeling pain in his heart of not being with both of them. One day he came to realize it was not Cheryl he was longing for, but for a Susan."

Cho lived a dangerous lifestyle. He was living in Cho footsteps with danger. Cho was getting married, soon. "Why couldn't he entertain such feelings for a girl. One argument kept winning over the other. That one argument that won, was that Cho been living this life many years and was ready to settle down. Me, I been at this just over a year and have many years ahead of me, before marriage. Not now. Not now," Mike shouted to himself, even as he looked at Susan with longing eyes.

"Cho will be married, maybe having children, I will be called upon for my skills, more often. I cannot allow father Cho, to put his family and happiness on the line. He deserves time to have love, me, I got years ahead of me."

Mike realized, "his thoughts were wandering to Susan often. He had to suppress those feeling, because of Cho and Laura. When he thought of Cheryl, they were mixed with memories of Susan. The two never seemed to be separate."

Every time Mike tried to hold Cheryl, to give comfort, she jerked away. It has been a long time for Cheryl to ponder her life with Mike, while he was away in the desert. Too long a time passed, she was using much more pain killers. Mainly, for the pain at first, then to conceal her pain for Mike not being home with her to provide comfort in her time of need. Her thoughts searched her soul. Those thoughts were not very kind to her."

"Some of the thoughts focused on her inability to stop using pain killers. Cheryl soon realized; she enjoyed them too much to stop. She remembered what Mike told her on the way back to the city, after visiting his family. Mike made a comment to her.

"I would never marry a woman, who drank or smoked. I lived with that person all my life. All that person can think about, is himself. My mom told us she would have gotten rid of us, if not for the government checks, we received, Mike, Mike said, said, said, and said repeating over and over in Cheryl's thoughts how he abhorred people that drank, took drugs, or smoked, or had any compulsive habit."

"Every month, more than half of their government check's income went solely to his mom's booze and cigarettes. She was going to drink and smoke. Her whole life, centered on her needs," Mike commented on his mom and their life.

"Why have children, if that is your sole concerns, to satisfy your needs and not your children. They interfere with those needs. Mike asked himself? Never a week went by, before his mom had to buy booze. Three or four days was the longest time she could remain sober. When she started to drink, after going without booze, was a catchup period. She would get stone drunk for weeks. Our lives would be hell," Mike told me.

"The one thing that Mike told me was, the worst times was when she drank hard liquor. She would scream, the whole time at them all day and night, until the alcohol was drunk. Beer was kind to them, it had not the same effect. Never, never would he live that way again," Cheryl recalled.

"Now, what will Mike do when he discovers, I have been talking all these pain killers, when I don't need to. This plagued Cheryl's thoughts constantly. She was quick to find another reason for Mike, to not want her. She noticed, when the first time they met each other. Mom and him, seemed to like each other a lot. Maybe she is trying to take Mike from me? Mom likes Mike. I saw the way mom catered to him. He comes to dinner and she makes his favorite meal. She asks me all the time, how he is doing?"

"Look at them on the dance floor. They are dancing really close. He trying to hold me, now. Trying to make me feel, he cares about me. Mom standing next to him, while he is holding me. They can't stay away from each other. That proves it," Cheryl realizing the truth, shouting at both of them.

"Leave me alone, get away from me," she screams at Susan.

"Cheryl, stop it. I'm taking you to your room."

"I'm not going with either of you two. I'm leaving here now," replied Cheryl with scorn in her words.

Bell stands and hurries over to Susan's aid. Mike steps away from the two women struggling. Bell grabs hold of Cheryl's arm. Together, Susan and Bell manage to calm her down.

Just as sudden, the yelling had erupted, came a quiet down. Cheryl allowed her mom and Bell to escort her to her room. Before they got to the dining room entrance, Cheryl grabs hold of her necklace, tearing it from around her neck. Holding the emerald and diamond necklace in her hand, quickly throws it toward Mike.

"Here, you can have them. I bought them, because I knew you liked emeralds. Now, I don't want them. You keep them. Maybe, they will show you what you lost tonight."

Mike bends down picking up the necklace. He looked at Cho and Laura for advice.

"Mike, my son, keep the necklace. Maybe with time passing, she will want them back."

"Mike," Laura rushes over to him, placing her arms around him then sits beside him. "Cheryl had to many drinks. She will be sorry in the morning."

"Laura," Mike turns to look her. "Cheryl knows how I feel about drinking. For some reason, this has been building inside her. I guess, all this time away has provided her with thoughts, she feels we don't share. She is right about Susan. I do have strong feelings for her."

Turning to look at the people sitting at the table, Mike realized he said to much. "I have care about Susan from the first time, I met her. I never wanted anything to blossom from that meeting. I kept my feeling in check. Cho was training me. I knew my life was going to change. I kept a distance from Cheryl. She made that easy at first. Her hated for me, assured that any feelings would never grow. It did, and I told her, I cared a lot for her. I also expressed that there could never be anything, other than friends."

"Susan and I had a sit-down conversation about Cheryl and myself. I told Susan how, I felt. She asked me to come to her, if there was anything more than friendship between Cheryl and myself. I did, but I told her there would never be more than that. I couldn't allow for those types of feelings, then and now." Mike looks at the leaders sitting at the table watching him.

"Cho, Chopper, Jack, Razor, I swear, I tried to maintain a friendship. I got the rest of my life to live and having a wife would put her in danger. I would be away for long periods of time. Just look what occurred. I've been gone for months. Now, this happens, only proves I was correct." Cho stood walking over to Mike.

"My son, I had the same thoughts, when I was young. I had many women that broke my heart. They could not accept my lifestyle. I found one. It took time, but she was worth the time."

Laura blew a kiss to Cho. "Got it babe," replied Cho snatching the invisible kiss coming his way.

"Better."

Chopper, spoke up, "Mike, it is a good thing it happened now. In a way, this was the best. You really had mixed feelings. To make a commitment with half-hearted feelings is not a good foundation to build upon."

"He right, Mike. It takes a special woman to deal with our lifestyle." Razor wraps his arm around his wife.

"Mike, Susan spoke to me when she first met you. She has feeling for you. It was too soon after Stephen's death. She mentioned that. Well, let's say she is a fine woman. Let time heals her wounds. Cheryl has made some serious remarks, that will need to be address between her and Susan."

"Thanks, Miriam."

"Hey kiddo, how you like your massage and haircut." Penny elbows Bone. He turns to her; "I'm just trying to change the topic and smiles."

"Massage; Cho, you said nothing about a massage. Was she pretty, quipped Laura?"

"No, she was a he, besides, I needed a good massage."

"I could have done that, Cho."

"Babe, you did plenty, besides, we got the massage while you women went shopping again."

"Well, my masseur was a woman. She wore me out. She found spots on my body to massage, I never thought were there. I will admit, after her rubbing my body, I felt much better. The haircut was great. She wanted to shave me. I told her there wasn't anything to shave on my face," commented Mike.

"You got that right, Kiddo. That baby face won't be growing any hair, for a long time. Ha, ha, ham chided Bone."

Upstairs, Bell and Susan got Cheryl to her room. Inside, they aided her in undressing. Soon, Cheryl laid in bed. Not long after, Cheryl was asleep. Outside the bedroom, Bell and Susan talked.

"Susan, why is she so upset with Mike? He just got home. I thought, while we were in Mexico, they were getting along fabulous. Then, returning home, all she could do was talk about Mike. Why this sudden change?"

"Bell, I think Cheryl has a problem."

Bell sits and takes Susan's hand to have her sit beside her. This was a swank hotel. Each room had a bath, bedroom, and a sitting room. All rooms were separated by a wall and door. Cheryl's door was closed.

"Bell, I'm afraid she has been taking more medicine, than the doctor had prescribed to her."

"How do you know that, Susan?"

"It occurred to me several weeks past. She constantly complained about her foot hurting. When she came home, the pain was nearly gone. After a week, the pain returned. I took her to the doctors. He gave her some pain killers. Now, now she is in constant pain. She takes pills every day. The doctor told me the wound was healed. He told me, he was not going to refill her prescription for pain killers. I don't know where she gets those pills. I asked her about the pills," she was taking. She replied, "they were candy."

"Bell. A short pause elapsed before Susan spoke again. Bell, she has been going places by herself."

"Judy told me yesterday, when they went to the beach, Cheryl told her to walk there and she would meet her. Judy placed the blanket out and went to look for Cheryl. She spied her on the street, talking to a stranger. She gave him something and he handed her something back. Judy rushed back to the beach to wait for her. When they came back, she told me what she saw."

"Susan, you need to check her stuff. If she is taking some drugs, it is best you find out now, before it is too late. We can still help her, before this gets out of hand."

"I want her to trust me."

"Trust is a two-way street. She lies to you and does this meeting with strangers behind your back. Trust, that is not trust, Susan! Susan, that won't do her any good. She is beyond that. She is beginning to care more about her drugs than she is for you or that matter, anybody. She is going to harm herself. We got to intervene now, while we can."

"I know, it hurts to think my little girl has gotten this way."

"It happens to the best of people. You have seen this, as I have."

Susan begins to cry.

Bell takes her in her arms. "Kids will break your heart or make you proud. We are family, Susan. You will not be doing this alone. We are here."

"Thank you. Will you tell the others for me?"

"Yes, when we get back. Tonight, check Cheryl's things. Tomorrow, we will enjoy the stay on the island. It will be a new day. With this problem, it is best to take one day at a time. We will get through this."

"What about Mike?"

"Susan, Mike is a bright man. He has proven himself to be that. He is a wonderful man. I wish I could get together with him. Believe me, you are not the only one in this club, who has not considered Mike as a sexy man." Bell winks at her.

Susan smiles back. "Yes."

MOUTH BLISTERS

Mike sat looking at Penny sitting next to Bone. Bone watched Mike sitting alone, pouting. Everyone was sitting around the large table drinking. Talking seemed to end once Bell and Susan escorted Cheryl upstairs to her room. It was quickly guessed after her explosion and accusation, that Susan and Mike were an item.

"How you doing big guy? The last we saw each other was at the river. You were being carried back to the Citadel after some pirate ambushed your rafts going down the river. You were bleeding from a gunshot wound. Jack and I went after the others held hostage by the pirates. We had to separate, when the pirate divided. Jimmie was taken by one group of pirates and Cheryl with the other group."

"Well, thanks for remembering me old friend."

"Hey, I just got back, Bone. You were never out of my thoughts. The long walks in the desert gave me plenty of time to reflect on my life. I learned how important this family is to me. So, don't go weeping tears about my realizing I love you all."

Penny slaps Bone on his hand. "Don't be like that. You been worrying the whole time Mike was away. Tell him that and quick acting like he was just any biker in the club." Penny turns to Mike. "Bone, he has trouble expressing his concerns, Mike."

"I know Penny, what he really meant to tell me is, he was happy I came home in his own way." Bone smiles.

"See the kid knows me better than you do, Babe."

"Gee Bone, you really been that worried about me, replied Mike making his words more in a sneer?" Bones turns to his wife with a rebuttal.

"Dang baby, why you go and tell him that? Now, he is gonna think I give a damn about him. He going to come and whine to me whenever he feels bad."

"You do Bone, and you love it when he comes to you with a problem. Why you got to keep this a secret, is beyond me."

Pretty breaks in, "it's a man thing, Penny."

"That's okay Penny. I like Bone too. He just can't get over me beating him eating that Chinese hot mustard contest we had," snickered Mike.

Bones head snapped back toward Mike. His eyes grew in size. Mike knew he got a nerve. He prepared for Bone's reseating him, a normal response he often got teasing Bone. Chopper had to put a halt to this slamming Mike down on chairs, when many of the club chairs were busted. It got expensive replacing the chairs.

"You cheated; you know it. I won. What was so bad, you go and let me think I won the contest. I ain't no pity case, kiddo. If not for Bell spilling the beans about it, you would let me go on thinking, I won. That is what boils my hemorrhoids and gets me mad."

"I never cheated. I learned how to eat hot mustard before the contest. By the way, it was with peppers; I wasn't sure it would work with mustard. Any ways you never said nothing about rules on what we drank."

"Hot is hot and you couldn't win now with hot tea or milk. If you drank milk, I could have excused that trick. You are still, just a baby, needing his milk." Now it was Bone that got to a nerve in Mike.

"You calling me a baby, who was doing the coughing with tears pouring down his cheeks? Baby, heck, you are the big baby. Next time no hot tea. I still will beat you and I won't let you win. I just didn't want to take your trophy from you. I liked you. Now that's different. This time, the trophy is mine to keep. Baby, am I? You going down, big man."

"Yeah, we see about that, Baby boy." Bone sticks his tongue out at Mike.

Mike stands, "you're on, man."

Bones stands, "Yeah, never happens, you are a wimp. You're be crying as soon a one of those hot pepper touches those tender lips." Bone slams his chair from the table. Hey waiter, you got any hot peppers in the kitchen?

One waiter walks timidly over to the towering giant fuming mad at a young man half his size. "Yes, yes sir. They have several varieties of hot peppers."

"You got ghost peppers?"

Cho abruptly stands. "Bone, those might be a bit too much for my son. He never ate them."

"Cho, this is between the kid and me. That is, if he is old enough and bad enough, as he thinks he is," snickers Bone wishing he made that response to Master Cho less harsh than what was said by him.

Mike responds, "the bigger they are, the harder they fall. Penny, get a stretcher ready for your man. They be needing to cart him off to the nearest hospital."

Mike returns Bone gaze with his own steely eyed look. Both stood face to face attempting to stare down the other. Bone had the advantage, being several feet the taller of the two.

Cho walks over to his son. "My son, you need to back down to this challenge. Those are the hottest peppers on the planet. They can be pretty rough to eat."

Mike turns to his father; "I will allow him to win without my tricks. I know I can't win but I will give him his contest. This has been brooding within him for some time. His pride was wounded. I want our friendship to be strong and not harbor any resentments."

The waiter returns with a tray loaded with peppers. All the waiters were putting bets on who was going to win. Soon, all the bikers were placing their bets. Bone was the sure thing with the waiters and Mike was with the bikers.

Mike looked at the peppers with trepidations. He whispers to his father, "might as well get this over so we can start anew, Cho."

Cho shakes his head. He understood Mike's reasons and agreed to it. Still, he had much concerns for Mike.

Bone steps next to Mike. A hard slap followed on Mike's back. "Well kiddo, we'll do this without nothing to drink. Just eat and swallow."

"Bone don't do this," plead Penny. Bone held his hand up to stop her pleading.

"Penny, I love you, but this has to be decided once and for all."

"Penny, Bone is right. He deserves a re-bout for the title. That trick of mine made him look bad. He might have won the contest if not for the hot tea. This will finally settle this. The game rules were, you could drink anything you wanted. I knew the hot tea would stop the mustard from burning and he didn't. This time, we both begin with the same understandings."

Bone began to feel bad about harboring his feeling about the contest. "Mike was correct. He agreed to allow any drink they wanted. Still losing was a bitter pill to swallow," was his thinking before the match began.

Mike looked at Bone, "hey big guy, one thing I should inform you about. I been in the desert for some time. Some of the foods I been eating, was very spicy. I got used to that kind of food. This ain't going to be no push over win for you, buddy."

"Good, that the way I want it to be." Bone lifts a pepper off the tray. Before he eats it, he turns to the waiter; these are the hottest you got, right?"

"Yes sir," responded the waiter staring up at the huge giant not smiling at him.

"Good, okay kiddo, pick your death."

Mike reaches into the tray grabbing a pepper equal to the one Bone chose.

Bone looks at Mike's choice; "good, see you chose a man size pepper. Hate to beat you with a baby pepper."

Mike shoves the pepper into his mouth. Bone quickly follows.

One bite, then almost a second chomp on the pepper with fire erupting in Mike's mouth. Mike swallows the pepper immediately, hoping that the burning would cease in his mouth. Bone continued to chew on his pepper. Mike marveled at the way Bone seemed to display no affects.

Bone watched Mike swallowing the pepper nearly whole. Mike was unaware that the pepper would not stop burning. Bone knew the pepper in his stomach could cause severe reactions.

"Mike, I see you swallowed your pepper, the next one you got to chew it. Grab a second pepper. I will give the hand signal for the both of us to swallow after we thoroughly chew on it." Bone was hoping the longer Mike chewed on the pepper will make him quick, before any harm to his empty stomach.

Mike nodded to Bone. His throat was burning. Talking would give Bone a hint to his condition. He was having trouble breathing. Mike thought, "even if he could answer Bone, he wouldn't be able to speak. Probably never again if he lasted through this contest."

Bone reached for another large pepper. Mike chose one not quite as large. It did not go un-notice by Bone nodding to Mike, before putting the large pepper in his mouth.

"Bone knew, the first pepper got to Mike right-off. It got to him. He had forgotten how bad these peppers could burn in your mouth. He started to have second thoughts. Unbeknownst to Mike, Bone was burning. He still had a few more he could handle. He looked at Mike's second choice determining, he was nearly through."

Both chewed on their peppers. Mike chew was much slower with fewer chomps. Mike's face was red, now it was becoming an ashen shade of pale. Both eyes were tearing. A cough, then another cough followed with some of the pepper spitted out onto the floor. Still, Mike would not concede, he chewed.

Mike was hurting bad. It showed on his face. Laura and Penny's concerns were valid. Bone was having second thoughts and began to consider letting Mike have this win.

"Mike is my little buddy and this was a silly contest to have, just as he came home, alive. This was to be a celebration and I ruined it with my pride. Besides, my belly really could not deal with this hot food. Being shot in the jungle and eating food gave me stomach poisoning. I never had the same hard gut, I once had after that mission. Bone knew sleeping would come with a terrible heartburn, keeping him up all night."

Bone watched Mike nearly hurls all his pepper. He could see Mike struggling to keep the pepper in his mouth. He chewed keeping the pepper in his mouth. Bone smiled at Mike. Bone swallowed his pepper. Mike saw his signal and tried to swallow his. His mouth was numb.

Bone was about to quit and give Mike the win. Bell with Susan returned to the dining room. Bell saw Mike reeling. Susan screamed. Each ran to Mike.

Mike turned white as a sheet and began gagging. Cho watched Mike knowing, he was going into shock. Bell also realized his condition. Susan saw Mike falling gasping for air.

Cho reached Mike first, cradling him in his arms before he hit the floor. Penny seized Bone's arm. Jamie quipped out a snide remark.

"Hey, the kid can't take a few hot peppers." He never finished the remaining words of his cute jest. Chopper slapped him on his head. Jamie felt the bump before he passed out. The table received a shockwave tumbling over several glasses of wine.

Cho began squeezing Mike's abdomen with strong inward thrusts. Pepper pulp flew from Mike's mouth across the table adhering to Bone's dinner jacket. Both Penny and Bone swung around the table to offer help. Bone told the waiter to bring hot tea.

The waiter quickly returned with hot milk. He thought milk would work better.

"Dam you, don't make me tell you again," shouted Bone to the waiter returning with milk. Bell took the glass and made Mike sip it. The waiter saw this giant snarl and ran back to the kitchen. He needed no second request. Swiftly returning with hot tea.

Mike drank the milk and several glasses of water waiting for his cure. The milk or the water was not having any effect on his burning mouth and belly. Suddenly, Mike's belly began to heave uncontrollably. Then, his body began to shake. Susan was crying. Bell grabbed her.

The hot tea arrived. Penny put the cup with hot tea to Mike's mouth. He spit most of the first swallow out. His shaking continued. Penny handed the cup to Cho's outreach hand. Holding Mike tight, he forces the tea in his mouth. Mike swallowed. Soon, the shaking ended. Cho stood lifting his son to his feet.

Mike spoke, "father, the burning has ceased in my mouth, but my stomach is burning. I can feel it bubbling. The hot tea, I can feel the tea getting to my belly. It seems to dilute the acid and pulp of the pepper. Still, it burns."

Bell could feel Susan shake. She speaks softly to her; "Mike is having an allergic reaction to the peppers." Mike doubled over with cramps in Cho's arms. Susan reached for Mike.

Bone takes Mike's hand, "little buddy, you going to be alright."

Mike turns to see Bone concern written on his face. He thought he saw tears. "Thanks Bone, you won fair and square. You are the winner and the best friend I got. I'll be fine in a few days. You can quit crying."

"What, me crying." Penny jabs him. Bone stops, then replies. "Thanks kiddo, you're my bestie, too." Penny hugs Bone's arm.

Laura could see the concern in Susan's face. She begins to explain what was causing Mike to be in agony. "Susan, it was that old contest Bone and Mike had back home. Bone challenged Mike to a hot pepper contest to determine the winner and still champion. You remember them eating hot Chinese mustard. Mike drank hot tea to help him win the battle of the witless."

"Somehow, that contest was brought up again and those two began to argue who really won the contest. It ended with this duel. Bone ordered ghost peppers."

"He what," exclaimed Susan!

"Who won this time," asked Bell?

Laura was set back to Bell's question. "Mike was in pain and all she could ask was, who won." Laura kept her thoughts private knowing her man might not like her making a comment to Bell.

Cho answered her question. "Bone won." Mike chuckled

"Yeah, he got me beat."

"Both ate two peppers apiece. Bone kept his down; Mike lost his pepper." Cho pointed at the pepper pulp sprayed across Bone's jacket. Bone Chuckled wiping at the pepper pulp. Cho continued to explain the event. "Mike went ashen and gagging for breath. He went into shock, falling to the floor. He's going to have a bad belly ache for some time. This is going to be a rough night. I'll tell the waiter to take some antacids to his room."

Bell replied, "Good, I'm glad this is finally settled between the two. Bone has been receiving a lot of needling from the other bikers, since that contest."

"How can you be so insensitive to Mike's pain Bell," retorted Laura.

"Look Laura, you weren't at the restaurant back home when all this began. This needed settling and if you talk to Mike, he would tell you the same thing."

Mike heard the two nearly beginning to fight over his condition. His throat had blisters and still burned. He was happy Laura felt so concerned. He knew he had to make the effort to stop the argument, before it went further.

"Laura, Bell is correct. Please don't get mad at each other, cough, cough, over this. Bone and I had to settle this between us. I felt he was still brooding over his loss and that might cause our relationship to be changed. This bitterness brewing between you two may cause harsh feeling between you two. I love your concern for me. Bell cares a great deal about me, Susan, Penny, and you all do. Cho warned me and agreed with my desire to enter this contest."

Mike, turns to Cho. Father return to the party, I will go to my room and rest for some time. Bell, please go with them. Susan, you." Mike was stopped by Susan before he could finish his sentence.

"Cho allow me to take Mike up to his room. I rather not be down here at this time."

Bell nodded to Cho and Laura. Bell turns to Chopper, lips speaking to him. I will explain, once they leave."

Susan takes Cho place holding onto Mike's arm. Both walk tightly together out of the dining room. Mike was weak and Susan was happy he was leaning on her, for support. Both went to the elevator.

The elevator door opened at his floor. Both walked out toward Mike's room. Susan reaches inside his pocket to fetch his room key.

Inside the room, Susan helped him out of his diner jacket into bed. Then, removes his shoes.

Mike objected to having his shoes removed. "I will be fine Susan. This party is for me. I will rest for some time and go back down."

The waiter knocked on the door. Susan went to the door taking a bottle from the waiter.

"Here, take some of these antacids. This should settle your belly. You are not going anywhere for at least one hour. Lay back and rest." Gently Susan pushes Mike back on the bed with her hand.

Mike was about to object but quickly accepted Susan's mothering. Susan grabs Mike's pillow to raise his back and head up. "This will keep the stomach acids from rising up into your throat. Believe me, that is not a pleasant thing to experience. Stephen had a bad stomach, after his last tour of duty. He got shot in the gut and had reflux."

"Reflux, what is this reflux, Susan?"

"You ever had heartburn?"

"Yes."

"Well reflux is, is similar to heartburn, but ten times worst. Your stomach acid rises up into your throat. It can cause some eating away of your throat lining over time. The burn gives a nasty taste in your mouth. Stephen would get it after eating too much, keeping him awake all night long. Never lay on your right side. The stomach is on that side."

"Stephen ate antacids with little help. He would try everything in the refrigerator. Drink half a gallon of milk. Pickle juice with vinegar cut the nasty taste. Soda crackers also worked, well. He was told that the salt was a base to the acid. The best trick to help, was warn salty water. He would slowly drink it. The taste went away a lot faster."

"Gee thanks, Susan. You can leave me here. I don't want you missing out on the party. I'll be down later. These parties go all night long."

"Mike, I don't feel much like partying. If you don't mind, I would like to remain with you and we both will go back down to the party."

"You know, I would love your company. Oh, I forgot about Cheryl. She okay."

"Yes, Bell and I took her to her bed. She was fast asleep. Still, that is not what concerns me most." A frown crept across her face. Mike thought it might be what he said at the table.

"Susan, maybe I should say what is on my mind at this moment. I feel, it is needed saying." Talking was difficult for Mike. His voice was horse but he had to tell Susan what was on his thoughts.

"Go on Mike, just say it."

"Well, I said a few things down stairs and, and well, I meant what I said."

"Huh," replied Susan not expecting that from Mike.

Mike saw Susan's confusion in her eyes. "I said you were a beautiful woman. Every man would turn to look at you. I cared a great deal about you. I know now, I meant it. Cheryl saw what I put out of my thoughts. I, I, maybe, well, I think I have fallen in love with you."

Susan's heart fluttered hearing Mike confesses his love for her. She wanted to say something. Mike stopped her.

"Please allow me to get this out, before I change my mind. I like Cheryl a lot. I really do, but not love. I was smitten with you, the first time we met. Cheryl was filled with hate for me. Not you. You have a loving, caring heart. That was what makes me feel the way I do for you now."

"Mike, I."

Again, Mike halted Susan speaking. "Please let me finish. This is not puppy love. We are not long between our ages. Cheryl told me your age when we rode to my home, after the Atlanta battle. I am old enough to know what I feel for you, is true. I have been through hell this first year with the Riders. More than most men, twice my age. This as aged me, matured me far beyond any person."

"I see how a man and woman treat each other in love. I see this love endure through their lives. I watched many who lost a loved one, the other moans greatly. I saw their pain. I guess you can say, I felt their pain as well. I know what it means to love and be far from your love ones. That pain, I to endured many times being far away from you. That memory of your face. The kindness in your eyes. You're caring and worrying over me. That was what sustained me in the desert. All my suffering was eased, knowing I would see you again. I had many long days and nights walking across the scorching desert to think on my feelings toward you. So, I tell you this after much deliberation."

"Susan, I know what it is to love. I saw children watching their dads and mom killed. I saw the same love, when the parent collapsed watching their child beheaded. I remember the pain of my dad dying and my believing my mom had died. I walked on a journey to return to my family. Love drove me. Not hate or the need for revenge. Love drove me to rescue those men in the prison. I killed not out of hate but out of love, to keep evil people from destroying good people. Susan, I know what love is. I live with love in my heart every second of the day."

Susan was filled with pride and almost in tears hearing Mike express himself. "Mike my love, I was trying to tell you after hearing my daughter shout out on the dance floor, her words woke me up to the fact of my true feeling. Like you, I have been reframing from admitting, I was in love with you. I realized that fact, then. A great weight was lifted off me. Cheryl knew I was in love with you. I am in love with you, Mike. I kept my distance because of Cheryl. I feel ashamed for my feelings."

"Why?"

"You are seven years younger than me. Then, there was the fact that I am recently widowed and Cheryl was in love with you. I talked to Bell. She said it was okay for me to have feeling for you. In fact, many of the women had the same feelings for you. You are a sexy young man. Mike you are smart, good looking, caring, powerful, rich, and who wouldn't desire being with you. You got it all."

"No, not all, Susan. I don't have a family." Mike looked down from Susan eyes. He didn't want her to see within his soul. He knew Susan could see into him with her eyes. I don't have someone to come home too. What I do have, is a dog and a ghost. There are the

Riders, who replaced my family. Cho, my father is more of a teacher than what a father is like. I know he cares a great deal for me. I believe he loves me, as I do him. Yet, I live alone."

"Susan, that is not the same as someone special. Cho has a family with Laura and both do their best to make me feel as family. Still, my life requires little attachments. I am in constant danger. How can I share that with a wife? Cho has done so for most of his life. He deserves his happiness. I am to take up this mantel, so he can enjoy his life. I have inherited his art. I will not allow him to continue to live this dangerous life. No, he has never said anything to me. This is my own feelings. Cho must never learn of this."

"Mike my love. Susan hugs Mike close to her. Then, kisses him on the lips. You can still find love. I did with Stephen. I accepted his life style. Look at all the members married in the club. Everyone had the same feeling as you do. Look at Bone and Penny, then at Chopper with Bell. Razor and Miriam, and Jack with Rhonda. Mike, Pretty and Judy are going to get married. Don't you dare tell anyone." Mike suspected this between the two of them.

"Yes Susan, you are correct, but there is one fundamental thing, I am young and they are older than me. I have."

"Stop it, Mike. They made that choice when they were young. If you truly love me, then respect that I know the danger you are in. I accepted this life, as did the others. We are a family. They give me strength and I give back to them in their need."

"Susan, can you sit and tell me, you never worried while Cheryl and I were in the jungle or when Stephen went on a mission?"

"Yes dummy, we all do. I will again and again when any family member leaves on a venture."

"Yes, you did, you adapted. Your inner strength is amazing. You are tough and strong, Susan. Cheryl is young. Look at her, she is not you. She is breaking. I see that now. Everyone sees her pain. That is why I am in love with you and not Cheryl. You been through hell and now that I know you have the same feeling for me, I put you through further hell on my ventures. I cannot bear to see you in pain. I cannot put you through the years of further pain worrying, about me. That is the cross, I wear."

"Mike, that is what love does to us. We love each other together or apart. I rather be together and share my love for you, than, be apart and not have you come back to me."

Susan hugs Mike hard. "Please my love, allow us the years together."

Mike hugs Susan, remaining silent. They remain embraced for an hour.

Down stairs in the dining room, the party was getting wound up. Jimmie and Jamie, with their dates, were whooping it up on the dance floor. Both wore their new tuxes and watches Chopper ordered. The tuxes might need some tending too, if they ever decided to wear them again. All three of the men was given money and a hotel room. Moss in another hotel. For reasons, he was not allowed to attend the dinner party. None knew he was on the island, except Chopper.

Both Jamie and Jimmie partied with Moss earlier before going to Mike's dinner party. Moss was left on his own.

Jamie stood by the table ordering drinks for all. Mike and Susan walked in, hand in hand. All the women took note. Penny whispered into Laura's ear.

"Finally, those two are together."

"I'm so happy," Laura whispered back to Penny. Bell had mixed feelings. Cindy realized, there went her chance with Mike.

Bell walks over to Mike and Susan. "I hope you are doing better, Mike?"

"I am Bell, Susan has been a great help. Thank you for helping me. Mike turns to Susan, excuse me, I need to speak to Bone."

"Hey good buddy. You ready to party?"

"Yep, replied Bone.

Mike tried to smile. He was still woozy with his stomach. Bone noticed Mike's color had not fully returned to his face. Jamie spotted Mike by Bone. Staggering over to where both were standing, he immediately started making jokes.

"Hey Mikey, Razor tell me you got a tummy problem. My woman can nurse you back to health."

"Yeah, I was in my room, Jamie. Susan been taking care of me. Bone and I were competing to see who retains the hot pepper record. I lost to the big guy."

"He sure did." Bone slaps Mike on his back.

"You mean this big baddie-waddie beat you eating sweet peppers," snickered Jamie.

Bone heard the sarcastic remark made by Jamie. Jamie never met Bone, if he had, he would immediately take what he said back. This was to be his first encounter with Bone. Jamie was about to make another remark about Bone being a meanie-weenie for burning Mikey's teeny-weenie tummy until he felt a powerful grip grasping his shoulder. A sudden twist, followed the pain in his shoulder was felt being whipped around facing a huge towering man. The big man had a most unpleasant look on his face, Jamie last remembered.

Mike stood watching Bone sit Jamie in his chair the way he done when they both met in the biker bar in the mountains. It was a cold night and he was soaking wet, shivering, and hungry. Chopper called him over to his table. Bone escorted him to the table. He made the same mistake Jamie done. He made nasty comments to Bone being escorted to Chopper's table.

The words rang in Mike thoughts of that night he said to Bone escorting him to Chopper's table. Mike smiles, recalling himself being lifted by the scruff of the neck by Bone. Both his feet dangled off the floor.

"I told Bone to get his paws off of me or was it, I'll slap you down to size. Whatever the words were, Bone didn't care much for them. He showed me the seat and helped sit me in my chair. My butt nearly shattered the chair from the impact of Bone's persuasive manners, he used to show me some manners."

Mike was nearly laughing at his recollection of that same incident Jamie was going to experience. "He recalled those two huge hands keeping him planted in the chair at Chopper's table. Bone sure had the knack of persuasion. Now, Jamie is going to learn some manners.

Jamie was escorted back to the table. He was politely seated next to the woman he came in with. She was about to wrap her arms around Jamie when the impact from Bone's persuasions kept that from happening. The chair was not built as sturdy as those in the mountain bar. It quickly shattered, driving all four legs apart. Four legs sprayed outward with Jamie planted like a potted flower on the floor. One good outcome to the impact was Jamie's woman falling into his arms. His butt was hurting from the slamming down on the chair but made worse when the chair seat hit the floor. The double whump made him feel the pain even though he was drunk as a skunk.

Penny walked over to the couple sitting on the floor. She handed Jamie his beer, he ordered for Mike. He needed it more than Mike. He only wished she gave him the beer to drink rather than pouring it on top of his head. His butt still hurt. Everyone roared with laughter.

Mike couldn't help himself having to make a little quip at Jamie. "Hey Jamie, I see you learned the same lesson I had to learn from Bone. My butt bone is still tender to this day from that seating he uses to get you to sit."

""He done this to you, too, Mikey?"

Yeah, on our first meeting and many times since that first time. I learned since then, to not to argue or make surrey remarks about him."

"I think, I have learned the same thing."

"If you ain't, Bone will gladly teach you again." Jamie waves both hands back and forth, then replies to Mike's remark.

"No, no, no, this one taught me pretty good."

"Can't say the same for the kiddo, Jamie. I had to reinforce that lesson to teach him proper etiquette three times before he learned. Then again, he was much younger than you and more pig headed. But he learned, didn't you, kiddo," Bone slapping Mike's backside followed by a thunderous roar of laughter.

"Yeah, and that was maybe seven times, not three. I learned another lesson this night, Bone old buddy. Not to try and beat Bone's records; ha, ha, ha."

Bone quipped to Jamie with his sly grin, "you wanna try and beat my record eating hot peppers, Jamie boy?"

Jamie looks at Mike nodding his head. "No, no, mister Bone. I got no stomach for hot food. Your record is safe from any attempts by me, mister Bone, sir."

"I like this guy, Kiddo. He knows when he is up against over whelming power, unlike some other folks that think otherwise. Bone gives Mike a wink. Well, my boy, the invitation is open for all comers."

Jimmie struggles to stand, walks over with his woman clinging to his arm helping Jamie off the floor. After some struggling, Bone helped. Both stood reeling with Bone propping them steady. After a minute, he lets them go thinking they were steady. He was wrong. They went reeling to the floor.

All the ladies got tired of their men ballyhoo. A signal was sent out to their men folks, a second time. None took notice of their wives look, so words were needed.

"Okay, you had your fun, we want to dance, before all your energy is wasted."

"Yes dears, came a resounding response by all the men folk. Even Jamie and Jimmie lying on the floor, answered stumbling to their feet with each woman doing their best to cover up their womanly assets from the free-for-all fall.

Razor grabbed his wife; Pretty took Judy's arm before Jimmie could ask her. Jimmie's lady sat in the chair, he placed her into, passed out. Next, Jimmie turns to Bell standing by Chopper.

"How about you, dear lady, care to dance with me. Chopper shrugged, then gave his approval. Bell hesitantly accepted. Bell was about to ask Mike.

Jamie took a cue from Jimmie, grabbing Bell escorting her to the dance floor. Jamie stood, walked over to Susan standing by Bell, alone. Mike was with Bone, talking. He taps Susan on her shoulder.

"It would be an honor to have one of the prettiest women here to dance with me."

Susan was waiting for Mike to make the first move. He was preoccupied with Bone bantering. Penny was attempting to take him away from Mike, so he would dance with her and allow Mike to dance with Susan.

Mike was just sitting down with Jack shoving a beer into his hand. Susan watched Mike take a drink reluctantly. Mike did not see Jamie approaching Susan.

Susan accepted. Mike saw them dancing on the dance floor. He had just pulled a chair from the table to have her sit, seeing her being escorted to the dance floor. The beer soothed his throat. He wished he had not taken the beer seeing Susan on the dance floor. Susan kept her eyes looking toward Mike while dancing with Jamie. Every step was with a toe smashed by a drunk clumsy Jamie attempting to dance. Susan's eyes called to Mike to come and rescue her from Jamie.

Mike quickly downed his beer. He begun to stand, until Cho patted him on his shoulders. Laura was next to Cho. Take my bride and dance with her. I have two left feet. In reality, Cho was an excellent dancer.

Mike stood and accepted Laura's hand walking to the dance floor. Susan had a look of disappointment expressed on her face. Jamie was doing his best to not step on her feet. He was too drunk to prevent what his feet kept doing over and over again. Susan did wonderful, not complaining or yelling from each misstep from Jamie's clumsy dancing.

Laura was an excellent dancer and immediately began to introduce Mike to some dance steps. After three dances with Laura, Mike acquired several good dance sets. Susan watched Laura teaching Mike, wishing he would swiftly swap with Jamie.

Every time Susan attempted to break from Jamie's hold, either Bell, Rhonda, or Laura would take up the next dance with Mike. All the men were happy to allow Mike to dance with their wives. They never liked to dance. Now that Mike was showing he was becoming a good dancer, all the ladies lined up to dance with him.

Judy and Miriam attempted to dance with Mike. Before either had a chance, Penny wormed her way to the front of the line. Pretty grabbed Judy taking her to the dance floor.

"Listen girl, you can dance with me. Mike got plenty of women to occupy his time. Me, I am alone or rather you dance with Mike?"

"No, you will do. I rather dance with you than any other man."

Finally, after each wife danced with Mike, Susan broke from Jamie's clutches walking over to Mike. Miriam was walking to the table once the dance ended. Susan immediately took Mike's arms. The last dance was hers and Mikes. To Susan, the dance seemed to last all night long. After several minutes, their dance ended.

Around three A.M. most of the ballyhoo was dying down. The men were telling crude stories. Many hotel guests were making many complaints to the hotel staff, they did not appreciate the ill manners from the table with all the drunks, yelling fowl words and telling nasty, ugly stories. Then again, some patrons enjoyed the stories and went to join the table. Those that did, were mainly American tourists and not the other European guests staying at the hotel.

The party was coming to an end after a drinking contest ensued. Many of the American tourists were lying across a table or lying on the floor, passed out. Many of their wives were on their way to joining their men or already there, passed out on a table.

The bikers were still in the game. Some were out. Jamie and Jimmie were among the first to drop out. Many of the bikers were gawking at the other non-bikers dropping out of the contest. It was worth all the drinks they bought them, to watch them get pie-eyed.

One man kept wanting to stand on a table attempting to do a strip tease dance. No one wanted to see that, not even the man's wife. He was too old and fat, to boot. The table born the worst of it. The table nearly gave in to his weight stomping. The table was saved after the drunken man was persuaded by the hotel staff to step down after three of the legs were snapped. If not for two of the bikers supporting the table, he would be joining the three legs on the floor. It was Bell that managed to pulled the fat, strip teasing, drunk from the table to the relief of the desperately tiring staff tugging on him.

Bell decided, "when the fat man was dancing, juggling a beer, while attempting to unzip his pants, was enough. It was the last straw, after some of his drink was flung on her new dress. It was the near beer hit of him tossing his glass that followed her gown getting beer splashed on it, caused her to act. Besides, he was about to pull his pants down."

Bell leaped upon the table with her red dress and matching heels. With one hand, she grabbed the fat man's belt from behind. With a jerk upward on the pants belt, the fat man yelped. The pain was felt in his crotch. He offered little resistance to Bell polite persuasion.

He was having difficulties un-zipping his pants while flying off the table. He landed in the arms of his companions waiting, passed out on the floor. They awoke laughing. The fat man kept attempting to un-zip his pants on top of the heap of drunks. He succeed with a shout of glee, "whoopie, I did it."

Many of the men were thrown out of the dining room after the second piggy back battle of bikers against the American tourists. Each man carried their wives on their back. When one wife was too drunk to continue holding onto her horse, another hopped on a back replacing the lady lying on the floor. After the second battle, it did not matter who was on whose back.

Each rider had to tote a beer in one hand and battle another with their free hand. Beers went everywhere. The floor was soak with beers. The object of the game was the carriers to get their riders to the opposite end of the dining hall with the rider on their backside. All this had to be done with their glasses still having beer inside, then return back to their side.

The first race was undecided. Many of the women were torn from their riders. Many never made it to the opposite side of the dining hall. Those that did, slammed into the wall and lost their drinks. Some did manage to keep beer in their glasses. No one checked. On the way back, many carriers slipped on the wet beer-soaked floor. More glasses emptied on the floor. Half of what was remaining went down. Their beautiful gowns were awash with beer.

The leader in the race, back slipped. That resulted in a chain reaction ending the first race without a clear winner, hence, the second race was required.

Those that were still capable, jumped on any back available. The floor was a large puddle of beers and fallen riders. The hotel manager watched with dismay. With the grace of God, the second race ended quick. Cho riding on Mike's back were the winners. Hell, they won the race before the other contestant made it to the opposite wall was noted by the staff.

Cho drank his beer. Some argument ensued, he won with an empty glass. Mike dropped to the floor, passing out. Cho wanted to prove he was the winner with a third race. The team that contested the win, went down joining Mike passed-out on the floor. Cho decided, he won from default.

"A win is a win," Cho said to all the people lying on the dance floor.

Bell watched from at a table along with Laura and Susan. All three were drunk before the first race. They drank cocktails. Neither could stand much less hop on the backs of their men. They sat at the table watching the first race. By the second, they never knew who won. Each lady applauded to a blur supposedly winner, before passing out. Cho reached down to pick Mike off the floor.

"My son, we won, best be getting to our rooms. Come, we need to get our women. Both found them sitting at a table. Chopper had Bell lying across him. Cho grabbed Laura, hoisting her over his shoulder. Mike grabbed Susan. He could not hoist her on his shoulder. Much less stand. He grabbed her around her waist. Both Cho and Mike staggered to the elevator.

Passing through the dining room entrance Bone and Penny were spotted by Cho, against the wall hand in hand in an embrace. Mike took Susan to her room next door to Cheryl's room. Inside, he laid her down on her bed. He removed her shoes and covered her with a blanket. He made it to the door, then out like a light to the floor.

Cho had better luck with his wife, Laura. Both fell in bed, without removing their clothes.

Down stairs in the dining hall, the managers looked with horror at his guest scattered like leaves everywhere he looked. He had no idea who was who among the bodies littering the floor. One order was given to his staff. "Clean the room and leave the guest where they laid."

Every window was opened, to air the room. Chairs taken outside to be clean. The last thing done, was mopping the floors. It was a long night for all the staff. One conciliation, the manager was looking forward to presenting the bill to Mr. Chopper.

GONE MISSING

The next morning, everyone met in the hotel restaurant for breakfast. Mike asked Chopper about the money, Susan said he had. Cho knew, but waited until they would get home. He was with his wife, Laura in their room.

"Chopper, it was brought to my attention, that I am rich. I got no money that I know of?"

"Mike, at the manor and at the Citadel, we came across a treasure of huge amounts of cash. At the Citadel cash and gold. We burned all the drugs. Come, let us talk in a private place before every one gets seated."

Chopper takes Mike to a corner of the dining room. "It is the custom of the club to divvy up the loot from our encounters. The last two ventures, netted us more money than we ever got. It was the biggest pay-off for our members. Thanks to you and Cho, our club is pretty well off, financially. I can say, you and Cho received an extra bonus. Mike, you might want to take a seat before I tell you how much. Cho wanted to wait until you were home to inform you."

Mike sat in a chair by the entrance.

"Well, to date, from the Manor, you received a half million dollars without your bonus. From the Citadel, two million and without the bonus. This does not include your monthly stipend for expenses, we allot to you. The club has banked twenty million after giving everyone a percentage."

"Huh, Chopper, does that include the wives and children of past members and their heirs."

"Yes, they all received a portion of that money. Some of the money goes into a college fund and an annuity for each child, when they come of age. Each wife will get half of their spouse's percentage in a lump sum. They will continue to receive a monthly stipend with a raise and other perks. We take care of our own."

Mike sat with a blank stare across his face. Come Mike, let's get some food while you ponder all the money you got. Susan walks through the door alone. Cheryl was not accompanying her.

Immediately, Mike stands and walks over to Susan. "Good morning, Susan. You look beautiful, considering last night's party. Cheryl, is she coming down for breakfast?"

Susan, like all the women were a tad bit untidy in their appearances. Susan much more. It was uncommon for Mike to see her not trimmed from head to toe. Laura was the only woman, besides Susan to never be seen any other way. Both were the type to look their best, anytime.

Susan sat staring past Mike in thought, thinking. "No, she never answered her door, when I knocked. I think she is still in bed. Maybe, she is afraid to confront us from her behavior, she displayed last night."

"I think that might be the answer, Susan. You think, maybe I should go up and check on her? Maybe hearing me talk, she would come down with me to eat breakfast. Bell along with Miriam walked into the dining room. Mike stood pulling a chair for each of them.

Chopper, nodded seeing Mike pull chairs for the two women. Bell looked away from Chopper. Miriam sat waving to a waiter to come taker her order. Jamie, already in the dining room made his typical quip to Mike.

"Hey Mikey, you gonna make the rest of us look bad." Jamie was referring to Mike pulling chairs out for the two ladies.

"Jamie, no one stopped you from standing, retorted Bell, meant for Chopper and not Jamie. Mike is a gentleman; he always pulls chairs for us. Some of you men should take lessons."

"Why retorted Chopper? Mike is doing a just fine."

Besides Bell, Cho said this was part of his training, Jack said walking up to the table Chopper was sitting with his companions.

Rhonda slaps Jack on his head, returning from the all you can eat bar before sitting. "Who trained you, then?"

"Mike, I would be pleased if you go and get Cheryl to come down for breakfast."

Mike stood, replying to Susan's request. Love to, be back soon. Mike was out the dining room, in the elevator, then at Cheryl room door. One rap, then another, no answer. Mike called to Cheryl.

"It's me Cheryl, open the door, please." Nothing. Mike knocked on the door again. Nothing. Mike was sensing a feeling of dread. A maid was cleaning rooms nearby with a cleaning cart.

"Miss, would you please open this door. Cheryl's mom is at breakfast and sent me to fetch her daughter. She won't answer the door. She had a lot to drink last night. The maid giggled. She heard about the riot in the dining room. I'll wait outside while you enter and check on her well-being."

The maid looked at the young man requesting her to open a door. He appeared to be a nice good-looking man. With trepidation, she opened the door. She calls inside to inform the occupants she was here to clean the room. No one responded to her call. "That was common," replied the maid.

Mike urged the maid to go inside and look. He waited outside the room. In the bedroom, the maid saw it was still made up. A blanket was thrown off the bed.

Mike entered the room after the maid called to him, there was no one in the room. He went to the bedroom. The bed appeared unslept in. He left the room wondering where and when Cheryl left. The maid began cleaning the room.

Mike fretted whether he should say something to Susan. Cheryl left early and spent the night somewhere other than her room was evident to his keen eyes. Mike began to worry. "It might be best to wait until everyone ate breakfast. Hopefully, Cheryl may pop back and join everyone for breakfast," pondered Mike with his dilemma. Mike left returning to the dining room.

"Susan, Cheryl did not answer her door. She might not want to be with anyone for a while. After breakfast we'll go back up and check on her, again."

"Okay Mike, that might be for the better," replied Susan with a sadden look.

Mike sat next to Susan. He put his hand on her lap. Bell sat staring at Mike. She knocked on Cheryl's door, before coming down the elevator. No one answered the door. She asked the same maid to open the door. She found the room emptied. Bell suspected Mike had done the same and was keeping this fact from Susan, as she was, hoping Cheryl would return soon.

Jimmie walked through the entrance with his date, Chopper provided for Jamie, Moss, and him. Jamie's date left the hotel once he hit the floor, passed out. He awoke early in the morning, when a mop swiped him in his face. He fell in his bed and yet to have come down to eat.

Breakfast went fast and quiet. No one wanted to talk much. It was obvious why, to anyone walking in. Most of the American guests were still in their rooms that partied with the bikers. Others came in the dining room avoiding the biker's tables. Their looks spoke volumes. Their eyes read death to all that talked or made any unwanted noise. It was plain to all; they were in bad shape, suffering from all the drinks paid for by the bikers.

After eating breakfast, Cheryl had not come down. Susan stood, immediately walked to the elevator. Bell called Mike over to her table.

Mike shouts to Susan, "I will be up, after I see what Bells wants. Yes Bell." Susan did not hear Mike's call to her.

"Mike, Cheryl is not in her room."

"I know Bell. I asked the maid to let me inside. She was gone the whole night. I don't know where she slept?"

"I know, I kept hoping, she would walk in the dining room during breakfast, Mike. Susan is going to be very upset, when she learns Cheryl is missing."

"I understand Bell. That is why I want to be with her, when she discovers Cheryl is gone. I kept waiting as you did for her to pop in for breakfast. Now, I am worried."

"I'll let Chopper know. We can begin a search party when you come back down with Susan."

Jamie walks in the dining room hearing what was transpiring. "Hey Mikey, count me in on the search. Bone listened intently to Bell's conversation. Penny nudged him to speak up.

"I am Babe, Mike, I will go with you and Jamie."

"Thanks Bone and you too Jamie. I think, we will need more than all of us to locate Cheryl."

"Good Mike, why don't you begin the search and I will go up to be with Susan. This is a girl thing, more than a man thing, she needs at this time."

"I'm going with you Bell," called Penny.

"Not without me," replied Miriam and Rhonda.

Outside Bone, Jamie and Mike looked in each direction. Chopper began organizing the others inside the dining room.

"Jimmie, you will remain at the hotel. The rest of the men will scour the town in small groups.

Jamie asked Mike, "should we split up? It could aid in finding Cheryl, faster."

Bone responded, "if we do, then how will the others learn if we located her?"

"He's right, we could be searching for hours after one of us finds her. Lets' stay together, replied Mike.

Chopper steps outside, "you three head north. Me and the others will take the south. The women will go west and Jimmie will stay here with the others."

"Mike, I think the beach is a good starting place to begin our leg of the search."

"Oh, why is that, Jamie?"

"Well, I overheard Judy and Cheryl went to the beach before we came back from the desert." Mike was not aware of the beach incident Judy and Cheryl told Susan. Bone heard about it from Penny. Penny learned from Bell. All the others knew, accept Mike.

"Bell told the others to keep this from you," Mike. Jamie continue telling Mike what he learned.

Judy said," she saw Cheryl with a strange man on a corner. They were doing some transactions. Bell learned last night what that transaction might be, hearing from Susan her worries concerning Cheryl's pain drug addiction. That realization came to a complete and utter surprise to Mike's ears.

Along the beach, Mike walked along the walk, Jamie on the beach, and Bone anywhere he wanted for two hours. Each stopped any person to inquire about seeing a girl wearing a green evening gown.

Not many people denied Bone's request. Each wanted to keep the giant happy long enough to get a safe distance from him. Jamie spent most of his time flirting with every girl he came upon. Mike entered every store and bar along the street.

By noon, all three met in front of a dingy bar from the beach. All three agreed, "the placed looked worst peering inside but the heat of the sun made the inside more appealing. Their thirst needed quenching. A cold beer is a cold beer no matter what the place looked like, or that was their thinking entering the dark poorly lit bar."

Opening the door, smoke poured out. The bar had a cloud of cigarette smoke as thick as a London fog. A vacant table was spotted at the farthest end from the door. Each sat at a table with every eye watching. After a few minutes and no waiter coming to take their order, Jamie stood walking over to the bar. His feet stuck to the sticky floor with each step approaching the bar.

Three burly unkept men sat at the bar. Jamie walked between two of the men. Blurting out; "hey barkeep, three beers for my table."

The bartender was a fat man, unshaven, wearing a tee-shirt soiled with beer and cigar stains. His craggily face was pot marked and both eyes blood shot. What hair on his head wasn't comb and laid disarray, plus oilier than a mechanic's rag. Jamie drank at bars with worst barkeepers. The beers were just as good.

The barkeeper pours three glasses of beer, then Walks over to Jamie slamming the mugs down on the counter. "That be three dollars, bub."

Jamie looked with disgust at the barkeeper's yellowed teeth. Many were missing. He thanked God, the barkeeper said little, any more, he would gag from the awful breath coming from his mouth.

The barkeeper took that opportunity to discard a wad of tobaccy, spitting it across the counter into a spittoon at Jamie's foot. He missed. Jamie was about to wipe his boot, when two other men walked to the bar. Each man stood behind Jamie. Each man looked at Jamie for a while. Each man smiled.

On top of the counter, all three beers sat half full. Most of the foam settled, after the mugs were slammed down on the countertop. The other half of beer flowed on the countertop. The two strangers standing behind Jamie kept smiling.

"I ordered three beers, not three half-filled glasses barkeep," responded Jamie.

"That still be three dollars," came a nasty snare with a bad smelling remark.

"I pay a dollar and a half for three half-filled glasses and no more, demanded Jamie."

The barkeeper grabs one beer and rakes the spilt beer off the countertop into the glass. After it was full, he proceeds with the other two glasses, doing the same.

"There, three full glasses. Three dollars bub."

Jamie drops three bills, grabs the glasses, and turns around. He never took the first step before one of the hands of a man behind him stopped him with his hand ramming into his chest.

"Where you going with them beers, friend? Jamie looked at the two men. He could count the teeth on one hand that both had in their silly grinning mouths.

"First, I'm not your friend. If I was, I would advise you to brush your remaining teeth. Second, those two men at the table are my friends. You need to discuss this with them. I cannot make this decision without their approvals. Jamie with his free hand slapped the big man's hand off his chest. Immediately, five men stood.

No one thought that Jamie was with the two men entering the bar sitting at a table. Neither did they looked to see who came in. Usually, it was only men they knew. No one dared entered their bar. The second man beside the man who got his hand slapped, grabbed for the three beers in Jamie's hand.

Jamie held tight to the three glasses. In the end he had to yield to the powerful grip the man was exerting on his hand. One finger felt like it was broken to Jamie. He held his pain without muttering a word. Bone and Mike watched keenly, until they saw Jamie was in pain.

Mike stood with Bone. Hold back big guy. We don't need to spend time in a jail. I think, I can resolve this without a fight. Mike knew, if Bone got in this, there would be a brawl. Bone shrugged with regret not to help Mike.

That was Mike's first mistake. Bone was a towering giant of a man. Anyone seeing him up close, usually deterred from any violent actions. Mike wanted to find Cheryl before she got into trouble. Jail, was out of the question.

Bone sat back down, knowing this was not going to be a peaceful transaction. He been in too many bar fights to expect anything else. He sat back wishing he had a beer while watching, what he knew was coming down. Mike walked over to the bar.

Bone smiled. Hey Jamie, let our friends keep those beers. Go keep Bone company and I will get us three new beers. Jamie left giving Mike a snarly grin holding his fingers. Walking over to their table, Bone says to him, "sit and watch the fun, Jamie lad."

"Mike thinks he can talk to those men nicey-nice-like and they would not bother him. Boy, that kid has a lot to learn."

Mike walks between the two men to the bar. Neither man attempted to part to allow Mike free, uninterrupted passage. Mike squeezed between the two men with ease. "Hey barkeeper, three new beers. Hold the foam, please."

"Please, hey bro, did you hear the kiddy say pretty please to Quince? Heh, heh, heh." Tapping Mike's shoulder, the big mouth man not holding the three beers asks Mike, "what you think you are doing? This ain't no ice cream parlor for children. This is a man's bar. You go along and fetch some sodie-pop down the street."

"I'm ordering three beers for me and my friends."

"You mean five beers. Big mouth points to the five men standing at the end of the bar. Make that seven beers. That includes the two of us you standing between." Mike ignored the comment and restated his order.

"No, I mean three beers," pointing to his table. All the men turn to look at a table in a corner. Two men sat watching with a smile creasing their faces. The big guy waves to Mike.

"You talking about that wimp that bought us beers and the other big doth sitting with a shitty grin waving at me."

"He is waving to me. I wouldn't let him hear you refer to him as a big doth. He is a sensitive kind of a guy."

"You mean he will start crying. He does look like a sissy, girlie type."

Bone perks up hearing himself called a girlie type.

"Well, because he would get out of his chair and come over here to wipe your butts on the floor. He does like a tidy place to drink his beers. This floor is a tad sticky. A good mopping will serve it good. Maybe, bring in a better clientele.

"Hey Quince, you got another spare apron for that big gutless girlie guy at that table."

"Sir, I do use that word sparingly with you. I told him, I would get new beers, so he would not be disturbed by you two dumb asses."

"You just called us dumb asses, Kiddie."

"I can see your hearing is good, especially with those dumbo large ears mounted on both sides of your pin head with a pea brain."

"Boy, that was your second big mistake."

"Really, what was the first mistake, shit for brains. Was it buying you two beers when I should have bought you glasses of milk to drink?"

Jamie was about to stand at the table to assist Mike, Bone grabbed his arm pulling him back to his seat.

"Hey, what's the idea, Bone? There are five men Mike might not have noticed in the corner. That makes seven to him. Don't you think, he might need our assist?"

"Jamie, did you not learn anything while in the desert about Mike?"

"I know all about him, I watched him take on an army of men with weapons. He and Master Cho took them on with only swords."

"Well Jamie, neither of them usually uses swords or any weapons. Just sit and watch. Just know it is taking all I got to not crack those skulls. Wish you brought the beers with you."

"But, but."

"Shh. Watch, the fun is about to begin. Keep quiet, I want to hear what they are saying."

Mike was aware of the five men standing in a corner and the other two men beside him. The two behind him were the closest of the nine men in the bar. Maybe ten, if I include the barkeeper, Mike pondered. Mike sensed the tension waiting for their first move. "He doubted for a second, they weren't going to do nothing, with the time it took them to decide to act, he decided to bait the big mouth to make his move."

Mike with his back to the two men, quipped out his remarks. Hey my back is turned, you two baby molesting cock sucking bastards scared of little me. I hope I don't have to turn around and let you see how scared I am, looking at my face. I can cry if that will give you two the courage to act like men. Maybe I should bypass this staring and put both you over my knees for a spanking. You two being nasty shitheads to my friends." Mike smiles at both men. Each man turned beet red with anger.

It was plain that both men were at their limits tolerating the verbal abuse being dished out to them, loudly. Also, in the presence of all the other men in the bar.

"Watch, Jamie, watch this. Ssh. Be quiet. Watch," retorted Bone squirming in his seat.

The big bruiser acted first raising his burly paw to strike Mike. Mike struck first, delivering a sharp crisp back kick up between the bruisers loins. The second man got the same but his kick went to his guts. He flew out the door onto the street. Mike turns around. Five men were quick to converge on Mike's flanks.

Both men on either side of Mike reached to grab him. Both received an elbow simultaneously to their jaws. Each jaw spit. Their knees gave way. Each man fell on both of their knees. Bone wrenched. Jamie grinned with sympathetic pain, hearing the popping sound of their kneecaps before they hit the floor on the floor.

"See, see Jamie. Keep watching, he ain't begun yet, shouted Bone wishing he had popcorn to go with that beer, he was still waiting for."

Next, the biggest of the five men at the end of the counter approached Mike. The others circled around Mike. The big man said nothing, then shot out a jawing snapping punch to Mike's head.

Mike blocked the blow with a wrist snapping block. Bones were shattered in this arm. Big man grabbed for his arm searing with pain. Mike did not allow him to find comfort in aiding his broken arm. Mike grabbed his arm, lifting him to his toes. The big guy screamed.

The other men watched this small kid drop four men and now making their main man tippy toe across the floor. Mike swung the arm down and back up in an arc. The big guy's body followed the motion, flipping him over flat on the hard floor. He never had a chance to get comfy before Mike lifted him to his feet throwing him through the door, out on to the street.

The next man was in awe, this little kid grabbed hold of his arm lifting him off the floor, spinning him around like top over his head. He felt his wrist break, the pain went away once the spinning stopped. He realized the little kid was flying him above his head, readying to let him fly to God knows where.

Mike took aim at the other two companions. Both ducked their friend's sudden flight path heading toward them. Mike leaped forward closing the distance remaining between them. A side thrust kick shot one man out the door. The other man, Mike swept both legs with a spinning dragon sweep. He went down. Quickly recovering. He went staggering to the bar. Mike skips, then spins with a wheel kick. Jamie turned away from what he imagined happened to the last man's head.

The barkeeper stopped what Jamie thought was occurring to the last man. He grabbed the man to pull him away from the coming kick. Several teeth went dropping out of the barkeeper mouth. It helped his smile, Mike thought. Each tooth sounded like ping pong balls striking the mirror before falling to the floor. Mike never stopped in his spinning kick. He continued with his spinning to finish off the last man, still standing.

Mike figured that was the last of them. He was wrong. That was number two mistake. One man walked from a back room or restroom. Bone saw the man and put out his big foot. The man was too busy looking at a kid, that downed his friends and not noticed Bone big leg. He tripped. Attempting to stand back up, he was met with Bone's hand. It was Bone's fist rupturing a disc in his spinal cord with a powerful blow raining from above. The man went back to the floor. He never stood back up. Or, none was aware he had later after the three of them left the bar.

Mike stood at the bar waiting for the barkeeper to get up from the floor. Blood was gushing out of his mouth. He grabbed a rag to stop the pouring out of blood. Three beers without foam were poured from the tap. Each beer was gently placed on the countertop. Mike asked, "how much?"

"No charge. Them on the house. All the beers are on the house. Just raise your hand, young fellow."

Returning to the table with three free beers, Jamie was quick to speak. "Mike, I was going to help you. Bone made me not to. He told me to watch. I see what he means, now."

"What Bone, you didn't want to help me? Mike stood staring down at his buddy holding three beers with disappointment at Bone's not interfering.

"Hey, hand over that beer, little buddy. Watching you made me thirsty. Hey barkeeper, send three more over. Why you look upset. I knew you could handle them, easy-like. If I thought otherwise, I wouldn't have remained seated. Besides, you told me not to interfere, remember?"

"Oh, I thought you would tell me, you were tire with a hangover. That I can believe, big guy. Besides when did that ever stop you from getting in a good fight. You need some further training. I'll aske Chopper to send you to the cabin for further training. Being married can make a man sloppy."

"I get the next beers," replied Jamie downing his first beers.

"No need," Mike replied. "The barkeeper said the beers are on the house. We got plenty of daylight left, to look for Cheryl. Another beer shouldn't matter, guys."

"Jamie, you take care of the tip. Better leave a large one. With his dental bills, he gonna need the cash," chuckled Mike.

Bone gives Mike a look of shock. "Mike never seemed so cold hearted before."

Mike called to Jamie. "Wait give the man, this. Jamie took the hundred-dollar bill Mike handed him. The barkeeper was stunned receiving three hundred dollars. Bone added a hundred and Jamie another.

SECOND TIME AT
THE SAME BAR

"Susan, I know Cheryl was not in her room all night." Susan was standing by her daughter's bed when she heard Bell's voice, walking inside. Next to Bell was Miriam and Rhonda.

"We are so sorry," replied both women at the same time.

'What can we do to help, Bell asked?"

"I don't know. Why isn't she in her room? Where did she go?" Susan was clearly worried over Cheryl's disappearance noticed by all three women.

"Mike with Bone and Jamie are out looking for her. Chopper has organized the others to take up a search. She will be found," cited Bell.

"Wonderful, thanks you, but I can't stay and sit in my room waiting for any news. I'm going out to look for myself."

"You're not going alone, Susan. I'm going with you."

Miriam is correct, girl, it is too dangerous for you to go it alone. You are not thinking right. We all will go with you," demanded Bell. Rhonda nods with support. Miriam said what she said hoping Susan would change her mind. She did not like to be put in any responsible act or in danger. She nodded with her consent with reservations.

Downstairs Chopper, Razor, and Jack were preparing to leave joining in the search in the lobby.

All three women walked in, just as they were exiting the main entrance to the street.

"Where are you three heading, asked Jack directing his question mainly to Rhonda, his wife?"

"We decided to look for Cheryl, dear."

"I intend to look for my child, Jack, cited Susan with defiance in her eyes. I will not sit waiting to hear any news trickling in."

"She is right, Susan will go nuts, I would, this is better for her and will help in the search for Cheryl," replied Bell.

Chopper knew better, not to argue with Bell, when she decides to do something. "You are right, the other team might not locate her for some time. Cho and Jimmie will remain behind. If she returns to the hotel, Cho will send word to us. We are just leaving. You three women go toward the hills and us three will head in the direction, Mike went. Chopper pointed to the direction they planned to head out too. We all should return back here in five hours."

The three women did not wait to hear the last remarks heading into the center of the city. In the same direction Mike went. "Damn hard headed women. They will be our deaths of us all," sniped Razor.

Chopper takes his crew along the beach. Within an hour the sun's blistering heat wore on all three men. The ocean breeze acted more like a wind stoking a fire than a cooling breeze. Chopper turned to the other two men looking no better than him in the heat. "You men feel the same, as I do. I think a cool beer in a dark bar to get away from this searing heat, would be in our wheelhouse, before we sweat away into a puddle on the streets."

No one objective to his request. Ahead was a seedy looking lonely bar on their street. "No other bar or establishment is nearby," replied Jack looking around.

"I guess this bar is what we got. Heck, this town don't look like many people drink," quipped Razor.

"Yeah, one bar does not make an inviting place to visit. We been walking for a few hours and this is the only bar," responded Jack.

"Your right, beggars can't be too picky," replied Razor to Jack's remark.

"You two stop your whining, a beer is a beer. Right now, I can care less."

"You got that right Chopper," snapped Jack. "Count me in Jack," added Razor.

All three men entered through a door barely attached with one hinge managing to keep it grip on the door. "It ain't much to look at," sniped Chopper pushing the door open. Out poured a flood of smoke making their seeing the inside difficult.

"Yeah, the hell with the door, let's get us a cold beer and get out of this heat," balked Jack.

Me too, I've seen worse, than this. If they got cold beer, is all I care about," Razor wiping sweat from his brow.

Inside the dimly lit bar filled with smoke several men were sitting at a table. Most of the tables were waiting for chairs to be returned to them. One other table was waiting with chairs. It was clear the bar had some cleaning from all the chairs and tables in disarray. Jack went to the bar to order three beers. A gnarly looking man holding a rag on his mouth, greeted him.

"Hey, this place looks like you just had a brawl with some unruly patrons. Jack looked in the corner at the men sitting slightly worn from a fight. You open."

"You think, bub. What you need mister, came slurry speaking words from the unkempt barkeeper to Jack's request. Both Razor and Chopper went to the bar after they attempted to sit in rickety chairs at the table. Razor pulls out a stool to sit on, Chopper asked the barkeeper where the head was. Rag mouthed barkeeper pointed to a hallway.

Chopper enters the head. Its smell reeked of urine. "On the floor, it appeared no one could hit the urinal taking a pee. It was wet and slippery. Chopper was tempted to added his pee to the pond, then changed his mind. He might have to make a return visit after several beers. He didn't want to swim through a lake. This pond was barely acceptable as is, he thought."

Chopper returns to the counter pulling a stool up between his two companions. The barkeep pours three beers, heavy with foam. Then, slides each beer down the counter. Jack reached for his beer on the wet slippery counter top. Chopper and Razor done the same, catching their speeding beers. Foam whipped off the glasses coming to a sudden stop.

No sooner than they lifted their beers, four men sitting, unseen to the three old men sitting at the bar, walks over to the counter near the three of them. One big bruiser with a freshly broken nose having a white strip of tape keeping it in place on his face, approaches Jack. He taps him on his shoulder.

Turning around to answer the broken nose bruiser, Jack notices the four men sitting as they entered the bar was now near the counter. "Hmm, what can I do for you?" Standing before Jack was a big man not smiling.

"My friends and me had a hard time recently. We decided you buying us a beer would make us feel better. This might make us more friendly with guest in our bar."

"Oh, I see, well, if I told you, we don't want you as friends and to go buy your own beers, would that make you not our friends? Maybe leave us alone, too."

Chopper kept sipping his beer along with Razor oblivious to Jack's friend requesting a beer for him and his friends.

The bent nose bruiser looks at his three companions at the other end of the bar. Jack saw the three men, I guess, if I should be friendly to you, I will need to buy beers for your friends, also?"

"You got the right idea. You look smart, even if you are a fat, stupid, American, we got visiting this place. Buying us a beer might make us change our attitude toward all Americans," he replied with a laugh and grin.

Jack turns to Chopper and Razor, "well, do you want some new friends with these dumb ass holes?"

"Not me, answered Chopper."

"Not me either, Jack," replied Razor.

Jack turns to confront the broken nose bruiser, "go fuck yourself, asshole. If that ain't possible, get one of your queery boys to do it for you."

"We tried to be friends, American. But now you go and insult our hospitably to you."

"Oh, is that what I did, I thought I was giving you three directions on getting yourselves fucked."

No sooner than Jack completed what he said, the big bruiser with the broken nose hauls off with a solid left punch to Jack's jaw. The other three men went to grab Razor and Chopper drinking their beers.

Jack block the slow punch to his jaw with his beer mug and returned his punch followed with a kick to the big bruiser' s groin. Jack's punch flatten what was left of the bruiser's nose. Blood slowly dripped out from the nose. Jack figured it was drain of all the blood from the first punch that broke his nose.

"Damn, that beer was sorely wanted. Now, I wasted a cold beer on you, dummy."

The big bruiser reached for his nose to realign it but the kick to his groin ended his attempts. He attempted to screamed before dropping to the floor. Jack ended his misery with a knee to his jaw. He fell back with a flop. He never made the scream he was saving from the second nose getting broke a second time.

Chopper sitting in the center shoved his palm out meeting the oncoming man in his chest. The approaching man stopped almost immediately. Chopper spun around on his stool delivering a similar punch to his man's nose, then followed up with a kick to his gut. His man bent over violently emptying his belly between Choppers spread legs onto the floor. A knee ended any more puking by his man.

Razor got lucky. He finished his beer when his man grabbed him. The mug shattered against the man's hard head. He was out before he hit the deck. The last man was Razor lucky number. He ended the first man quickly and never had an opportunity to unload like both his friends.

Before Razor could administer a welcome to the man hastily attempting to land a blow, Chopper had grabbed hold of an un-occupied stool. He offered the fourth man a stool to sit on. Instead, the stool missed it's mark pinning the head between the legs of the stool that came crashing down on the fourth man. Razor sighed with relief.

"Damn Chopper. I was counting on giving him, a welcome."

"I knew that Razor, I missed his head on purpose."

"Sure, you did. Anyway, I can still welcome him."

"Your welcome Razor." Chopper handed the stool to Razor. He twisted the stool. The sudden twist on the stool jerked the head down. Razor yanked on the stool shoving his man's head into the bar counter. The head poked through to the lower counter. The legs of the stool didn't break. Each of the three legs were jammed tight in the bar counter top.

"That is one well-made stool," Chopper quipped with a laugh.

Jack had just enough time to get his first swig of beer when two men entered from the street. One man race to accept a beer from Jack. Jack offered his empty mug as Razor had done with his second man. Jack was in a hurry and missed the jaw of the first man charging them at the counter. Luckily, Jack caught the next man racing for his beer behind the man he missed. The mug impacted squarely in his face, knocking him backwards, hitting a table, then rolling over it to the floor.

"That was beautiful Jack," chided Chopper.

The first man Jack missed with his mug left Chopper eagerly waiting to offer his empty mug to him. He needed a refill. Jack leaned when he should have swayed with the first man rushing at them from the street. The man hit the bar. He quickly corrected his miss, turning around to make another attempt at one of the old farts standing at the bar. A knife hand strike to the man's neck was followed by a mug upper cut to his jaw. The fight ended with another old fashioned American left hook punch spinning the man around on his heels.

Razor handed him his new beer on the way down after Chopper made his acquaintance with his old Fashion American beer mug left-hand punch. The mug shatter splitting the man's skull.

Razor turns to Jack, "that is the least I can do for my new friend, is to treat him to a cold beer."

"Thanks, good buddy," replied Jack.

"Me too Jack. I had an empty mug and nowhere to put it. You going to give me a cold beer," requested Chopper?

"You two are the best."

All three men sitting at the bar re-ordered another beer. A third man was about to enter the bar. He saw six of his friends lying on the floor. He had several options to choose from. "One, to turn and run out the door, two, make a dash for the bathroom, and three, take on three old farts sitting at the bar," he pondered with great anxiety.

Chopper stood. The man ran to the head. Outside, someone might spot him running away was in his thoughts. Chopper undeterred, followed the man to the head. A loud flushing sound was heard at the bar when he walked out of the head.

Chopper returns to his seat. All three men turn around simultaneously ordering a third round of beers. The barkeep loss several teeth earlier and decided to abstain from entering this fight. He grins through his bloody rag. He replied with a muffled sentence, "coming right up." He made sure the mugs had no foam. His first thoughts seeing the three old men enter his bar was they were going to be easy. Plenty of beers for his men, all around.

Chopper quipped to Razor and Jack, "that was what was missing on this trip. I bet the others wished they were here?" Both men agreed with Chopper.

"Yeah, for once, we get to talk about our adventure, instead of Cho and Mike recount theirs. That was getting a bit tiring, letting them have all the fun, of late."

"Yeah Chopper, we get the bragging rights this time. Let get going. We stay here any longer, there might be more patrons to offer us their friendship."

"Your right Jack, we can't stay here having fun. Maybe after we find Cheryl, we should come back."

"That's a great idea, Chopper."

Chopper flips out a hundred dollar-bill. Both Razor and Jack did the same. The barkeep took the money with a sudden feeling this was somewhat like the first encounter, he had earlier. He pondered for a few seconds on the coincidence of both fights occurring in his bar on the same day. He fingered through the six hundred dollar-bills, dismissing the thought, as the three elderly men walked out of his bar.

A THIRD TIME AGAIN

Bell, Rhonda, Susan, and Miriam found themselves walking in a circle. Miriam kept telling them they were walking the wrong way. She was right. They followed her advice and now was walking in a circle but not in the wrong direction. After a second time around the city, even Miriam began to recognize the same buildings. Their third trip convinced them; indeed they were traveling in a circle.

Girls, I'm hot, tired, and thirsty, quipped Miriam. Where is a place to get out of this heat and get a cold drink?"

"Bell, I saw some stands by the beach, selling drinks, quipped Rhonda."

"Which way do we head, Rhonda?"

"I think it is that way, Bell."

Rhonda points the way thru a narrow passageway between tall buildings. She spotted the bar earlier. It was a small dingy bar with a door barely held to the frame had a sign painted on the window. The first part of the name was hard to read, the second word was all they needed to know, bar.

That place looked like a slum, commented Miriam. Miriam was feeling scared hearing Rhonda recount her seeing the same bar she saw and wanted no part of it. All four women paid little attention to their direction leaving the hotel. They went where Cho pointed Mike and Chopper were going. Their path went the opposite direction.

After an hour or maybe longer, three women were seen coming in their direction. Bell was the first to spot who they were. "Hey girls, looky there."

Penny, Laura, and Judy saw them, as the others spotted them. What are you three doing out here in the middle of nowhere, asked Bell?"

"We went down stairs to eat breakfast and discovered Cheryl was missing. Cho said a search party was begun. One with Mike, Bone, and Jamie. A second team with Razor, Jack, and Chopper. When we heard Cho say the third team was you girls, we decided to head this way."

"Where is Pretty, Judy?"

"Oh, Cho made him stay at the hotel. Since there were four teams out scurrying about and only one man to run informing the search parties if Cheryl was found; Pretty was volunteered to be a second runner."

"We were walking around in a circle. We decided to look for a watering hole. It is hot and we are tired and thirsty."

"I know where we are. Cheryl and I walked this way to the beach. A few blocks from here, is a bar. We can go there to rest, get a drink, and cool off Miriam," said Judy.

"Good, lead the way, Judy."

"Hey, why is Susan so quiet like?"

"She is worried about Cheryl being alone in this city, Penny. Wouldn't you be." Laura puts her arm around Susan to comfort her.

"Thanks Laura, I'm okay, said Susan."

"See, right where I said it would be, girls."

"Yeah, you were right, wish you were a little more descriptive of this place, announced Laura. Miriam looked at the seedy bar. Smoke poured out of the door barely hanging on a hinge. It wasn't so much as the rundown appearance that bothered Miriam but more so the scruffy, fat, oily haired man attempting to repair the door.

Bell made the first attempt to approach the repairman. "Is this place a bar, where a girl can get a cold drink, Mister?"

The fat, oily hair, scruffy man looked to where the voice was coming from, spitted tobaccy on the ground before answering. "Yep, go on in. Got plenty of tables for pretty girlies to sit. I'll be in soon."

All the girls walked passed the scruffy, oily haired man, unshaven, unkempt, wearing a torn shirt and sporting a bloody rag over one shoulder. Miriam turned her head from looking at the man entering the bar. He spoke to each lady passing through the door.

Evening girls. His breath nearly made Penny heave. Laura held her nose. Bell paid no attention and the rest hurried past him.

Inside, five blurry men sat in a corner. Each man had a bandage across a bent nose. One man had a rag held to his mouth. At the bar was two more men, sipping beers through what looked like a straw. One man kept bent over drinking his beer.

All seven women entered through the door. Every eye turned to watch them sash-che to a table. Seven women walked in. The first was a tall, well buxom red hair. "A real eye catcher," whispered one of the men sitting at the table in the corner.

Next, was Susan. A whistle ran out. Laura followed and more whistles followed. Penny and Judy walked in. One man attempted to stand. He was forced back into his seat. Rhonda and Miriam were the last two. Both were older than the other girls but still caught the eyes of many men.

"Hey, that's my kind of a woman," shouted one man sitting. Bell remained standing after the others sat. She walks over to the bar counter. The oily haired scruffy man rush behind the bar. What ye pleasure, cutie?"

Miriam was near panicky. Rhonda held her hand to calm her. "Why so nervous. In your day, you would flaunt yourself back at them. Then, if any man got fresh, you wouldn't hesitate to slap the shit out of him. I guess, Razor was always nearby. Yeah, I see he has babied you too much."

"Don't be upset with me, Rhonda. I'm not like I was when I was younger."

Bell answered the barkeep. Seven cold beers. She didn't trust any alcohol this bar might serve. Looking about the bar, she figured any booze was distill in the back, inside a car radiator. Not fit to drink."

Miriam was panicky again, when a man at the table pointed at her and smiled. The next thing occurred, had her ready to bolt, was him standing walking "to their table. "Standing was a polite thing to call his stagger, thinking Penny.

He walked toward a table near theirs but never made the trip to sit down, instead, toppled over onto their table. Miriam screamed when the man's face landed between her breast. He looked up smiling with most of his teeth missing. All the men roared, watching him face plant his face between the lovely lady's breast.

Laura, Susan, and Penny weren't laughing. Rhonda was doing her best to calm Miriam. Bell acted first. She grabbed the man from behind by his belt. Then, jerked up. He stood quick. Bell slapped his face with a force that swung him in a complete circle before hitting the floor. His friends laughed louder.

The drunk swiftly rose to his feet to confront the statuette red hair. He should have stayed down. Rhonda uncrossed her legs. One leg went up between the two legs that supported the drunk. He went back to the floor. Stupidly or too drunk to know better, the man holding his groin attempted to stand again. Bell aided his attempt with her knee. He went up making flipped back toward his table. Every beer was flung on each of the laughing men sitting, now standing. Their laughing stopped and a nasty look took place on their faces.

A lone man at the bar awoke from his stupor. Miriam made oohs and aahs watching the drunk get slammed by her friends. The lone man looked at the table with the women and his friends by another table. He reacted without thinking. Charging at Bell.

Bell side-step, Laura was waiting. Her forearm moved under his chin. Both legs lifted into the air, his head led the way for both feet. He went crashing down on the floor. Laura stopped any pain he was feeling with a snap kick, to his face.

Four men stood and moved toward the table where all the women were still sitting. Another man from the opposite end of the bar. Penny met the first most daring man to arrive at their table first. He felt her side kick in his guts. Everything he ate dumped out. She followed her kick when the man was stooped over with an axe heel kick to his back. The cracking sound was agonizing wickedly sickening to hear.

The second man to get within range, was closest to Susan. She vented her frustration and fears that one of then, might be with Cheryl. He reached to grab her breast. They were the perky type not the melon or tear drop shaped. He noticed them bouncing pointy boobs with lust. He was going to get a feel, even if it killed him. It nearly did.

He got his wish and a feel. Susan allowed his lusty grab as a last wish granted to him. She wanted him focused on her boobs and not on what was coming his way. He managed to make a comment before the blow came. "Hey, babe, these boobs feel really good."

"Glad you like my boobs, Susan replied with a grin. A knee rammed up between his groin. Both sacs were crushed. Before he could move, Susan reached under his arm, tucked under the man, thrusted her hip, and threw the fool over her shoulder. He landed on a table with a loud whack. Then, before he could comprehend what happened, all four legs of the table snapped. He went to the floor on top of the table. He didn't have a long wait. Susan delivered her next kick. His face caved in from her heel.

Judy stepped away from the table. The door was nearby. Rhonda told her to run. She made it to the door, only to run into another man, entering. She didn't hesitate. Neither did the incoming man. Both swung at the other. Judy was first to make her hit. The other guy folded from her knee cap dislocation kick, followed by a wheel kick slamming him into the newly fixed door.

One man was left. Bell moved to take him on. Miriam shouted to her. Bell he is mine. Bell turned looking at scarcity cat Miriam, stunned to hear her say that.

Rhonda too was amazed at Miriam's sudden change. Maybe what she said, sparked a toughness inside her, still remaining. Miriam walks up to the smiling man waiting to see what she was going to do. He heard her scream and panic. He wasn't expecting much. That was his mistake.

Miriam kicked between the man's legs. Not at his groin but a nerve bundle inside the thigh. Another man recovering, stood, grabbed Miriam from the rear. Bell stopped Rhonda from acting to aid Miriam.

"Let her be, she needs this."

Miriam felt the arms wrap around her chest from behind. One of three thing happened in a blink of an eye. One, was a heel kick going down on the top of the man's foot. Next, was her butt slamming into his guts followed with a knuckle strike on the back of his hand gripping her. Then, both of her arm spray out shooting her holders arm out releasing the tight grip the man had around her chest. She dropped down, reached under her legs, grabbing hold of both of the man's leg. He went down. He was followed with a sharp side kick to his groin.

The other man was in severe pain from her nerve kick. He was lucky when Miriam dropped him with her version of an axe heel kick to his crown of his head.

Rhonda stood amazed at Miriam's skill. Her man began to stand. She thought he wouldn't, after what she done to him. She wheeled kicked him with a crescent kick. He spun like a top on his knees. Bell watched waiting for him to stop spinning. She decided to end the monotonous spinning with another crescent kick. It only made him spin longer.

"The barkeeper watched with astonishment. These men I got can't even beat women in a bar fight. I need some new blood," he silently remarked to himself.

Another man stood up to run out the door. Penny grabbed his belt. She lifted the man to his tippy toes. Susan and Laura were staring at the fool that stood up. "After you, Laura."

"No, no after you Susan. You need this far more than I do."

Thanks Laura. Susan shoots an open cupped hand into the fool's throat. He gasped for air. "Your turn, Laura."

"With pleasure, Susan." Laura watched for a second to make her decision while the man struggled, to breathe. She decided to try a move Cho taught her. Grabbing hold of his oily hair, she spins him around, then shoots her hand filled with oily hair downward. The impact halted him gasping for air.

Bell turns to the barkeep. "Where are our beers?"

The barkeep grabs all seven beers in both hands, gingerly walking around the bar carefully avoiding any fallen man. After watching those women, he did not want to spill their beers. He placed all the beer down on the only table still standing. Susan noticed the barkeep looked to be crying.

The barkeep wasn't crying. "He was thinking the damage done this day was going to ruin his reputation. He would have to endure all the jeers from the town's people. They once feared him, now, that was gone when the word got around, how a kid beat every man up in his bar. Then, later that same day, three old men farts did the same, again. Now, to further humiliate him, women repeated beating up the most fear band of thugs in this town. He hoped no one was watching to tell."

One lone man witnessed the last fight. He was passing by the bar. A beer would be nice. The bar was open, after a certain time for any locals. He stopped from entering, hearing a ruckus inside the bar. He figured some tourist went inside. They often did to their regrets. He stood across the street waiting for him to be thrown out. Instead, seven women walked out of the bar.

Once everyone's thirst was quenched, Bell handed the barkeep a hundred dollar-bill. Susan, Laura, Penny, Miriam, and Rhonda followed suit. Judy waited at the door. All the women walked toward the door. Bell turned around to make one last remark to the barkeep.

"Hey, with all that money, you might want to get this door fixed."

Once outside, a lone figure emerged from the back room. He heard the ruckus and was in the head. He remained in the back, hidden. Walking out, the barkeep gives him an order.

"Follow them dames. See where they are staying. See it any others show up. Return here quick. Got that." Something wasn't right. Three times his men got whupped. Each time, he was given hundred-dollar bills. Somehow, all that must have a common denominator, he reasoned.

No Good to Run and Hide

Three men were walking along the beach on the boardwalk. "Hey guys, look over there, shouted Jamie. Jamie halted while Mike and Bone walked on. They stopped and turned to his shout. They saw him ogling several women bare chested sunbathing on the sandy beach. Both of them walked to Jamie leaning on the rail toward the beach from the boardwalk. Two topless babes walked near, where he stood. Both of Jamie's eyes were transfixed on four well-tanned boobs approaching his way. Each topless girl giggled, watching him drool.

"He is cute. He must be an American. They never seen any women boobs before. American women are only simple flirts. We are better flirts."

"Yes, yes, you are correct, my girlfriend. I bet he offers us a drink. They always do."

Jamie heard nothing but saw plenty. Mike spotted the girls before his companions had. Two women walking toward Jamie spotted the handsome young man with the two older men. They stood to walk over to him. Jamie thought it was to greet him. That changed, when the tall giant turned with a growl across his face. The giant appeared to have a case of bad indigestion. They turned from walking over to tease the young man. Jamie was disappointed.

"Hey, why don't our girls walk around the beach, topless. They got just as good as them chicks with the boobs," sniped Jamie watching the two girls turn away.

Bone quipped back; "they do at a place in San Diego, called Black's Beach."

"When we get back, Bone, I'll remind you to take me there."

"Can't Jamie. I'm a married man. You talk to my wife, Penny. If she says it is okay."

"What, you a big guy having to ask your old lady?"

"Jamie, the next words out your mouth, might be the last you speak for a few months, snarled Bone."

"Sorry man, didn't mean no disrespect to you or your wife. You can go ahead and punch me. Just not too hard, please."

Mike wasn't paying much attention to the scenery, as was Jamie. Looking around, he saw a familiar sight.

"Hey Bone, you and Jamie take that direction, I go over there. Mike pointed to an alley.

"We can go with you, kiddo."

"No, night coming quick. We can cover more ground, if we separate. I'll meet you two in the plaza, before darkness."

"Whatever you say, kiddo."

Bone, lets walk on the beach. Never know some chicks might have bumped into Cheryl. She might even be lying on the sands, getting a tan."

"Who you kidding, you just want to check out the girl's naked bodies?"

No sooner than Bone and Jamie walked on the beach, Mike darted off across the street. The person he spotted, was walking into the alley. He saw Mike, just as Mike spotted him. Mike did not want Bone to catch sight of this man. It didn't take long to catch up with Moss, aka One Eye. Moss looked like he was homeless to Mike.

"Moss, wait up. Why you walking aimlessly around? You look like a mess. Didn't Chopper get you a hotel room?"

Mike stopped short of hugging his friend, there was still a little unforgiveness left inside of him. Still, he was happy to see Moss. Cho was aware of Moss on the island. He reported Moss's involvement in the desert. Moss being alive, was a good sign, Chopper had not told the others.

"He did and now, I am on the street. I got no money and been asking for hand-outs from the tourist. I can't get back home until I make some money for a plane ride."

"Yeah, I would say, fly with us. Cho and Chopper wouldn't object but the others might toss you off the plane. Razor, Jack, Bone, and Pretty are on the island. Susan is here."

Moss looked quizzical about hearing Susan's name.

"Moss, Susan is the wife of the man your men ambushed at the warehouse. I wouldn't give you a plug nickels of a chance for your life. Stephen was well-loved, and respected, and Susan's husband."

"Thanks, but there ain't much I can do about that. You know, I got no ways of leaving this isle, Mike."

"Come with me. I will get you a meal and we can discuss the future."

"You done enough for me, Mike. I can't keep letting you help me anymore."

"You got that all wrong, Moss. You helped me see inside myself. I found forgiveness and God through your teachings. Besides, there are some bad people on this isle."

"I know Mike. I want nothing to do with my old life. That is my I am begging."

"We can talk further, after you get a meal in your belly. Down this alley is a café. We go and get a meal. I'm hungry too. After a big meal and several beers down between the two, Mike relates his problem to Moss.

"You see Moss, I believe she is taking drugs. I hesitated to tell her mother, Susan. If she contacted some drug dealers on the street, they could, well, I need to find her before that happens."

"What does she look like? I will help you."

"Cheryl is sixteen, taller than me, nice figure, has long, straight, blonde hair, and blue eyes. She walks with a slight limp. I believe she is still wearing her green evening gown."

"Mike, I have some bad news. I did see her. It was early this morning, just before sunrise. She walked pass me in tears. She stopped me to asked about, well, she wanted to buy."

"What, go on and say it?"

"Drugs, Mike. I told her I couldn't help her with that need. She walked on passed me. I decided to follow her. She met a man on a corner. I saw the man deal drugs throughout the night. He left Cheryl at a corner. He returned, both left just as you spotted me."

"What, where, Mike inquired anxiously?"

"Mike, this guy would walk away from a client and return later to fill a big order. I think Cheryl made an order, he had to make a special trip to get. This guy, I dealt with in the past. He came to the states with a partner. He made his money collecting young girls, to, to sell as sex slaves. He bragged about drugging tourists, hide them on his island until, he could ship them off to the mainland."

"You believe this is what he has plans for Cheryl?"

Moss nods his head, then points down a street. "Around the corner, he would meet his client in a van. Rumors on the street is, that was the last time they were seen. The local police do little to deter this market in drugs and sex slavery."

Without any words said, Mike slaps a hundred on the table, jumps up and raced toward the street corner.

A truck was stopped. A hand reached out of the side door. A girl entered the side doors. She turned to look back. A blur of a person was seen racing toward her.

Cheryl was waiting, as directed by the drug dealer. His boss wanted to talk to her, before giving her what she wanted. The door shut.

Mike reached the van as the door shut. Cheryl saw who the blur was. Mike was staring at her. The van sped off. Cheryl screamed, seeing Mike. She realized her hidden secret was now, not so hidden. She felt ashamed.

Mike grabbed for the door handle. He was to slow. The van ran down the alley, he came up. Mike chased after the van. Cheryl called Mike's name. The driver looked in his rearview mirror spotting a man chasing his van. He was nearly upon him. The driver floored the pedal.

The alley was to narrow and had trash cans. The driver had little choice but to squeal his brakes to a halt. Smokes rolled around the wheel hub from the burning brakes. The driver swiftly reverses, backing toward the stranger following.

The van was nearly upon the stranger. The driver prepared for an impending impact. None came. Again, Cheryl screamed. Another man in the van with her, fought hard to restrain Cheryl struggling to get out of the van.

Meanwhile, Mike at the last-minute, leap up onto the van's rooftop. Inside, the driver and the two in the rear heard nothing, when he landed on top. When a fist came crashing through the cab of the roof, the driver saw and heard the stranger. The driver began to swerve the van back and forth across the narrow alley street. Mike grabbed hold of the roof ripping the lid off like a can of sardines lid being rolled back.

The driver slammed hard into the wall of a building watching this stranger peeling the roof on his truck, off. He wanted nothing to do with him. Mike wasn't prepared for the sudden jarring impact of the van into the building. Sparks flew from the side toward the rear of the moving van. Mike lost his grip and footing. He slip toward the rear of the van. He would have fell off if not for the driver believing he was still on top of his roof. He jammed on his brakes to attempt to throw the person from the roof of his van.

Mike stopped sliding back to the rear of the van and was flung forward. He stopped, landing on the hood of the van. Mike lean over the windshield to get a look at the driver. The driver saw the face of the stranger staring at him through the windshield. He was a young kid. Still, the face had two eyes filled with death. That look, he hoped to never see again. Both eyes glowed red. The windshield shattered.

For the first time since that night, the driver witnessed his own vulnerability with a near death experience. That night changed his life. He knew death was closing in. The driver was young with few options to make a better life for him and his poor family. He was either destined to be a fisherman or a tourist guide. Not much to inspire a young man, he constantly fretted about. He could move to the mainland but that too had difficulties. With no friends and skills, he was left with begging or fishing.

One night, a man appeared from the darkness, holding a gun. He pointed it into his friend's face, demanding all their money. What money they earned fishing was swiftly gone. A week of hard back breaking work gone in a minute. He knew right then and there; back breaking work, wasn't worth it. There was an easier, more profitable way.

The next day, the driver recalled, "him and his friend went to the boss. To request a job. It wasn't much of a job, they got. It was every nasty job the men teased them constantly for doing. Still, the pay was better for one day's work than the meager amount allotted to them for a week doing fishing. His friend finally quit. He knew he had to prove himself to get a promotion. One day, that changed.

He was being constantly teased by one man taunting him every day. It was so annoying, he decided he had enough. He walked up to him without a word said, and punch him smack in his face. The teasing man was stunned and shocked that the kid had the guts to take a poke at him. The punch barely made him whence.

The man looked at the punk with some disappointment. If his punch dropped him, he might have more respect for the effort. His friends stared at him, not expecting him to take a punch without dropping the kid soon after getting punched. They listened to Big Bruno for a year poking fun at the kid. They sat silently, stunned, the kid had the backbone to punch the biggest, baddest of all of them.

Bruno's first reaction was to hit the kid. All bets were on Bruno to drop the kid setting a new record. What they got was Big Bruno laughing then wrapped his arm around the shoulder of the kid. Bruno announced to all he was his best new little buddy. The best for him and no more poking fun by anyone.

The driver rose up the ranks with Bruno advice and training. This job he was working was to be his stepping stone to a better job on the mainland. It took three years to get to where he was, now. He was the best. Besides, all the girls were from rich Americans. All, were spoiled brats. The money poured in. He was making tons of money.

He jerked on his steering wheel into another wall. Mike lost a hand hold. The next slamming in the wall made him lose the other hand grip on the fragile remaining windshield. Glass crumbled in his hands. Mike went falling off the truck. He landed on his feet. The driver looked back, amazed to see the kid still standing.

Mike's feet struck the wall. He pumped his legs shooting off the flaming wall before being squeeze between the wall and the van sparking side panel. Mike slid across the hood grabbing hold to the fender long enough to project himself up into the air making a flip, to his feet.

"Who the hell is that guy, yelled the driver?"

Cheryl replied, "he is my boyfriend. Whatever you do, don't stop."

"Hell girl, I ain't a dummy or crazy. After what he just did, all I want is as far away from him as I can get." Quickly, the driver floors the gas pedal. The truck sped up. The driver watched the guy chase after the van.

"Damn, he is gaining on us," screamed the other man in the rear looking out the windows.

"I know, I can see him in my mirror, replied the scared driver."

The driver ran into everything in the alley to slow the stranger chasing him. Trash cans went flying. Mike leap over or spun, and flipped over each flying can, never slowing. A clothes line got ripped off the wall. Mike rolled on the street to evade the tangle line and clothes.

The driver never took his eyes from his mirror. What he saw, scared the be-jeevies out of him. That was when he recalled his first near death experience being robbed at gun point. He watched this stranger evade any debris coming at him. He seemed to defy the laws of gravity. He leaped, twisted, bounced from a wall, then back on another wall appearing to run across the wall. Then, by some magic, he would appear to walk across some of the flying trash cans in mid-air.

The driver was in a panic. Cheryl kept screaming at him to speed up. "Don't let him catch us."

He yelled back to the girl. "Who the hell or what the hell is that guy?"

Finally, after hearing Cheryl constant screaming, he shouted, "shut up girl." After the third or fourth banging his van against the wall didn't slow the stranger, in fact, he was gaining ground, the driver realized he was the one slowing down. Each bang slowed the van. He put the foot to the pedal speeding up and stopped ramming into the wall. It worked; he could see the stranger fading back. At the end of the alley, he turned sharply. The van tipped to one side almost flipping over.

By the time Mike made it to the corner, the van was far up the road, making another hard turn. "He lost his one chance to get Cheryl, sighed Mike not wanting to tell Susan, he loss Cheryl."

Moss followed Mike into the alley losing sight of him around the corner. He had to dodge a van speeding into the alley. The van came to a sudden halt, then backed up fast. That was when he spotted Mike. "It was amazing to see Mike do his thing, spoke Moss to himself."

Mike leaped on the van's roof, ripped the cab's roof nearly off, almost was tossed off, slid back to the front hood, punch a hole in the windshield, again, nearly thrown off, when the van slammed a building wall and somehow Mike flipped up in the air clearing the wall and van, landing on his feet in the alley street.

Walking on the wall came as a shocker to Moss watching Mike, resume his chasing after the speeding van. Next, was walking on top of all the flying trash cans flung into the air. He walked in mid-air on each can like stepping stones crossing a stream. A memory of him chasing Mike on rooftops in the city flashed in Moss's thoughts. Back then, he survived a warehouse blast. His face was burned, and wounded. He made an easy trail to follow with blood dripping on the ground.

Back then, he never knew Mike's skill level. In the desert, he learned how dangerous, he really was. He was lucky in the city and again in the Mexican jungle. He fought off the whole Cartel soldiers, until Master Cho came to his aide. At the prison city in the desert, Master Cho wasn't there to help. On the road leaving the city, Master Cho wasn't there to help. He took on all those soldier single handedly. No one would ever believe him, if he told them what Mike can do.

Walking back through the alley, Mike spotted Moss coming the other way. "Moss, she was in the van. It got away. I got a favor to asked you."

"I know exactly what you are going to ask. I think I can get what you need. Where can I contact you?"

"If you show up at the hotel, you might not leave, Moss."

"I'll worry about that when the time comes."

"Moss, you do this for me and I will get you off this island and fill your pockets with cash. Mike reaches into his pocket pulling out a wad of cash. Take this."

Moss looked at the wad. "I can't take your money. I owe you more than I could ever repay, now."

"Take it Moss. You are going to need money to learn any intel from those you know. What is left, use it for food and lodging until I get you off this island. I'll be waiting at the hotel." Mike dashes off before Moss could say a word.

Mike wanted to get to Bone and Jamie. He figured Jamie would be on the beach. He was right. Jamie walked around ogling all the bare breasted women. Bone was nearby keeping an eye on him.

After telling them what happened and Cheryl's getting away, a loud shout was heard. Bell spotted Mike, Bone, and Jamie on the beach.

Miriam quipped to Rhonda seeing them on a beach with naked women, all around them. "I wonder what Penny would say if she was with us?" She giggled.

"Ssh, you two." Bell greeted the three by the boardwalk. Jamie blurted out what Mike did.

"Mike spotted Cheryl getting into a van." Susan was walking a few feet behind the women. She heard Jamie's remark.

"Susan, listen, I allowed Cheryl to get away. She entered a van. I chased after it. I couldn't stop the driver. He went north, out of the city."

"Was she okay?"

"Yes, she looked good, Susan. Mike, did Cheryl enter the van freely, asked Rhonda?"

Mike hesitated before answering her question. "Yes and no. Bell gave Mike a quirky look. I think, she was not going inside the van freely. Maybe spotting me, she changed her mind and jump inside on her own accord."

"Why Mike would my child do that? You, you."

Susan, all I can think, is she felt ashamed seeing me with those men she was with. One other thing, I should tell you all. My friend said, that person is a known sex slave seller. The good news is, he will keep his women lock away on the island until he can set a time to ship them to the mainland. Time is important. We got to be ready when my man learns anything, to act quick. If we continue this search, me may lose that opportunity to amass enough people to go after her."

"Thank God, Bell snapped. Miriam held Susan as Mike continue telling his story. "I got a friend who knows people on this island. He will use his contacts to find where the driver is. He will meet me at the hotel. No need to continue our search, until we learn more."

Susan wanted to continue her search. Mike, I can't wait at the hotel for a maybe intel coming."

"Susan, we got no choice. My friend said to continue with the search and asking questions, will make her captor harder to locate. They will dig in, or hurry up their time table or something bad."

Miriam squealed once she figured out what Mike meant, saying something bad.

Bone asked Bell, "if she saw his wife? I left her at the hotel before telling her about Cheryl gone missing. Her and the other ladies found us on the street. We went to a bar. Some men hit on us. We had to straighten their attitudes out. She was with us girls. We left the bar and split up. I think her team should be making their way back to the hotel."

"Who was with her, Jamie inquired?"

"Well, there is Penny, you know of, Judy and Laura. Mike was surprised Laura went with a search party, without Cho. Bell saw his look. Cho stayed at the hotel and didn't stop Laura from going. I don't think he had any choice Mike, chuckled Bell." Everyone decided to walk back to the hotel, together. It was a short walk from the beach. Jamie lagged behind.

Everyone was coming or entering the hotel about the same time. Most met in the lobby. Cho arranged for their dining. Mike went straight to Chopper and Cho.

"I found Cheryl entering a van. She is being held as a sex slave captive. Moss helped me find her. He has contacts. He is going to learn where this sex slave trader keeps his girls. Moss said, he would have a time table to ship his girls to the mainland. He will meet with me here, tonight with news."

Cho asked Mike, "you did tell Moss about the other bikers here. They will cut him up in to so many pieces, he will make great dog food."

"He knows, father Cho."

"He is still going to help Mike, Chopper asked with a surprise?"

"Yes."

"I smell food, Chopper said turning to look toward the dining room.

"Dinner is waiting Chopper, I want a private talk with Mike. Please go to the bar and tell the others, dinner is ready, requested Master Cho."

Mike follows Cho outside the hotel. Night was ebbing at the horizon. The sky was aglow with an orange tint. A silent figure creeped toward the hotel main doors, but not un-noticed by both Master Cho and Mike not standing far, shielded from any eyes wanting to look at them talking by a row of tall shrubs.

"Is there something you have not told me, my son?"

"I found Moss on the streets, begging for money. I thought Chopper got him a room. He had no money and wouldn't take my money until I made him. I told him to use the cash to learn what he can about Cheryl. I promised to get him off the island, later."

"Hmm. I would expect nothing less from you. Is there more?"

"Yes, I allowed the van to get away. I chased it but I couldn't save Cheryl."

"Did you do everything you could, my son?"

'Yes."

"Then, keep not this thought to weed into a garden of regret and fear."

"I will wait outside; you go and get a bite to eat. When you finish eating, come and relieve me. Laura steps outside and begins to talk to Cho.

Mike turned to enter the hotel. Moss was at the front door. The doorman was stopping him from entering. Mike calls to Cho, "he's here." Mike takes Moss back to the shrubs.

Cho tells Laura to go back inside and keep all the others from coming outside. Laura waved to Moss entering the hotel. Laura sees Susan by the front door. Susan heard some of their conversation.

Cho entered the lobby hearing Susan shouting at Laura. Mike remained with Moss to learn what new intel he has founded out.

"Who was that? I heard a name, Moss. Do I know of him and how does he fit into this, with my Cheryl?"

Cho motioned Laura away. Susan, Moss was with Mike and me in the desert. He helped Mike fighting the black Muslin terrorist before my team arrived at the mountains. He has proven to be a good and trusted friend. He is teaching Mike about God. He is a man of God, now. He was a very bad man, until he found religion. That is all you need to know for the time being. He is helping us fine Cheryl using contacts he has on this island."

"What has he learned, Cho?"

"Mike is learning that now." Cho sensed Susan was content with what he shared with her. Cho realized, he and Mike was going to need to tell her the rest. For now, it was better to not tell her anything more than what concerns their search for Cheryl. If she learned Moss was One Eye, the man responsible for Stephen, her husband's death. Shit would hit the fan. Every biker in the hotel will be wanting blood. Finding Cheryl would end before it got started."

THE SPLIT UP

Mike was correct about Moss, watching him help their family, knowing if discovered would mean certain death for him, proved he was a changed man, thought Cho. Master Cho reflected on all that occurred with Moss returning outside to learn what was discovered.

"Once this beggar was a leader of a large Atlanta street gang raking in millions from his drug empire. Just days ago, he was in a desert city prison rescued by Mike. Then, fought alongside my son and me against an army of terrorists. My son says, he teaches him about God. Today, he ekes out a living asking for hand-outs from the tourists, thought Cho seeing Moss and his son talk.

Outside the hotel, Moss quickly informs Cho and Mike all he has learned. "This is worse than we thought. The man selling Cheryl drugs and kidnapped her to sell as a sex slave has taken her to a safe place on the island we feared, to hide. Mike, your attempts to rescue Cheryl has sped up his timeline to get his girls off the island. That alley chase put the fear of God in the man, he is running scared."

"Moss, how does he plan on doing this and when. Did you learn any of this?"

"Master Cho there is a small boat preparing to launch within hours, located on the opposite end of the isle. There are few homes. Just a tiny fishing village."

Cho swiftly takes a wad of cash from his pocket shoving it into Moss's hand. After you take Mike to the place on the island, quickly return here. That money is for you to continue your investigations. Moss, before you leave is there another way off the island, other than a fishing boat?"

"Maybe a landing strip not far from the fishing village."

"Good, Mike, you and Moss make to the village. I will inform the others and meet you there. Don't wait on us. I will take men to the landing strip. Two men will remain here. The others will leave to aid you or go with me." Pretty walks outside to stand by his leader, as a second is to do.

Cho turns to Pretty and Moss, "once you return, help Pretty keep an eye on the women. They might try something, especially one tall, brown hair, pretty lady. That will be Cheryl's mom."

"Master Cho I am your second, I 'll get Jimmie or another."

"No, I need someone I can trust, Pretty." Pretty saw Moss and suddenly realized who he was. Now, Master Cho's orders made sense to him. He was to be quiet on this matter without being told by Master Cho.

"Master Cho, I was informed that this slave boat doesn't depart until there is a boat load of girls. It is expected to meet its quota in a day or so."

"It is like you said Moss, I might have hurried things up trying to stop that van. We cannot take that chance, interjected Mike."

"Are you up to a long run, Moss? I noticed you have acquired a limp."

"No, my legs have yet to heal enough to keep up with your running, maybe never. I saw how fast you can run."

"I don't intend to wait for you. I've seen many tourists ride scooters. Where can we rent scooters in this town, Moss?"

"We are in luck, there is a small shop to rent scooters down this street."

Mike grabs Moss dragging him behind to a small rental shop. Two scooters were rented. Twenty minutes later, two scooters eased up to the edge of a village. Darkness was beginning to settle over the sea. Lights flickered on in the small homes. Several lanterns were spotted being carried to a small boat near the shore. Fishermen were readying their boats for the night. All, accept one boat left in the water.

One lantern went away from the boats into the trees. Mike and Moss silently crept toward the homes. Night came with a cloak of invisibility, shrouding their approach. They walked away from the lantern's lights shining from beach and the sole lantern heading toward the trees.

The moon was out but covered with a heavy layer of clouds. It only peeked through seldomly, given the opportunity by the reluctant clouds. A lantern hung on a tree branch. A trail was spotted through the trees. Mike motioned Moss to remain behind.

"Shh Moss, I need you to keep an eye out for others. Don't want any party crasher until we know more. You wait here, I will scout ahead."

Moss nods watching Mike sneaking along the edge of the trail, swiftly fading into the darkness. Moss eased into a covey of trees bundled tightly watching the stillness of the night pass. His eyes kept a watch on the small homes lit for anyone coming out and walking toward the thicket of trees.

The trail wasn't straight. It twisted for hundreds of yards, Soon, another lantern appeared ahead. Mike approached the opening. He spotted a large shipping container. It was covered with a blanket of mess webbing interwoven with leaves and such.

"This was the place," Mike thought. "Why else would a shipping container be parked hidden down a long twisting path in a secluded spot, far from town. Plus, covered with a web of camouflaging, Duh."

Near the storage container was a small fire and two men sitting on chairs around the fire. Mike crept closer, just beyond the fire's light. Then he sudden froze, halting his forward movement.

Mike notice spotlights under some webbing on each corner of the container. Then, a rustling of leaves coming from an area to his left. A man stepped out from a tree, zipping his pants. Both lights on the container lit the area. Mike suspected the lights had sensors. That proved it.

"When you think they will get here with the food? I'm starving, "said one man sitting near the fire.

"You always starving," replied the man next to him holding a lantern.

Mike crept closer to the opening. He spotted several more flood lights within the trees pointing inside the open area. Mike assumed they were sensors aimed at the container. Against the container, was two rifles. Both men sat away from their weapons.

"Careless," Mike thought.

Mike could here talk within the container. Two people, both girls, one he recognized. He crept closer to listen in on what the men were discussing.

"Damn, that new girl just won't stop her yapping," complained one guard sitting.

"Yeah, that last girl Rico brought us, won't stop her bawling."

"What she saying," asked the man still attempting to get his zipper up.

"Something about a boyfriend. She keeps saying, "he was going to find her. They need to hide her, if not, there will be hell to pay. He will kill us all."

"Just one boy, he must be some super hero type."

"Rico said, he could walk on walls."

"Well, you know Rico. He can't keep away from the stuff."

"I know but I saw the roof to his van. Something tore the roof open like it was nothing."

"Hey, you two bozos, what's all your yammering about inside the container? Besides, what's this about a super hero boyfriend," asked the man zipping his pants?

"It's that new girlie in the box. She keeps screaming, her boyfriend is coming to rescue her. When he gets here, we all are going to die."

"Yeah, Rico said, "she was a druggy. It's just hallucinogen from the drugs."

"No, no Rico said, "this boyfriend can do all kinds of weird stuff. He showed us the van. Something had punched a hole in the roof, then tore it half off. Ask Sal, he saw the truck, too?"

"No, you were the only one to see Rico's van. I waited here, to keep an eye on our new girlie."

"I heard enough, thought Mike. He was about to take the three men out, until he heard the roar of an engine driving to the campsite. A truck appeared from another road. It was a tan 1962 Chevy. Three men squeezed out of the front seat. One man stayed behind with the truck, while two walked over to the men by the campfire.

One man sitting speaks up, "I see you got us nothing to eat."

"No, we were told to get here quick. Something going down. The boss said, "there was going to be visitors."

One guard sitting spoke, "that might be this boyfriend we been talking about."

"We don't know about any boyfriend," said the driver of the Chevy truck. "We are to get here quick, was all we been told."

"What are we supposed to do, wait here, starving for some boyfriend to arrive?"

"You best be glad we came to help, than your empty bellies being filled."

"You saying that because you ate already. We been here all day with no relief or food."

"That's because of this incident happening, back at the bar. Seems, some kid came in, beat the hell out of your relief. Then three old men did the same and a third time by some women. The reliefs are in bad shape," said the driver.

"The boss is having some men from other areas to get here soon," spoke the second man beside the driver.

"Well, that's just dandy, now you take the truck and git us some food. The others can stay here."

The five of us should be enough for one little boyfriend. The big man that zipped his pants held up a rifle. The other two sitting guards walked over to the container taking their rifle s in hand.

"See these, them men in the bar didn't have these with them, I bet. We do. I think these should make a big difference, if this boyfriend should show."

"Yeah, even if he brings those three old men and women with him. What you think?"

The driver nods his head, then turns walking to the truck. He sits for a minute waiting until a song was finished sung on the radio. Mike rushes back along the trail to Moss.

Mike spots Moss within the shelter of a clump of trees. "Moss, we got some trouble. More men arrived. The word was sent out, that their bar was attacked. They are expecting us here."

"What we going to do?"

"We are in luck; the guards haven't eaten. One man is driving away to get food. There are five men only."

"Mike, I think I got a plan. You say they are starving and one man is sent to get food. He hasn't left, yet. Why don't we go to that village and wrangle them some food? I'll deliver the food to distract them. You do your thing, then."

"One thing wrong with than plan, Moss. If I don't dispatch them fast enough, gun fire will erupt. You would be caught in the middle. That might be a quick way to get yourself killed, this night. When the actions begin, take cover."

"Don't fret about me, Mike; God will protect me. I am against unnecessary killing, especially mine. The good book says, it is wrong to commit murder."

"We aren't committing murder, Moss. Many times, the Lord has sent his people into battle against their enemies. These men are killers. God sanctions killing evil people, read your book."

"I know the book. I hope we can avoid killing."

"Moss, I will kill if I have too. I will do my best to disable any man first." I do not relish killing people, anytime."

THE NIGHT WENT ALL WRONG

In town, Chopper was organizing his teams. Razor was about to leave, leaving Jack, Jamie, Bone, Magic, and Pretty still talking to Chopper when Cho came up to Razor. Razor said, he and Jimmie were going back to the bar to confront the barkeeper, he informs Cho. I assume Cho, you will take Jack with Jamie going to the airstrip. Did you learn where the strip was, Cho?"

"Yes, I got a good idea where to locate the strip. It is not far from the fishing village along the beach. Not far from where the girls are being held, Moss reported." Bone was next to both the men. He listened to the plan with a keen ear. Razor and Jimmie departed and Cho went to discuss his plan to head out to the air strip with Chopper.

"Who is this Moss fellow Cho," inquired Bone walking briskly toward Cho? Master Cho turned to Bone answering his question.

"He came off the plane with us. He is with Jamie and Jimmie staying at another hotel. He escaped the desert prison. Mike rescued him and other prisoners. You were told the story, Bone. They helped Mike and me fight this Iranian army attacking the cave people, we had discussed."

"Why is the air strip so close to the container, asked Jamie? Jamie stood by Bone anxious to get started. He prodded Bone into the lobby seeing Chopper and Cho talking about another search team.

"Jamie, if they are spotted by the police, they can make a quick get-away," snapped Chopper.

"Ho."

"I'm going where Mike is, quipped Bone to his leader, Chopper. Bone left shortly after his discussion with Cho and Chopper. Chopper allowed his second to go where Mike was heading, reluctantly. Bone wanted to go with Mike. He spotted Cho and Mike outside the hotel. When he returned inside telling Penny his plans, Mike had left with the stranger. Bone recognized the man.

Not long after Mike departed with Moss, Bone had rented a scooter. He was traveling at a slower rate. His massive size was not intended for a scooter. Bone arrived at the beach just as Mike was informing Moss about the guards.

Walking up the beach, Mike spotted a huge dark shape emerge from the road, where they left their scooters parked. Mike realized they had little options to hide or get away from the unknown person advancing where they laid planning their move on the men at the cargo container. He prepared to meet the huge man. Before the huge man reached the two of them, Mike recognized him, it was Bone.

"Bone what are you doing here," Mike said just loud enough for the big man to here and not so loud to alert the guards.

Bone was startled hearing a voice reach out to him in the darkness. He halts listening to the whispers greeting him. He hoped to spot where the words were originating without attempting to fathom what was being said.

Slowly, he advanced toward a lantern. Suddenly, a lone figure emerged behind the light. He could make out the man approaching him, once the lantern's light was behind the man. It was Mike.

"You gave me a scare there, Kiddo."

"Well Bone, I'll keep that our secret. Don't want the others to think you were scared of the dark, do we. You know, one little man on a lonely beach in the dark."

"Hey, you still ain't big enough for me to take you over my knee and give you a spanking, kiddo." Both hugged the other.

Suddenly, Bone caught sight of a second man emerging from the darkness. Bone could not believe his eyes. "It was One Eye, the man responsible for terrorizing Mike and his family, and killing Stephen, Marcus, and nearly killing Mike on several occasions. What the hell," he shouted. Mike swiftly put his hand over Bone's mouth.

"Shh, we got company, Bone." Bone grabbed Moss by the throat just as Mike put his hand over his mouth. He lifted Moss off the beach sand with his one hand. Moss dangled for a moment. Mike quickly yanked Moss from Bone's grip in the nick of time. His massive fingers were squeezing Moss's life from his body.

"What the hell you think you are doing, Kiddo. This man killed our men, Stephen, Teddy Bear, and Marcus. Dang, and you, I can't even count how many times. Hell, you been chasing this punk across several continents."

"Hold on a second, Bone. I know how-well you feel about One Eye. Cho saw him earlier, as did Chopper. Both have allowed him to live."

"That don't matter none. He gots some answering for."

"I know Bone, let me explain. Moss has helped me and Cho in the desert. He is helping us here. He was the one to locate Cheryl. He has put his life on the line, doing so. I will explain more, later. This is not the time nor the place. Just trust me and stay your hand for now, please." Mike looked up at his giant friend with begging eyes.

Bone eases his anger nodding his acquiesce to his metering out death to an enemy. "Kiddo, this better not be no trick."

Moss nodded his understanding of Bone hated. Moss recalled, "how Mike was filled with the same rage for revenge. Mike warned him, this might happen and stay clear of any of the Riders."

"Bone, those guards have not eaten and are starving. Moss came up with a plan. We are going to the village for food. Moss will take the food to the guards distracting them for me to free Cheryl. If I am spotted before freeing her, then, all hell is going down. An extra pair of hands is going to come in handy for the plan to succeed with no one getting harmed, well just those guards."

Bone looks at Moss. "You know, a bullet might take you out, doing this."

Moss silently nods. Mike discusses his plan to both men.

"I don't think they will ask many questions. They are pretty hungry. We can surround them. On my cue, we go in. I'll make for the container. You take the truck driver out. Try not to kill all of them, please," Mike begged.

Cho with Jamie and Jack asked for a car at the hotel. A jeep was waiting outside. Soon, they were at the opposite end of the island.

The road was sandy. Cho was glad the hotel gave them a four-wheel jeep. Their first attempts to locate the air strip was a massive boo-boo on his part.

Cho turned down the first sandy road. It led to a beach. The wrong beach. The night offered little light to guide them. The jeep got stuck in the liquid sand covering the road. It took twenty minutes to turn the jeep and push through to the road.

That wasn't the first time, nor the second time they went down the wrong road and again and again shruggingly through the liquid sands back onto the road. The final turn proved to be their last. The jeep turned onto the road, then a tire went flat.

"Shit, this night is not going good, carped Jamie. I hope we don't have the same luck, when we get to that air strip?"

Cho decided to race down the beach while the other two remained to change the tire. Jack persuaded him to stay. That proved to be another mistake. Their head lights were spotted by the aircrew on the strip. It turned out, Cho was correct and should have went ahead. Now, they were spotted.

"Hey guys, do you see them lights back up the road," asked one crewman by the plane. The men were prepping a plane and two more guarded with rifles. News was delivered to expect company. It seems the bar was attacked by some Americans was the gist."

The barkeep had the last of his attackers followed. It seemed too coincidental that all three bar fight encounters, gave him the same tip in hundred-dollar bills. All three groups were at the same hotel. Inside, his man saw all three groups meet in the lobby. There was the kid, three old men and women kissing some of the men.

Back at the bar, the barkeeper watched three different men walk in. One was a big man, he recognized as one of the older men. One standing beside him was tall and thin, he too was one of the older men. The third man to enter was new. He was the youngest of the three.

The barkeeper just sent word out to all his men to expect company. He mentioned a kid and three older men. All were Americans. Now, two of the three older men walked into his bar. Where was the kid and the third older man was on his mind, looking at his guest? Eight men sitting, stood with a wave of his hand.

Chopper had called to Razor to wait for him as he was about to depart the hotel. Once he completed his talk with Master Cho he hurried to catch up to Razor and Jimmie. Chopper spotted the tell signal, quickly. All eight men made their way cautiously toward one end of the bar. Jimmie went to one side, near the eight. Razor on the opposite side and Chopper down the middle walking toward the bar. The stage was set for what might occur.

"I see, we meet for a second time in the same day. You got new men. Are we to meet with the same hospitality? Chopper girded himself for the barkeepers replied.

The barkeeper leaned on the countertop glaring into the eyes of a man twice his age but nearly not as aged in his appearance. What he saw was a man with no fear. A man who has been in war with death following him. Next to him, two men with the same stench of death. They had guts entering his place outnumbered. This man speaking with authority and demanding answers galled the barkeeper. Still, he had a way about him the barkeeper couldn't help respect this man defiantly walking up to him. Chopper not taking his eyes from the glare of the barkeeper spoke softly.

"Where is the girl?"

"What, you come in my place and make demands? If you come for the same, you'll get the same as before."

"I no doubt that you will, and you will get the same from us."

"I think you make too many boasts. This time you are out matched. The barkeeper eases back straightening up off the counter top placing both hands flat on the counter top. He dared Chopper to attempt something.

Every man standing at the bar opens their coat to revealed a weapon tucked neatly in a belt. Some didn't tote a gun in their belt but had a knife.

Chopper turned opening his belt. Both of his companions done the same. Under their coats was a belt holding their pants up.

"Ha, ha, ha, we, we have you at a disadvantage, replied the barkeeper."

"No, you got that all wrong, again, sir. I revealed we were not carrying a gun to you. If you had any common sense, the reason would be clear to even the tiniest brains among you all."

"The barkeepers look with a queer expression written on his face at Chopper. Chopper seeing the barkeeper was indeed possessing a pea sized brain, explained his remarks.

"The answer is simple, against this motely rift-raft crew, we need no gun or weapons." Jimmie laughs at the eight men waiting for the signal while Chopper was berating the barkeeper's men.

The barkeeper stares at Chopper while making a thin curled snarl under his ragged beard and swollen chin. The smile slowly peeped through his grotesque distorted face, revealing to Chopper take action. Choppers next moved startled the barkeeper and those men reaching for their weapons. Before Chopper did what took all by surprise, the barkeepers acted first.

"Here now, lets' have a beer before we begin, mister, mister, you know, I never got to know your name, friend." Three beers were placed on the countertop in front of Chopper. The barkeeper said nothing. Chopper signaled his two companions to approach the bar.

Years of this kind of fighting made the Rider weary of any free beers. They approached the bar taking a mug in their hands. The eight men closed in, still with their hand on a weapon not yet pulled from their belts The boss man had no intentions of talking to this old man further. "He and his two companions were not long for this world. The drinks was a goodbye gesture," thinking to himself.

Chopper said to the barkeeper; "First, I'm not your friend. Second, the name is mister Chopper. Third, all the hell with it." Then, came the surprise no one expected at that moment.

It was too late for the barkeeper to realize he was being played the fool. His mouth was busted open. Teeth rained down to the floor. The blow had split his lip and re-opened his swollen nose. Next, came a sudden jerk on the barkeepers head yanking his face into the countertop, then back up by his oily hair shoving his head into his newly purchased mirror over the liquor shelves. Bottles went shattering to the floor. The barkeeper dropped down. Chopper grabbed the head slapping it downward to speed up its descent. It came crashing back down on the countertop, again. Then, bounced back up only to be slammed back down a third time. Both eyes rolled back into their eye sockets. Chopper did a basketball dribbled with his head on the bar top.

Both Jimmie and Razor were doing their thing. Once the barkeeper's head bounce off the countertop the first time, two beer mugs, empty, smashed against two of the eight men.

A third and fourth man were giving a stool by Razor and Jimmie they assumed to sit on. "They objected the stools to sit on," Jimmie quipped to Razor.

"Did you see that? They thought we were offering them stools to sit on." Both stools came traveling down on number three and four guys. They laid on the floor quietly at peace with the world.

"See that Jimmie, how ungrateful can you be. We offer a stool and they rather laid on the floor."

"Yeah, boss man, replied Jimmie with a giggle. Just a bunch of ungrateful sorts. No manners."

Chopper picked up his beer; finished it, then throws the mug at number five man. He ducked, the stool didn't. Number six stood to close. One leg of the stool stuck him in his open mouth. Both men fell backwards. Neither rose, until the morning.

When the barkeeper's head hit the countertop a third time, number seven and eight men remaining, were introduced properly. Number seven was greeted with a punch by Razor. He accepted it with a polite response. He never raised his hand to block the hit. He was too busy looking at his friend smiling up at him from the floor. Razor expected number seven to lay next to that man with his hay maker punch delivered to the jaw of number seven.

Number eight was only looking when Jimmie made his introductions. He was like his comrades, stunned by the old man sudden move, not reacting and by the grace of God, did not pull his gun," thought Jimmie. He swung first. The punch was blocked by the man. Jimmie expected him to block the slow punch. It was a feint for what was to follow, a round house kick to his head. Number eight went floundering toward the counter where chopper was patiently waiting.

Chopper halted number eight's attempts to rise off the counter-top with a snap on his shirt collar. Number eight went upright then straight down to the floor. Razor followed with a swift kick landing between the man's legs. His face went an ashen color. He curled up holding his jewels. Whatever else transpired in the bar, number eight could care less.

Number seven was still standing to Razor's utter surprise. He was big, roughed, and definitely could take a punch. He attempted to punch Razor. Chopper standing near Razor, stopped the punch with a block. The first stool broke easily on the man chest. Razor was about to thank Chopper.

The stool wasn't well built, cited Jimmie to both Chopper and Razor. Jimmie knew a good piece of furniture better than Razor. He built furniture before entering the service. The stool he sent to number seven did not break.

"Damn Jimmie, you can pick nice stools. Mine must have been of poorer quality."

"You think Razor, I thought you would know better than using inferior furniture in a bar fight, being older and wiser than this young buck, jived Jimmie?"

"Where you fine that nice stool? Got's to git me one."

Oh, I don't know, it was just sitting by that table all alone. I'll look for a label. Hey Razor, it got no label, sorry.

Huh, Chopper, you going to hold on to number seven all night long. That stool I plowed him with, shouldn't need extra support.

The barkeeper regained consciences. Two men entered the bar. Chopper turned without rebutting Jimmie's comment. Both men drew their guns upon seeing every man lying on the floor. Chopper spotted the guns. He grabbed a stool number seven was supporting. The bullet struck the seat of the stool. Wood splintered out the bottom of the seat. Chopper felt the splinters and saw the hole. He felt for another hole on himself.

The hole was as big as Chopper's fist in the stool seat. There was no hole in him. He felt the slug's impact. Apparently, number seven intercepted the slug meant for him. The stool had little effect on him. The bullet did. Chopper smiled with glee. Razor patted him on his back. Jimmie shouted. Both shooters halted their fire after seeing one of them, get the intended bullet.

Gentlemen, there is another man, plus, there is that first man that took a shot at you, Chopper.

All three men spun in unison grabbing empty bottles from the countertop. One, two, three, each bottle flew toward the door. One bottle hit the shooter man. The number two bottle, the second man, number three got what was left. The first bottle rammed into the chest of the first shooter. It was broken when Razor grabbed and tossed the bottle The third bottle followed the first into the shooter.

The second bottle entered the mouth of number two man entering the bar. He was about to squeeze the trigger to his gun; it fell from his hand. The trigger was released when he landed on top. He fell on top of his gun with a beer bottle partly protruding out the rear of his skull. "A once in a million throw," Razor announced. The gun fired. The second shooter lifted off the floor, then came a fountain of blood from his back before he return to the floor for his final rest.

The first shooter was still standing, blood oozed from the wound around the bottle sticking out of his chest. He tried to squeeze his trigger, again. The trigger was hard to pull. It seemed stuck to the first shooter's thinking. Jimmie walked up to the man, still standing. He grabbed his gun. The man let go easily. It seemed holding the gun was the only reason for him to remain standing. He dropped to the floor after Jimmie took his gun. Bang. Bang followed his descent.

Chopper was still feeling for a gunshot hole, he expected from the shot fired at him. Razor went around the countertop and poured three beers. The barkeeper was leaning over the counter. Razor shoved him out of his way.

"Here Chopper, take a drink. That was a close one, old buddy."

"Dag-nab-it, if I got shot again, Bell would kill me herself." Jimmie parks at the bar and quickly receives a mug of beer by Razor.

"Heres to Chopper, he didn't get shot, nor killed by Bell, Ha, ha, ha."

At the hotel, Susan was getting anxious. She wanted to go after Cheryl. She overheard in the lobby, Bell telling Penny, Laura, and

Miriam, Mike was heading to the opposite end of the city to a small fishing village.

Chopper told Bell to maintain the fort at the hotel. That job was increasingly becoming more difficult. It was made more difficult when a man came off the street screaming, gun fire. Shooting was coming from a bar down the street, he screamed. Panic erupted inside the hotel lobby. Patrons ran for any cover, wives screamed, and hotel staff hid. The only persons not in a panic were the drunks Americans from last night party.

Bell knew her man with Razor and Jimmie were going back to the bar. Miriam grew concern hearing gunfire. Then return back to the hotel. When was the million-dollar question?"

"I'm going to check on my man," shouted Miriam in a near panic as the quests.

"No Miriam, you are not leaving. Chopper gave explicit orders for everyone to remain in the hotel. So, stay put. Our men are capable."

"You can stay, Bell. I'm leaving. Bell, Chopper went with my man. Neither had guns."

A growing fear was easily seen in Miriam's eyes with every passing second. Bell worried that Miriam's fears would spread as she was attempting to bring calm and some order to everyone inside the hotel.

"Wait Miriam." Bell walked over to her. Rhonda watched and made an attempt to follow. Bell stopped her. "Rhonda, someone has to remain behind. Your man is with Cho. You need to be here when they return to report this."

Bell saw Susan go to the door. She knew she couldn't stop her. Penny ran after Susan. Miriam and Bell skirted out the front door of the lobby, heading toward the bar

"I'm coming with you, Susan. Then Laura followed.

Me too, Susan, Laura replied. Both women met up with Susan outside the hotel. A rental car was parked nearby. It was a hotel car for their use. They piled into the car. Laura drove. Laura had asked for the keys. Susan had the keys. She took the keys from Bell earlier to have a private talk with Cheryl when morning came after the party.

Bell and Miriam knew where the bar was. Arriving in front, some people were outside, looking in. Two men were spotted lying dead in the entrance. Blood covered the floor and oozed out onto the street. The police had not arrived. It was their policy to stay away, until a call was made. No call was made. It was an arrangement made by the police and the barkeeper. He paid them well.

Miriam rushed inside. Bodies littered the room. Two men were standing drinking beers. One man sat on the floor drinking a beer. One man standing was bleeding. It was Razor. Miriam screamed.

"Someone, call an ambulance."

Bell spotted Chopper on the floor. Broken tables, stools, chairs, and bottles were flung everywhere in the bar. It was a total war zone existing inside the bar.

Jimmie began assisting Chopper to his feet spotting Bell standing in the bar doorway. Chopper had blood on him.

"Not again," she wanted to desperately scream out. Jimmie spoke.

"Bell, he is not wounded, the blood isn't his. A bullet hit the stool after passing through that man lying on the floor. He's dead. In a way, that man saved Chopper from being shot. He was in the direct line of gunfire from that man by the front door. I shot him."

Chopper listened to Jimmie explanation with dread. The way he explained the incident, made it seem he was shot at. Jimmie, maybe you should say nothing was what he wanted to tell him, but the cat was out of the bag. Bells eyes grew in size hearing Jimmie say, he was shot at, again.

Bell saw the gun still in Jimmie's hand. Jimmie let the gun drop. Bell bent down to pick up the gun. She lifted the gun, wiping the finger prints away, then drops the gun on the floor.

"Thanks Bell, plum forgot about fingerprints. He shot Chopper. Pointing to the second shooter Jimmie says, the other man hit Razor, when I took his gun. I shot that SOB with the second shot."

Bell examines Chopper's chest, pulling his shirt open. A bright red spot was seen, dead center mass. Bell turns to Jimmie, "thank you. Turning back to her man, Babe are you okay?"

"Yep Bell, just a bruise. This beer helps."

"How many is that?"

"I figure three, not enough," replied Chopper.

"Make that five Bell, quipped Jimmie. Miriam, I looked at Razor. It is a flesh wound. He had four beers. Really, he's fine, Miriam."

Razor did the same tearing his shirt open that Bell done to Chopper's shirt. "Look honey, it went in here and out there. See," a tiny bullet hole Razor pointed too. Miriam looks at the little hole exiting the back of Razor shoulder. It grazed the fresh.

"See, tiny, not worth screaming so much honey." Razor finished his fourth beer.

Jimmie hands Miriam a clean towel. "Hold the towel tight against his body. The blood will stop, soon enough." Bell removes Razor's belt and lassoes it around the towel Miriam wrapped him with.

The barkeeper finally stands up. His face was a bloody mess. Both mouth and nose had stopped bleeding. Jimmie immediately grabs the barkeeper's shirt, dragging him over the countertop. He wanted a private talk with the man. Bell watched Jimmie drag the man to a hallway. Chopper told her, it was the head.

The head was nasty with urine spread everywhere. The toilet had not been flushed for at least two dumps. The barkeeper was slammed down hard onto the toilet seat. "This should have been Bone's forte, Jimmie chuckled to himself."

"Okay, you and I are going to have a little talk. Don't know anything is not an option." Jimmie wails back and slaps the barkeeper across his already swollen face. Blood trickle out of his nose and mouth anew. Both ears rang inside the barkeeper's head. Jimmie slaps the man a second time on the opposite cheek. Then a third and fourth, before he asks his first question.

"Stop, stop, the barkeeper holds up a hand, please, no more, plead the barkeeper."

"This is only going to get worst, before the night is over. I will ask only once." Then, Jimmie slaps the barkeeper, again.

"Stop, why you hit me again? Ask, asked me your question."

"You didn't answer the first question."

"What question, you never asked me one." You just slapped me over and over again. Pow. Jimmie slaps him again.

"Stop, please stop. I am begging you. I will answer any question you want me too," meekly replied the barkeeper. The barkeepers head dipped down. Jimmie jerked on the oily hair, snapping the head back up.

"That is to let you know what will happen, if I ask again. Chopper asked you where is the girl?"

"What girl are you talking about?"

Bam. A tooth went flying. One ear began to bleed. The barkeeper raises his hands to stop Jimmie. He received two more slaps. The barkeeper slipped off the seat. Jimmie stopped him with his leg planted in his chest.

"No, no lying down. Keep awake."

The barkeeper wasn't passing out. The toilet seat was slimy with shit. The floor was wet with urine, made slippery. He never used the patron's restroom; he had his own private restroom, the barkeeper wanted to say. He kept that quiet. He wished he hadn't, when the next wrong answer was forthcoming.

The water to flush the commode was brown in color. Not fit to drink, bathe, or give to the patrons drinking anything other than beers. On the walls was writing. Foul words and nasty poems. The odor was beyond describing.

"Rats avoided this place," quipped Jimmie to the barkeeper.

The barkeeper wanted off his seat. That wasn't going to happen. "Ask your damn questions," he retorted with anger to Jimmie.

Jimmie slaps him hard. "You didn't say, please."

"Please, please ask me a question."

"I did." Pow, pow, two more slaps rang in succession across the bloody cheeks of the barkeeper.

"We got several girls. Which one?"

"You don't listen to well, do you."

Another slap. The barkeeper went flying onto the wet floor. Jimmie lifts him by his shirt collar slamming him back on the commode seat. The barkeeper splits blood. Some of the blood landed on Jimmie's shirt. It was a new shirt. That offended him. Two more slaps, followed.

"Better not spit. Swallow your blood, mister," Jimmie said with a nasty growl.

Tears filled the barkeeper's eyes. I didn't want my boys to start anything with you people. They got the wrong message, believe me. They reacted from what you did to their friends. They wanted some payback, I guess."

"Is that so. Why you have us followed? Why you signaled your men to attack us coming inside this bar? I am not stupid. Plow, another hard slap. More teeth went flying. Only a few remained. What you really meant to say, was your boys were shamed when women kicked their butts. The three old men did the same. And before that, a kid by his lonesome."

"Okay, anything you say, just not slap me again."

"Well mister, you picked on the wrong bunch of Americans. For your sake, choose your words carefully, before you speak. Have you targeted my friends?"

"What is this targeted, you speak of?"

Two more slaps followed. Both ears rang. Blood flowed from each ear. Next, Jimmie raised the barkeeper off the toilet seat and raised the lid. The commode was filled to the brim with human excrement. The smell rose up quick. Jimmie turned the barkeeper around to look inside the bowl of shit.

"So, it has shit in it. What you want me to do, flushed the damn thing," replied the barkeeper with a smart ask remark.

"Yeah, your right. I wanted you to flush it. You think I am going to shove your head down in the bowl. No, no not that at all, man. What I do plan is to take my hand, grab some shit and feed that ugly face of yours. I figure by the third swallow of this shit, you will talk. What you think?"

"I think you are crazy. You really think that will make a difference?"

"I don't know until I try it, Jimmie grins. Let's fine out together."

Without a second thought, Jimmie's hand pokes through the slimy, gelatinous, smelly, sticky globous brown goo. His hand whipped the mass into a pungent odorous smell swiftly rising permeating both their noses and mouths, giving each a bitter taste. A taste Jimmie would come to regret and the barkeeper a flavor in every morsel he would ever eat. Joy of good food was forever lost to him after this day.

Jimmie's hand came out of the bowl dripping puddles of filth through each crack between his fingers. The barkeeper could only watch the brown odorous goop quickly come to his mouth. He held his swollen lips as tight as possible. It was to no avail. Jimmie jerked on his oily hair. His head bent backward causing his mouth to begin separating. The slimy concoction found many openings into his mouth. Jimmie pressed his hand tightly over the barkeeper's mouth, nearly suffocating him with shit oozing from his fingers.

Thank God his nose was broken, gasped the bartender thinking to himself with some comfort to having his sore and broken nose. It helped prevent some of the taste. That was good only until, the gooey globs became to flow down his throat. The barkeeper's words echoed in Jimmie's ears. "You ain't shoving that down my mouth." Jimmie laugh recalling his words. That help him stomach what he was doing. He laughed and laughed making the bartender gasp from each handful of shit fed to him.

"Please, nasty shit splatter from his mouth with each word he utter. I had enough, my friend. Friends, we can be. Friends, don't treat each other like this. We can come to an understanding among us, as friends," whimpered the barkeeper.

"That would be true, if you were a friend. Since you ain't, then I got no hard feeling watching you gagging on this shit. Besides, you made me stick my hands in this crap. Friends don't make friends do that."

Cough, cough, cough, Shit went flying out of the barkeeper's mouth. "Enough, I tell you. Spit, spit, and spit again," was his reply.

"Better make this quick. I'm reaching for a second hand full. Another spit came. Jimmie rammed the barkeepers head down into the toilet bowl. Shit rose up and over the bowl spilling on the floor. The barkeeper's body went limp. Jimmie jerked his head from the bowl. He coughed. Shit covered his entire face.

"Had enough to eat. I got a dessert waiting."

The barkeeper was semi-conscience. Jimmie reached back into the bowl and took what he grabbed rubbing it onto his face and every part of it where he could get down the mouth. The barkeeper woke quick. Another handful was at the ready, dripping off Jimmie's hand.

Now mister barkeeper, I can keep this up all night or until this toilet bowl is emptied. Since there are two of them, it will take a while. The second bowl is filled to the top. Hey looky, it has a darker color. You know, I bet someone puked on top of that shit. Its' got blood mixed in with it. That might give it a better taste.

Jimmie had lied. The second bowl was dark brown water filled with pee. It seemed the patron did not know to flush the commode after they emptied their bladders. "No shit, oh well, maybe a cocktail to help swallow all that shit will go nice with his supper. This may work out better this way," Jimmie pondered.

The barkeeper waved his arms in surrender. He had enough. Jimmie moved his head over to the second bowl. Before the man could ask why, he learned why. Jimmie dunked his head into the pissy brown water of the toilet. He lifted and re-dunked several times, until the barkeeper's head was somewhat clean of the brown gooey mass clumping in small islands over his entire face.

Jimmie stood the man up. He could barely remain standing without his support. The man's legs gave way. He appeared to pass out.

"No freaking way you going to black out on me. Jimmie re-dunked the man's head. He awoke coughing pee out of his mouth. He desperately tried to wipe away the brown encrusted goo surrounding his mouth. Jimmie held his hands in one hand above his head and with his other hand the oily hair of the barkeeper.

"That encrusted goop is better than another mouth full. Talk asshole. I don't want to hear spit, spit from you, got that." Pow, a slap behind the barkeeper's head followed his remark.

"Remind me of that question, uh, please. He suddenly remembered the magic word, "Please," before Jimmie could remind him."

"Did you put a hit on my people? That is a simple question, a yes or no will suffice."

"Who are your people?"

"Wrong answer. What, no, sorry, please. don't," asked Jimmie not hearing the same banter from the barkeeper. Quickly Jimmie grabs hold of the man's oily hair from behind. With a hard yank, a cluster of hair was yanked out. The barkeeper screams. He felt a tug on his head. Then, he saw the shitty first toilet bowl below his knees.

"I got the message. Yes, I got your people targeted. You going to kill me or let me go. If you don't, they will be dead before the night ends."

"If I let you live, what guarantee do I have? Why would you let them live, when I set you free?"

"You got my word."

"Your word ain't worth shit."

"I control this town. The police, the government, and across the sea to the mainland. When the word gets to them, they will stop."

"You coming with me. First, I need to make you more presentable. Ladies are present."

Jimmie turns the hot water on in the sink. Brown water shoots from the spigot. Jimmie assisted the barkeeper to wash his dirty face holding his head under the scalding hot water. Once his face was presentable and a dark red from the scalding hot water bath he received, Jimmie handed him a soiled cloth hanging in the stall to dry his face.

With a yank, Jimmie escorts the man tugging at his belt outside the head to the counter. Jimmie stops long enough to wipe his man's face on the cracking wall paint. Chips of yellow stain plaster remained covering the barkeepers face confronting Chopper. The barkeepers face was dry but Jimmie felt it needed an extra drying with the ladies present.

Chopper was downing another beer. Bell tended to his needs. Miriam was with Razor. He was downing another beer. No police were present. Jimmie knew there would be none after his debriefing with the barkeeper.

"Listen to this man Chopper, he has something he wants to get off his chest."

Chopper smelled him before he got to the bar. Bell back away, holding her nose. Shit covered the barkeeper's clothes. His pants were soaking wet. Chopper suspected pee. The head floor was drowning in urine the last time he made a head stop.

Bell gagged looking at the brown circle around the barkeeper's mouth. Along with shit covering his clothes, she could only image what Jimmie did to aid this man to talk.

"Tell them," demanded Jimmie. Jimmie slaps the barkeepers head from behind. Now or so help me this next trip to the head, you can't even imagine. Jimmie whips out his knife. The blade was opened. He places the blade near his crotch. The threat began real, when his pants were ripped down to his ankles. The barkeepers began talking.

The barkeeper was wearing frilly women's panties. A nice garter belt held his fish net stocking up. Every woman in the bar gasped. Some outside onlookers were peeking inside. Laughter erupted outside the bar. Many of the onlookers made jeers and called out to him.

"This is the man we been fearing. He is just a kinky old man."

Bell began to laugh, then Miriam. Soon, everyone was laughing. The barkeeper tried to hide his face. He was glad not one of his men could see him. That changed suddenly, one of his men began to awake. He heard the laughter and the jeering. The boss man held his head down out of shame.

The hired man stood slowly, near Razor. Razor put his hand on his shoulder. He went back to the floor on his knees. He watched the crowd outside grow with increasing laughter at his boss. He no longer struck fear in their hearts. He remained respected to his boss. He had to live in this town and work for the boss. It was difficult to not laugh. He put his hand over his mouth, to hide his grin and muffle his chuckles.

"You and your people will be dead by morning, chided the shamed barkeeper. I had my men planned to attach the hotel before dawn. They are men waiting at the container and air strip. There is no escape off this island without my say-so."

Miriam attempted to slap the barkeeper. Bell halted her hand. Razor spoke.

"Honey, we will need this man."

Bell asked, "when and where is this attack to come?" The barkeeper quickly spilled his guts with fast talking.

"The container is near a small fishing village three miles east outside the city. I sent them there anticipating you would go there. They got machine guns. A mile from the village, is the air strip. They got machine guns. The others men are surrounding the hotel as we talk. The plan is to enter inside from every direction. No one is to be left standing." Chopper took those words that everyone inside the hotel was going to get butchered, with no one left alive to retell the incident.

"I hope you got a car mister," demanded Bell.

"It's behind the bar. Here are my keys. The barkeeper reaches inside his dripping pants lying on the floor. Removes the keys, hands them with trembling hands to Bell.

"Jimmie, grab Razor. Miriam get the car, I will assist my man up. Choppers stands. Bell turns to the barkeeper, you come with me. Jimmie, make sure he behaves himself," demanded Bell.

Everyone begins to walk to the rear of the bar. The man on his knees that awoke, went back to sleep from a kick delivered by Miriam assisting her man out the rear of the bar.

"Hey, I gave you what you wanted. You were to let me go" carped the barkeepers.

Jimmie turns back to look at the barkeeper keeping pace with Bell. "Get ahead of me, barkeeper. I lied. So, kill me." The barkeeper stumbles ahead of Jimmie.

Chopper listened to this man tell him, they had a hit on his people. "How stupid is this man? His men get their butts handed to them three times and he wants to start a war with me,' he thought?

Choppers waits until the barkeeper get close, then delivers a haymaker to the man's ribs. Crack. The barkeeper bends over screaming. The crowd outside the front of the bar saw the people within the bar, leave out the back door. Many knew the alley behind the bar and swiftly ran to the alley to glimpse what was happening. Outside all heard the barkeeper scream and went wild with laughter.

Jimmie had to let go of Razor, to assist the barkeeper walking. Razor did fine, without his help. "Not so with the barkeeper, he was acting like a sissy about a few broken ribs," thought Jimmie.

Jimmie stops long enough to prop the barkeeper on the countertop and walks behind the bar. He grabbed two bottles of vodka before he assisted Razor. He turns and smiles at the barkeeper looking at him, with curiosity.

"Hey, you owe me for them bottles," squealed the barkeeper.

"Okay with me. I was going to use one to kill that smell reeking off of you, I will use it on me. Jimmie opens both bottles pouring the alcohol over his shoes and then hands and face. What was left, he took a swig and poured out what remained.

"Why you not give me some?"

"It was my booze, bub. Get your own. Now move it."

Jimmie slaps the barkeeper on his head. He slid off the countertop he was clinging on for support, to the floor. His hand halted his full fetal sprawl on the floor. He did not want the gawking crowd outside to see him laid out on the floor, from a slap.

Jimmie kicked the barkeeper's elbow. He slammed face down on the floor. The crowd roared with laughter. He looked up at Jimmie, filled with rage. Jimmie put his foot on top of his head and raised his arms in triumph for the crowd's benefit. The crowd roared louder.

Bell, hearing the shouts, turn back to see Jimmie clowning. "Jimmie quit fooling around and get that piece of shit, moving. We got a war to stop."

Jimmie tells the barkeeper, "get up followed with a swift kick to his rear. You are my prisoner. Be glad you are, this night, your services might be needed to fix it, or you better be able too."

The man, Razor kicked walking out the rear, awoke. He watched his boss drop to the floor and get a kick in his ass. He laid pretending to be out. After the Americans went out the rear door, he stood. The crowd saw him approach the door. They knew him well. He hurt many of them and their family members.

The awoken man reached the door filled with people eager to get a look inside. He shoved against the mob, until he was outside the bar. That was a terrible mistake he made. Several men waited, with clubs. The crowd parted, then reformed in a circle around him. The man had little time to make a connection to what was coming next.

What came next, was sudden. One hit to his back, another to his arm, and again to the other arm. Back, guts, arm, leg, the other leg followed in succession with every blow. Non-stop, this continued until he dropped to the street. The men with clubs back away, the crowd squeezed inward. Kicks, spit, and more kicks rained down on him. The crowd stopped, when one man called out.

"Let him live. He will tell the others what will come next for them and their families. Follow me. We will go to his home, and the other homes. This night, we will burn them out of our lives. Years of suppression has given us the courage, finally we have a chance get pay back. We must not let this chance get away."

By morning, the beaten man awoke in pain. He had nearly nine months of treatment to regain some of his abilities. Nine months in a hospital alone with not one visit from comrades or family members. The doctors told him, every bone in his body was broken. He said, he was lucky to be alive. The man did not feel the same. He sat in his bed, feeling pity for himself. The doctor had one tad bit of info to tell him.

"You will never walk again. You will need someone to care for what needs you may require."

The pain filled man thought about who he could get to care for his needs. No friends he had, would. They cared little about anyone, accept their families. The next blow came hard to him. His family home was burnt down. His father and brother were killed, fighting a mob. His mom was missing. Some conciliation was his home was not the only to burn, that night. Many of the men he knew, lost their homes and love ones. The message was clear.

He was dismissed from the hospital. He had little money. His boss did not pay retirement. He wished for death sitting in a wheel chair rolling down the street, he often walked.

Behind the rear of the bar, the barkeeper was given the best seat in his own car. After the trunk was shut, his life was in darkness. He heard the car start up. The car filled with people bouncing up and down with each person entering. His car was moving, where, he had no idea?

TO MANY ON THE BEACH

Susan, Penny, and Laura managed to find a road they believed, took them to a small fishing village by the beach. They turned to drive down the road, then a sudden jolting impact hit their vehicle, broadside. A truck spotted the car begin turning. It was parked opposite of the road watching for men to come. The warning came from the top, it said, "stop them at all costs."

Inside the large truck, men were waiting for several hours parked off road, under a clump of trees. Headlights were spotted just as they decided to leave, to get a bite to eat. Their boss sent word, "men were coming to get the girls." They were ordered to stop them.

The impact from the truck caused Susan to hit her head against the door window. The blow temporarily knocked her unconscious. It was Laura's scream alerting Penny, allowing her to react soon enough to avoid flying through the windshield. Laura braced for the impact and was left unscathed. The car spun from the truck's hit, jarring the passenger side door open. Laura went out the door screaming.

The driver of the truck purposely hit the rear end, to make the car spin. The only thing preventing the car from flipping over, was a second impact into a tree. Mike was the only one to hear a car getting hit by a truck and a scream, a woman's scream that followed. Bone and Moss heard nothing. Neither doubted Mike's ability to hear the scream, while he pointed to where the sound originated from.

"Over there, boys. A car got smacked by another vehicle."

"Mike flew down the beach to where they parked their scooters, with Bone and Moss doing their best to keep up.

Mike, what about Cheryl in the container?"

"She will need to wait a little longer, Bone. I hope those women are not who I think they are? If so, you will be glad we are going to their rescue."

The night was upon the three men charging up the sandy path toward the intersection cut-off to this fishing village. It was pitch black running on the road. Mike could see well enough; Bone and Moss slowed their run. One light was visible up the road. Laura's car lights went out, after hitting the tree. The truck had its lights shining. That made the run up the road for Bone and Moss easier, as they neared the cut-off in the road leading to the fishing village.

Mike halted beyond the sight of the men approaching the car. Both men had rifles in their hands, walking to the car. Mike spotted a woman lying on the ground away from the car. One armed man went to her. He lifted the woman onto her feet. Mike gasped, seeing the woman was Laura, Cho soon to be wife.

She was shoved toward the car. Another woman was jerked out of the car by her hair. Her scream was heard by Bone. He knew it was his wife, Penny. Bone ran past Mike watching, onto the open road. The third person pulled from the car was Susan. She slapped the unarmed man pulling her from the car. Blood trickled down the side of her face. The unarmed man returned the slap to Susan, then threw her to the ground.

"That was a shame, you went and done slapped my face, like you did, pretty lady. His snarly perverted grin changed from a lust to a mean look. We were thinking of letting you three join us in a party, we were planning. That is, before we killed you."

Susan realized the truck hit their car on purpose, it wasn't an accident, to her horror and dismay.

Penny was the second person to lash out at her attacker. He was about to set his rifle down against the car fender. Before he grabbed her, Penny punched the man hard on his nose. Once she heard they planned on killing them, she reacted with more hits at the man. He let go of his rifle grabbing his nose. Bone arrived just when Penny opened up on the man

Bone grabbed hold of the man Penny punched. Mike was on Laura's attacker at the same time. Her man grabbed hold of his rifle spotting a giant charging across the road. Bone was big and in the dim light of the shining truck headlights, he was barely visible to get a clear look from the light's glare. He was glad he couldn't see what took hold of his friend but was happy, the giant took hold of his friend, then him.

Bone had charged at Penny's attacker screaming like a wild beast. The man attempted grab for his rifle to shoot the screaming giant rushing at him. He couldn't even, if he could. The suddenness of the hit, sent his rifle flying over the car. Bone lifted the man above his head, tossing him, God Knows where, into the foliage. Tree limbs went snapping was the next sounds heard.

His last thoughts were, "if not for this crazy woman's punching, kicking, and yelling at me, I could have dropped that big galoof." That was maybe what he was thinking flying through the air. Maybe a second thought might have occurred to him, I wished I had buckled my seatbelt before this flight began. Seatbelt, what seatbelt? Then, before the first snap of a tree branch, it dawn on his weary-fogged brain, he was flying in the air and assumed he boarded a plane and not buckled up. No one would never know his mistake, when the second branch snapped his backbone.

"Bone pondered, assuming the man had insurance for his flight. It wouldn't apply on this flight. He wasn't wearing his seatbelt. Besides that, the flight Bone put him on didn't have seatbelts. He was flying solo. Still, he should have put his landing wheels down for the landing. Again, Bone dismissed that thought. He broke the man's leg before lifting him over his head with a kick. It was going to be a rough landing with or without landing wheels or leg, thought Bone with a snicker.

Mike was about to give the same treatment to the first man attacking Susan. It wasn't necessary. "She was unloading her arsenal of fighting skills he taught her. He might have wished for Mike to deal with him. Mike would have ended the battle sooner, than Susan. Susan was taking out some frustrations, it seemed to Mike, watching."

Susan hit the man with a devastating hammer blow to the side of his head. Both eyes of the man, went blank. It was swiftly followed with another to his jaw. Teeth went everywhere. Before he could find safety on the ground, Laura smacked the man between his legs with a vicious front kick. She regained her footing after being thrown from the car, then raced to where Susan was inflicting much pain to one of the two men from the truck. The man laid on the sandy road with both legs sprawled out, an easy target for a well-aimed front kick.

"Now, have some fun with those useless sacs on any woman, bub," snorted Laura to the man cowering in a fetal position on the ground in front of her. She bent down raising the man to his feet. Susan stood waiting her turn not yet satisfied.

Once Laura was satisfied, Susan took up where she left off. The man had little time to take a rest break. Susan began with a spinning crescent kick. Both arms went up into a protected posture, after Laura's beating ended. His two arms went dangling after Susan's kick. Next, Susan shot another spinning back kick into the man's guts. He went flying toward Mike.

Mike greedy accepted the man to exact his revenge, for attacking his girls. Mike decided to send the man on an airborne flight, like Bone had done. "This man will have his destination routed. He is going to do a solo flight for free. Plus, with no extra boarding fee, there was no plane. He wouldn't have to be afraid of a terrific landing. He was on a collision course with no survivors, all curtsey of OZ package plane flight," Mike said to the dazed frightened man.

Susan turns to see Mike standing behind her. "Well, when did you plan on offering a girl a hand?"

"Didn't need to, you were doing just find, without my aid. In fact, both of you did great," Mike smiled.

"Where is Cheryl, snapped Susan?"

"Down the beach lying inside a large cargo container. We were going to get the guards some food. They been all day without anything to eat. While they were being served meals, I planned on sneaking Cheryl out of the container. That was until, I heard a car get hit. We came to offer help. Guess we came for nothing."

"Don't be silly, you are always needed."

"That goes for me too Mike," chided Laura.

Both women walked toward Bone and Penny embracing. Susan swirls her long dark hair at Mike, then slaps Mike's behind walking past him.

"You two planning on coming with us. We still got a frighten young girl to rescue," chided Laura to Bone and Penny.

"Wait, you three don't think for one second, you are going with us. Those men are well armed," snapped Bone to all three women?

"Yes, retorted Laura. I was told that any attempts to rescue the girl, they were to immediately kill her."

"You hear that, you big lug;" quickly followed by an elbow into Bone's side by Penny.

"That is my girl and try and stop me," snapped Susan.

Mike raises both hands. "Not me. Bone is the only one here making that request."

"Thanks a lot, kiddo."

"Hey, you the one that made that demand. Own up to it, big guy." Mike was going to say the same thing, to the ladies. Now, he was glad Bone made that remark.

Susan, Laura, and Penny our plan still has merit. Instead of one of us delivering their meals, it will be you pretty ladies. Who would not be distracted by beautiful girls? Mike spoke fast to change the subject. Bone quickly pick-up on what he said. Penny's name was said.

Mike's right, this will work out much better with Susan and Laura keeping their eyes on them serving their meals," replied Bone. Penny jabs Bone in his side, again.

"Ouch, what that for, babe," responded Bone? "They been trained to fight and you haven't been taught how to fight."

Shyly Penny turns to Mike. "Well, for a matter of fact."

Mike interrupts Penny's poor attempts to explain what she was eluding too. He caught her shy look at him to help her tell Bone, her little secret.

"Bone, for your information, I been training her with my students at the cabin."

"You see honey, Mike been giving me lessons for some time."

Bone was stunned.

"It was my surprise, to you."

"She pretty good, Bone."

Bone looks at Mike. Suddenly, a huge smile broke across his stoic face. "Thanks kiddo. I was going to ask you to teach my girl some self-defense. Don't want my woman to get herself in trouble and not know how to handle herself."

You mean you are not mad with me?

Heck no, I'll never get mad at the ones, I love. Both hug the other. Secretly, Bone did not want Penny to learn how to fight. He liked having Penny depend on him to keep her safe.

Yeah Bone, at the bar we went in, some men tried to take advantage of us girls. Penny decked one man, all by herself.

Bar, what bar you talking about, Laura?" There is only one bar. We went there and had a bit of a trouble from the barkeeper. He had his men try and strong arm us for free beers. That old nasty fart wouldn't try that again after Mike busted his nose and a few teeth went missing.

"Hey, that wouldn't be the bar down the road from the hotel. The door was partly off its hinges. We walked inside, thick cloud of cigarette smoke filled the filthy place," cited Laura.

"That's the place, Bone said with awe. Mike took on all eight men by himself"

"What were you doing Babe," inquired Penny?

"Me and Jamie watched, of course. He didn't need our help."

"Yeah, I bet you two sat drinking beers watching the show."

"They did just that Penny," Mike replied.

"Heck, it was a chance for Jamie to see Kiddo in action."

"Yeah, Jamie saw plenty in the mountains."

"We would have jumped in if he needed help, babe."

Mike noticed Susan felt out of the conversation. "Was Susan with you two," asked Mike?

"She sure was, snapped Penny. She laid out two men."

Mike puts his arm around Susan and smiles. Both Penny and Laura saw their reaction, taking notice of a connection brewing between the two had arose.

"Once we get to the village, Laura and Penny dress up for your part. Susan can prepare the food. We need to make sure you keep their eyes on you."

"Kiddo, you look embarrassed. Just tell them to dress like hookers."

"No Bone, I'm not embarrassed, I'm not as worldly as you are. I wasn't sure how to tell them to dress up like tramps."

"Oh, oh, touchy we are to getting called tramps. Hookers is a better word than tramps, I beg your pardon," chided Laura at the inferred difference in either word chosen to refer to their role in this plan.

After some quick snickering, everyone goes to the village. Moss was standing by one hut. He spoke the language of the people. Inside, two women were tending to a grill hanging over an open fire pit. Fish was being cooked. On a table was flat bread and beans. Moss told the ladies, "the guards wanted to be fed. He also made sure to them, to not say anything to their spouses, until later." Moss motions to Bone and Mike with two rubbing fingers. Bone pulls his wallet.

Laura began to dress the part. Penny and Susan watched. Laura ripped her skirt on one side, then, opened her blouse to just before her assets were falling out. Next, she slid her bra out of her blouse. Mike stood shocked watching her transformation. Susan and Penny quickly followed Laura's lead. Penny opened her blouse. Bone stopped her just one button short of what Laura done.

"That will do just fine, Babe."

Susan nearly popped out of her dress's top. She didn't have buttons to undo. She took a knife and cut a slit from neck to, well below where she should have stopped. Laura pulled a pin out of her hair to unfurrow, handing it to Susan. With the knife, she cut her hem above her knees.

Mike notices, if she sat, more than the top of her stocking would be revealed. Penny took the knife from Susan and Bone grabbed it from her.

"I'll do the cutting Babe."

Both women watched grinning at Bone pampering Penny, doting on her modesty he expected her to have.

Walking up the trail, each lady made last minutes corrections to their appearance. Penny opened another button on her blouse. Mike went around the container with Bone heading to the parked truck on the other end. The night was pitched black. Some birds ceased their nightly songs once three women approached the campfire.

Bone prepared to take the two men standing by the truck closest to him. Mike would do the same at the container and campfire. Moss's job was to take the driver of the truck down and get the keys for their quick get-away.

Susan was the first to emerge from the trail into the light. All eyes turned to her. Next, came Laura sultry walking behind Susan. Penny followed last emulating Laura's walk the best she could. Penny hiked her dress as high as Bone allowed, her. It was a tad higher entering the campfire light, Bone took noticed.

Laura and Susan were less restricted. Their breasts were hidden only by a thin veil of blouse. All their buttons were opened. Each step was ecstasy of motion from two breast vying for their release. It did not go unnoticed by all the guards and Mike.

Both skirts on each lady was high as modesty would give them. Each step, a hope for the men their hemline would inch just a little higher above their thighs.

Laura was used to men gawking at her on planes. She often was tempted to slap every man that attempted to peek at her breast serving them meals. She could feel their eyes follow her walk up and down the plane's aisle. After time, she would add a swish to her walk just to make them squirm for their naughty behaviors.

Moss picked up a large rock on the trail. The driver stepped from the truck to look at the women at the campfire. The plan was going as expected. Moss whacked the driver on the back of his head. He fell without a sound. Moss searched his pockets for the key. He found them in the truck when his search came up empty. If things went sour, he was to drive the truck into the camp and wait for the rest.

Bone was at his position, ready to take his men out. He spotted Penny walking into the campfire light. She was baring more than he expected. He hesitated to strike the two men. That hesitation nearly caused the plan to fail.

Mike saw Bone hesitation and reacted swiftly. Susan was grabbed by one man. He attempted to grope a feel. Penny was snatched by a second man. Laura was bent over serving one man his meal. Both breasts were ripe for the picking. Her man pulled at her blouse. Both fell from their perch.

Bone watched Penny closely. Her man cupped both her breasts; Bone's eyes nearly popped from their sockets.

"Damn it Bone', Mike thought. Bone was about to lunge at the man before taking out his two men. Mike had no choice but to attack earlier than was expected. He dashed from the side of the container to the first man closest to him.

Laura beat him to his intended man. Her man had pushed her onto his lap. His hand was trying to push through her tightly shut thighs to no avail. She slammed her plate of food into the man's throat. He gagged. Food flew on his face, blinding him momentarily. Laura stood facing her naughty man. A kick to his face knocked him back onto the ground.

Mike was on top on his two men. He struck the first man below the left ear lobe with his finger tip. The carotid was blocked, the man fell dead. Then, Mike pivoted around Susan to strike at his second man. He had to shove Penny from his path to make a second strike between the third man's eyes. The punch shattered his facial bones. Fragments went into his brain. Death came quickly.

Penny getting shove, awoke Bone from his rage at his girl being grope. Not too soon. Both guards were readying their rifles. Both heads came crashing together with a loud thud. A third man remaining sitting at the campfire that cupped Penny's breast, met her husband. Bone greeted the pervert with a hammering fist coming down on top of the crown of his head. The man was shorter, with his three crushed vertebrates.

The last man, attempted to make a dash to the trail. He spotted Susan and swiftly reached for her. Susan slammed an elbow into his face. He reeled back. Mike was standing in front of the man holding his face.

The man was stunned to see a skinny kid looking at him. Two red glowing eyes filled with death, returned his gaze. Fear filled his heart and mind. He would remember seeing death, the rest of his life. It was a short-lived life. He knew his life was terminated feeling a finger piercing his chest. He could feel the hand grab hold of his beating heart. It stopped beating. His eyes glazed over. His last vision was seeing the kid's hand pull out of his chest. Darkness filled his mind.

Mike had for years condition his hands, hardening them as tough as steel. He could break bricks with a finger strike. The human chest was not made of steel. At the Rama theater, he practiced striking a concrete wall, per Cho's instructions. Bob an usher would often make a nasty comment watching. One day, he watched Mike practice striking the wall with his finger tip.

"What you trying to do, punch a hole in the wall with your finger, ha, ha, ha, he would laugh." Bob laughed every day he saw Mike practice on the wall. Every day, until this one day. A piece of concrete splintered from Mike's finger jabbing into the concrete wall, went flying to Bob's face. A small cut proved Mike was not pretending. Bob stopped his mocking. Mike turned walking away. Bob went to the wall feeling where he was striking. He felt a small hole in one spot. It was the same spot Mike was punching with one finger. He put his pen inside the hole. It went half inside the hole. Later, Bob mentioned to an usher, "Mike made the hole with a hammer and nail."

His man went down, Mike smiled recalling that memory popping into his mind. That was when he saw Susan's expression on her face. She stood agape from his act. She never saw Mike in action. His speed was unbelievable. He dropped three men with a finger. She could not fathom what Mike was doing. Death came swift to each guard. He was as deadly as a man with a knife or gun. She shuttered with trepidation, seeing his awesome power.

Susan heard stories about Master Cho and Mike. She doubted many of the things, said. Now, all those doubts went away. She knew now, the truth. Fear was slowly replaced with awe and finally a weird sense of security. Mike was more than she expected. He was no longer a young man, several years her junior. Her feeling grew stronger that day, for Mike.

Mike wiped his fingers of the blood and gore. Then bends down to assist Penny to her feet.

"Sorry to have knock you down, Penny. I had to react before earlier than expected. Bone was about to come to your rescue. Bone reached both guards as Mike was assisting Penny to her feet. One guard froze, seeing his friends being downs in quick succession. Within a second, that young guy took them out, touching each with his finger. He peed in his pants, seeing the guy turned to face him. Two red glowing eyes met his. Bone was behind him and the man next to him.

Bone saw Mike turn facing him. He saw Mike's look at him. He knew he had almost ended the night with tragedy, not acting when he should have. His petty jealousy seeing that man grope his wife, made him think unreasonably. Both heads smashing into each other ended the one man's fears seeing a demon and him glad the battle end.

Mike, with his red glowing eyes, nearly cost Bone to make a second mistake hesitating to smashing the two truck guard's heads. He almost forgot the red glowing eyes were not a demon, but Mike. The same was true with all the women. Moss was the only one unphased by the sight. He fought alongside Mike in the desert. The red glowing eyes was how Mike brought fear to the Black Muslim terrorists.

"Whoa," came from Bone's mouth. He was startled to see Mike's eyes. Bone wished he did not say that. For the first time, he showed fear. All three ladies saw what he saw. Each experience the same emotion. Penny ran to Bone's arms for comfort.

Laura was the only one not afraid. Cho told her of Mike's disguised and that he also used the same disguise to enhance the local's fears. Still, the sight before her, startled her. Susan grabbed hold of Laura. Mike flipped the red light off.

"I am glad you saw my disguise. From now on, you will not fear the rumors being passed around of a red glowing eyes demon. You will know it is me, and how this struck fear in my enemies. I am sorry, you saw this now. I much have preferred a less dangerous time.

Bone, why you scare the women with that silly remark, "whoa." This is not the time to joke."

Bone knew what Mike was attempting and glad of it. The girls were familiar with our jokes between us. This should calm their fears seeing Mike as a red glowing eyed demon," silently spoke Bone to himself knowing, he too, was scared and glad Mike made it seemed, he was joking.

"Hey kiddo, I didn't mean nothing by it. I thought a little levity would ease the tensions."

Mike winked at Bone. Later, he would rub it in, that he saved face for him. Still, that allowed the women to calm down. Susan giggled, soon afterwards, Penny and Laura were giggling.

Susan stopped giggling, "asking Mike if Cheryl is in the container."

"Yes, I believe so." Susan could not look Mike directly in his eyes. She feared he would see the panic within her.

Unbeknownst to Susan, Mike could sense her emotions. Bone was at the container door. Moss stood near him. The door was cracked open to reveal a light within. To the rear of the container stood two women. One was Cheryl. Chairs lined the walls with one table central between the two rolls of chairs.

Cheryl stood hearing a person entering the cargo container. Susan shoved both Moss and Bone away to follow Mike through the door. Both Mike and Susan were not expecting Cheryl's, reaction. She looked at both of them, with dread.

Susan ran inside ahead of Mike. Quickly, she embraced Cheryl. Cheryl seemed unresponsive to Susan's embrace. Both arms kept down to Cheryl's side. She was unemotional with a detachment to all the people entering the container risking their lives to save her.

Cheryl had a secret, it filled her with shame. That shame made her run away into the night. She wanted far away from the ones she loved. Her being a disappointment and them finding it out. That was too great a burden for her to face, once they learned what she had done. The drugs was just a small part of her hidden shame, she felt.

Mike called inside the container to her. Cheryl did not look up to his calling. Mike entered the container. Everyone else, remained outside. Cheryl was wearing her green evening gown. Mike seeing the green dress made him recall the incident at the party. He patted his pocket. Cheryl spotted his hand patting his pocket. Mike had picked up Cheryl's emerald necklace off the dining room floor. She tossed the necklace at him, before running upstairs to her room. He placed the necklace into his pocket. Cheryl saw him do it.

Mike forgot to remove the necklace in the morning. "I need to return the necklace to Cheryl at breakfast, recalling Mike feeling the necklace in his pocket.

Cheryl felt more shame seeing, Mike had her necklace still in his pocket and was attempting to return it to her. She didn't deserve his gift, not after what she had done, to him. Her betrayal, how could she accept it back, from Mike.

CHERYL'S DILEMMA

Inside the container was Cheryl and Susan embracing with Mike entering inside. Cheryl remained as dead as a mackerel the whole time. Susan sensed Cheryl did not want to be found.

Cheryl felt her mom's concerns for her. She knew mom suspected why she was uncaring toward her. She prayed it was only her motherly senses and not the reality of the truth she was hiding.

A memory of when all this began, flooded Cheryl's thoughts. It was back in the jungle, coming home. She received a gunshot wound. Mike went after One Eye, escaping on a cargo plane. Mike was gone, maybe lost, or dead. News concerning his where-about took days. Her wound ached making her concerns for Mike worst. The doctor gave her pain killers to ward off the pain. They helped and made her feel good. She liked taking the pain, pills knowing it was wrong. They were additive. The more she took the great her addition and the more she made the concerns for Mike her excuse to continue taking the pills.

Cheryl recalled men selling drugs in her town. "Her and Bobby fought with them. Mike came and saved both of them that night in the woods from the three drug dealers. That was the night, she killed a man. Afterward, came a showdown with the neighborhood moms and the biker chicks. The biker chicks had enough of their snobby neighbors attitude toward their members. Bell led the bikers to confront the women. She told them how they intervened many times with drug dealers around their neighborhood. It all came to a head after Mike save two of their children one night from to dealers, recalled Cheryl.

"Both boys made a mistake taking a short-cut through the woods to Cheryl's home. They ran into a drug drop-off. Both boys were badly beaten and were about to be killed, then Mike arrived, saving their lives. Cheryl thought many times when she went to the drug dealers to get her pain killers about that night. Now, the same thing could have happened to her."

Cheryl giggled, thinking, "both boy's mothers went to Bell and Susan to confront them. They blamed Mike for their boys getting beaten, until Bell straightened them out. Once Bell finished, mom laid into both women. Later, they came running back to beg the biker moms to continue their vigilance." Susan held her daughter tight. Cheryl was unmoving, almost non-reactive to her embrace deep in thought.

Cheryl continued her reminiscing of her father's death, at the warehouses. "Dad and other bikers went to end the threat to Mike's family and the neighborhood. They were ambushed by the drug gang. Dad was killed by drug dealers. The leader was One Eye, the man Mike had chase into the jungle and then to the Mid-East deserts. Then, there was the last attacked on the warehouses. Marcus was killed in an explosion. Mike lost his memories and was chased through the city with men bent on killing him. He fought for days wounded and burned. He made an incredible walk back to the club."

Cheryl smiled, unseen by her mother embracing her, thinking, "how all the bikers returning looking high and low everywhere found Mike in his cabin, in bad need of care. That night, drug killers came to finish their handiwork. Mister Casper saved them all from those men. Again, and again, Mike went off to battle with drug dealers." Every recall about her past sparked another memory inside Cheryl brain.

"I remember following Cho and Mike to the manor house. Both took out the entire army of men, staying there. That was the first time I witnessed Cho and Mike fighting. It was awesome. None of the Riders helped. Even if they wanted to assist them, the battle was over, once the Riders entered through the gates. One Eye escaped to Mexico. Mexico, Huh, that was where I got shot." Cheryl whence thinking about the burning truck, her stuck inside, Pretty coming to the rescue, and the pain from the gun shot that began her addition.

"Now, look at me standing in this container, feeling sorry for myself. Mike often said, "shame was a heavy burden to carry alone. It is far smarter to confess and asked for forgiveness. Then and only then can one earn back the respect of their peers."

Those words echoed into Cheryl thoughts. She slowly realized, she needed to confess her shame. Still, now seemed the wrong time. She woke when Susan shook her shouting, "look at me, Cheryl!"

Cheryl looked up seeing the concern in mom's eyes. Then felt Mike glare boring a hole through her. Thinking to herself, "how you like me now, mom and you Mike, and the Riders, when they learn what I have done?"

Mike sensed something was eating at Cheryl. He suspected it was her drugs and shame of her weakness for them. Mike instantly became alerted to Cheryl's addition, the first moment he stepped off the plane. He knew another thing. Cheryl was not in love with him, anymore. Something has changed her feeling toward him.

Mike's senses have grown over time. He could use his senses far above any man. Cho said this would come about. His sensitivity in all five senses had grown. He could look at a person, meeting them the first time, and know much about that person. Maybe, even more than the person themselves were aware of.

"A close attention to details can reveal much to a man, that learns to see with all his senses, was one of those many adages, Master Cho cited to him on a daily basis. Many people never take the time to use their senses, they were intended to be used for. Over time, that lack of use eroded their abilities to learn from their senses. The more man became civilized, living away from nature, the less he depended using his senses, another adage from Master Cho, recalled Mike.

Every encounter Mike had with a person, he would take note of their posture and walk. He sees how they dress and wore their clothes. Every word they uttered, provided clues to that person's identity. Even their hygienic care. Make-up was a way to hide your true self from others. That was a major clue to women. The more they covered or changed their appearance, the more info was to be learned. Paint applied to cover imperfections and shape others thoughts. Adore themselves with tattoos. All to hide what is ugly to them. A widow into their true selves," thought Mike.

Mike watched how a people combed hair, which side they parted it, or did they dye their hair? That revealed whether the person was left or right-handed. Did they comb their hair straight, curled it, or had it styled? Was that person a natural free spirit or a self-centered person worrying about others opinions? One could see if that person was a nurturing or a self-egoist looking out for themselves. Those were just the tip of the iceberg in understanding, the true nature of a person.

Mike saw in Cheryl a change within her. She needn't say a word to him, he knew much about Cheryl, seeing her in the container. Cheryl learned much about Mike's extra sensory perceptions in the jungle.

Cheryl reflected more on Mike. "His mom was a drunk and smoker. She often cared little of what they were doing. She was weak and Mike was strong. His mom once said to her, "she wished she never had her kids. They were a burden on her keeping what she desired to do. She had more knowledge in her little pinky, than they all had together. The only reason she kept them, was to get the government checks."

"How can I go to Mike, with him thinking that way about his mom? He will see his mom, in me. He will turn away from me. I will lose him. I see him look at my mom, before we went to the jungle. Now, he openly stares with lust in his heart for, mom. She returns her lust for him. Even if he did care, once he learns what I have done, he will turn from me, with disgust."

"I couldn't bare his disdain or hate. All of the bikers will hate me. Mike left me to go after this One Eye man, when I needed him the most. This One Eye was more important, than me. I fought alongside of Mike. I got shot, helping him fight the Cartel soldiers. Without me, he would be captured or dead. He came back to my mom's arms. He danced with her. They held each other, the whole night embracing on the dance floor. The way they were holding each other, they should have gotten a room. How could they do this to me?"

"Bobby, Bobby, he loves me. He will do whatever I asked him. I asked him to help get me pain pills? He did. He would do anything for me. Not like Mike. I had to throw myself on him, to get his attentions."

"Bobby told me, he knew some dealers standing outside, around the school, by the fence. They sold drugs to kids walking home. Him and his friends would sit in the smoking area outside at school, during lunch, watching them peddle drugs. No one went to report it to the principal. They didn't want to be known as squealers. Maybe, they could have told their parents and let them to the dirty work of informing the law?"

"What was that Mike told me, Cheryl pondered on Mike's words before they came to her? Oh yes, if you are walking down the street with a friend and he decides to throw a rock at a window, breaking it, and the police came and caught you, would you tell them, your friend threw the rock? Do you think your friend considered your feelings, before throwing the rock? Will he take the blame or allow both of you to go to jail?"

"In another way, Mike said the same thing; if I asked my mom to go with my friend rambling around and we both promised to stay out of trouble, then went and got into to trouble. You go home, do you tell your mom? Who is the guilty person? The person hiding the wrong or the person doing the wrong. Both lied and neither was willing to confess. Then, both are just as guilty of the wrong. I told the friend I would keep my mouth shut. I would never squeal on my friend. That added to the lie."

"What Mike said after my response, has often been a reminder to me and my conscience. Your friend threw the rock either for fun, mischief, revenge, or something to prove to you. Whatever the reason, did he think of the consequences of his actions on you? Did he consider his promise to your mom? If he broke his promise, then he has no honor and why would he consider confessing to the law. He lied to the police and your mom and you. What kind of friend is that? He cares nothing for other people's property or anything about that person. Why would he care about you?"

"All I could say to Mike was, I ain't no squealer."

Mike replied shocked me, "neither was he."

"What is that to mean, I asked him?"

"One must know the difference between what is right and what is wrong. If you think you are right, who am I to tell you what right is? We need to find the truth for ourselves. To find the truth, is to seek wisdom. Your friend felt he was right, in breaking the window and cover up his wrong doing with a lie. He allowed you to take the rap with him. He cares about you, is that what you are telling me, Cheryl?"

"Cheryl, Mike said to me, who loves you, cares for you when you are hurt, feeds you, will defend you with their life, and keep faith with you? Is that a person who you can trust or a person you do not want to be a friend? Will they call you? Be there for you, when you are troubled?"

"No, Mike answering his own question. You said that person who lied, put you in trouble, will let you take the blame with him, push you to take drugs, or drink, so he can bring you down to his level. He is weak and wants others to be weak, to justify his own weakness. He will say, "see, they take drugs or drink, why not me and you?" Does he care more about you, than your mom? Who wants you to be, all you can be, successful, strong, and caring, etc."

"Mike stood that day in the park, then walked away. I hated him for making me feel bad. He made me see myself and what I done without blaming me and my friends destroying his camp, near the clubhouse. He came to my aid at the store when those boys tried to cop a feel. I never knew he was there at the store watching me. After the boys knocked me down to the ground, he acted, staying hidden from my eyes. I came too, the boys were gone. I figured they were going to rape me."

"Bobby told me about the dealers by the fence. He said nothing to anyone. I knew I could count on him to get me what I wanted but not what I needed. He was my friend. He was in love with me. Whatever I asked for, he couldn't help me fast enough, especially after I told him, Mike and I was quits."

"I remember the first time Bobby came to see me. I was sitting on a swing in the park. My foot was wrapped and I was still using a cane to walk. We swung together, side by side on swings all day. We went to a bench. I leaned over giving him a kiss. Bobby touched the place I kissed, telling me, he wanted to make sure it was real and he wasn't dreaming. I knew, I had him. He would do whatever, I asked of him. He begged to have me asked, for anything."

"Later that day, Bobby returned with a bag. Inside was what I wanted. We met in the park every day, since then. We would go for long walks in the woods. I forgot about Mike. Bobby and I would make out. One day, I told him to try one of my pills. Mike was right. I was feeling low and needed to justify my low self-esteem. Bobby took a pill. I convinced him," why would I try and hurt him, if I didn't care about him, after he first rejected my offer."

"For a long time, we were alone. Our friends began to follow us. Liddea and Skip were my next victims."

"Hey, we thought we were a group? Why you two been avoiding us? We want to hang with you, they carped often following us around, like little puppies."

"Bobby told them, we were tripping with pain killers. He said, they would go and tell their parents. They promised not to tell anyone. I told them the pills will make them feel good. They took pills with us. Soon, Lou came and joined our group. Together we all hung at the hobo campsite, taking pills. The only one we kept out of our group, was little Macy. We knew she would tell her parents."

"Once my leg was healed, we started on other drugs. Money was hard to come by. After all the money came in from the raid on the manor and Citadel, our parents left money lying around. It was easy to take a few dollars or asked them for spending money."

"Liddea would go directly to her dad. She was daddy's little girl. He loved to spoil her. My mom was different. She asked why I needed the money. Lying was hard, at first. Soon, it got easier. Skip had to work for any money. His dad often said, earn your money, if you want it. Skip knew his dad left his wallet lying around the house. It was simple to grab a few bills. His dad kept a large wad of money in his wallet, Skip told us. Lou had the easiest method to get money. His parents handed out money to him every day to get him out of the house. Come back before dark, was their only request."

"One day, Liddea got sick from taking pain killers. I got scared. Really scared. Bobby and I remained past suppertime at the hobo camp before she came off her trip. Mom hit the ceiling, when I came home late that night."

"Mom asked me once and only once, concerning Bobby and me. She spotted us in the park, several times. She watched us go off together and return at dusk. It appeared to her; we were a couple again."

"I told mom, Mike and I were still an item. Bobby was just a friend coming by, to keep me company. That's all mom, I told her a lie. Mom seemed to accept my answer. I thought, boy would she be shocked to learn Bobby and I were more than friends."

"Bobby was my first. It happened before the five of us friends were hanging together in the woods. We got high and it happened. It happened many times after that. I like drugs and sex with Bobby. Cheryl smiled, thinking of her and Bobby together."

Seeing Mike at the airport, she had planned to tell him about her and Bobby. Somehow, seeing him walking toward her, made her change her mind. It could wait. Mom and Chopper had plans for a big welcome home party. Why spoil this good time for them? Besides, I liked good times."

Then, a sudden realization occurred to Cheryl with her mom still embracing her in the container box. "Mom had been unusual tight reigned on her before coming to this island. Was she suspecting her drug usage? She caught her mom looking in her room. Mom said, "she was tidying it up, or was she," Cheryl pondered? After that time, I set traps to catch her looking for my drugs. If mom found my stash, it would reveal her looking around in my room."

"It was a simple trap. I used long strains of my hair, laying them across my hidden cash. Just a strip of tape to hold the strand of my hair in place. I never kept my stash in any of my places, I usually hid it in other places outside the house. That was after I saw mom sneak around my room."

"I heard mom talking to the doctor. He told mom he wasn't prescribing me any pain killers. That was the first time I began suspicious about mom. That and her questioning me. Her inquiries were other signs mom suspected."

"I told Bobby. He and I had accumulated a lot of drugs. We were selling them to make money. Neighbor kids, only. It was too risky to sell to kids in the club. Bobby was left in charge, when I came here. I was the leader and brains of our little dealership. Maye that was a bad idea," thought Cheryl?"

Suddenly, Cheryl was snapped from her thoughts when Susan pulled away. Susan stared into the eyes of Cheryl. There was no emotions to be found. She was far off in a world of her own.

"Baby what is wrong," asked Susan?

"Nothing. Cheryl shouted in Susan's face. I want out of here. Why did you come? Leave me alone. I going away. I don't want any of you in my life. Why can't you understand this? Go, go, please go."

Susan began to cry. "Why," she asked Cheryl?

"Stop mom. I want to live my own life. I am old enough to make that decision. Don't try and stop me."

Mike steps forward. Cheryl, why do you behave this way to your mom and to me? Is it because you are taking drugs?"

Cheryl was stunned. Mike knew and now her mom knew. "You left me alone with a bullet in my foot. You went after One Eye, instead of remaining by my side. He was more important to you. You been gone all this time, leaving me alone and in need. Bobby was there. He helped me. He cares about me. Where were you? I was in pain."

"Pain, I know of pain, myself, Cheryl. I gave up my family to protect them. One Eye was going after them. He killed members in the club and your father. He had to be stopped. Pain, what do you know about pain? All you have to do is look upon my body. Look at what I have to do. Look at my life and training, I endure."

Cheryl hears nothing what Mike says. She sees the man standing behind him. It dawned on her who the man was. It was One Eye. Him, is that him, she blurted out with hate in her words?"

"Yes," Mike was caught off guard by her request. He knew Moss was behind him. He thought Cheryl could not see him outside the doors. Cheryl reacted.

"Stop Cheryl. He has helped me in the desert. He put his life before mine to aid me and Cho. It was him, that helped us locate where you were at great risk to his life. I have forgiven him. He was at my mercy. I could have killed him easily. Instead, he did not resist and told me he was waiting for me to get my revenge. He deserved it. He told me, he has accepted Christ in his life. He is teaching me about God."

"Oh, I see, he is to get an out of jail free card."

"No, he still has a lot to answer for. It weighs heavy on me about Stephen, Teddy Bear, and Marcus's deaths every day, what Moss had done in the past. I have forgiven him and expect others to find their own peace. While he is with me, no harm will I allow to come to him. Moss knows he is a wanted man. He still came to our aid. He might not make it off this island, now, that all knows, he is here."

"Screw you, Mike. I don't need or want anything to do with you. We are finished, especially if you won't kill that man," screamed Cheryl.

Susan turned to see Moss at the doors. Hate filled her heart. This was the first time she saw One eye, since Stephen's death. She met him at the intersection on the road, leading to this village. She did not make the connection. She listened to Mike, telling Cheryl about Moss's helping Cho and him. She heard him say, he found the Lord. Mike had the chance to end this man's life, but didn't. He forgave him, after all he did. He was responsible for many deaths and his uncle being slain. Still, it was hard not to hate this man."

A scream came from outside the container behind Moss. It was a woman yelling. She said, he has a bomb.

THE BLAST

The sound of the blast echoed through the container. It was louder than what was heard outside the big steel box. Moss turned to see a man approaching the door. He was walking from the container listening to Cheryl's remarks.

A grenade was spotted in a hand of one of the men, he knocked unconscious at the truck, with a rock. He was holding a grenade with the pin pulled. Moss knew, he could never kill, again. The man raised his hand to throw the grenade. Now, Moss had to decide; him or his friends?

Moss reflected on many bad things he done in his life, at that moment. The one good thing he done, was to accept Christ in his life. He vowed to atone for all of what he done. If he ducked, the man would throw the grenade. It would end many troubles he would encounter later. No one would know he had not been killed in the desert. If he attempted to stop the grenade thrown, every Rider would be after him. He had a death mark on him for the rest of his life. He would be looking over his shoulder afraid, until he died.

Moss made his decision before he went to the hotel this night. He knew it would expose him to the Riders. Mike gave him money, with more to come. He said, "stay away from the hotel."

Moss accepted God and his fate. "I promised myself, I would not fear death for my past sins. Even through, I walked with death lingering close. I want to show God how truly a changed man I become. What time I had left, it was to do God's work, regardless of the consequences, I swore."

Moss leaped at the man holding the grenade. Both spun around into the container doors. One door slammed shut. Moss held the man against the door with his body. The grenade was pinned between the door and the man's body and him. Behind him were the other women. Moss prayed they would be protected with his body acting as a shield to minimize the blast. He wasn't long to find his answer.

The blast went off with a shattering loud blast. The blast tore at the man's body before ripping through to him. Moss last thoughts were the pain from the searing heat, then the concussion from the blast. He felt the hard ground buckle against the impact of his body. He could smell the burnt flesh and feel the impact of the concussion on his skin. Seconds to think, was he dying or going to live before unconscientiousness came upon him, ending his questions. He heard women scream, blood splattered on the doors, and a tall man standing above him. Darkness came, before he recognized the tall figure.

Inside the container, everyone was thrown toward the rear. Mike remained standing and unmoved. He felt the struggle Moss was having with someone outside the container. The blast ended any speculations, he had. He looked at Susan and Cheryl and the other girl. All four were safe. Susan was shielded by his body. The others were stunned from the loud sound and knocked off their feet.

Bone yelled to Mike inside the container. "Is everyone okay?" Moments passed slowly before an answer returned to Bone's call.

"Yes, what happened," replied Mike?

"Moss jumped at a man caring a grenade. He slammed the man against the door, shielding us from the blast. The man is scattered around the container. We won't have any problems with him. Moss is lying on the ground. He saved our lives, Mike."

"Is he dead?"

Bone swiftly scanned the body. "He is alive, barely. His arm is partly torn away. His heart is beating, kiddo." Bone halted his talking to examine Moss. His thoughts wondered where Penny and the other women were. He quickly spotted his wife. She was alive. Penny was kneeling by a person lying on the ground.

"Kiddo, I owe Moss for saving my wife's life, also mine."

Mike comes out of the container. He spotted Moss on the ground, bleeding. His arm was barely hanging on.

"Quick, give me your belt," Mike shouted to Bone.

Moss was perforated with small holes leaking blood on his entire body. None were deep. Bone handed Mike his belt. It was then, he noticed the person Penny was tending too. It was Laura.

"Dear God," Bone yelled.

Mike wrapped the belt across the shoulder and rotor cup of Moss to prevent further blood loss. "Bone, he is going to need medical help, quick. It was at that moment, he heard Bone shout, "dear God."

Mike saw Penny kneeling by another woman. It was Laura. "Oh my God," Mike said softly. He races to Penny's side. To his horror, Laura was lying on the ground. The blast Moss attempted to shield from the others, was not entirely successful.

Laura was standing to one side of Penny and Bone, outside the container. The blast never touched them. Laura received a partial blast indirectly from the two men struggling by the door. Penny turned to look at the two men beside her. Moss yelled a grenade. Bone grabbed her, throwing both to the ground. He laid atop of her, shielding her from the intended blast.

Laura caught the blast on her face. Metal from the container flew out from the torn body of the man holding the grenade. It was a small shard that struck her on the face. Many were minor cuts, quick to heal. One eye would never see again Penny feared, applying a cloth against the wound.

Penny imagined the wedding, Laura had planned. She would never see how beautiful she looked. Her only pictures would be memories to remind her. Mike could see what Penny was thinking tending to Laura's face and the cut above her eyes.

Susan came outside standing, then kneeling to aid Penny. Cheryl walked out of the container box, still in a daze. She spotted the torn remains of a body strewn over the area. She saw One Eye, with many wounds, bleeding and his armed nearly torn off. She spotted everyone by a woman, lying on the ground. It was Laura. Her face was cut. Penny was gently peeling a metal shiver from her face.

Cheryl watched her mom, help Penny. "Why wasn't she helping her. Damn you all," shouted Cheryl. This would never have happened, if you let me be. You are to blame, not me." Susan held her hand up.

"Cheryl, not now. Laura needs help."

"I'm leaving. Don't try and stop me." Mike and Bone tended to Moss. Everyone was getting help, but not her. "Damn that man. Damn all of you." Cheryl was filled with anger. She could not accept it, as her fault. They did not have to come looking for me? Cheryl watched no one coming to stop her. She dashed quickly into the darkness. She had the keys to the truck. Moss dropped them before hitting the ground from the blast. They laid near the doors.

A truck starting was heard. Mike and Bone quickly realized Cheryl was taking the truck. Mike stood attempting to chase after Cheryl. Bone stopped him. "She is too far away for your attempts to halt her." Mike knew different. Bone stopping him, gave Cheryl the extra time to get away.

Penny calls out, "is there another car? We need medical for these two.

Susan cries out, "how could she leave. How could she abandon us? She saw Laura was wounded and Moss near death's door. She drives off knowing this. I didn't raise her to be like that. That can't be my daughter."

Susan turns to Penny tending to Laura, "I'm so sorry." Tears ran down Susan's face. She stands looking at all the death about. The screams from the wounded were coming from everywhere. She puts her hands to her ears to shut the sounds out.

Mike takes hold of Susan in his arms. He places her head against his shoulder. "Calm yourself, Susan. This will pass. Cheryl, you raised but she is her own person. Her choices are hers. She is not herself. Drugs have changed her. I will find her. She will come back to us. It will take time and love, but she will be with us again. Have faith, please."

"Why?"

"Susan, Cheryl blames others for all the wrongs she feels. She made choices. She doesn't yet want to accept it as her fault. It is weakness she experiences, this, she never thought, she possessed. It is why she seeks to blame others. She was aware, help was here, if she asked for it. She didn't. She allowed herself to feel pity for herself. When she comes to her realization, acceptance will come. Then later, she can accept our forgiveness. She is hurting and wants to rid herself of this pain. Fleeing is her only choice she thinks, there is. Her fear is great and continue to eat at her soul. The longer she doesn't face her fears, the deeper and harder will it be to save her. Her problems will compound themselves the longer she runs. If we let her get away, she will be lost and maybe to the point, we won't be able to help her, is my fears." Susan looks up at this young man she was in love with hearing words of a much older and wiser person.

"How can we help her, now? She has run away, Mike?"

"Know this Susan, I will find her. We can help her see our love is still there."

Susan looked at Mike and cried. His words hurt. Hearing them, hurt much more, knowing he was right. Cheryl was lost to her. "Mike, please find her. Tell her all will be forgiven. We all make mistakes. We can overcome anything, if we believe in forgiveness."

"Bone honey, a truck hit our car. I think the truck can still be driven."

Before Penny completed telling Bone about the truck, Mike leaped into a run toward the two vehicles crash site at the cut-off to the village. The keys were still in the truck's ignition. Entering the truck, Mike prayed the truck would turn over. He turned the key; a roar was heard. The truck was drivable.

Lights were spotted at the container campsite, first by Susan. She screamed, seeing Mike driving. Bone lifted Moss and Penny with Susan grabbed Laura. She was conscientious. She moaned reaching for her face. Penny stopped her hand. Her eye was barely in the socket, the other eye was covered with blood. Penny assumed the eye was lost and afraid to attempt to clean it.

Susan removed her dress blouse shrouding Laura's naked body. Most of her clothes were torn to shreds from the blast. The only clothes still worn by Laura was a half bra, panties, one shoe and remains of her skirt. Surprisingly, there was little injuries to the rest of her body, other than her torn clothing.

"It hurts, cried Laura. Why is it so dark? Where am I? Who is holding me. Penny, Susan are you here?"

"Laura, it is me, Penny. Susan is beside me. You got hit by a grenade blast. Moss shielded us from the blast. You were not covered by his attempt. He is badly hurt. You have many small wounds. Many will heal quick. One eye is damage. I am not sure about the other. We are going to the truck. Soon, we will get to the hospital. Don't try and touch your face, please."

Penny holds tightly to Laura. Susan takes her hands, both assist Laura through the trees to the waiting truck.

"My wedding. My face. Cho." Susan wanted to cry. She wanted desperately to plead for her forgiveness. She remembered Laura looking at wedding pictures to make plans for her occasion. Now, Susan blamed herself, "Laura will have only those pictures of what might have been."

Penny recalled how she often would look at her wedding album pictures. How much they brought her joy. She cried, "thinking Laura would never see her wedding pictures."

Then, came a thought occurring to Penny. "Maybe she won't see her pictures, but she can listen to the sounds. I can make recording from all the guests. Music and her vows. Her memories will not be pictures but of sounds."

Both women kept trying to ease Laura's fear. At the truck, she was leaned up between Mike and Susan in the cab. In the rear, Moss was tucked between Bone and Penny. Mike sped as fast as he dared on the sandy meandering road back to town. Moss was heard softly praying. Penny heard him pray not for himself, but for Laura and all of them.

AN EXPLANATION

Inside the fast-moving truck Susan sat quiet holding onto Laura's head. Laura passed out again. It was a good thing, Mike said to Susan. The truck turned onto the main road leading to town. Susan broke her silence.

Mike that man in the back of the truck, Moss; well, now that I know who he really is, why did you not kill when you had the chance. Mike did not want to have this conversation with Susan concerning Moss. Maybe this was the best time to tell her. Bone and penny could hear with the cab rear window lowered.

"I found him in a church on this island. I was mad enough to make the killing blow. It was that church across from the hotel. He was kneeling by the cross. A priest was kneeling with him. When the plane landed, after we departed the jungle, I snuck off and made my way into the town."

"I followed the road straight to him in that church. That surprise me he would go to a church, considering his life style. He went inside. I waited several minutes before entering. I believe the Pilot's spotted me entering the church. He set a trap outside the church. Later, I learned the details on the plane, crossing the sea to the desert."

"I walked up to One Eye, kneeling. He turned, expecting me. His first words from his lips were to tell me, he was sorry, for what he had done. He went on to say, he found God and that was the reason, he sought out that church. He said, he understood my hate for him. Months earlier, he would have killed me without hesitation. Those words made my killing blow to come, much easier."

"I looked down at that man, ready to make my killing blow. Something inside me held my hand."

"He went on to say, before I made the death strike, he forgave me. He told me, Susan, he deserved his death. He came to church to prepare for his dying. He wanted me to know, he had accepted his death and asked God to forgive me, when I killed him."

"I couldn't make the strike. I turned away lowering my killing hand, walking out of the church. That was when I sensed the Pilot and his crew, waiting for me. While I was fighting the Pilot's crew, he took aim with a dart rifle. I went down. They toted me to the plane. I was told by the Pilot; he knew Cho flying over the sea. He learned of Cho adopting a son. He was training the boy. He said, if any harm came to me, Cho would not rest, until he was found. Knowing Cho abilities, he decided to kidnapped me. He feared, I would follow and interfere with his plans."

"One Eye or Moss his real name sat beside me on the plane. He did not know that I wasn't going to kill him but knew I held my hand in the church. He was no longer my enemy. The plane crashed in the desert. Sand pirates attacked us with rockets. The crew had some injuries. I went off to deal with them. Later, we walked after burying the plane's cargo of weapons. Moss taught me about Christianity and Islam while we walked out of the desert."

"Several of the crew were hurt. The going was slow. We had water for a few days, at best. The Pilot and I talked. I told him I would journey ahead to find help. A sand storm came. For days, I walked without food or water. I stumbled upon an oasis and passed out. A man named Gungi found and nursed me back to health."

"I remained with him and his wife for several days. I told him I walked in the desert for a week or ten days with no food and little water. He said, that was impossible, few people could survive three days. He said, the survivors of the plane crash were most likely dead. I never believe that to be so. He taught me his religion, Hinduism."

I left, heading in a direction I sensed I should head. Someone needed help, I sensed. Cho said to listen to my senses. Part of his training was to develop my extra sensory perception. It was lucky for Jimmie and Moss, I had. On my journey through the desert, I saved some soldiers being ambushed. Rescue both Jimmie and Moss from a Prison. Cho caught up with us at the Twin Mountains. We battled an army of Muslin soldiers. Moss was there, helping us."

"I never knew any of this, Mike. Does Chopper know, replied Susan?"

"Yes, Cho has been in contact with Chopper during his hunt for me. Chopper was going to fill everyone in on the details back home. You learned some of the story here. There is much more to hear. That can wait, until then. I will tell you this. Bone, Razor, Jack, and Bell came to my room with Cho and Chopper to learn the whole story." Mike recanted some details he left out of the short narrative giving to Susan.

"Susan, the mountain folk living in caves, were starving. I told Moss and Jimmie; I was going to help them. Both agreed to help me. I told them to take the truck and leave. They stayed. Moss was a big help. When Cho arrived, he wanted to kill Moss. I stay his hand. Cho excepted my explanation."

"It was a good thing that we spared Moss's life. He has helped us find Cheryl at great risk to himself. He saved all of you, from being blown apart. God is with him. It was fate, that I held my hand. This day, he lies bleeding to death saving you all."

"Susan, he did all that knowing, he was putting himself in harm's way. Remember Susan, you are not the only person wishing for this man's death. Life is funny that way. You think you know your purpose in life and wham, God throws you a curb ball. Moss was a dead man with Cho and me, after him. When the time came, I couldn't. God, I believe stayed my hand. Now, I see why. I am glad God had stay my hand." Mike smiles at Susan. Mike hoped Susan would understand and see the good Moss was doing to make-up for all his wrongs.

Down the beach a plane was being readied for flight. Mike and Bone were making their way to the hospital, with the women. Three men waited at the plane. Cho had Jamie slow their vehicle and dimmed the headlights entering onto too the sandy beach. They got a flat tire and made a quick tire change. It was too late; their vehicle lights alerted the guards at the plane.

Cho hopped out of the truck nearing the plane. Jack ordered Jamie to blink the headlights. Jamie was about to ask why. Jack spoke first, "on special missions, it was best to allow men spotting them, see a signal. They would ponder on who was sending the signal long enough, for them to get within range. Who else would make a signal, but one of their own?"

"That made good sense," Jamie thought approaching the plane. Cho was now sliding up close as the men watched the truck get nearer. Three men walked toward the truck. The truck stopped. No one came out of the truck. All three men raised their rifles. Two doors creaked open. Two men emerged out of the truck into the darkness on each side.

Cho was waiting. He rose up from a crawling position giving the closest man a chop to the back of his neck. Then, in a fluid move, spun delivering a second blow to the middle man. Both went down in a second.

The leading man saw Jack. He knew this was not one of their men. He squeezed his trigger. Before the round left the chamber, Jack was on him. A front kick to his groin followed by a block on the rifle. The round went astray as the man fell to the ground. Jamie raced to the fallen man striking him many times until, he stopped moving. One man was left. He was a mechanic coming up the rear. He watched with astonishment all three guards downed in seconds. He froze where he stood.

The mechanic stood alone looking at a big man facing him. He heard a second man behind him, he couldn't move, pain filled his mind. Thinking, where did that man come from." He suddenly realized; these men were the ones they were warned about. Their orders were to kill any strangers coming on the beach. "Another truck was to arrive. Why weren't they here," he asked himself, looking at the three men?

"The pain seared through his body. With every breath, the pain will worsen. See Jamie, the mechanic tries to breathe, he wants to scream, but can't. That is Cho's touch," Jack explained.

The mechanic looked at a small Asian man smiling at him.

Cho asked, "how did you know it was us coming?"

"Why were you told to kill us, asked Jack?

The man was scared, "they know. Now, they will surely kill me." He wanted to lie down and cry like a baby. His body couldn't move.

Cho spoke, the pain you are experiencing will get worst as time goes by. You will live with this pain, if you do not answer our questions. Your time is short. After a certain elapse of time, I will not be able to reverse your condition. You will die in terrific pain."

The mechanic realized they knew everything. "Why not tell them anything they want to learn? He hoped the Asian would keep his word and end his pain. The Boss put the word out to take out all of the Americans at the hotel. We are to wait with the plane for the Boss, in case he needed a quick get-away."

"You mean, the women too," asked Jack stunned hearing what was said?

"Yes, everyone inside the hotel. Tonight, by midnight at the hotel. The Boss has spies, watching the hotel."

"How is it going down?"

"Several men with automatics will rush through the front and some from the rear entrance. Others will wait outside, for clean-up. No one will escape. Anyone in their way, is going down. The Boss said, to not take any chances. If any live, we will pay the price for failure. After what you people did at the bar, it put a scare into the Boss man."

"Damn Cho, our wives are there alone. Jimmie and Pretty are the only men we got guarding the place. We got to get back, fast."

Cho taps the mechanic, his pained ended. Cho turns and walks back to the truck. Jamie remained long enough to put a bullet in the mechanic's head. He lowered his pistol to the man's head. The mechanic looked shocked.

"The Asian said, he would stop my pain, plead the mechanic looking up at a rifle barrel stuck between his eyes."

Jamie answered the mechanic's question. "He did stop the pain." Pow.

Quickly, all three men entered their truck. Making a sand splattering turn, they were speeding back to the main road. Two trucks met at the same intersection. Bone and Penny were thrown to one side of their truck. Mike served in time to prevent both vehicles from colliding. Both trucks swerved just in time to avoid a second crash. Jack cursed at the driver; he nearly ran into.

Mike looked at Jack and saw Cho in the other truck. Susan yelled, "it is Jack. We need to stop."

"No, Mike replied to Susan. We got little time as it is, now. We need to get both of our friends to the hospital. "Mike shouted at the truck riding beside theirs on the road. "It is Laura, she is hurt, father."

Cho was quick to react. He was out of their truck, walking across the roof then leaping into the rear of Mike's truck rear bed. He looked down at Bone and Penny cradling Moss between their bodied. He saw Moss's arm nearly severed. He leaned down to examine his wound. There was little he could do, that wasn't already done.

Cho lean through the rear window into the cab of the truck. Laura was covered with a cloth. She was out cold. He gently peeled away the bloody rag covering her face. He wiped gingerly at the eye covered with blood. It had a slight cut over the brow. The other eye was far worst. Cho crawled out the back to the side door, on Susan's side of the speeding truck. He entered, sitting by Susan. Mike spoke.

"Father, it was Moss. He saved them from a grenade blast. He threw himself onto the man shielding the women. Laura was farther away than Penny or Bone. Susan and I were in the container box, we found Cheryl hiding. Moss caught most of the blast. I am rushing to the hospital. When we get there, you remain with Laura and Moss."

Cho interrupts his son. "Mike, my son, there is to be an attack at the hotel, before midnight. All the women and Americans there are going to be slaughtered by the Boss man at the bar. He ordered everyone to die."

"Father, remain with Laura, I will do what is necessary. Cho was about to object. I am in charge, ordered Mike. Someone is needed to stay at the hospital to protect them. You don't need to concern yourself with the others."

"Mike my son, the Boss man has a hit on us all. We are not to leave this island alive."

"I understand, father. First Laura. When she is safe along with Moss, we can discuss your participation. I need to prepare the others.

This night is going to be the beginning of the worst night, this Boss man wished he never had. No one attacks our family. They will know who Oz; the red glowing eyed demon is. He will make his visit on each of the leaders."

GATHERING STORM

Two vehicles come to a sudden halt in front of the hospital. It was a small single-story building with an overhang drive through awning. Two wings, branched off either end. One wing was for emergency, having one ambulance. The other wing, the patient wards. Not aware of the two wings to the hospital, Mike drove under the awning to the front.

Two men opened the trucks doors. One carried a woman; the other went to the tail gate door. Bone jumped out of the bed of the truck. A second truck arrived behind the first. Jamie assisted Bone lifting Moss from the rear. Both women followed their men inside. Jack remained outside to keep watch.

Moss screamed when Bone lifted him from the rear. Jamie caught the half-torn arm dangling from ripping off. He looked at the arm barely attached with a weasy feeling rising up in his gut.

Jack recognized One Eye in Bone's arms. This man called Moss, was him. Jack listened to Mike and Cho telling of their adventure in the hotel, when they first arrived. They all agreed One Eye should be given a trial, before any vengeful action was taken. He deserved that for his part in the desert.

Jamie walked alongside of Bone into the hospital. Both were greeted by a nurse and one doctor on call. Laura was taken to the ER. Moss was tended too in another room by an intern. He decided the arm had to cut off. Another doctor arrived at the hospital. All work was halted on both patients. The Boss sent word prior the arrival of the two trucks at hospital donot accept any people from the hotel. That meant Americans. Any Americans.

Cho made a persuasive argument to the head doctor to make exception. Bone added with his own personal persuasion. Both the intern and nurses readily agreed to Bone's request. The head Doctor needed some encouragement from Cho. He quickly acquiesced to the Cho's polite request, that, and a finger touching him on his back. One minute, maybe less, the doctor became a good doctor, again.

Mike called to Bone and Jamie. Jamie, you remain with Cho. Bone come with me. You women come with us. Penny, and Susan went out of the hospital without a word said. Cho orders Jamie holding a rifle on the staff to go to the ER and stay there. "No one is to leave or come inside, period."

Cho walks with Mike to talk to him alone. "Mike, report to Chopper. He is in charge. Listen to his advice and don't go lone wolf, until you report back to me. Our top priority is to our family."

"I know Cho."

Jack enters the lobby, he was anxious. Bones points to the ER wing. He meets with Jamie by the operating room doors. Inside was both Laura and Moss lying on tables. The intern was administering to Laura. The Doctor to Moss. His injuries were more serious. The intern told the Doctor, he examined the arm. It had to come off. The Doctor agreed.

"Jamie, never leave them alone. There is a hit on the family and any Americans at the hotel seen. That means everyone there will die. A team is position to raid the place, before mid-night.""

Yes Sir."

Jack returned to the lobby. Cho, Bone and Mike were talking talk. "Jack, Bone and I talked with Mike. He has his orders to report to Chopper and back to me. Not to go lone wolf. Do you agree with us?"

Both nodded. Jack turns to Mike; I'm going with you." Cho knew why. Both his wife and daughter were at the hotel.

"Me too," replied Bone.

"Okay, get going. Mike, I will see you later," replied Cho. Both hugged, then Mike walked out of the lobby. Cho shouts to Mike, "when both are stable, I will be with you, my son."

Outside, Susan met with the men leaving. She goes to hug Mike, saying, "I am staying here. I need to know both of them will be okay."

Mike understood her concern. "Be safe Susan, remember, I will find Cheryl."

Penny sat up front in the truck. Mike with Bone were relegated to the rear truck bed. Jack drove. It took less than five minutes driving to get to the hotel. Bone and Penny went inside. Mike held Jack back at the truck.

"Jack, Moss saved our women lives this night. He put his life on the line getting the intel to locate, Cheryl."

"I know Mike and for that, I am grateful. This and other facts will be heard, before any judgement passed on him, I swear to you."

Another car was parked by the front of the hotel. Mike heard a loud thumping sound in the trunk. A yell was calling out to let him out. Mike walks over to the car trunk. With his finger, jabs a hole in the rear hood.

"Quiet, you have fresh air. Any more noise and you will not speak ever again." The man inside immediately shut up. Mike walks away contented the man understood his meaning.

Inside the lobby, all four went. Mike went inside the dining room. Chopper with Bell were sitting at a table. Jack went directly to his room. Mike walked over to their table. Chopper was shot again. Not bad. Bell smile at him.

"I see you heard our Boss man in the car trunk. He has been noisy for some time. I see you stopped that."

"Yes Chopper. We learned there is to be a hit at this hotel before mid-night."

"I know. The Boss man said, "he put an end to that.""

"Not so sure that he did, Chopper. Everyone, Cho and I talked, we believe the hit is still on. I spotted some men outside, coming here. They weren't the friendly type. They carried rifles and I mean, not shot gun for doves, but the automatic type, for people."

"Damn that asshole. Mike, Bone, get the Riders down here for a conference. We a lot to do with a short window to prepare." Jack was in his room. Rhonda filled him in on what happened at the bar. He told her to remain in her room but tell Razor and Miriam to get down stairs.

Razor was lying down in his room being tended to by Miriam when a knock came to the door. It was Rhonda. Razor heard just enough, then abruptly ordered Miriam to remain with Rhonda and Judy.

Pretty, Magic, with Jimmie were in the dining room when Razor came in. Chopper was telling them to go to his room. "Two large bags, get them. Inside are weapons." Pretty with Jimmie ran to the elevator.

Magic, Mike second noticed Mike's expression on his face every time Chopper mentioned the Boss man. He quickly jumps in to the conversation. "Mike, the Boss man Chopper keeps referring too, he is the same man at the bar, you and Bone had a run in with."

"Oh, is that who is in the trunk of the car? I thought the voice seemed familiar. After the last visit to the bar, Jimmie asked the barkeeper to explain his meaning of an impending attack on our people. He liked his polite, well-mannered request, eagerly answering his questions. Chopper was just passing out this intel to all, still here in the hotel. You just confirmed what we learned."

Choppers nods his head with a sinister grin. "Mike, what do you plan on doing? We can take care of the hotel. Jack, standing next to Bell and Chopper, he will get all the staff and other patrons informing them of the danger coming. Jack, tells them to remain in their rooms. Do not try and leave the hotel. Death will come, once you leave the hotel. Tell them that, Jack."

Mike waited until Jack was given his orders before returning his answer to the question, Chopper asked him. He was interrupted again, before he answered.

"There is seven less men to deal with Mike," sniped Pretty.

"Yeah, make that five more added to that list," replied Bone.

"Jack reported, they took out four at the landing strip," answered Chopper. That takes care of nine we got not to worry about. Those at the bar we encountered before returning to the hotel; several will not he in this fight, the others will not be able too." I cannot imagine there are many men still employed by this bozo, coming here to our hotel."

Mike continued his report to Chopper. "Cho, along with Jamie and Susan are at the hospital. Moss threw himself between the women and a grenade toting guard. His actions saved everyone outside the container box we found Cheryl hiding in. Laura was not as lucky. Some of the shrapnel hit Laura in her face."

"Before you asked, Chopper; Moss took most of the blast. He is going to lose an arm. Cheryl took off in one of the trucks. We went straight to the hospital with both Moss and Laura."

Bell listened intensely to Mike's reports, then heard Laura's name. "Mike, how did this man get to the container? Didn't the guards get taken out?"

"Bell, Moss used a rock on the driver. He assumed the man was out cold. He woke, grabbed a grenade. Moss spotted the man coming at the container. He intercepted the man. He slammed the man into the doors of the container using his body as a shield."

"Laura."

"Bell, one eye is seriously injured, the other we thought was worst. Cho cleaned the wound discovering it was only covered with blood and not serious."

Bell felt a bit relieved hearing Mike's report. "I want to go to the hospital."

Chopper quickly nixes her request. "No way Babe. Outside are men hell bent on killing every man, woman, and child in this hotel. I am going to need every person we got. You leaving, will get picked off or worst, taken as a hostage. I don't need this group scattered, wandering around. We need to act as a cohesive team."

Bell was visibly upset from her man's objections to her leaving. Bell's thoughts, "we are apart. Cho, Jamie, Susan, and Laura are at the hospital."

Razor lying on the table in pain, spoke. Bell, you know Chopper is right. We need to fortify this hotel. You go upstairs with the other women. You and Miriam are good shooters. Do sniping from your rooms."

"With what, Razor?"

Chopper interrupts Bell. Babe, in our room are two large bags. Rifles in one and small arms in the other."

"Pretty with Jimmie immediately dash to the elevators. Their going to get those bags." Inside our room Bell, are two large bags in a closet. Bell walks inside the room. Pretty had opened both bags removing and categorizing the weapons on the bed. "Here Bell." He hands two of the four rifles to her. Then, took out four pistols from the other bag. Jack walks in the room hearing Pretty shouts. He looks at the two bags, realizing the danger was real. He grabs two grenades from a bag.

"Bell, get all the women in this room. There is an adjoining room. You barricade this room and prepare a sniper's post on the balcony. Have one of the women post at the front door. Then, do the same in the other room. He hands both grenades to Bell. "You know when to use them."

Pretty, get those weapons down stairs. Jack turns to Rhonda and Judy. Love you two. Pretty lifts one bags, Judy kisses him before he walked out of the room.

Jack, Jimmie, and Pretty enter the elevator. Bell takes charge. Miriam, make a barricade in the other room. Rhonda, take the pistol and guard the front door. Shore up the whole room. Judy, you with me. Get your ass moving and block the door. Take this pistol. Anyone entering, shoot through the door. Penny, you take charge of the ammo and provide first aid if anyone gets a bullet."

Bell was a good shot. She pushed a large sofa to the balcony, tipped it over then, put a blanket on the floor to lie upon. She readies her sights and begin to search for targets. Miriam was doing the same thing in the adjoining room on her balcony.

Before Mike arrived at the hotel, two ushers approached Chopper. Many heard the bikers talking about the hotel being hit. Everyone was a target. Both asked Chopper if they could help him. Bell was glad for the assistance. Chopper told each man to keep an eye, as spotters.

Chopper calls Bell to one side. "Babe, these men live in this town. They got families. When trouble begins, we can't rely on them. They are like fair weather friends. They will turn on us or run. Don't get cozy with them."

Bell understood, nodding back to Chopper. The others did not need told this, except Judy. She was the youngest member of the Riders. Now Judy was assisting her sisters, fortifying each room. Bell sensed her anxiety.

"This sofa will prevent a grenade from being tossed inside the room from the outside. All that furniture you moving around will keep any one out of the rooms. Judy eased up with her nervousness hearing the rooms were secured after Bell's explanations.

Outside the two rooms, Jack secured the stair well. He placed and axe across the door. The elevator was different. He rigged a grenade wired across the elevator door. He made it a point to tell Bell and his men leaving with the bags of weapons.

"Listen, don't forget, I got a wire running across this door. You forget and walk out of the elevator, well, shame on you. Both passed the word to all others in their teams. The hotel staff was told to not go to that floor, under any reasons. Jack made one last adjustment. Once they were on the main floor, he opened the elevator control box. With his rifle butt, slammed it hard. A few sparks flew out. Now, this elevator is secured. Anyone wanting to go upstairs, they going to walk up the stairs. One way in and out easier to guard."

Jack reports to Mike and Chopper. "All the rooms are secured. The stair well and elevator are out of use. Bone knew Jack would do a great job securing the rooms. His fears for Penny, lessen.

"Chopper, I am going to the hospital to report to Cho."

"Damn, nearly forgot about the Boss man in the car."

Mike knew what to do before Chopper replied. He swiftly went outside to the car. With his fist slamming into the lock, buckled the door. It opened. Mike swiftly covered the man lying face down with a cloth, lifting him from the car tossing him over one shoulder. Inside the hotel, Jimmie grabs hold of his friend, the Boss man.

"I'll have all you killed for this." Boss man rarely made empty threats. He looked at the man that released him off his back, like a sack of grain, flopping him down on the lobby floor. It was that little skinny kid. He was the same brat that wiped his bar clean with his men, single handedly. He knew right off, he said too much. One thought rolled about in his head; how he would enjoy watching the kid, looking at his family, while he slowly strangled life from him. Before the squirt died, he would take a baseball bat and bash his head in. Boss man grinned with that thought."

Many a times, Boss man had done the same to a town person that went against his rules. He used a baseball bat, as a little child, he loved the game. He wanted to be a baseball player. That never came to be. Still, he enjoyed swinging a bat.

Jimmie took the Boss man from Mike. "I'll take him to the women's room." Boss saw his old friend. That thought about the bat on the kid went to the bat on his friend, called Jimmie.

"That ain't happening, Jimmie. Jack blew the elevator control panel and put an axe in the stairwell door. Take him to the office. Make him secure and lock the door. We might be needing this ass for asking terms, if things begin to head south for us."

"You really think he will honor anything he promises, Mike?"

"No. But Cho or Me will remain behind, we should give everyone time to get off the island with our women folk." Pretty was talking to Chopper.

"Chopper, I was thinking, me being upstairs, would give the girls some comfort."

I get it Pretty. In a battle, I sometimes forget about the collateral. We got family here. In the heat of battle, I think about my comrades and now, I have to consider our women.

Jimmie dumped Boss man in the front office. No window or back door was seen. He added some duct tape to his mouth and both hands and feet. "Now, I am going to tape you to the desk, you SOB," grinned Jimmie at the man pleading with his eyes to not kill him but fantasizing all their deaths.

Pretty passes out the other rifles and pistols. Chopper takes two pistols. "Here Mike, take this." Mike shakes his head, implying no. "Just in case," replied Chopper to Mike's nod. He places the pistol behind his back, inside his pants turning to go to the front door.

At the front door, Mike spotted a rifle barrel in the ajar door. He leaps, then rolls to his feet beside the door, waiting for the man to step through.

The door blasted open with three men emerging side by side. One turned to Mike. His rifle was grabbed. The barrel was bent up curving back to the man's face holding the piece. He squeezed his trigger. Nothing. His rifle butt was shoved into his chest. The hole was vast. His rifle pointed from his chest like a weather vane to north. With blinding speed, the next man felt himself spinning. He stopped hitting the next man beside him.

Mike often tried to perceive the thoughts of the men he fought. This was so for the three men bursting inside the front doors of their hotel. The second man saw the weather vane pointing him in another direction. He turned to see where he was to go. It was at his comrade beside him. He was confused seeing where he was being pointing too. Mike decided to do a round house kicked at his knee caps. Then, before he could react, a spinning heel kick shoved his nose down his face. He coughed. Then saw his final destination. Mike was pleased he gave the second man a sense of direction to his final days.

The third man pulled his trigger, a short burst sounded out. The beautiful chandelier hanging in the lobby blew into millions of sparkling shining glass shards raining down. Chopper and Razor clapped their hands. Jimmie stepped out of the office locking the door turning in time, to see the shower. Jimmie was stunned. It was amazing to watch Mike do his thing. He was at awe seeing Mike move with blinding speed and skill. He thanked God, he was on their side.

The third man halted pulling his trigger. He was awed watching the pretty little sparkling glass rain down to the ground. The desk manager had no time to duck behind his desk. He knew the three men crashing through his door into the lobby banishing rifles. Word was passed to him, by a friend. The hotel was to be attacked. No one will live through the night. He knew that him and his employees were dying this night. He didn't have much time to get the word to the others. Now, it was too late.

When the sparkling shower of glass ended, so did the third man. Somehow, the third man replaced the chandelier on the ceiling. He hung with all four arms and legs draping down, dripping blood. It wasn't as pretty as the sparkling glass chandelier.

Quick, Chopper ordered all to their posts. Jimmie ran to the rear door entrance with his rifle and a hotel volunteering aide. He had placed many large boxes around the door. Some against the door. Others to offer a shield for him against a grenade and flying bullets, once the door was bridged.

Pounding came from the door. Pretty shoved his aide down behind a crate waiting for the explosion. He didn't have a long wait. Chopper, Razor, Mike, Bone, and Jimmie heard the blast. Jimmie remained by his post near the windows. Razor behind the desk and Chopper with Bone in the dining room. Tables were turned over making a fortress wall. If it got to hot, everyone was to get to the fort in the dining room.

Mike switched his hood light on. Both eyes lit with a red glowing light shining out. The front window shattered from a grenade. It erupted, spewing damage in all directions.

Pretty waited until the man was about to leap through the broken window. He met the man with his rifle barrel. Pretty recalled Mike ramming the barrel down a man's face. He tried to emulate the same with his rifle. It didn't make it all the way down the man's face as Mike's had. Still, he thought it was a good effort on his part.

A man leaped inside through the broken glass window. He wished he kept his mouth closed. Jimmie hadn't need to worry. The man was ready and willing to swallow his rifle barrel all the way down into his belly and out the asshole. Jimmie stood looking at the man hanging from his rifle. His only concern was, how to get the man off. He dropped his rifle and took the man's rifle. "The hell with trying to get this slime ball off my rifle, Jimmie was heard saying, before all hell broke out.

Another man entered the lobby. Mike waited as he neared the dining room. One more step and Mike would act. Chopper was waiting. Bone jumped from his place rushing to the man. He wanted some man for himself. Mike spotted Bone charging at the man pointing his rifle at Bone. Bone wasn't going to make the distance to his man. Mike kicked a rifle. It went upward slamming into the man aiming at Bone. The rifle went floundering away from his shot to drop the giant. Bone cleared the distance grabbing the man by his throat. One squeeze, that's all. His man eyes popped from his head. Bone slammed the man into a wall.

Another man dashed inside. He spotted two red glowing eyes. He lifted his rifle to shoot, disregarding the giant shoving the head of a man in to the wall. Bone turned, reached out to grab somebody. It was the other man. He quickly received a welcome from, Bone. He was happy to join his partner in the wall. Bone turned to Mike smiling. Mike nodded, then was gone.

Jimmie stood firing his rifle at any moving object entering through the remains of a fragmented rear door. Once the three men entered the front door, and before Mike dispatched them, an explosion tore the rear door. It remained on its hinges, barely. Any man entering had to make it inside weaving through a jagged steel door. A hail of lead sprayed the door. Two men dropped dead. Another man outside, fired into the open door. Jimmie duck as bullets ripped at his crate. He handed his pistol to the aide. He was shaking before the fight with fright.

"He is no use to me," Jimmie thought looking at his aide shivering, covering his face with his hands behind another large crate. He took his one grenade tossing it through, the open rear door outside. A man shouted.

"Grenade, run." The blast sent smoke through the door.

Mike shouted to Pretty by the window in the dining room. "Grenade!"

Pretty leaped toward the band stand. He just made the place, when the explosion came. All the instruments covered him like a blanket. The fortress of table shook but held.

Red flashes of gun fire litter the outside of the window spraying bullets everywhere. Bone was trapped in the lobby. Razor was behind the counter with the desk manager. Bullets perforated the desk, barely missing both manager and Razor lying flat on the floor. Bone held his rifle out the door. He pulled the trigger, until the rifle was emptied. Then, quickly dropped a clip and reloaded. Razor stood to return fire, as Bone was reloading. Chopper followed with his return fire.

Upstairs in the room, both women used the gun fire to spot shooters outside the hotel. Bell dropped the first man. Then, another before Miriam found a mark. He ran across the road to a shrub. He went tumbling into the bush. Miriam fired her rifle at where the man went. He never came out of the bush.

Bell screams to Judy to bring the phone. Bell calls down to Chopper. "Babe, we took out three men. We can't do much more, up here. I am coming down."

Chopper screams back on the phone. "You can't. The elevator doesn't work and it is booby-trapped. The stairs are the only way down. We got fire coming from the rear. It is too dangerous. Keep up, sniping. Babe, there is a third case under your bed. Get it. Inside, is a rocket launcher."

Gunfire outside cease. Quiet was disturbing those inside. Mike waved to Chopper, then leaped out the front door. Several men were reloading their weapons when a strange person stood before them. His eyes were glowing red. They hurried to get clips in their rifles. Some men fumbled, dropping their clips. Mike replied with a haunting chuckle.

"Your training is lacking, heh, heh, heh." A two finger jabbed left the first man sightless. The second man tried to call out. His throat was torn from his neck. The third man was picking up his clip. He never got to an erect position. Mike lowered his leg on his back. The vertebrate separated. He went limp and fell face down on the concrete sidewalk.

Jimmie recovered from a second grenade blast, momentarily stunning him. Five men were entering the rear door entrance spilling hot lead everywhere. His crate vanished into dust. He dived to another box. The aide kept lying on the ground cowering. Jimmie could only crawl from one crate to another with lead following him, He came to two crates. Jimmie decided to make his last stand behind them.

Outside, Mike saw men running to the rear of the hotel. He heard hundreds of rounds. Inside the lobby, Bone with Razor went to the fortress. Magic went to his window. Bone followed to the other window. Each saw men going around to the rear of the hotel. The they spotted a red glowing eyed figure dashed across their view, heading toward the rear.

A man dropped from a gunshot above the dining window. Bone said to Pretty, "bet it was Bell."

"Got that bet covered. That came from Miriam."

"How you figure that?"

"that man was on her side of the room. Bell was facing up the street. I watched them drop several men. Remember, I helped them set up their sniping area."

Mike Heard men across the road. He pointed to Bone and Pretty to cover his run. They saw men in hiding. They opened up, spraying the area with hot lead. Mike made it to the alley behind the hotel. Men were scrambling up the rear of the hotel to where Jimmie was holed up. Some men slowly snuck hiding behind trash cans. Gunfire was erupting inside the rear of the hotel.

Gunfire suddenly stopped inside the rear of the hotel. Jimmie was glad he stacked more crates. He stood. Several men were loading their rifles. They stopped to listen to what this man standing was saying.

"Bad move to stop what you were doing. Should not be distracted, while in a gun fight. You should be loading your rifles. Let me give you some advice. Better and more training is always required. If you bozos were better trained, I wouldn't be standing up advising you of your stupidity. While you watch, I try and instruct you how to shoot those rifles. You missed with every shot. Use short bursts. Don't waste rounds shooting at empty boxes and crates. See, now you got empty rifles. Not me, see how I shoot at you. Too late to learn, now."

Mike heard two short bursts, knowing it was Jimmie. He learned one thing about Jimmie in the desert. He measured his shots. He said, "make them count. Hit your targets." It was the same lesson, he was taught by shooters back at the club house," Mike recalled.

Mike had several men to deal with in the alley. He walked up the center of the alley to his first man. A hand grasped the man hanging back near a large trash can. He was dumped in the can. The lid came down hard. Next, was two men that turned, hearing the lid bang shut from a trashcan. Night was dark in the alley. They saw two red glowing specks walking toward them. They raised their rifles. Two red glowing specks went up a wall. They followed with their rifles. Then, the two red glowing spots flew across the alley onto another wall. It remained still on the wall. One man cried out to the others.

"There, what is that?"

The red glowing speck slid to the street. One man aimed his rifle. The eyes quickly dashed toward them. His rifle was jerked from his hands. His friend saw two red glowing eyes beside them. His friend's head went missing. He knew this when blood came raining down on him.

It was his turn, thought the second man. "He knew this, because there was him and just his friend walking beside him. His rifle was yanked from his hands. He momentarily saw it fly toward the other two men ahead. It looked to stop in mid-air. That was weird, he thought. He kept peering in the direction of where his rifle was floating in mid-air. Night was getting darker. He could barely see the rifle. Darkness was forever in his eyes," was his last memory.

One man of the two froze, dropping his rifle staring at two red glowing eyes. He watched in horror both men behind him, lose their heads. Both were still standing when something touched him on his backside. He turned. A fountain of blood was geysering out of the two soldiers not far behind him. He was a young man in the gang. It was his first time holding a rifle. He shot several rounds through a window, inside the hotel. His family was poor, only his mom and sister. His dad was killed one day exiting a local watering hole. He got into a fight, a typical norm for him, drinking. One bottle side on his head, was all it took. He and his mom went to the hospital when an officer came late one night, rousing them from their beds.

He was fourteen years old. Only one option left for their family. Quit school to find work. Many odd jobs, making little money, just enough to eke by. Two hard long years of misery was all he had, before getting this job. It paid much more for less work. Joey was what the men called him. His first pay check was followed by a celebration at home. More money than a year's pay was welcomed, gladly.

To keep his job, Joey decided nothing was too wrong, to keep earning this kind of money. Joey came to a horrible realization, staring into the red glowing eyes of death, this night. His partner didn't freeze with fear, reacting immediately once the two red glowing eyes came close. He saw a man. Just a man. He would come to wish; he froze like his young partner had done.

Mike watched the man squeeze his rifle's trigger side stepping the path the barrel was pointing at. With his forearm, Mike blocked the rifle. It swung away from him. Mike took a second step closer to the first man. He was side by side with him. An arm wrapped around the neck of the first man. Mike completed his third step with a heel pivot spinning him and the first man away from Joey.

The first man's feet went flying into the air following the arc of the spin. His legs halted at the same time his body impacted the steel railing of the step leading into the rear door blasted by a grenade. His body spun around the hand-rail like a cork screw.

Joey turned slowly to view what happened. He spotted the man standing beside him with his rifle wrapped around the rail beside his companion. After that sight, all he would remember waking in the morning, was his partner cork screwed on a rail. It was not a dream waking up. Before him was his partner still wrapped around the rail with his rifle. Himself, was alive. His rifle was where he dropped it.

Mike was going to touch the young man but seeing him faint, was just as good. He took off down the alley to the main road. The threat to Jimmie was no more. On the road stopping near a truck by the bar before getting to the hospital, two men attempted to wave him off. Mike assumed they were asking for help. He slowly walked toward the truck with his head down. One man offered a hand to him.

"What you want, asked Mike. Does everyone in the town want a tip from the tourist. The street was dimly lit. No street lights to aid seeing a person. Mike was glad for that. Neither man could see what was waiting for them, once they realized who they were talking too."

"No, we don't want a tip. Get your ass over here and help us unload this truck." He points a rifle at Mike.

"Yes sir."

Inside the truck was boxes of rifles and ammo. One box was lying on the street near the tail gate. Mike bent to lift the crate. The other man kept watch down the street. The gun fire had ended.

"Hey Luweidgie, I guess they got them Americans? You think we should continue to unload these crates?"

"You heard the Boss's orders. He said," unload the boxes in the bar." You can do what you want. Me, I doing what the Boss told us to do."

"Yeah, you better do what your boss orders you two bozos to do," touted Mike.

One man helping Mike was toting a big knife. He cut the ropes binding the boxes. He turned pointing his knife at the man, calling him a bozo. "Hey mister, I was using this to cut the straps to these crated, maybe it will be better to cut that tongue out of your mouth?"

Mike stood, both eyes glowed red, the man with the knife froze. Word was getting around, about some demon with red glowing eyes. The guard watching the street turned hearing the word bozo, he saw the glow. He threw his rifle, before running down the street.

The knife man was a tad dumber or braver. Never was he the one to hesitate. He often acted first, then made his regrets, later. It was a careless trait he adopted but one that had served him well. He never came up against a man that could make him regret, after he began using his knife. He instantly regreted thrusting his blade. The second and third thrusts were just instinctive. He lashed forward with a stab. Mike, simply leaned his head out of the blade's reach. The man sliced once, then twice like a windshield blade on a car.

One slice was close. Mike was quick. The next cut came wickedly close to his chest. He twisted, watching the blade pass harmlessly by. Mike watched the man foolishly continue to strike at empty air. He decided to stop his folly of wild swings with his knife. The finally attempt came, when the man raised the blade above his head suddenly bringing the dagger down at Mike.

"I do this to stop you from hurting someone or yourself sir, Mike said as he took hold of the wrist holding the knife. He allowed the man to complete his downward thrust, then reverse the direction. A vise wrought grip raised the blade upward. Then Mike made it come speeding down between the eyes of the beholder. He looked like a unicorn with a knife handle poking from between his eyes. Mike propped the man alongside the truck's tailgate.

"What am I to do with a truck filled to the brim with guns," Mike pondered. Inside the truck was a third man watching. He jumped down from the rear, just as Mike was completing his unicorn interpretation. Mike spun around shouting into the face of the man. It was his Kia shout. It was powerful, the man froze momentarily. Then, he quickly grabbed his chest. He dropped to his knees. Mike was dazed watching the man drop to his knees. He felt for a pulse on the man's neck. There was none. He was dead. He looked about in his fifties, a bit over weight, and had a puffy face.

Mike reasoned that his Kia was the cause for the man's heart attack. Cho said to him, "the kia can be used as an offense weapon and not just a defense." This night, he proved Cho was correct.

A fourth man was coming out of the bar holding a box. It had liquor bottles inside. He dropped the box. Mike turned, saying, "he was aiding a man clutching his chest. He thought the man was having a heart attack."

The man did not believe Mike's explanation. Then it dawned on Mike, his eyes were still glowing red. That, or the man leaning on the tail gate, looking like a unicorn with a knife protruding between his eyes. The man pulled a knife.

"Not again," Mike thought. Mike grabbed hold of the unicorn man's knife, throwing it at the man coming out of the bar. The tip entered his knife free hand, pressing it into the thigh of the bar man. Mike moved as he threw the knife both arriving at the same time. He was swiftly standing face to face with the man walking out of the bar.

"Shit," was all he had to say. Urine ran down his pants. Mike took hold of the man's throat.

"I got one question to ask you. Is there anyone else in the bar.?"

The man gurgled, "a no." Mike squeezed harder.

"Yes. Men are coming down the street. Maybe twenty or more. You got seconds to get away." His neck felt fingers digging deep into his throat. They burned like fire. More urine ran down his pants legs.

"Thanks, I am one of the men you are attempting to kill this night." The man began to pray. More urine ran down his pants. Mike slaps the man. "Keep awake. Listen to my words. I come to kill those that come to do harm to my friends. If you come in peace, you may leave in peace. Those that don't, will join in my feast. You, I will allow to live to tell those coming. Look upon the faces of your comrades. They have my mark, OZ. Beware of my mark. It means death."

Mike touched the man, freezing his body, but not his mouth. Pain entered his entire body. Blood trickled down the man's face. One man lying dead on the street was witnessed by the frozen man, he watched a demon slicing the head from the body. He went to the truck with the head and inscribed two letters, then to the bar, inscribing the same two letters on the door, and a finally inscription on his forehead. The cut burned, like it was coming from hell fires with each letter. He knew what the two letters were etched into his forehead, OZ. The demon disappeared into the dark.

A road fuse was lit. It burned for a few minutes, but not before the bar man frozen, was taken inside the bar, to get a drink by his comrades. They thought he needed one, the way he was standing still, not moving.

The head was spotted by twenty men racing up the street to the parked truck at the bar. It was a gruesome sight to behold. A head, dripping blood, both eyes staring into the night, stuck on a pole, entering onto the beach. Many poles were lining the beach separating the street from the beach on the boardwalk. They halted coming to where the truck was once parked, now re-parked up against the beach walk pole.

Mike had released the parking brakes. The truck was slowing rolling down the street. Several of the men chased after it. They followed the truck to its re-parked place. Some stayed to hear what their comrade had to tell them. He was frozen in the street. A knife poked through his hand into his thigh. He slowly with a shaking voice, murmured the demon's warning.

"A demon with red glowing eyes came. He done this to me. He said, "tell all that he will let us live, if we stop attacking his friends. If we don't, then he is going to eat us all. I need a drink. Then he did something to me."

None dared to question the man's word. He was a good fighter. Besides, some saw the red glowing eyes person racing away from the bar. He turned, before he took off. That was all any wished to see again. A glimpse of two red glowing eyes would haunt their dreams for a long time.

Mike turned the next corner to the hospital. The truck struck a pole on the boardwalk and stopped. The hospital was a block from Mike. The explosion was loud. The buildings shook. The night lit up bright. A fire ball rose into the air. Many smaller blasts followed the main one. The truck was no more nor the soldiers that chased after it. The explosion was near enough to the bar. The force from the blast cause much damage to the front. The Boss man would need more than a paint job to restore the bar to its original appalling street appearance.

E R STAT

Inside the lobby of the hospital blood, covered the floor. Two dead bodies, laid like two stiffs on a gurney in the middle of the pool of blood. Hundreds of bullet hole riddled the front desk. Mike, slowly made his way across the slippery floor, to the front desk. Another body, a nurse was sitting upright staring into the void. Her face was flush. Her white nurse's dress was stained all over with her blood. She was dead.

Mike turned to follow the blood trail down Through the double doors were three men, not doctors, with machine guns were lying silently on the floor. A fourth man was poking through the walls with both legs hanging like drapes. There was no window at that place in that room.

"Now, the hospital has one, Mike chuckled. Definitely father."

The further Mike walked; the more bodies laid dead. Some with bullet holes and others with no signs of death, was evident. One fact Mike did discover, each man without bullets holes had mangled bodies. "Definitely Father."

Inside one room was a body mangled with some body parts nearly ripped off, hung in contorted positions. Mike instantly recognized the man lying dead at his feet. His death was similar to the torn man at the container box. Moss was shielded from most of the devasting blast of the grenade by the man he pushed against. This man had no shielding. Why, was evident to Mike. Jamie sacrificed himself, to save two nurses cowering in a corner of the room.

Entering the room, Mike saw the open window. The bed was emptied and was moved near the window. Mike walked to the bed lifting the medical chart of the patient. "The name said it all, Laura. Father was here."

Mike looked out the window, no foot prints were seen. He knew Cho could walk without leaving signs. In the middle of a fight, even Cho might not be able to escape carrying Laura and not leave a trail. Mike decided to not follow the obvious attempt to convince his attackers to chase after a false trail. He turns to leave the room. By Jamie's body, he saw a sign, he overlooked. A small circle in a pool of blood by the body, It meant someone kneeled. Cho was checking Jamie's vitals or saying goodbye to a good friend. Mike was convinced, Cho was still inside the hospital.

Outside the room a nurse darted pass Mike in a frantic. He stopped her. She was in tears, shaking, and covered with blood.

"Is there anyone in the hospital alive, Mike shouted not expecting a response?"

Mike felt the small cuts and abrasions covering her arms. She was in shock. She looked at Mike with his red glowing eyes shining, screamed jerking her hand free of his grasp. She ran down the corridor. Mike was tempted to give chase but decided to go in the direction from which she was running from.

Mike switched his red lights off, not wanting the same reaction from other staff he came across. Every room, the door was opened or torn off its hinges. Many were patients riddled with bullet holes still lying in their beds.

"Why, Mike asked himself? Are they that afraid of us?"

Ahead was a corridor of gurneys and men with rifles lying dead, strew all about. This was a war zone of biblical proportions. Everything was damaged by rifle fire, grenades, or scattered haphazardly, Mike viewed it with awe.

"To survive this, would be a miracle. I hope father and Laura are still alive?"

One door laid ahead. Surprisingly, it was the only room with a door not torn from its hinges tossed at the men. Other rooms the door was used as a flying projectile. Men received a door ending their day, early. One room door was still implanted in a wall. The soldier looked like a taco. He was the meat wrapped between sides of a door folded by the wall to each of his sides.

Mike went to the open door with trepidations. He could sense people beyond the door. Two men laid dead attempting to enter the room. Definitely Cho.

"Father," Mike called.

Cho hearing his son, called back. "My son, come inside."

Mike ease the door open. Blood covered the floor. The room was in dis array. The bed and cabinets were used as barricades. A doctor with two nurses were crouching, then stood, once the older Asian man called to a voice outside the room. Mike entered looking at the scared staff.

"Everyone has left the hospital. It is safe to leave." The hospital staff didn't need to be told a second time. Both nurses flew past Mike out of the room. Mike held his hand halting the fleeing doctor.

"Stay for a second, Please?"

The doctor wanted out of the room but deferred to this young man. He watched this lone Asian gent take out men with rifles. One by one, he did amazing unbelievable feats no human could possibly have done. When he heard the Asian call to his son, he figured this person was just as dangerous. He remained as he was told.

Inside the room was Cho cradling Laura in his arms. Neither were injured.

"Father I am glad that you and Laura are safe. I spotted Jamie. He died saving lives."

"Yes, I will sadly miss him."

"I to, Father."

"We were attacked at the hotel. All are safe. Some staff were the only casualties. I don't think we will be eating in the dining room for some time. Bell and Miriam did a great job sniping from their balconies. Jimmie defended the rear position against overwhelming odds. The main lobby was my domain. Once I ended the threat, I signaled Chopper, before going outside. I found a team attempting to reinforce the first assault team."

"Oh yeah, I found that barkeeper in the car trunk. I handed him to Jimmie for safe keeping. I was told he was an old friend to Jimmie. Then, I came here. I spotted a truck loading crates, of weapons."

"I heard the explosion, my son."

"There were twenty or more men coming to the bar. I don't this battle is at an end." Mike made his report then realized Cho was sitting on a bed cradling Laura head in his arms. "I am sorry, father. Is Laura, okay?"

"Laura was unconscious from the surgery. One eye is damaged. Time will tell if she will see from that eye. The good news is, she is fine." Mike smiled and reached to hug his father.

"Father what of Moss? Did he survive?"

"Look under the sheet, my son." Moss was lying opposite of Laura on the bed. Mike pulled the sheet back. One arm was missing.

"The doctor had to amputate it, replied Cho. He is doing fine. He got a ton of drugs running through his body. He ain't feeling, nor caring about much right now. I owe this man much, for what he did this night. No matter what he done and his aid in the desert, he has earned my forgiveness, my son."

"I am glad to hear that, father. Someone stayed my hand that day, I like to think it was God's hand. He wanted me to allow Moss to live. Laura and the others are alive, because he is alive to have saved them."

Cho looked at Moss lying on his bed beside Laura. He reached down and grasped his hand. Mike saw another side of his father at that moment, cradling the hand of a man he hated.

"Mike, I came to this room with those dogs on my heels. This doctor and his nurses shouted, to be let inside. I opened the door in time. They fell into my room. Two men were standing behind, them at shoving them. I had to act swiftly. Their mistake was not shooting when the door was ajar. Fortunately for us all, they did not, not so fortunate for them."

"I shoved the doctor back into them. The first man was closest, doing his best to get the doctor away from him. While he was distracted, I snatched his rifle from his hands. The foolish man was using his only weapon to direct the doctor, instead of using it as it was intended for."

"I used his rifle for its intended use. Well partly, I took the barrel and whirled it around. I made two hits with one swing. The first hit was a home run. A loud swat or was it a thug, I was in a hurry.

Either way, the head went mushy. A thug sound. The second man got a tip hit. He was a tad farther away. He had the drop on me, with his rifle. That momentary tip was time enough for nurse Juanita to grab a fire extinguisher off the wall. Her quick thinking, spraying the extinguisher out the door, made the second man cover his face. I took his rifle and returned it back to him. That man was not one bit thankful, my son."

"I too, have often encountered the same unthankful behavior from many men, when I was generous returning their weapons."

"It is this new generation, I feel. They have not been brought up with the same manners, we were taught. I am glad you have good manners, my son"

"I owe that to your wonderful teachings, Father."

Nurse Juanita halted walking out the door, when Cho spoke her name. Mike thanked her. "You were very brave to do what you did." She was young and attractive, Mike thought. No wedding ring decorated her finger.

"My son, Mike turns back to Cho. As I was telling you, I leaped out the door slamming into the second man. I shoved him into the wall. That hole is where he was stopped."

Mike looked at the human shaped hole before entering the room. He saw the mangled heap remains of a distorted man, all twisted. He died in misery. His rifle was in his hands.

"My son, the other man shot many of the staff chasing us into this room. I gave him time to reflect on his misdeeds. He was the one you may have stepped over entering this room."

"Quick my son, we must take our friends to the hotel. You are going with us, Doctor." The doctor was about to object to Cho demands. There are other doctors that will tend to the wounded here. You will be needed at the hotel."

The doctor witnessed this Asian taking out many men, while caring for his two friends. "He ran down the corridors with both injured patients in his arms. Somehow, he was missed by all the rifle fire, flying at him. He told both nurses hiding, to follow him, and then me stooped in fear behind a gurney, thinking the doctor collecting his medical bag. The Asian man helped him filling his bag with medicine from a wall cabinet in a room they took momentary refuge in before arriving at this final room."

"The Asian tossed many objects at the men chasing them. It was amazing that each tossed item, found a man without this Asian man taking any aim. It was the last object thrown, it allowed them to dash from their room to this room. Next, the Asian man saved them from the last two men. The doctor realized his career was over, once he went against the orders of the Boss man to help the Americans. His oath was a stronger reason to provide aide. He was glad he made that decision."

Cho suspected going to the hospital, "they might not tend to them. The Boss man had total control over this town. Jamie was told this fact and relayed it to him, before he was killed. Cho sensed their apprehension entering the lobby of the hospital."

"Rest assured doctor, your career will not end and neither will your life, after this battle is over." Before Cho and Mike could walk from the room, Pretty and Bell walked inside.

"What, where, how, are you two here," retorted Mike with a surprise look seeing the two.

"Well, that is a happy how do you do Mike," responded Bell.

"I didn't mean it the way it may sound, Bell. The last thing I remembered, was Chopper telling you to stay put in your room. Oh, thanks for making that shot at one of the men aiming his rifle at me."

"You know that was me?"

"Yes. The attack is not over. I spotted about twenty men heading to the bar. I destroyed a truck laden with weapons and supplies for a long siege. They are planning for a second attack."

"We are aware of that. Razor spotted them gathering on the beach from our perch. He came up to survey the battle field, responded Pretty," Cho's second.

"What about the axe in the stair well door jack planted to prevent anyone coming and going, asked Mike?"

"I removed it to go down stairs. Miriam was in a panic about Razor. He met me after the door was freed of the axe. He was at the bottom of the stairs preparing to come up as we were coming down. That is why Pretty and me are here. Chopper didn't object but had

Pretty come with me, for extra security. Such a dear man I married. Also, we figured you might need an extra set of hands, getting the wounded to the hotel."

TWO ARE BETTER THAN ONE

Inside the hospital preparing to depart, Pretty, asked Mike about the scene he left at the bar. Bell went to find a gurney for Moss. Cho was carrying Laura to the lobby.

"Hey Mike, what happened at the bar? There was a truck blown to smithereens by the boardwalk. A couple of dead men nearby and this one guy frozen stiff like a popsicle."

"Oh, he will begin to move within a few minutes. I wanted him to tell the others my message."

"Oh, you mean that spiel about, leave in peace, not and you join in your feast, or something like that. Shit, you going to do that thing here?"

Correction Pretty, my son and I will be doing that thing," Cho said walking in front of them carrying Laura to the lobby.

"Yeah, something like that. Pretty, did you not spot men on your way here. There was about twenty men coming down the street to the bar."

"No Mike, the street was clear of any men."

"Dang father, you know what that means."

"We need to hurry; the next assault will begin soon."

"Master Cho, you got a flashlight with a red filter like Mike's?"

"Don't leave home without it, ha, ha, ha. I carry one with me every since our time in the desert, Pretty," quipped Cho.

Bell returns with a gurney. Both Laura and Moss are transferred to the mobile bed. An I. V. bottle dangled from a pole attached to the bed. Pretty went to get an ambulance. It was at the front, in seconds. Both patients were loaded inside. The doctor was given orders to remain with the patients going into the hotel.

"Pretty keep close to the doctor," commanded Cho with a worried looked clearly written in his eyes.

"Got it, Master Cho. I don't need to ask what you two got in mind this night. Wish I could be with you."

Your good Pretty, but you lack certain skills for this kind of killing, my son and I possess. Besides, if we fail, your skills will be badly needed at the hotel. I will rest in peace, knowing you are there."

Bell and Pretty rode with the doctor. At the hotel an ambulance stopped at the main entrance. Many eyes kept watch in the darkness behind shrubs along the beach front. One man raised his weapon. He was stopped by a superior.

"Wait until all are together. We begin to soon; it will alert the others inside."

Meanwhile, Cho and Mike prepared their plans to fight the remaining soldiers attacking the hotel. Inside the lobby, Cho speaks first.

"Pretty will get his wish. We will not be able to stop all those men advancing on the hotel. Mike, Pretty asked about Jamie. You know, they got close in the desert? He asked, how he died before leaving. I told him, I went to secure the main lobby. Some men entered through the rear. Jamie was guarding Moss and Laura in the room. I got them together after escaping her room, when men broke inside. I had went to Moss's room with her. Jamie was there to keep them safe, while I took care of the front of the hospital."

"A soldier tossed a grenade into the room. Jamie caught the grenade, tucked the damn thing in his belly running outside the room into the men waiting. It took all three out. He saved Laura, Moss, the doctor, and nurses in the room."

Pretty walked outside to the ambulance into the rear. Bell heard Cho talk to Pretty, about Jamie. She like Jamie right off, in Texas. She persuaded Chopper to let him join the East Coast Riders.

"Father, we have much to do this night. I have two pistols and two machetes, choose what you want.

"I will take one of each. What is your plan, my son?"

Mike hands Cho a machete and one pistol. Cho tucks the pistol into his belt and held the machete in one hand. He inspects the edge of the blade. It was sharp.

"You think, I would hand you a dull blade father, Mike chuckles."

"Tonight, we will confuse them. They will think there is one red glowing eye demon they face. We must act as one man, keep them from suspecting there is two. They will truly believe we are a demon. We will be everywhere at the same time."

"I understand, I hoped you would come to that plan of attack, replied Mike already having the same plan in his mind."

"My son, handle the blade with deadly seriousness. Fear is our greatest weapon. Use the gun as a last measure. It can serve us as a tool and do little to enhance fear. They will question, why a demon requires the need of a pistol. Let the blade do our work."

"Trust me on that, father."

"You did well in the desert. We will do the same on this island. A ghost that will not be forgotten. Tonight, we avenge our friends and teach these fools a deadly lesson."

"Father, I think it would be best, if you take the hotel, if that pleases you?"

"It does. You think I worry about Laura?"

"Yes, and you should be. I know that will not distract your task, at hand. Still, our friend needs your expertise fighting in buildings. I have little of that expertise. I have mastered open areas. I will head toward the beach. I intend to enter the water and approach them from the sea. This way, we will have them between to two of us."

"Excellent plan, my son. It is what I would attempt. God keep you safe."

"And you, father."

Cho checks his gear. The red flashlight works, then darts away into the night to the hotel. Mike saw Cho disguise with his red light lit. It was difficult to distinguish either of them, as not the same person.

Cho reached the rear of the hotel in silence inspecting for signs of soldiers. None were station anywhere near the hotel. Cho knew that was going to change, soon enough. After checking with Jimmie stationed in the rear, he goes through into the dining room. Pretty was with Chopper and Razor.

"Pretty, take Mike's position he had when he was here. Before you do, help Razor and Bell get Laura upstairs and take Moss behind the front desk into the office, barked Chopper.

Cho reported to Chopper their plans. I will be out front. Pretty don't let them get upstairs."

"That ain't a happening unless, I'm dead Cho."

That goes for all of us, blurted Chopper, and Jack. Jimmie poked his head out to report the rear was secure and heard Cho's remark. Me too, Cho. Cho felt proud he was with men of that caliber and courage.

"Master Cho, Bone is in the lobby, Magic near the windows spotting. I sent Bell and Razor back upstairs with Laura, they will do their sniping from the balconies."

"Thank you, how is your ammo, Chopper? Mike took care of their ammo supplies before coming to the hospital?"

"Was that the explosion we heard earlier, inquired Jack?"

"Yep."

"Good lad," Jack replied.

After Jack's remark, Cho stealthy left the dining room. Outside were men gathering to make a siege on the hotel. Each man prepared their place to shoot from. Not so many were outside and too busy to notice Cho noting their positions. He spotted a hidden approach to the hotel, not viewed from the rear or the front of the hotel. But, one could from a third-floor window. I'll need to inform our women sniping, about this position."

Cho quickly climbed up the walls, grabbing hold of terrace railings. On the third floor, he surprised Miriam lying in watch. Cho swiftly grabbed her mouth before she screamed and alerted the men below.

"Ssh Miriam, it is me, Cho. Say nothing, just listen. Look to your left. Below, barely visible is a small alley. Keep a sharp eye for any men coming from that direction."

No sooner than Cho appeared, he jump from the balcony into the night. Miriam startled was not sure Cho was there, beside her. She looked down toward the alley he pointed at. Sure enough, she spotted the barely visible path. After fixing her sights at the alley, Bell walked in with Razor.

Miriam called to Bell and Razor coming in the room, motioning them to her position. "Cho, just left, I think he was here. He jumped off the balcony. He told me there was a small hidden ally below. I spotted a path. He said men would come that way."

"That was what I wanted too here. I'll take up a position to guard the alley. You two have already got your stations covered, stated Razor leaving to his station.

Cho landed softly on the ground, then swiftly made for a spot near the rear and front of the building. He watched men approach, where he was hiding. They went where he suspected, they would go. Cho waited until they passed by and stood, following.

"If only they knew I was standing behind them, wouldn't they shit a brick, Cho chuckled. Should I, or should I not take them out now. If I do, I might alert the others. My son might be spotted. Yeah, I think it is best to hold my hand for the time being. I'll let my son make the first move, before I act."

Meanwhile, Mike had entered the waters below where many men were gathering to get their weapons and directions. Mike spotted the boat pushing on the sands without motors roaring. They used their oars to keep quiet their approach to the beach. Some men remained by the boats, unloading what was left of their ammo. It was needed, since the truck was blown up.

Two trucks came to a stop by the boardwalk. Little light shined from the city. Many street lamps were put out. The stars shined little with the cloudy sky. It was a good night to attack the hotel. Many of the men felt assured and many lost their fear of the stories going around, about some red glowing eye demon. A call went out for everyone to come to town, after the airfield and fishing village raids were reported.

The local law was told to stay away from the main street and hotel. They were told there would be a disturbance. The chief of police received orders, go to the other end of the island. He took all his men. He was told to expect to be there all night to stop a disturbance.

Mike swam silently to the last boat. One man was standing, waiting for others to return to assist with the last two crates. Mike would assumed that man's identity. He rose from the waters dripping wet walking like a zombie to the man with his back to him. He tapped the man on his shoulder.

The guard was amazed turning to see someone was still at the boat with him. That amazement quickly was replaced with shock, then fear, then death. Mike stood still waiting for men to return. Many men were marching down the street to the hotel. Mike still waited for men to return to the boat.

Several crew men spotted the dark silhouette by the boat. It appeared more like a wisp or cloud floating where their comrade was standing. They turned to see where the others were, before deciding to move closer to the figure. When they turned back, the wisp was facing them. Two fast strikes sliced through each man's throats. Both heads landed in the sand. Mike placed each head with the boat guard. All three had OZ etched on their foreheads piked on one of the boardwalk posts that lined the beach sands.

Mike shoved the two boats into the waves before following the main party of men to the hotel. It wasn't long, before he caught up to their slow walk. The hotel was not far from where they departed the boats on the beach. Mike sensed their fears of the red glowing eyed demon was returning with every step they took closer to the hotel. Mike decided to begin his slicing and dicing. Slowly he eased into the rear of the line of men. No one looked to see who it was. They were all focused on what was going to be seen at the hotel and not in their ranks. Mike listened to the orders given to the men by their leader.

"Listen to me, softly speaking to his men; when we reach the hotel, remain in groups of three. The leader begins to point to each trio giving them instructions. You take up on the left of the main doors. You by the right side. You and you go to the rear. You and you get close to the shattered glass windows. Make ready to charge inside, when you get my orders."

Mike heard enough. One head and another fell silently from the shoulders of the two men in the rear. Mike caught each head before hitting the ground. Since they were by the boardwalk, he decided to continue his ghastly display with each head shoved onto a post inscribed with the letters, OZ.

The leader continued his rant on how his plan was to be played out. The night was pitched black. Two men standing in the rear was not seen. We will attack first. Our goal is to keep those Americans distracted. Then, our second team will use this as a diversion making their way along the alley. Our last attempt failed. This attempt will catch them off guard. We discovered a hidden alley path, few use. I will send several men to keep the hotel rear guard occupied, while I take that team, entering the hotel from the fire escape.

Whack, whack, two heads came sliding off the shoulders of two other men in the rear. Mike caught both heads like he done before. Each found a new shoulder on a boardwalk post. Five heads total, counted Mike.

"Going to have a lot more heads before this night comes to pass," chuckled Mike completing his etchings.

"Listen men, there are only a few American men inside the hotel. Don't take chances, they are tough. Kill any one, you see. We will make restitution with the hotel, later. These Americans are lazy, mainly the typical fat type. This battle will end quick. I estimate five or six men and five to six women. I am not sure if the men are all hiding, shivering in fear on the main floor of the dining room or if the women are in their rooms and the men on the main floor. The women we got nothing to worry about. They are cowering like sheep where ever they are."

"Like most Americans men, they use their women to fortify them with strength. They fight like girls. They even sent their women to our bar to try and get the boss to forgive their men. They paid hundreds of dollars as a bride. The boss brushed their puny attempts away. They came to save face for their men, leaving embarrassed and more shamed."

"What stories you heard, were lies. They can't get off the island and spread this tale to make you fear them. Bah, who do they think we are?"

The men all roared with laughter to the words coming from their leader. All but two men standing in the rear. Two heads were missing. No laughing came from them. Two boardwalk posts had companions topping off their bland appearance. Blood oozed from each head to the deck, bleeding into the wood. Mike returning to the gathered soldiers swiftly removed the corpses, dumping them under shrubs. The night helped conceal them.

All the men heard the stories of a small boy beating eight men single-handedly. Then, came three old men later, they beat the eight men in the bar. Finally, there were six women that came to the bar. The same thing was told. It got to the point, the people were laughing at the Boss's men, where ever they were seen. By end of the day, everyone was telling the story.

The group of twenty men was whittled down with six less. Another team had departed before Mike joined the ranks of his team. Their number, Mike could only guess at. They departed to the front of the hotel.

It was now or never Mike thought, looking down at the two rows of men in front of him. Seeing them, made him recall a similar situation in the desert. Cho and him faced the commander and his army. That time, there was four rows to each column of men. He recalled with clarity every man stood still, frozen from their slices severing their heads. Then, with a thump on the ground, all heads fell in unison, like dominoes.

Now, Mike was in a similar position, this time, he was behind them. Two red lights lit up his hood peering down the column of men. The leader turned to a frightful sight. At the end of his shorter column of men, was two red shining tiny orbs of lights staring between the rows at him. A shiver ran up his spine.

Mike was contemplating how to precede with his attack. "This had to be done swiftly. Not one mistake. I will need an escape if this goes wrong. He looks around and spots a balcony. That fire escape will do nicely. With a quick jump, hop, and twist should do the trick getting up to the fire escape, imagined Mike. Good, that is go."

No sooner than Mike turned to face the men, he spotted the eyes of the leader peering down the column. He said nothing. Mike could see the frighten stare in the leader's eyes.

"One loud shout would end my surprise," Mike thought. Mike drew his blade.

Swiftly, his blade began its gruesome task. One head, then another fell from the shoulders of a man. With each slice, a memory was recalled about the army column. He couldn't see the man in front of him, until he sliced the head. Not one man moved. Him and his dad move, was so fast, not one head moved from its perch on top of the soldier's shoulder to give away what was transpiring to the soldier next in line waiting for his slice. Mike had one thought on his mind with each slice he was making.

"Dang, should have sharpen my blade. Each whack isn't as clean a cut. The heads fly upward, instead of remaining nested on top of their shoulders. Got no time to sharpen it, now."

By the third man, the leader shouted. Mike made the fourth cut; all four heads were in the air coming down. They hit the ground as he leaped, hopped, and twisted into the air onto the fire escape rail spotted for his get-away. Grabbing the rails, he jerked his body up on to the deck and readily ascended to the roof before any eyes noted where he went in the darkness.

The leader looked at the few scant remains of his now much smaller group of men, with a ghastly stare. Mike heard the screams of the men below. Each head rolled on the ground bumping into one leg, then another man's leg in the column. They looked down and saw a comrade staring up. After the fourth man head was severed, one soldier spotted his leader gaze transfixed toward the rear of the column. He turned to see why. He saw two red glowing eyes, then pissed in his pants. He stood pointing at the rear of the column screaming.

"It's him, the red glowing eyed demon!"

Mike was looking down from his perch on top of a two-story building. He was spotted. Quickly, he leaped a wide span between the building he was on to another building. Below, the soldiers gasped at seeing the red eyed demon flying across the great expanse, between the two buildings.

One man shouted," it is the red-eyed demon."

Below, all the headless bodies remained standing that Mike did not stash away under shrubs. Suddenly, together all limp bodies slithered to the ground at the same time. One soldier bolted down the street. Others were about to follow.

"Hold still, men, cried out the leader. You leave and your families will suffer. That man will wish he remained with us," angrily shouted the leader to the remaining scant few men of his command.

One soldier shouted from the darkness. "They all fell at the same time. They bodies waited until we looked at them. It was if they were commanded to fall right then."

"Enough of this shit. You are soldiers, not scare little children. He attacked us in the rear. It was an act of a coward. He will not attempt that again. We are on to his tricks. That isn't a demon or ghost. He wielded a sword. Why would a demon need a sword? Don't be fools. That's what he wants you to think." Silently thinking, the leader thought differently. He saw the eyes and speed of this red glowing eyed demon. He began to doubts himself. The leader, undaunted led what few men left in his command up the hidden alley. Mike watched from the roof tops.

Meanwhile gun fire was heard coming from the front of the hotel. "The diversion has begun men, shouted the leader in the alley."

Cho was ready and waiting. Two men approached where he laid. Orders to men with hand signals were used to not alert the people inside the hotel.

On the roof top, Mike couldn't help his impulse to toss a rock down at a trash can below. The clang coming from the can, made one man shout. "He is by the trash can". The trash can, never had a chance. Bullets perforated the can into a sieve. The trash can would never hold water again.

Mike could see the men storm the can. He could see and feel their fears. It was so great and palatable to his senses, even up on the roof top. Stephen said to him once, "imagine a lion stalking its prey hiding among the tall grasses. The sweat from fear alerted the beast to where it laid hiding. So too, was the odor coming from the men below. Fear, much, much fear."

The leader repeated what he said prior to entering the hidden alley. "He is a man, not a demon. A demon needs no sword. We got guns and are many to his one."

The men listened. The leader made good sense. Still, they knew this man killed their comrades, without one seeing or hearing anything. They feared the demon but dreaded the leader's anger. Either way, this night, they would die from the demon's sword or from their leader's anger.

Mike was working his way down from the roof-top while the men listened to their leader instill them with new courage. Mike went to slice another head then toting the head, made his way pass the men watching their leader. He could have easily taken one, maybe two more heads, but decided to complete his task. With the bleeding head, Mike marked the walls ahead with the letters, OZ. Everywhere were letters written. Doors, trash cans, hanging clothes, nothing was spared from his bloody mark.

Before the men marched down the alley, Mike decided to plan for a second escape route. He spotted another balcony. Swiftly ascending the ladder to the floor, he discovered the window had bars. He was glad he checked this escape route out, before the soldiers came. He tested each bar. The wood was rotted. One bar easily came out, the other with some effort. Now, he could slither through the small animal opening.

Inside the small opening, Mike laid waiting for the men to arrive. "He planned to drop down, take a man, quickly return to his nest. His plan was to make each step the soldiers took, a step walking into death. Fear will fill their hearts and mind. Dying would be easier, than living before the night passes into day light. He decided to leave one man alive, to tell the tale."

One lone man was seen entering the alley, below Mike's perch. He quickly spotted the letters written on the walls. He looked around for signs of the demon. He spotted more bloody letters everywhere his gaze happened upon. He shouted to the leader. His scream alerted the team but scared the shit out of most of them. The silence was so great, only heart beats could be heard among the men beating from their chests.

One man approached the wall. He rubbed a finger across one letter. It was still wet with fresh blood. His foot touched something. Looking down was the head of his comrade. He knew the man, he stood next to him, when the demon made his fourth slice. Three heads were spotted on the ground before entering the alley. Now, they knew where the fourth head went.

He reached down to pick up the ghastly head. Another man shouted, "leave the head be." Silent followed his demand. Blood spurted up from the headless man shouting his warning. Then, a second man spurting blood standing alongside of the man given the warning by his comrade to leave the head alone. Two bodies stood frozen among the few men remaining with the leader, with blood spurting up from their torsos. Once the blood stopped shooting upward, the bodies fell to the road.

Mike was climbing into his hole with both heads. He waited until the team below, calmed down. The leader did his thing each time an attack came, to calm his men. Panic was at his footsteps. All his men remaining were about ready to desert.

The men slowly reformed into a tight group. Men stood so closely; it would be hard to drop a dime between the gap that was between any two men. The small band of men slowly made their way to the place to begin their climb. Two heads rolled down the alley. Both halted just as two men dropped dead. A loud bang was heard. One man's chest exploded, another man, his right arm flew off.

Mike looked up at the hotel third floor. He spotted a lone sniper taking the two men out. It was Razor. Below, men were dancing around the two heads rolling in and out of their formation. None realized two men, were shot. Mike thought, he was watching a soccer game being played.

At the front of the hotel, half the number was alive. One by one Cho snuck up to a group of three men hiding. They were so intent on firing their rifles, not one man in the group of three noticed his comrade was dead. Cho rammed his finger into the first man. He froze. With his sword arm, sliced the vertebrate of his spine. Neither moved or screamed. With the third man, he grabbed hold of his rifle and clubbed the man between both rifles.

By the third group of three men, Cho grew bored. He decided to try different methods to end their firing and his boredom. One man was stomped down on his neck. The second head was lopped off, and the third man, Cho yanked the rifle from the man's hands, then made a putt. The head went flying through the hotel window. Chopper shouted out the hotel.

"Cho, you made a hole in one."

Cho lifted the second head and with the rifle barrel swung the rifle butt into the head. The rifle butt-bat slammed into the head, sending it through the front door. Bone called out.

"Home run," Cho.

By a window, one man attempted to rush in. He fell with a knife protruding in his chest. He remained lying face up, with a head stone knife sticking up, marking his grave. Magic left his knife with the man.

Gunfire filled the lobby, after the knife dropped the rushing man. Chopper and Pretty poured lead out the windows. Slowly, gunfire was becoming less and less out front. Jimmie listened to the explosions of gunfire coming from the front. He waited silently, knowing his turn was coming.

Bell spotted her first man. He dropped holding his leg. Miriam shot twice at another man. Both missed. Now, the men below were aware of snipers on the third floor. Bullet ran up through the windows. Judy screamed. Penny ducked crawling toward Miriam. Rhonda went to Judy to check on her. Razor turned to check on Miriam. She was safe, hiding behind her barricade holding her rifle. None could return fire down at the men advancing to the rear door. Jimmie was alone to face the men coming his way. The hotel volunteer did not return to help him.

Men raced to his door. Jimmie set booby traps again, at the door. The entrance had little to stop the men from coming inside. The first attack shattered one door and left the second barely hanging. He piled as many crates he could get into the opening. One grenade would end that barrier, that Jimmie.

Men pile at the crates pushing hard. One booby trap went off. Crates fragmented but little was done to the men outside. Too many crates lessened the carnage Jimmie was hoping for.

In the room, Razor's wound reopened. The doctor with Laura went to examined his bleeding. Razor had to stop until the doc rewrapped the wound. Below, Mike noticed Razor not being at his perch. Gunfire rained from below up into his room window. Mike hoped Razor was not hit.

In the room, Bell asked the doctor about Razor's wound.

"He will be fine, but needs to rest." Miriam left her posted rushing to Razors side.

"Miss Bell, these men are going to kill us all, before night ends."

"Listen doctor, they are messing with the wrong people. Before the nights end, so will this threat. You and your nurses will have nothing to fear about. This town, will be as clean as a whistle with dead remains of all those thugs ruling your city. You going to need a new election afterwards."

The doctor pondered her words. Bell saw his doubts. "Listen, two of the men outside, just a week ago, took down an entire army of two hundred men by themselves, armed with a sword. Do you really think they would have any problems, dealing with those untrained thugs, toting weapons? Hell, they can't shoot straight."

Razor watched outside into the alley. He noticed their number decreased each time, he took a count. His first count was seven, the second count six, and now, four maybe five remained.

"Mike or Cho is down there, he thought. Good, I can't help much now."

Below, the leader saw only one room lit. That was where the women were likely to be in. Razor realized too late; "his room was the only one lit. It did not occur to him, before the doctor treated him. Now, once he was out of the fight lying on his back, the sudden realization his light was still on, alerted him that they knew where they were, now."

The leader called to a man. Both looked at the room. "There is where we go," whispered the leader. Razor spotted the leader talking and pointing to his room. He grabbed his rifle. Pain coursed through his side. He readied his sight and fired. The bullet flew straight, grazing the forehead scalp of the leader. Razor cursed himself for missing.

Men scattered below. Gun shots rapidly came into the window where Razor laid. The one light was shot out. "Good, that ends their visibility," Razor sighed.

In the dining room, Magic peered outside to spot any men advancing. That was a silly mistake. A bullet whizzed through the broken window. One zipped past his head. A second nabbed him in the shoulder. It winged him good, spinning him around. He fell to the ground winching in pain, without a word said.

"To do so, would alert the shooter, he was hit. They had few defenders now and that idea would embolden those outside," was on Magic's mind grinning his teeth, to hold back a scream.

Magic rolled to a table, ripping the table cloth off. He tore it shoving the rag into the bullet hole. Chopper was about to call to him. Pretty waved him to be quiet. He understood the meaning, keep the window covered for any further thrust at the hotel. Pretty sped to the undefended window to replace Magic.

Magic accomplish one thing for that costly look out the window. He reported there were soldiers clustered by the window. The front door looked to be unguarded. Pretty wondered if that was Cho doing his thing. Most of the bullets being fired, was coming into the dining room. He crawled back to his position.

Outside, the leader in front, noticed firing at the front entrance ceased." Get ready men," he shouted.

Cho ended any threats at the front door. Bone remained in position by the desk. He suspected, as did Chopper, a main thrust was coming soon.

Across the street, many men cluster at a central locale. One man was not part of the group. He stood behind watching. Above, overlooking the front of the hotel was Bell and Miriam sighting the large group of men below, shelter from their rifles by many trees and shrubs.

Men coming up from the boardwalk, saw the heads with the letters OZ, etched across the foreheads. They spread the word among the group gathering. Fear rose up within many. Whispers of deserting, was heard by Cho. Those that remained, were more afraid of their leader, than this demon. It was known that to not follow orders was death, not just to you, but to their families. No one had the guts to run.

The leader stood facing his men, waving all forward. Two men darted toward the hotel entrance. One man fell after two steps. Bell dropped the man. The second made the door. He fell back riddled with bullets from Bone's rifle.

The leader waved again. No one moved. Cho touched one man. That was to keep him alive, to report what happened this night. He needed a witness to spread fear throughout the city. Others that might want to exact revenge when they departed this wicked island would think twice.

Cho stood with all the others. Everyone charged forward. Two men remained behind, headless. Bell took aim. She missed. Miriam missed her man. Jack watched both women feel disappointment with each miss.

Bell quipped; "my man was too fast, then another man ran across the road. They are going to get inside," she screamed.

Both ladies rained bullets down at the charging men. Panic filled them, with each miss. Jack did his best to calm them.

"Listen, that is okay, even our best snipers would have a difficult time hitting moving targets this close. It did little to ease their disappointment.

"Our men are going to get overran, Bell yelled back to Jack. Another man popped into her sights. Again, he avoided her shot. Every shot Bell made was a miss. Despair was setting in."

Chopper watched three men charge at the window. Magic was managing to prepare for a shot but was having difficulties holding his rifle with his one good arm. Chopper fired; the bullet spun the man, throwing him toward the lobby entrance. He wobbled out the door into the arms of the other two men.

Bone was reloading his rifle. Both men saw their chance to charge through the door. That was until their comrade fell into their arms. Bell spotted one man catching the wounded man by the front door. It was her chance to redeem herself. She slowly pulled the trigger. A second man went spinning, exposing a third man. He stood in the open to anyone to shoot. He had little time to contemplate what to do. Miriam nailed him. Both women were smiling.

Jack said, "see I told you."

The third man laid staring at the third-floor window. He saw the red hair of a woman. "Damn, killed by a woman. We were told their women were hiding in fear." It was his last thoughts before death came.

Cho had nearly halved the men he was with. Heads fell like rain drops. One man turned, just in time to shout; "It's the red glowing eye demon." His head went sailing among the cluster of men huddled advancing to the window. Pretty was prepared for the charge. He mounted his rifle on top of a table placing towels on either side to stabilize his shots. Chopper, Magic was beside him.

The leader with some men, were plastered to the wall outside the window. He turned to check his men's positions. No one was anywhere in sight. He spotted several men lying on the street. One had a hole in his chest. The others looked oddly. It suddenly became evident, why, their heads were missing.

One man with him felt something wet on the wall. He wiped his fingers over the wet spot. He returned the finger to his lips. It was blood. He leaned back to get a better view at the wall. Two Letters appeared. OZ. He stepped away from the wall a tad too far. Bell dropped the startle man with one round.

"His last thought was how was this possible? He saw the letters everywhere along the road and on walls. But, how could these letters appear right now, where they stood?" The realization of that question was never answer by him. The leader did have the answer, though.

Leader man asked the same question, how could these letters suddenly appear on this wall? They just got here. His question went unanswered by his only remaining soldier behind him. He turned to asked the question a second time. His man looked different, to him.

A dark figure loomed behind him with no face. Slowly, the faceless soldier raised his head. Two red glowing eyes appeared.

This red glowing eye being spoke several words to the leader man," staring at him. You were warned. You come in peace; you may leave in peace. To come killing, will bring death. You will join in my feast, tonight. Cho tapped the leader. He urinated in his pants with pain coursing throughout his body.

Cho stood up waving his arms. Miriam was about to shoot.

Jack yell, "it is Cho, hold your fire."

In the rear of the hotel along the hidden path, the battle was about to draw to an end just as Cho laid neared the two men at the wall. The rear door blew once the man wiped his finger on the wet blood in front at the wall. Jimmie laid behind many crates, expecting the blast. It came with a huge bang.

The smoke filled the back room. Jimmie spotted a hand reach through the smoke. He waited until the shattered crates were pushed aside readying his weapon for the charge. Four men pushed inside.

Mike was attending to the leader on the hidden path leading to the rear and the upper balcony windows, where the women were sniping. He just froze the man, when the explosion occurred. He made a request to the leader to remain with him. The leader offered no objection, but he did winch with a smile or grin. Mike was busy ducking the blast to notice which expression was on the leader's face.

Jimmie stood peppering two men coming in. Both went flying back out the door. A third man squeezed past the hail of lead. he unloaded his machine gun into the crates. A fourth man flatten to the deck outside the door. He charged in once the third man opened up with machine gun fire. Both men were inside the back of the hotel with Jimmie.

Unbeknownst to both men firing their machine guns, Jimmie was prepared for such an eventuality. He set one booby trap to detonate with a push of a button. The blast cleared the rear door and everyone hiding behind crates, shooting at him. The battle ended with bang. The blast tore through the two men like shit through a goose. Jimmie walked out the rear door or what was left after two attacks. He almost shot Mike stranding with his red glowing eyes.

"Damn Mike, them red eyes scared the bejeevies out of me. I almost shot you."

"Thanks for not doing that. Susan wants me to locate Cheryl. A bullet in me would make that difficult and have Susan on both our cases. She is a woman we don't want to piss off."

"Mike, where are the rest of the men. I was under the impression, to expect a whole damn army."

"Oh, there was, but many of them are still by the boardwalk along the beach. I got some more heads to mount with them. You can be of use right now assisting me, before morning."

"Oh, I get it. You want to send the same message we done at the Twin Mountains in the desert. Jimmie spotted one man in the alley alive. Mike, why keep this man alive?"

"He is their leader. Got to keep some one alive to tell the story. I'll leave him here, for the time being. Mike stops, turns to face Jimmie. Hey, you got some sacks? We got a few heads to pick up."

"Shit Mike, how many did you take down?" Mike did not answer. Wait here, Mikey, I got some bags back inside."

Night was beginning to lighten with morning coming. Jimmie returned holding several bags. Everywhere he looked, heads laid on the ground. They formed a neat straight line up the alley toward the rear door of the hotel. Five heads fill his bag. Mike was finishing his first bag and beginning on the second bag when they reached the main street by the beach.

A vivid memory came to Jimmie seeing the row of heads at the beach. Head stuck on post led, down the beach. It was the same scene on the mountain pass. Both walked to where the last head was mounted. Next, came the gruesome ugly act of placing a head on the posts.

"Mike, once a reporter sees this along the beach, a story will be in print on the front page. Hell, maybe before we leave this city, it will go worldwide. This might not be such a good idea. The Riders might get a ton of questions, back home. Probably from the government."

"That is a good point you made, Jimmie. I had not considered that. Cho supported this idea. He feared the mob would take revenge on the people. He told me, it was better to get some heat back home, than to allow these people to live in fear."

"Hope so, kiddo."

Mike left Jimmie to clean up the mess. At the hotel, he spotted Cho by a window. A man was sitting frozen by his side. Chopper was talking to Cho through the window. Dead men litter the front of the hotel. Some with bullet holes, most missing heads. Cho heard Mike's footsteps approaching. He turns to meet his son.

"I see you have been busy, as have I. I left Jimmie cleaning the mess up, at the beach."

"You already been mounting heads?"

"Yes, father."

"I came to see how many you had to complete our display? We got maybe an hour before morning and people will begin to emerge from their homes. Mike hands Cho a sack. Bone walks out. Mike hands Bone a sack. Hey big guy, we got some work to do, before the sun rises. You can be of great help."

"What you want me to do," little buddies.

"Just look around, see any heads without bodies, put them in your sack."

"Huh, you got to be kidding. Why?"

"Bone, remember what we told you at the mountain pass. We lined the road with the fallen soldier's heads. Then, floated the bodied town to the city. We intend to do the same here. We want this mob to get a clear message of what to expect, if they seek revenge on the people or come after us."

"That will surely send a message, Cho. Huh Cho, what we do with the bodies," asked Bone?

"We will get the hotel staff to drive trucks to collect the bodies. They can dump them into the sea."

"You think that is a good idea?"

"Sure Bone. This way, they will keep their mouths shut. They helped with the fighting and disposing of the bodies."

"What about the news and local government?"

"We will destroy all names and details they have on us in the hotel and at the hospital, before we depart. We will be on a plane, before the news media ever gets hold of the story."

"Jimmie made a good point to me, father. He said some people might report about the red glowing eye demon, killing all these men."

"That's fine, my son. Let them tell this tale. It will keep them from finding out the truth and plus, spread fear about this avenging demon protecting the meek."

"You think of everything, Father."

"Been around for some time, my son. Now let's get this job done before the sun rises."

"Bone, tell Chopper to get the staff collecting the bodies. Make sure they do it quick. Also, get Pretty a bag."

"My son, you and I will make a stop at the local newspapers. I think some persuading will be required. They are good at spreading mistruths without facts. Selling a story, is worth some little missing facts. Money and fame are their motivation. Why ruin a good story of a demon wiping out a mob family on an island?"

"The local government will go along with the story. They don't want to rock the boat. The mob rather keep the truth from getting out. That might send the wrong message to people. The mob bought off the official and they will do as they are told. Either way, everyone benefits from this lie."

Mike asked, "what about this socialist island."

"My son, power is socialism. People are made to believe this wonderful tale, that all are equal and should share in the wealth. In truth, they will but the rulers will always reap the wealth. They will enjoy all the benefits of having power and control of the masses. They will eat high on the hog, dress in the finest clothes, build and army to enforce their rule, and maintain their power."

"It is an illusion. The whole system is rigged against the common man. It has always been that way. There are people who believe they are more deserving than others. Then, there are those who will follow them. That is where their true power lies. It is those that believe in them and support their rise to power. Then, an ugly realization sets in, too late, by then."

"My son, socialism is another scheme to control the people. Look at all those nations that adhere to this garbage. The people wait in long lines to get food or buy things in scarce commodities. People will not work for little. If one man works hard and another sits, why should he have to share with that lazy person. See, that is the reason why socialism will always fail. People are different. Why work hard when others don't. The incentive to produce is loss. Does a person working harder get a raise or a promotion? Even if he gets a promotion, will he get more benefits. It he does, then that is not socialism. Things become scarier. Hence, the long lines."

"In our system, those that work hard benefit with their efforts. Those that don't work, have less or the government will support them. Why work. Our system is like socialism in many ways. We pay taxes so those that don't want to work, can live the way they want."

"Why is that wrong, Father?"

"I said, the poor slob does not get any benefits he deserves, for hard work. He is equal to all the workers, but not to the elite. They are special. Why would anyone bust their asses off, to get nothing? They could work just like the lazy fellow and reap the same rewards."

"Do you think the elite politicians, military, and rich will eat the same food you do? Hell no. They live high on the hog. They always will. They believe they merit a better living. Socialism is about equality, but not for them. That is the true lie people won't see."

People that are smart, hard-working, have abilities, are gifted with talent, goal-oriented want to be rewarded for their efforts. If there is no value in their accomplishments, why do them? There go advancements in science, and in the arts. People need something to aspire too. It what gives meaning to our lives. Without them, we are cattle grazing in the fields. We eat and wait to be slaughter."

"Socialism is just another scheme to control people. The weak-minded people that cannot achieve anything, want what they cannot get themselves. They clamor for those things; they are not willing to work for. This is why many will fall for this scheme. They want something for nothing. It is their only hope of getting those things, they desire."

"Education, is the key to teach them. There are many ways to earn their goals of a better life. One does not need to break his back, toiling the land or a job they are miserable at. They can better themselves and change. People make the strong, weak, by shoving that system in their faces. Over time, people will think that it is the right thing to do. Help the weak. Help does not mean supporting their lifestyle. It is to aid them to improve their lives. In time, you get a welfare system, much like socialism. One small step, then another, and soon you have socialism replacing our system."

"That is why the government and news will do as the mob tells them too. They are scared people will learn the truth. Their power will be weakened. People will learn to fight back to end the power of the elite controlling their lives. Fear is a strong motivation to overcome, my son."

"That is why they must never see our faces. These men, we spared, will be our strongest supported. The fear we instilled in them, will keep m afraid to speak the truth, the truth is what we don't them to know, just like the reporters and government. I played this role, as you, my son. No one saw my face and lived. I disappeared into the shadows with every strike. What they saw was two red glowing eyes of a demon, killing them at will."

Mike spotted a pothole at his feet. "Father, I have an idea. These men, we have stayed our hand, are frozen with pain. Let them see us."

Chopper called to Jack in the room with the women. "The battle is over, bring the barkeeper down. Blind fold the asshole."

Jacks turns telling the women, the battle is over. In the lobby, the barkeeper was dragged out into the dining room, near the stairwell. Many staff persons were cleaning the area. Some were outside, lifting the dead headless men into the rear of trucks. They knew that if any of them were spotted doing this gruesome task, it was a death sentence to them and their families. They hurried to collect all the dead men from the street, before dawn.

Mike quickly explained his plan to his leaders, Chopper, Jack, Bell, Razor, and Bone. Take them outside and leave them standing together. Uncover their eyes before you depart. Bring the doctor and nurses. Also, blindfold them.

Many of the bodies were collected in the rear of trucks within an hour. Those with bullet holes were collected along with the headless men. Outside, the scene was set for the frozen leaders with the doctor and nurses.

It was dark near the spot chosen for the witnesses to see the act, both Cho and Mike had practiced, before they arrived. Bell did the honors of removing the blindfolds from each person. Mike stood near the hotel. All eyes saw the Americans run inside away from the demon standing by the front entrance of the hotel. Many staff persons screamed, seeing the red glowing eye demon. They scattered away into the hotel. The scene was set, for Mike's plan. Mike recovered his face with the hood.

All the leaders and doctor and nurses blindfolds were removed. They opened their eyes seeing a lone figure standing in the shadow of darkness, feet from them. They stood frozen in pain, even the doctor and nurses. Cho touched them inside the hotel lobby before blindfolding. Each person stared at this dark figure with no face. Slowly, the head emerged from the darkness as the hood slowly peeled back. Two red glowing eyes shot from his face. Each person was filled with fear wanting to run, but unable to move.

Both leaders captured along with the Boss man and the doctor and his nurses watched with tears in their eyes. Each wanted to scream, but couldn't. The demon slowly walked closer. Their blood felt like liquid fire flowing through their veins. Mike stopped and spoke. Each word echoed through their minds like a loudspeaker was near both ears. They winched from the loudness coming at them.

"Those who come to kill, will be killed. Those who come in peace, will leave in peace. All the rest, will join in my feast. I allow each of you to live this day to spread my words. Some doubt what I am. Some believe I am a demon. You witness my words come to beings. Those that came to kill, are dead. Their heads will remain a reminder to you. Believe what you may, know this and believe this, I will return, if you go against my people and friends. Each of you have felt my power this day. Your blood burns within as I come close.

My touch is pain incarnated, your minds will see terror in the night, when there is none. You will walk in fear, until I deem it shall end. There is more pain to come, if I return. Much, much, more. There will be a second chance. When you see my mark, beware my coming. Death is on its way. Leave or die when it does come. I will etch my mark on those that should fear me returning. Beware."

Suddenly, the demon raised his arm to beckon another. From the shadows appeared another red glowing eyed demon. The demon moved as if he was floating on air to the first demon. Both appeared to merge into one. With a clapped of his hands, and a puff of smoke, he disappeared from their sight.

Bell with the other leaders immediately blindfolded all the watchers. Next, the blindfolded persons were taken to the lobby. Mike along with Cho reappeared from the pothole, they dropped into. The streets were cleared of all the dead men.

"I got to tell Magic, his trick worked wonderful, chuckle Mike to Cho.

THE NEXT DAY

Within the hour the sun rose. Morning was here. Every wall had OZ written in blood. The streets were cleared of the violence the night had experienced. People in their home hesitated to open any window or to emerge from their homes. One hour quiet was the only sounds outside their homes. One by one a window opened. Then, a door and a person. Soon, many eyes dared to look out of their windows, fearing what they might see.

Four violent men waited in the lobby of the hotel. The staff was told what to do. Each man was unblindfolded. The office manager of the hotel told the men that the American left. They were tied and held prisoners.

The four leaders were taken to a chair and coffee delivered. Neither man drank his coffee. All three stood walking out of the lobby. They could move again. The pain remained. Each agonized with every step toward the door. The pain was horrific. The hotel staff watched three men walk slowly down the road to the beach with the four guards in escort. Along the ways, they saw all the men's heads mounted on posts. Not one body was seen, that a head was attached too.

As the men continued their walk, screams were heard. People looking out the windows saw all the bloody heads lining the sidewalk along the beach. The sun led the way of the three leaders down the street. Like a beacon, showing them the way.

People with children going to the beach, spotted the gruesome sight. They quickly shielded their eyes. They ran swiftly pulling their children back to their homes. They saw thirty men's heads mounted on posts. Some they knew, some they wished they did not know, and those they wished they did not know and glad for it.

Three men were spotted making the long walk down the boardwalk. One man in particular was viewed wearing a bra, panties, and fish net stocking. It was the barkeeper Boss man. Everyone once feared the man. Now, they held their laugher as he passed by. Many feared the news of this event would keep tourists from coming to their isle.

A plane flew from the direction of the rising sun to a landing field. It was the same field, the Riders departed to greet their missing son and his father returning from the desert. Men and women loaded unto the plane's ramp. A woman hugged a younger man. The Asian did the same. Both said words to the one younger man remaining behind.

Susan hugged Mike. She plead to let her remain behind with him. Mike responded; "Susan, I will do better searching for Cheryl, without having to worry about you here. I know you can take care of yourself. I will need to move fast, with silence. You are not trained to do what I can do."

Cho places his hand on Susan. "Susan, I know your fears. As I spoke earlier, this is a lone wolf action. There are many men on this island, we have not met, that will seek revenge. I to want to remain with my son. So do the others. But the more men remaining, increases the odds against finding Cheryl. They know we are searching for her. Now, after this incident, they will try harder with their own search."

"I know Master Cho, I can't leave, her not knowing I love her."

"Susan, Cheryl knows that. This is one reason she has run away. She cannot deal with her shame."

Cho hugs Mike, then turns taking hold of Susan's arm, entering the plane. Both wave farewell, as the ramp is raised.

Mike sped off, before the plane was in the air. Susan watched from a bay window his running back to the city. Mike contemplated his plan running back to the city.

At a bar, across from the beach, four men sat drinking a beer. The barkeeper remained behind the bar in pain. He could move again but the pain was every second, a bane to him.

"God, the pain, what did that demon, OZ do to me? This is more than a person can bare. I agreed to his demands."

"Hey boss, go home and soak in a hot tub of water. That always helped me."

"Yeah, you may be right. I can hardly think straight."

"Why don't go see a doctor," shouted another man drinking.

"I would, but that demon Oz said, if we tried to make the pain go away, it would get worse."

"Any worse than it is now, Boss."

"No, no nothing can be worse. I'll go home and try that hot tub of water, first."

"Yeah, do that, we got the bar taken care of. Besides, he left with those other Americans on that cargo plane."

"How can, you be sure?"

"We saw all of them get on the plane, boss. We gonna chase the girl down. Get some pay back?"

"We will wait a day or so to make sure. If there is no sighting of that demon OZ, we get the girl. You are sure she is at the hotel?"

"Yes sir. Why wait, you don't believe that was a demon, do you?"

"I just want to make sure. You ain't the one in pain. We wait for a day to pass. Got that!"

Mike was standing at the end of the bar listening to the men banter back and forth. "He knew, he and Cho were correct. This man needed some more convincing."

The Boss man walked out of the bar, not suspecting, he was being tailed. Entering his large home, he ordered the maid to prepare a hot bath and a masseuse. The hot tub felt great, but did little to ease his agony. He stepped from the tub drying himself with a towel. A masseuse was waiting at a table.

Each muscle was kneaded by the masseuse. Pain shot through his body with each knead. It continued to increase with each grind from the masseuse. The barkeeper endured the pain for a minute, before he believed what the demon said was true.

"Stop, stop with what you are doing. I can't stand the pain, anymore."

The masseuse continued. He attempted to rise off the table but was slammed back down by a powerful thrust. "Let me up," he demanded.

A mirror was below the table. His table had a hole to place the face down into. He looked at the masseuse, two red glowing lights shone back. Fear followed by a chill squealed up his spine. His breathing quickened. Words escaped his lips.

"You believe me an American, did you not? I said, I would return and to not think, I wouldn't. Already, you plan to take revenge, after my warnings. You foolish mortal. Where is the girl hiding? Tell me, so I know you believe in me. Tell me to make me believe you truly want to live in peace. I know her where-abouts. To do otherwise, will prove you will lie and betray our pack."

"She is at a hotel, near here. I swear this to you. I don't know what room."

"That is a shame. That is not what I requested from you. You give me crumbs and expect me to bend to your lies. You made your bed, now lie in it. I will be back. You have until that time to learn more. I have to speak to the others. They may be more forth coming with answers."

"Please, don't leave, no, no, I swear I am telling the truth."

Mike touched him, the pain amplified ten-fold. The barkeep passed out. Mike left through the window, once he tapped the masseuse. He was put into a sleep state. Mike stared down with his red glowing eye, ablaze. Fear made the masseuse shiver in terror. He heard stories of this demon standing before him.

The demon spoke, "my name is OZ. I come in peace, tell me where the girl is. go tell the men in the bar, why I come. They falsely believe I am an American. Tell them, they can believe what they want, but give me the girl. She is under my protection. Do this quickly or you will merit, the same as your boss is enduring, when I return."

Mike pointed to the man lying still on the table. "He is alive. Do not continue with your rubbing him. It will make the pain far worse. Do so at your own risk. You have been warned."

The masseuse listened to stories with no doubts. Urine ran down his legs. This demon is, far worse seeing him for myself, he thought. He could not move, until the demon ended his speaking. He was a demon. Swiftly, after the masseuse blinked, the demon was gone. He stood, shaking. Quickly out the room, he ran. Down the stairs to the street. Soon, he was running in the bar panting for his breath. Four men stood, pushing the chairs away with a strong force knocking them over. Each feared the demon had returned. They joshed the boss, but inside their thoughts, they hoped it was not true.

One man got a beer for the masseuse. "What happened? Was the boss killed? Was it by that demon, with the red glowing eyes? Speak up, man!"

Slowly, after a huge gulp of beer, the masseuse spoke. "It was him. I saw the demon with my own eyes. He is real. He froze me, like the others. He said, to tell you, to believe what you want about him as an American. She is under his care. Give him the girl."

"Is that all?"

"No, no he said his name was OZ. If you see his mark, beware, death has come for you."

"Don't think that will happen. We had every wall and door cleaned before noon. Not any OZ is written anywhere in this town."

"He, he came to me, while I was giving the boss a back rub. He, he touched me. I watched him begin rubbing, the, the Boss's back. The Boss tried to rise up. The demon slammed him down on the table. He, he told me not to continue rubbing the Boss. His pain will increase with each effort to relieve the pain. He was out cold, when the demon left. I ran here, as, as I was told to do."

"Continue man."

"He asked the Boss where the girl was. He told the demon; she was at a hotel not far from here. That was all he knew. The demon replied, telling him, he, he wasn't leaving the island until, she was found. One other thing, the demon said to me. He left the boss with a ten-fold pain and he was coming here soon. Give him the girl or each of you, will live with more pain than anyone could bare. That, that, or death."

"So the boss is alive?"

"Yes, only for a short time. His pain will endure for weeks or months before he dies a most horrific death. He said, something about a feast, he will have for those that come to kill. The masseuse looked at the four guards with a queer look."

The others knew what that meant. Each man looked at the other. "I don't know about you three, I'm leaving this island before night."

"You forgotten about the mainland boss. He finds out you deserted and your life, wife, and kids are going to die. Besides, how far you think you will make, before that demon gets to you?"

"I doubt that."

"So did the boss, now he is lying face down on a table in his room. He wants that girl and that is all he wants. Let get him the girl, before he fines us. No one will know, we gave in to this demon's demands. Just keep our mouths shut and we will be safe."

"I got a better idea. We blame another man for telling the demon where the girl lies. We get one of them new lads to take the blame. Easy-peasy."

"That's a great idea. Get us a newbie, barkeeper."

One man shouts out. A young man comes inside the bar from the rear entrance, just as the four guards told the barkeeper to get a man. Everyone looks at the newbie standing with no idea, what they had planned for him.

Listen and listen, good newbie. You are to go out and search for a man. You will know him, by his red eyes. Do not fear him. You bring him good news. He will not harm you. We will, if you fail at this task. Tell him, the girl he is seeking, is in room 311 at the hotel on the corner of third street. Take her and leave."

"Sure, the girl is in room 311, at a hotel on the corner of third street."

"Say please, to that man, dummy. Now, repeat what I told you."

"Sure, the girl is in room 311, at a hotel on the corner of third street, please dummy."

"One of the men slapped the delivery boy. Where did we get this dummy?"

"Listen you, say please and leave out the dummy, if you want to live, got that!"

The boy walks out of the bar. One of the men yelled to him. "Get moving, fast."

By high noon and walking down several dark alleys calling out the name OZ; a lone figure emerges in front of the boy. OZ followed the boy leaving the bar. He heard one boss tell the others, "he was taking the next boat off the island. That wasn't going to happen," Mike thought.

"You called my name, boy?" The boy halted, freezing where he stood. He looked at the strange figure wearing a long coat, with a hood. Slowly, the head rose. Two red glowing eyes appeared. The boy began to shake. He heard the stories told.

"I, I, got a message for you."

"Is that message to inform me, the girl is in room 311 at a hotel on the corner of third street?"

"Yes, yes, sir. How you know this?"

"I know many things. I know those men, plan to make you the patsy. You are to be blamed for giving me the location of the girl. They fear the boss on the mainland. You are going to get blamed. Fear not. This will not happen. Go in peace. If you remain at the bar, you will die, I have warned you."

The boy left with a yellow stain on his pants. The smell was obvious to anyone, he approached. All four leaders noticed the smell at the bar, when he returned.

"I see you found the red glowing eyed demon, OZ. The smell and yellow stain on your pants, is proof of that. What did he tell you after you told him where to fine the girl?"

The boy was hesitant to speak. The demon said to tell them. "He knew where the girl was. He told me where she was. He said to tell you, that your plan to make me a patsy, wasn't, wasn't going to work. What is a patsy?"

"Leave us. Go back to the kitchen."

"Damn, he knows everything we said."

"That breaks it. I'm leaving after, my next beer. Any of you coming with me? Number two boss replied, not without me, you don't."

"The boy heard the two bosses talk about leaving. He turns to make one last comment."

"Hey Boss, that red glowing eyed OZ said, he knew you planned to take a boat off the island. He said, that wasn't happening. Not until he has left. To do so, will definitely be your last thing you do."

"You two still want to leave," said the third boss man.

"What, you got a better idea?"

"Yes, I intend to sit here and get good and drunk all night long, if necessary. I am going to be so drunk, that OZ demon can poke me all he wants to. I ain't going to feel nothing. I'll die a happy drunk."

"That better than my idea. I'll join you."

"Me, I'm still leaving this rock. I 'll wait until morning. Maybe, he got the girl and will leave by then?"

"You're a dead man once you put a foot on that boat."

I'm a dead man if I stay here. Neither way this leaving gives me a chance. Staying here; I got no chance. Barkeeper hold that drink. Number two stood, pushed his chair under the table, bid farewell and was out the door in a few steps.

ROOM 311 ON THIRD STREET

Mike ran down the alley to third street. Before him, across the street was a seedy dump. "this is no way as nice as the one Chopper had for them. He chose the best on the island and Cheryl gave that up, for this dump. This looks building looks to have been spared its final death blow, after the earthquake happened. How it remained standing, is a mystery to me? Its barely standing. One small shove or beath from a breeze would finish what the earthquake was supposed to have done," pondered Mike.

Mike crossed the street to the hotel. A smell met him, before he reached the door. Opening the door, cigar smoke flowed out. Inside, at the reception desk, sat a fat, balding man, with a scraggly beard reaping in cigar ashes. Each ash stray on the counter top was over filling with unemptied ashes. It was apparent, he had a bad habit and not just a smoking habit. Mike figure a three or four pack a day habit.

The clerk hands were darkened from smoking each cigar down to the stub. A blister was swelling on one hand from the last good burn, he got from a cigar. Both eyes were red, having bags under each lid. Mike noticed the large knot on his forehead, a result from falling asleep many times on the countertop. The reason was evident, once Mike spotted empties, filling the wastebasket.

"Definitely a heavy drinker, too. A half dozen bottles were spotted. I bet that is what he eats, I mean, drinks for supper, Mike thought. Hand me the keys to room 311 Mike demanded in not so friendly request to the bent over clerk."

The clerk slowly raised his balding, uncombed, oily haired head from a bent position to what he would call an upright, direct stare at this stranger, demanding the key to room 311.

Mike was wrong, "I thought bags but saddle bags under each eye is a better description. The desk clerk must have lost his razor and the beard seemed to have stopped growing. That could be for the lack of a proper diet, or just his nasty look. Looking down at the man's arm reaching for a key in a covey box, Mike saw dirt so thickly applied to his arm making it look darker. He first thought the dark skin was from too much sun. That did not make much sense, seeing the man never left his desk. Every pore on his skin had to be clogged with dirt. That would be cause enough to stop his beard from growing, reasoned Mike not yet finished with his survey of the man.

"This man was old before his time. He once combed his frizzy, oily hair was evident attempting to cover the bald places. There were spots peppering his head not common to a man going bald. He pulled his hair out with his comb, was Mike's first thoughts looking at a newly bald patch. A large scab was replacing the missing patch of hair. Either that, his clientele living in that rat's nest on his head was disturbed and made a complaint, biting his scalp."

The old man slowly managed to say, "why? Who are you?"

Mike stood amazed; he could speak at all. Both the desk clerk's lips were parched and cracked. His shoulder remained in a stupe position, when he raised his head. He could play the hunchback of Notre Dame if he hadn't taken root to the chair, he was planted in."

Mike first thoughts entering the hotel, "it was the building giving off an odor, but changed his mind after the man spoke. His breath nearly dropped Mike; it was awful. Other words could be used but none could describe it any better."

Mike entered the building with his red glowing eyes not knowing what to expect. The desk manager saw the red glow looking eyes at him. The cigar went down his throat, in one gulp. It was still burning with red embers. It didn't matter to him, seeing those eyes, he would gladly swallow ten more. Urine ran down his pants legs. It smelt of stale beer to Mike. It was a welcome smell, compared to what he was smelling.

Mike reached out with his hand to get the keys to room 311. He had little time to wait. The manager swiftly pulled the keys from the wall and tossed them to him.

Before walking away to the room, Mike replies to the manager. I come in peace and will leave in peace. If you seek other, then you will die and join in my feast."

The old codger nodded a reply back. He was a no-account, but still like living. "Why," he often wondered, himself.

Mike left the front desk with great pleasure to be as far from that derelict, as he could get. Three steps up and the fourth step buckled under his foot. He realized each step on the stairs was a challenge on their own. Many creaked from his weight, even with the merest of pressure. Some were broken in half, others waiting with boards laying at a slant. If not for his abilities to shift his weight, the stairs would be off limits. Near the third floor, all the steps were missing to that level at the door. Mike leaped on to the ledge, still remaining. Each level had no rails for a person to hold on to.

Landing on the ledge required a balancing act by him. Mike looked at the stair well, he lit onto. Someone went crashing down, them recently. That was the reason for missing steps and what was left of the rail dangling over the ledge.

Next time, I should take the elevator, he pondered. After saying that, he changed his mind. If the stairs are in this condition, the elevator must be a death cage. The door was within reach, one thing prevented him to walk through the door. A hole was dead center of the stoop, he was standing on. After a little hop, he grabbed the door knob. He was glad to get out of the stair well on to the third floor.

Mike spotted the first resident living on the floor. He was caught by surprise by the sudden intrusion of an unexpected visitor. The large brown rat was well fed and scurried off with a wiggle and a wobble to the nearest hole in the wall. "He can be picky with all the choices of holes to choose from," chuckled Mike.

Mike counted the holes down the corridor. Every room had a rat hole. Sixteen holes and sixteen rooms. Walking down the hall, he thought about knocking on the door nearest to him. He wasn't sure which room was which. Many of the numbers were missing.

A baby cries is heard at the first room. Across from that room, a man and woman were fighting. It was a cacophony of noises greeting Mike at each door. Two rooms had a number. On the right, an odd number was hanging on the door and the opposite side had an even number. With a little math, Mike determined which room was 311.

Mike approached room 311, it was the only room without some noise emancipating from inside. "It figures," Mike thought. It was at that door Mike took notice of each door's color. The light was sufficient enough to see the dingy, faded color. In the center of the panel, was a square patch of yellow paint. Each door across from the adjacent door, bore the same color. Two red, two green, two blue, and so. Mike looked at his key. It was yellow. "It figures," replied Mike.

The hall was recently painted. Paint ran down the walls leaving streaks. One touch, left paint on his finger tip. Mike knocked on the door. Then again, when no one answered. Mike tried the key. It wasn't needed. The door creaked open. He entered closing the door behind him.

Mike spotted Cheryl sleeping on a couch, near the door. It was a one room flat. No air conditioning. A sink, one refrigerator, a table, two chairs, and a gas stove. Another room appeared to be the bathroom. A quick inspection revealed he was correct. Walking to the table, he spotted white powder in a bag among half eaten-rotting food, along with several empty liquor bottles. He was happy that the bag had not been opened.

"What was that saying, candy is sweet but liquor is quicker, No, no, that not it, sugar is sweet, but liquor is swifter. No, that not it either." The rhyme kept rattling inside his brain. It stopped, looking at Cheryl lying asleep on the soiled couch.

"I suspected you were taking drugs, Cheryl. Now I know the truth. Several needle marks are on your arm. I am glad you are unconscious." Mike felt her wrist for a pulse. There was a faint one present.

Mike looked at Cheryl, "how could you drop to this level, Cheryl. He thought of many reasons people choose this way. Some did it for fun, others were teased into taking the drug, some out of spike to their parents. Some were weak and felt like failures, and others felt, they needed it for some medical reasons. Cheryl had none of those excuses.

Cheryl, you are a strong person, with a purpose in life, enjoyed adventures, a leader, not a follower. You couldn't be goad into taking drug. You killed a drug dealer. Maybe Cheryl's your shame drew you away from our group. Without a support group to help you manager this problem, you attempted to go it alone. Shame can be a mighty potent reason to avoid facing the truth, dear Cheryl."

Mike thought about the kids in the club looking at Cheryl. "Many of the kids in our club were around drugs and dealers in the neighborhood and school. They saw the effects drugs had on them. We kept a strict code and watch with all of them. We constantly stated, we are there for them. They all knew how easy it was to be drawn into the drug scene by others. Why, Cheryl?"

Mike stared down at a girl, he once knew but now a stranger. "I can't take you home in this condition." He sat beside Cheryl stroking her hair pondering his options.

Mike stood and walked around the room. There were signs all about, "she was not alone. Someone has been coming to her room on a regular basis. On the table were several glasses. One with lipstick. Many liquor bottles had different labels. Then, there were cigarette ashes in ashtrays. Cheryl hated the smell of cigarettes. Mike picked up several butts laying on the floor. Neither had lipstick. One had a filter, another without one. Two men," Mike determined.

Suddenly, Mike realized, "Cheryl was held in this room drugged by those men. Sex slavers usually drugged their girls. There was hope for Cheryl. She was forced to take the drugs." Mike went back to where Cheryl was lying. He looked at her arms. There were indeed bruises on each arm. Not from drugs, but by someone restraining her.

"This might be a good thing, Mike pondered. She was forced. Cheryl wasn't taking the drugs, willingly. Mike begins to clean the room. A fresh start, begins with a clean environment. Remove all the ugly reminders. Next, I need to clean her. He went into the bathroom and drew a bath. The tub had rust stains as did the water pouring from the tap. After several minutes the color cleared. The tub was full of stained, rusty, cold water. No hot water was available.

The next item on his to do list, was to search the room, to see what other things he could use. She smelled and so did her clothes. There was nothing but her soiled dress. She had changed into a t-shirt and jeans. Mike striped Cheryl of her jeans and t-shirt, leaving on her panties and bra, before dumping her into the cold water. The shock snapped Cheryl awake.

"What the hell, shit, who, who the hell, let me out of here," shouted Cheryl. Mike held her down in the icy cold water. She fought tooth and nail attempting to get out, not realizing who was holding her down. Mike received many nail scratches and teeth bites for his endeavors.

"Stop Cheryl, stop fighting me. It is me, Mike. I found you in this rat trap of a hotel. Everyone has left the island. I remained, to look for you. Stop fighting me and bathe yourself. Either you do or I will. Cheryl quickly calmed down. She looked up into eyes filled with love. She began to sob.

"Mike, why did you come for me? I told you to stay away. I don't want any help."

Cheryl, this town nearly killed your mom and all the others, two nights ago. There was a terrible gun fight at the hotel. Laura was almost blinded trying to rescue you in that container box. Both Chopper and Razor were shot. Moss or One Eye, the man you hated so much, saved all the ladies at the container. He did so, losing an arm. Jamie is dead. He got blown up saving Cho and Laura and some doctors and nurses at the hospital. They done all that for you. That was their choice. Don't you get it? They care about you. They love you. They will forgive you. They are family and family does this. All they done was love you. That is what love truly is."

Cheryl was about to respond, but Mike knew what she was going to say and spoke first." I know, you told us to leave and their hurt was not on you. Shut your mouth and listen to what I am saying."

"It is your fault, period. You did what you did, because you wanted to. It is no one's fault, but yours. People got hurt and some killed, all because you did not come to your family with your problem. Don't you dare, blame others, for your lack of faith, in our family. Your ego and pride was yours. That led you to take drugs. I can only guess; others are involved with your habit. Usually, one rarely does this alone."

"You want me to leave you here, go back and tell them, you do not love them. You want nothing to do with them. Your love is false. You corrupted all who love you. Your friends were tools to provide what you wanted, drugs. All this was just, lies. I will not do your dirty work. You tell them. Then I will take you away.

"When I leave you here, I will never seek to find you again. You will be dead to men. I cannot love someone who cannot forgive. Your mom and everyone will be told you are dead. This is your last chance to come home and ask for forgiveness. It will take courage. The Cheryl, I once knew had that courage. Does this girl, I am with, have that kind of courage?"

"Before you answer me, think hard on what your life will be like. You will be a drug addicted sex slave. Be abused, misused, degraded, and trapped alone forever. All your hopes, dreams, experiences, children, you will give up, and for what, a life of misery? Remember this, Cheryl, everyone makes mistakes. Would you condemn a person you love or would you forgive them? There are bad days, we all have them. There is a light at the end and a new day bringing hope. Night comes and daytime follows. You are in the nighttime. There will come a morning. Nothing stays the same. Life is always changing, some for the worse and some for the good."

"Cheryl, think back to the jungle. All those children and women loss their husbands and fathers. Then, their homes were destroyed. They went into the jungle with little. We found them, barely making a living. We brought daytime to their nighttime. We left them with hope."

"God created this world to adapt to change. Nothing remains the same. This is not the way to find salvation. Think how you have changed into this person, why not make another change, back to what you were or a better person learning, what you did and giving back to others this knowledge."

"Understand this Cheryl, nothing is worth that. This is not the way to find forgiveness. You cannot heal your hurt and what you done to others going this route. If forgiveness is what you truly want, just ask. That is all you have to do. It's that simple."

"Mike, I have done terrible things."

"Cheryl, I know what you have done. The others are aware of what you have done, and still they care. They came to help you. Bad, this is not that bad. Killing is bad, destroying the lives of others people is bad. I have done all those things. You are not alone with this guilt you bear."

"I found forgiveness. My ego is not so large nor those that love me, to not forgive me. I try to find reasons, to allow me to see everything I done, has a purpose. That purpose is to aid others, rid them of evil that has entered into their lives. Allow them to change and heal from their tortured life."

"I live life for that reason and replied no, to possessing wealth, power, or fame. I kill to protect, to help those unable to help themselves. Murder is the sin. The Lord sent his people to war. They killed their enemies in the name of the Lord with his blessing."

"Animals kill for food, to defend themselves, and to protect their families. We are animals, that is God's law. It is the law of this world, among all living creatures. We are part of this world and of these living creatures. God's laws govern them and thus, us as well."

"You think you are above this law and cannot face what you have done. I do every day. I make choices of life and death. You can never justify your crimes, against mine. Yet, do I quit and give in to my sins to quit. I don't surrender, nor allow shame to keep me from living. There is hope and a new day. Change will come and so will salvation. Your good works will help others. One thing I know that you don't."

"What, mister know it all?"

Mike looks at Cheryl. His eyes softens when he speaks. In each of his words was a loving tone. "I know the sun will set and rise each day, anew. God will give me another chance with each new day. Love is the choice; I give you on this new day. God gives you this day, to make that choice. If you don't choose this day, guess what? There is another day, to come. He will never give up on you. He gives you every day, after this day, to find your way back into his loving arms. How long it takes for you to come back, is up to you. Why waste time making this choice? The sooner you forgive yourself and accept our love, the sooner you can begin living your new life. Don't let this chance go by. Don't allow anger, fear, and hate stop you. Please come back to us."

Cheryl see Mike before her. He is so caring, loving, and strong. Everyone want to aspire to be like him.

"I did once. Why did I go down this path? I can't go back; I can't face them," Cheryl fretted with agonizing pain in her heart. The shame, what I did, I can't, I just can't, cried Cheryl.

Mike saw the tears and what Cheryl was thinking and replied. "What is so hard to look at family and say, I love you? I am sorry for what I have done. Loves gives us the strength to overcome much. Have you lost that love in your heart for your family? Don't forget, how to love, Cheryl. Don' think they have lost their love for you?"

"Cheryl, tell me truly, do you wish to go home? Do you wished it never happened? If that is the case, then, you do want forgiveness and to return to your loving family. Just say it." Cheryl looked at Mike. tears ran down her cheeks.

"Cheryl, our pride can get in our way, just like shame can drive us apart. Pride cometh before the fall. It was pride and shame that holds you back. Let your pride and shame pass away. Don't let it rot the love in your heart like fruit on a vine unpicked."

"Think of it this way. When we make ice cream. We add cold to freeze it. Cold removes the heat. What was left, when the heat went away? A tasty treat. When loves leaves us, Hate fills the void. The same is true, when hate is gone. What is left, love?"

"Doubt, not knowing is replaced, when we learn otherwise. Not giving up, when we constantly fail at a task. When the failure ends, what is left? Success. Stay the course and success will be your reward. That is what come from struggling and hardship, rewards."

Cheryl sits in the cold rusty tub of water thinking on the words Mike spoke to her. Cheryl stands crying. She reaches out to Mike. Both hold the other. Both get sopping wet. Both begin to laugh.

"How can I fix what I have done?"

"Cheryl, I cannot answer that question. With many wrongs comes many solutions. I will help you to find solutions to all the wrongs. We will together. The way, will make itself clear, as we go forth. Every day, we will begin with hope and a second chance. Some days, will not go well, but the good news is, we get another day to try again."

"Cheryl, your faith will fade, your strength will faulter, that is the way of things. It is never easy. Each day, a little pain and hurt will be lessened. Finally, a day will come, that there is no more hurt and pain. This hurt and pain will last as long, as you let it reside inside you. Heal thyself first, this will aid in helping you heal others."

"This memory will fade with time. The sin will never truly go away after ridding oneself of it. There will be days, that make you recall what you did. Then there are others days that will bring it up. When it does, do the right thing. Do good and help others. That will cure many wrongs."

"What did Jesus say to men throwing stones at a whore. Let you among you that has not sin, cast the first stone. Did any man throw a stone?"

"No."

"True. Others are quick to throw stones, to cover their sin and show others they are faithful. Weakness breeds weakness. People use excuses to mask their failures or for not doing what is right. They point at others, "see, they too sin, they did it too.' What hypocrites, people are."

"Cheryl, get clean, we are leaving, now."

"I can't, people are coming back to take me off."

"Cheryl, you know me, do you trust me?"

Cheryl pauses then answers, "yes."

"Why the doubt, see, it is easy to slide back and surrender to weakness. Stand up, have courage and face your fear. Serve the Lord, by serving yourself. We are invincible, together. Trust me, as I trust in you. We will overcome all obstacles, like we done so in the jungle. You stood by me, when I was hurt. You endured much, to bring us to safety."

"We will take our time to make the journey back. Each day, you will gather your strength back. It will be an adventure. This will build strong roots to build you back up. You will look back on all this as a foundation providing strength to overcome any future hardships."

"Yes, yes, you are right. What I did, I can fix. My friends and family are important to me. Mike, I want to go and tell them, I am sorry."

"Cheryl, not everyone will be as forgiving to what you done. Some will harbor hate. Those that have love in their heart, will forgive you. With others, time will heal their pain. Remember, don't give up, keep trying and doing your best. That will do much. That is life, no matter how much we give, it will never be enough, to some. They will want more."

"Just giving, should be enough Cheryl. It is Cheryl, because it comes from a good place, your heart. A little is a lot to a starving person. I know this, many times I was starving. The little help I received was more, than I expected and greatly appreciated.

"Mike, just keep reminding me of that."

"That is why we walk this together, Cheryl. A journey is best remembered, when it is with someone. To go alone, is not fun. I was so alone for a long time. That is not a path for many people. It is tough on you. It, can break many. You are broken and to make this journey alone, would be more than you could accomplice alone and solve nothing. Enough of this, let's get out of this pig stie."

"I'm with you, Mike."

Cheryl was back, Mike could sense a spark of hope in her.

Swiftly, Mike took the dried clothes he handwash from the window rails. The sun dried them quickly. Cheryl took the clothes, Mike turned around to allow her to put them on.

"Here Mike, take my underclothes and place them over the heater, they are wet."

After several minutes, Cheryl checked her under clothes. They were dry enough. Mike was in a hurry to leave the room. Mike stood on the veranda over-looking the city. It was a warm sunny day. Many people were doing the same thing. It was as if nothing had happened two days before at the hotel.

Outside, Mike spotted a car stopping in front of their hotel. Cheryl stepped outside on the veranda. She saw the car come to a jaunting halt below.

"Mike, that is the car, I was brought here in."

Several men stepped out of the car. One had a rifle. Another held a pistol. Mike quickly pushed Cheryl back inside the room. It was too late. One man spotted the girl he brought to the hotel on the balcony. He raised his machine gun. Several rounds were leveled at the window.

Plaster splatter off the walls by bullets. Cheryl swiftly donned her underclothes. Mike went to the door stepping into the hall. He heard three, maybe four men race up the stairwell.

"Cheryl, four men are coming up the stairs, make that three. Mike heard a crashing sound. They didn't see the hole," Mike thought.

"Quick, we will take the elevator. Both ran from the room toward the elevator. Another yell was heard from the stairs. Mike smiled.

"Cheryl there are two, now." She looked at Mike with quizzically.

One man fell. "I guess he couldn't make the leap over the large hole on the ledge to the third-floor door, Cheryl." Both entered the elevator. The door closed. Two men walked out of the stair well slowly checking each room. Neither had been to the room.

Mike earlier switched numbers with two other rooms before entering Cheryl's room. Cheryl's room was no longer 311 but changed to 309. He checked to make sure both rooms 309 and 310 were not occupied.

The first room the men came too, was 309. They kicked the door in. Machine gun fire peppered the room. After some rearranging of furniture, it was decided that room was empty and not the girls.

Outside the room, one of the men looked at the room number. "Hey Jose, this is not the correct room number. I think the numbers have been changed. This room is out of order. It is nine, should be an even number."

"So?"

"Look dummy, we went in the wrong room. That is the right room, pointing at 309. Both rush to the room; Jose kicked the door open. Again, they peppered the room with lead.

"Hey Rico, it is empty."

"You think, dummy. They must have taken the elevator. They heading down. Both ran to the veranda. Below, they spotted a man and girl getting in their car. Another man laid by the car.

Hey Rico, ain't that our car?

A One Eye Mama

Many hours elapsed on the plane home. The first stop was a large city. The military base was on the edge of a metropolis. Exiting the plane was a gurney carrying a woman. She was swiftly ambulanced away with a passenger riding inside with her. She awoke with him holding her hand.

At the hospital, doctors and nurse were prepared for her arrival. Cho saw her hours later. In the waiting room was his friends, he called the family. All but two were there. Bell arranged quarters for them on the base.

Cho, what is the news, bellowed Razor standing when Cho walked into the waiting room. Jack, Rhonda, and Judy sat next to Miriam. Pretty was getting coffee for all of them, with Jimmie's aid. Chopper stood by the hall watching Cho pace by the ER. Penny was embracing Bone standing by Chopper. Magic stood watch outside the room. Chopper went to sit down, next to Jimmie. Somehow, that made Jimmie feel more like a part of this new family he was accepted in.

"Jimmie, you did good back there. We decided to asked you to join the Riders. You will make a great addition to our team. That is, if you ain't got nothing better to do? Can't guarantee how much money, we can start you with. But I will say that with all the help you given us, we are going to reward you with a large bonus. You don't mind getting rewarded with cash," asked Chopper with a slight smile.

"Heck no, Chopper. Could use the money. My last gig, went sour. I hired on with the Pilot and he got shot down in the desert. My pay, it will be long in coming from that job. My luck's been going south. Now, I see it turning."

"I see your point, Jimmie. Great, I'll inform the others. They will be pleased. We will continue with this, when we get home." Chopper turned to watch Bone and Cho wear a streak in the carpet.

Bell sat by Chopper and Jimmie sipping her coffee given her by Pretty. "Babe, I know this might not be the best time to bring this up, but maybe it could help."

"What's that, Bell?"

"Mike. Think you should call him."

"Can't babe, no phone. He could be anywhere on that island. Cheryl took off to God knows where. She might not be on that isle."

Susan walked out of the restroom. She been crying. She hadn't stopped crying since leaving the isle. She lost both the ones she loved. Mike, she finally accepted she loved him and missed he was by her side to give her comfort. Then Cheryl, like her own daughter. She and Stephen had no child of their own. Still, Susan raised her as if Cheryl was her own child, since, three years of age.

Bell waved Susan over to sit with them.

"Bell, can Chopper phone Mike to check on his progress. I am worried."

"Susan, I just asked him about that same subject. He told me, "there was no way to contact him. Mike will have to contact us." He will soon, knowing how much you will worry, not knowing. Be patient."

Jimmie spoke up, "Chopper, maybe I can help. I'll take the next flight back to the island."

"We just landed Jimmie. Thanks, but where will you look. By the time you do locate him, Cheryl might be found and they be returning."

Susan stands walking over to Jimmie, giving him a kiss on his cheek. "Thank you, you don't know how much that means to me."

"I think I do, Susan. I have a kid and know if that was my child, how much I would be worrying. That is what family is for."

In this family Jimmie, there is never any doubt about that. Family comes first. I tell the others of your plans.

Before anyone could hear what Jimmie was planning, a door opens. A doctor walks down the hall. Cho and Bone meet the doctor. Cho turns smiling at the others. Everyone assumed Laura was going to be okay. Cho walks over to them gathered in a cluster, waiting for the news.

"Laura is doing great. Her eyes are fine. The one eye will need further surgery. The damage can be corrected, "Cho paused.

"What else," Bell and all the women asked in unison?

"I am a father. Laura is with child."

"Is that all," chided Bell. Cho looked stunned to hear her say that. "We knew about the baby weeks ago. She was going to surprise you, when we got home. Don't you dare let on to her, that you know. She wants to surprise you herself."

"I can't see her. She is being moved to a room. When she wakes, we can all see her," replied Cho relieved.

Bone stands by the doctor. "How long will that be, doctor?"

The doctor looked up at this giant asking him a question. He turned to answer, having to allow his eyes towed to a new height rising up to the ceiling, just to see the face of this man mountain. He had a look that could scared death away. It nearly done that to him.

"Yes, yes, she is doing good. It will be very soon. We are moving her to a room. When she wakes, we will let you see her."

"That is good." The giant smiled, if one could call that a smile, thought the doctor. The way Bone was smiling, made the doctor believe the man mountain was thinking of a meal. He hoped it wasn't him, being inviting to the table. The doctor swiftly turned hurrying down the corridor. Shortly, a nurse came to inform the party in the lobby, they could visit the lady.

Laura awoke with Cho by her side. He kissed her opening her eyes. Then, was greeted by all the Riders standing around her bed. Smiling faces greeted her weary look. The doctor entered, before anything was said. Laura reached for her face. Bandages were covering one side. Before she could inquired, the doctor spoke first.

The doctor cautiously made his way around the people, especially avoiding Bone. You are going to make a complete recovery, Laura. That bandage is for your eye. It received some damage from the blast. I think it should heal fine. You might have some vision problems for a short while. If it doesn't improve, you will need to wear glasses? I will not worry. I believe that will not be necessary."

Bone heard news different from what the doctor said earlier. Cho too was curious. The doctor excused himself, being as polite as he could. He walked out of the room. Bone followed after Cho signaled him.

"Hey doctor."

The doctor came to a sudden halt. He hesitated, before turning to face the man mountain. He wished he hadn't said what he said. Now, he had to tell the truth. He hoped they would be gone before the truth was revealed.

"Listen, er, er, I said that to give her hope. There is a good chance the eye will improve. Time, time will tell."

"She asked you a question said a booming voice down to the doctor from the man mountain. She is a Rider. We understand the nature of our business. There is no need to soft soak the truth to her."

The doctor felt the fear rise up inside his throat. It suddenly became hard to swallow. You, you want me to go back inside and tell her the truth. I don't know the truth. There is hope, mister Bone. You should leave that to time. There is no need to deter her recovery with the feelings, she has no hope."

Hmm, Bone pondered the doctor's words. "Leave, I will discuss this with Master Cho." The doctor left quickly.

Inside the room, Bell with all the other wives swiftly turned the subject to Laura and Cho's wedding plans. "Laura, you need to get your ass out of this bed. You got plans to make for our wedding." All the woman crowded around the bed choking Cho away. Cho steps outside with the other men. Bone reports what the doctor said.

"Laura, we got your wedding dress sent here. We want you to try it on. When we get home, the cake should be ready. Penny has been doing checks on your wedding to-do list. We all been preparing. This is going to be the best wedding, we ever had," joyously spoke Bell.

Penny steps near the bed. "I spoke with the priest. He asked if you two have your vows ready?"

Penny, Cho and I have made our vows. We were just waiting to get home with Mike. Cho and I want him to be at our wedding. Where is Mike," Laura asked looking around the room?"

Bell spoke up with trepidation, "Laura, Mike is not here. He remained behind to find Cheryl. We hope he will return soon."

"That is best," Cho replied to Bone outside the Laura's room. All agreed to keep what they learned a secret, until time comes that the truth must be spoken.

Jack looked concerned watching the doctor making his hasty leave. "I believe the doctor is correct. Laura is going to make a great recovery, Cho."

Cho walks back into Laura's room, as the women were leaving. Outside, Penny asked Bell what that was all about. Bell asked Laura, just before Cho returned in the room, did you tell him?"

Laura replied, "not yet."

"Why not?"

"No reason, haven't done it. I want the time to be right."

Cho knew what they were talking about. The doctor spilled the beans to him," replied Bell.

"Oh that. Then Laura doesn't know, he knows, replied Penny?"

"I guess not, and none of you better tell her, either, demanded Bell. I hope Cho won't go after Mike."

"He won't," sniped Rhonda.

"I spoke to Jack about that. He agreed, Cho should stay here. Mike can take care of himself. Razor agreed with Jack."

"Jimmie told me, he was going. Chopper told him to stay here."

Cho sat softly by Laura's bed. Laura spoke, before she could change her mind. Dear, I got some news I been keeping secret, from you. I, well, I am pregnant." Cho sat motionless and quiet. He knew but wasn't sure how he should react.

"Dear you aren't happy, would you rather this child not be born?"

Cho stops Laura from continuing her sentence. Shh with all that nonsense. I am the proudest man alive. I hoped so much, that we would have children."

"Mike."

"Shh, Mike is my son. That is all that is needed said. I will have another child. This will both of ours." Cho bends over and kisses Laura.

Laura saw Cho loving eyes. For the first time, she realized how much she really loved him.

Whispering into her ear, Cho says softly," I'm going to be a daddy, me a dad. We will have a son. Mike will have a little brother."

"Ahem, dear, this baby might be a girl."

"No matter a boy or girl, I will rejoice with great happiest."

Bell, you going to Susan's room to tell her the good news. She been upstairs by the phone, most of the night, waiting for a call. She went back to her room after seeing Laura."

"I think, she is making herself sick over that girl," sniped Penny.

"You are right, we got to do something, before she has a breakdown."

Bell, just got news from Jack and Razor. They told me when we walked out of my room. They got news about a boy and girl, held up in a hotel. They matched their description. Some shooting took place. Both of the them, fled in a car. No one has seen hide nor hair of them, since. That was a day ago."

For the next two days, Laura annoyed both doctor and nurses about her wedding. "When am I leaving here?" That day came soon, afterwards.

Outside the room, all the Riders waited to enter.

It was Laura's request to the nurses to keep them waiting, until she was ready. Even Cho had to wait outside the room. Inside, she dressed and stood at the mirror with her back to the door.

The door opened and all poured into the room. Laura waited, until she felt all were inside. Cho was at the head of the line. She slowly turns to face all. Her eyes were perfect. One still had gauge covering it. The doctor had her sit. Slowly, he peeled the gauge away. Sitting was a beautiful woman. Smiles were on every one's faces. Cho rushed over to Laura, kissing her.

"You are the loveliest wife in the world. Also, a mother."

The doctor speaks up, "her eye healed wonderfully. There will be some scarring. He looked at the man mountain with a sigh. He was glad the giant was smiling. She can leave anytime. The doctor hoped sooner than later.

TROUBLE BACK HOME

Two young boys came running out of a cabin. A dog was barking rapidly. The door opened for them to leave, then quickly slammed shut once they were outside. It was early in the morning. The sun was just peeking over the tree tops.

One boy was new to the subdivision. He befriended Bobby and Lou at school. They introduced him and the other kid to the rest of their club. Both of them were hanging with the club of five. Cheryl, one of the leaders had left to meet some person across the ocean. Bobby was left to continue their club business.

The older boy, between the two newbies was expelled from another school. The other boy's father was transferred. Both boys had acne and long hair. The younger lad had a severe case of acne. He saw a doctor regularly.

Bobby mentioned the cabin to both of them. It was the mention of a ghost that got their attention. Each doubted Bobby story about a ghost. One day, they decided to check the cabin out. Bobby and the other members often went to the cabin without them. That made the new boys feeling left out, that and a pervading thought, the cabin was where they were hiding their stash of weed and drugs.

Bobby, along with the others were walking to the cabin, to tend to Boo. It was a chore; they all were responsible for. Bobby and the others knew, "if Mike returned home and Boo was not there? Well, that was something they preferred not to think about. It did not matter that they were family or kids to Mike. If they failed their duties, dire consequences from the Riders themselves would befall each one of them."

Both boys laid hidden near the path, leading to the cabin. They followed the group one day. It was on this day, they walked up the tail and heard voices behind them. They knew if their friends spotted them, it might not bode well. They hid in bushes, to one side of the trail. Both spotted the five approaching the cabin down the trail. Bobby spotted them. It was too late to hide further. They stepped from the bushes, waiting for the five to get nearer.

The bigger boy told the smaller boy, to keep quiet, I'll do the talking, see. I will tell them, we wanted to see the cabin. Never say we been in the cabin to them. We were just taking a walk down the path, to check it out, see. This way, they will not suspect, we been inside the cabin."

"Hey Bobby, what's happening," shouted the older boy.

As expected, Bobby answered with why, "you walking down this path to the cabin. We don't like anyone coming down this road. It is only for the Riders and us. Never let us or any Rider see you on this road or at the cabin. Got that!" Bobby suspected something. No one told them about this road. How did they get to it?"

"Sure, sure no harm done, Bobby."

"Good, see to that. Next came an unsuspected request to both the boys.

"Both of you can come with us this time. We are going to feed the dog and take him for a walk."

"Lou watched both of the boys. Their faces betrayed what they said about walking to the cabin. Lou decided to make them reveal more. "This cabin is not a place we stash any drugs. It is a friend's home. We are required to take care of it, when he is off on a mission."

Mandy spoke, "something he seldom does, he rarely leaves, but when he does, we are to take care of his home. There is nothing inside. This will be a chance to see this for yourselves."

"There is a dog, inside the cabin. You better never hurt that dog, let him out of the cabin, or anything, else. Your lives will depend on that. I am not kidding you about that, it ain't no joke. I am really serious. That dog gets hurt, so do you," replied Lydea. Her eyes blazed with intent. It was a scary look to anyone.

Bobby spoke, "you are our friends and are in our group. You get the real stuff. All we ask from you, is to keep away from this cabin. The bikers own this place. They are our family. They don't look kindly on any trespassers messing around. Ask around, if you don't believe me. Several men have been found dead near the cabin. I don't mean years ago, neither. Like real recent," replied Bobby.

Bobby looked at Lou, both came to the same conclusions. "We know what you are thinking. This cabin is where we stash our drugs. We aren't. This is just a cabin and nothing more. It is haunted. The ghost will attack you."

"Yeah, that is why we are going to take you with us. Inside the cabin, you will meet the ghost. If he doesn't like you, you will learn pretty quick. Never return," Skip said.

"Hey guys, we believe you. We don't need to go inside. Really, we will just wait outside the cabin, huh, until you finish with what you do," said the older new boy.

"No, we want you to go inside to meet Mister Casper for your-self. Then, you will understand," insisted Bobby. All seven begin the long walk to the cabin. Lou took hold of the younger, newest boy's arm. Macy and Skip took the older boy's arms walking toward the cabin.

At the cabin, all waited by the door. Slowly, the door creaked open with no one's help. Boo did not bark. Everyone walked to the open door. Both boys began to struggle to get free from their companion's hold on them. Neither could free themselves from their escorts. Inside, the door slammed shut. It was dark within. Still, Boo remained quiet. The younger boy began to cry. Then begged to leave.

"Please let me go. I'm sorry. We didn't mean no harm. Please let me go."

Bobby suddenly turned to look at the older boy. The older boy knew what he was going to ask him. He knew, they were in the cabin. The lantern lit by itself. The younger boy screamed with fear. The light flickered, brighter. No one was near the lantern. The room inside was brightly lit.

The young boy peed in his pants, watching the light grow brighter. His crying ended. "Please don't kill me," he begged.

Bobby looked at the older boy, still quiet and turns to the wall over the bed. A note was written on the wall. Lou shouted, look Mister Casper has written us a question. The younger boy broke free of his escort's grip racing to the door. One, two, three jerks on the door and still, it remained shut. He dropped to his knees, fearing what was to happen.

The older boy read the words on the wall. Earlier, when they first came inside the cabin, nothing was on the wall. It was like the first time; they entered the cabin. The door shut without any one touching it. They tried and tried to open the door. The damn dog, kept barking. It was pitch black in the cabin. The dog stopped his yelping after he threw several objects at him. After what he was told outside, coming back to the cabin, he feared for his life.

Bobby read the words written on the wall," check on Boo."

The older boy began to sweat, then tremble. Salty water dripped into his eyes. He kept from wiping the burning salty water from his eyes in fear, the others would think he was crying or he was scare. There was little need to sweat in the cool cabin. Outside, the leaves were changing colors. It was Autumn.

Bobby swiftly went to Boo, lying in a corner of the cabin, near the bed. He gently rubbed Boo's side. Boo whelped. Bobby felt around his ribs. He noticed blood coming from his nose. Boo was breathing, with difficulty.

Bobby turned to the older boy commanding the others to get Boo to the club, ASAP. He stands walking over to both boys on their knees, pleading.

Lydea lifted Boo gently walking quickly to the door. It opened. Both Macy and Lydea departed with Boo, then the door swiftly shut before either newbie had a chance to dash for the door.

Bobby grabbed hold of the older boy' arm, making him standup. Lou shouted. Bobby, Mister Casper has written a message, again."

All turned to read the note. "They hurt Boo."

"Bobby, we came to see the cabin. The door was opened. We walked inside. The dog attacked us. I threw a can at it. That's all, I swear it. It ain't hurt bad," replied the older boy.

Bobby turned to the younger boy, "are you going along with this story told to me by your friend?"

Lou examines the door. It revealed someone tried to Jimmy the door with a crowbar. He looks at Bobby.

"Listen carefully to what I am going to ask, either of you. If what you say is a lie, I am going to leave the two of you in this cabin, with Mister Casper. I am going to ask him to tell me if you tell the truth. This is your last chance to confess."

"Believe what Bobby is telling you two. This is not what you want to happen," spoke Skip.

Bobby didn't need to hear them speak. In his mind, he didn't need to do anything. When Mike returns and learns of what happened and what these two done, sent a shiver up his spine. Bobby recalled what Mike could do in the jungle. On the march with Cheryl, he would take a pirate, rip him in half, tossing the two halves into the air. All that was done without ever being seen. Men went flying in the air, left and right of him. That went on until night came. The pirates separated into two groups. The Seal team led by Jack, rescued him. Mike went after the other group alone, for Cheryl.

The older boy looked at the younger one. Neither spoke to Bobby's question. "That was the wrong response, friends. It going to prove to be the worse decision you made, before the night comes to an end, both of you will be locked inside with a mad as hell ghost, tending both of you."

Chopper listened to Magic's report on the phone, when Cho walks in.

"Hey Cho, I'm talking to Magic on another phone. What he is telling me, is something we all need to hear. It concerns Mike's dog, Boo."

"Oh God, I pray something isn't wrong?"

"You better listen to this report for yourself." Cho takes the phone after Chopper telling Magic to repeat his story, to Cho.

"Chopper, the girls got Boo to the vet. A tin can was thrown at Boo by a new boy at school. The can bruised some ribs and another can, cut his nose. He will be fine. Apparently, two new boys joined a club Cheryl and Bobby had. They got curious about the cabin. It was mentioned to having a ghost haunting it. Mister Casper locked them inside. Boo starting barking. Both boys were trapped inside the dark cabin, scared. One through a can to shut Boo up. Lydea said, "she was keeping Boo at her home, for the night."

"Tell me more about the two boys," demanded Cho.

"Well, from what I could get from Bobby, the two boys were left in the cabin overnight. They were discovered, the next day cowering in a corner near the door. I had the bikers search for the two boys after a mother came to the club. Tall said, she told them, the boys went to check out a home with a ghost. I figured the only haunted home was our cabin. Tall searched most of the night around the cabin and the trail. At the cabin Mister Casper refused to open the door."

"After forcing Mister Casper to open the door, the older boy told his story, to Tall. Bobby has some answering for what he done. He locked them inside the cabin, with Mister Casper. Both of the boys were pretty shook-up and scared. They thought, we were going to kill them."

"Tall questioned all the kids with Bobby. He asked them a second time, after finding the two boys. Not one, said a word. We got another problem to deal with after we deal with the two boy's parents, Chopper?"

"After both boys were taken from the cabin, a note was written on the wall. It said, Boo better be okay. Mister Casper was upset, to say the least. We spotted a spiral of smoke coming from the fireplace. Mister Casper lit a fire for us to come to the cabin."

"Arriving at the cabin, Mister Casper was reluctant to open the door. We could hear the shouts of both boys inside. The door finally opened. On the wall was written a note, "do not take the boys, yet". The door slammed shut. Those two boys sat in their own pee for the whole night, shivering in fear."

"Did the boys tell you what happened to them?"

"Yes, and who did it to them and why. For what transpired in the cabin for the night, neither the boys or Mister Casper said anything. It has been a day since the incident occurred and both boys returned home. We got Bobby's group together, to explain."

"Bobby did most of the speaking. He told us, both kids were new to the school. One was transferred, being expelled. The other was at their school, because his dad was transfer by his company. Both joined Bobby's group. I think there is a drug connection. They wouldn't say much to us. We did learn why the two boys were in the cabin."

"Go on."

"The older boy, the one that threw the can at Boo, went to the cabin after hearing stories in Bobby's group, about a ghost living there. That and with some prodding on the younger boy, they believed drugs were hidden by Bobby's group. That is how we learned of the drugs, the group is involved in. They are taking drugs and selling to others in the neighborhood we live in."

"Then, older boy confessed everything to us. Both him and the younger kid went there to look for drugs and check out the ghost in the cabin. Entering, the door slammed shut trapping them inside. Only when Boo was hurt, did Mister Casper opened the door to let them out. He feared for boo's life."

"Yeah, I am surprise Mister Casper let them out at all. I guess we can be lucky, he done that. Those parents might cause trouble."

"Well, they ran out of the cabin. Bobby and his group were going to the cabin to feed Boo. They met on the road. Bobby suspected the two boys had went to the cabin. It was the way both boys acted that caused an alarm to go off with Bobby."

"Both boys protested being taken back to the cabin. Bobby forced them inside. They confessed to being there earlier. They lied about, why they went there and how Boo was hurt. Bobby left them in the cabin with Mister Casper to teach them a lesson."

Cho broke in to the conversation. "Why didn't Bobby tell you all this sooner? Why let this go on for two days? Did the police come?"

"Yep, but we kept them searching somewhere else. Both parents are upset about the whole thing. After informing them, we were constantly patrolling the neighborhood for any drug dealers, by the way, they moved here because of our good work. They would rather keep this private and not involve the police."

"The two boys are not speaking to their parents, yet. We did."

Cho takes the phone from Chopper a second time. "Magic, what are the parents saying. Do they know about Mister Casper?"

"No, and they will never know. Those two boys got the message from Mister Casper himself. He left a final note for them, before we left the cabin. Basically, it said," never speak of this, to anyone." Later, Tall added for good measure, the ghost would come for them, if any word of this gets out."

"Good, what about our group?"

"Bobby and the others are in detention. We got the whole lot of them under strict house arrest. Their parents will keep them home, until you get back. I got Riders posted outside the homes, for added assurance, in case one tries to sneak out."

"Great, sounds like you got everything under control. Tell Tall, he did good."

"I did. Tall asks, how is Laura? Is Mike, okay? Is the island under control? Everyone here are on pins and needles, ever since you told us about the mob trying to make a hit on Mike."

"Laura is doing fine. She removed the bandages this morning. Some minor scarring on one eye. Still, not serious. The doctor says, in time, she is accepted to recover fully. Cho is happy. The women are working on wedding plans with Laura. Cheryl is missing. Mike remained behind to search for her. Last we heard, he and Cheryl were in a hotel. Some thugs came. They escaped in a car."

Many of the Riders were listening to Chopper conversation with Magic and Tall. They gathered around the phone. Cho filled them in on anything they might have missed. Everyone was stunned to hear Bobby and his group was selling and taking drugs. They became more shocked, when they heard Boo, was hurt.

Bell gasped, Miriam and the other women murmured concerns of Mike's learning of how Boo was injured. Some suspected Mike, might harm the kids.

Cho knew better. Those kids will be dealt with by the governing counsel, he told all. Chopper hung the phone up. No sooner than he done so, it rang again. A nurse picked up the phone. She handed the phone to Chopper, "it is for you, sir."

LEAVING IS HARD

It was a sunny Autumn day on the island. Waves swept the shores of the beaches with an emerald sheen. People began to exit their homes pouring onto the beaches. It was a marvel to witness how rapidly people adjusted to the night before, the violence that took place. Dead men littered the streets and the boardwalk. By morning, all the bodies were removed of the streets. The boardwalk was a different matter. Head dripping with blood were mounted on posts or poles down the entire length of the boardwalk. It was a gruesome sight to behold. It took the police an entire day pulling the dead heads off the poles.

Many people went to see the dripping bloody heads. They were enthralled looking at the gruesome sight and watching the police pulling head from their tombstones. It was done with much reverence, for each head. One officer would lift the head from a post, hand it to another officer, he placed it inside a bag. The bag was passed to another officer to be stacked in the back of a pickup truck. Once the truck was filled with the unholy sight, it slowly drove away with a long line of followers in tow. Not mourning followers but curious to where they were taking the heads.

"It was a sight," commented one town person to another watching the precession of ghouls following the truck. They were talking about another truck with police, not so filled with reverence for each head, plucked from its tombstone post. One by one, a head was tossed into the rear bed of their truck. Boos were shouted by followers after a head missed the hoop mounted to the cab of the police truck. One person was heard saying, "damn, there goes a two-point score to another man, taking bets."

One man, a tourist commented to a town's person. "That is a horrible thing to say."

The town's person replied, "You would not say that, if you lived here in this town, with those thugs, mister. A third truck followed the second truck. Two officers pulled the posts and poles out of the ground. Later, they would be placed back, after cleaning.

One office was heard complaining to another. "It amazes me, how swiftly these heads were mounted to each of these posts. It took seconds to put them on the posts and now it takes us the whole day to pull these posts out of the ground." All the posts were thrown in the rear of the third truck.

All this occurred two days ago. Mike looked at the beaches as his car was speeding through the city, toward the airport. People were crowding the beaches, as if nothing happened. Little evidence was seen by Mike in the car of the heads mounted on posts, he so meticulous took time to achieve his intended effects.

At the airport, word was already sent ahead by the local mobsters. "No plane is allowed to take off. He was met by the same man, when they landed coming from the desert. Bell, Susan, Cheryl, and Rhonda stood by the hangar, as he exited the plane with Cho, Jimmie, Pretty, and Jamie. The man said he could not get any flight out of the airport." Now, his plans has changed.

"I need a plane, as soon as possible leaving this island. Can you rent one to me or provide a transport from our source?" Source meant the military type.

"So sorry, no planes can land or take off, sir, replied the man showing fear in his eyes. Mike looked around. Many planes were on the tarmac. Then, it dawned on him. That meant no planes for him and the girl. Mike thought about taking a plane by force. He ruled that out. It would be tracked by the mob and shot down. He would have no chance. Besides, Cheryl was with him, any chance he had was less now, with her in tow."

Mike takes Cheryl's hand, dragging her down the stairs to the tarmac below. Hey, you are hurting my arm. Why the rush, Mike?"

"Cheryl, remember the hotel, a gun fight erupted, there. Those men are after us. Mike recalls his learning of Sun Tsu's lessons. An army must be capable of a coordinated movement in accordance with a detailed plan and responsive to systematic signals. Therefore, communications must be a primary concern in any force movement in the field."

It was apparent to Mike, "the Bosses in command lacked this important precept of Sun Tzu. If they attack with coordination, there would be many men at this airport to prevent any coming and leaving. Most armies rely on professionally trained soldiers. These men were not professionals," Mike pondered.

"They did not adhere to the lessons learned from days past. They act without thought. Reckless, trying to avenge a wrong. Their leader gives orders, after each action has been taken. He should be preparing for such actions, before they occur. They care little of the dangers, they face. Either that, or are not informed of their adversary. Such careless actions will lead to disaster, that I can capitalize upon. If they only approached the hotel with some stealth, the outcome of capturing Cheryl and me might have been different," thought Mike and glad they didn't.

"Mike, what are we going to do," asked Cheryl?

"Cheryl, that is not my concern. You are. Look at you? Your hands are shaking. Once they did not."

Cheryl was about to object to Mike's assessment, until she looked at her shaking hands. "Okay Mike, you can't just dump me here and go off to fight them, alone?"

"True Cheryl, this Boss man has little skill in fighting. If he had, this airport would have been sealed off, before we got here. No one was here, when we arrive. He acts after the fact. Many of the other places to get off the island are now, being put off limits, once the controller makes his report to the Boss. I saw his men approach, the hotel you were staying in. That proved to me, we have time to still reach a way to leave this island."

"Mike, isn't there a consulate on this island?"

"I am not sure. Many places, I was told by Cho, had an American consulate."

"Then, take me to this one. That is American soil. They wouldn't dare attack that place."

"That is a great idea."

Mike returns to the control room. After a few questions asked, he learned there was an American consulate on the island. Within minutes, two fugitives fleeing in a car drove up to a gate, guarded by Marines.

The ambassador was notified by one of the Marines. He had been expecting this to come. Both were escorted to the ambassador's office. He was reluctant to act in their behalf. He feared the fallout to come, from holding two fugitives from the local law. Earlier, the same day of the attack at the hotel, law officers came to the consulate. They had warrants for all the Americans fighting at the hotel. He informed them, they left by plane, that day. The police returned later, to issue two new warrants for a girl and young man.

Before the ambassador could explain to Mike and Cheryl his concerns, a small band of men crowded at the front gate. They were toting weapons. One man stepped forward making demands. He was aware of the two people that entered through the gate.

Mike listened to his demands. One Marine reported what was said to the ambassador. Mike swiftly demanded asylum for Cheryl. He mentioned Chopper and Cho's name to the ambassador. The Ambassador knew their names. His response was immediate. He was informed, if people came to him, help them with speed anything they requested. That command came from the highest levels. Mike wished he had mentioned Chopper and Cho's names earlier to the ambassador.

Outside the gates, the crowd grew larger. A chant arose. The police remained off to one side, removed from the crowd. The ambassador watched from his window. The police had no intentions to get involved. He knew the officers were there to apply the warrant and not keep violence from occurring. He was aware all the law, was bought and paid for by the local mob. He tried to remain out of the local affairs, now he had little choice.

He turned to look at Mike. Mike knew what the Ambassador was about to tell him. He spotted the scanty Marine force guarding the ambassador and this compound. His Marines were outnumbered. He knew they would put up a great fight. The marines would make them pay a high cost of their own men. In the end, the crowd would win the day.

Mike watched the ambassador stand looking out the window. He knew his concerns, he faced. There were no good options, except one. Mike made the option easy for the ambassador.

"Sir, I will go outside and meet with them. They want me. If I don't, then all of you will die and they will have me. I cannot allow you to sacrifice yourselves for me."

Cheryl screamed, "no, no, you are not going to give yourself up for my sakes. They will kill you."

"Cheryl, Mike turns to face her, I got no choice. I knew this was to happen, coming here. They will rush in, kill everyone, and still get me and you. This way, you all have a chance. The ambassador can get you to safety. They will play with me for a time. That should allow the ambassador time to get you off this island."

Mike turns to the ambassador. "Tell the Marines to fire three rounds to inform me that Cheryl has left the island, please. Once you are away and safe, I will make my escape, Cheryl."

The Marine stares at the young man making this strange request. "Who is this kid? Stories were heard at the consulate about a red eyed man making hash out of many of the local mob men. This young man had no red eyes."

Cheryl contemplated Mike's words. "It was sound. She knew Mike could make good his escape with ease. She thought, if the ambassador could get her away quickly, Mike would not be in much harm. Okay Mike, I will agree and leave."

Mike nodded his answer to Cheryl. Turning he looks at the top sergeant in the office, Tell your Marines, I will be out soon. Do not mention the girl."

"Are you sure, you want to go this route with those men, asked the ambassador? He heard stories of a man with red glowing eyes attacking Black Muslims in the desert. They were too unbelievable for him to take stock in. Besides, this man had no red glowing eyes. Then, stories came to him on this island of a red glowing eyed man fighting with the locals. Maybe, this red glowing eyed man will come to this young man's rescue, if the stories are true," thought the ambassador.

Mike reached over giving a kiss on Cheryl's cheek. She began to cry. "Don't worry Cheryl. I will be fine."

The ambassador listened to Mike's reply to the girl. He suspected Mike had some connection to the red glowing eyed demon. "Young man, do you expect this red glowing eyed man will come to your rescue?"

Mike was shocked to hear the ambassador asked him about the red glowing eyed man. "You heard of this demon, Sir?"

"Yes, I thought you may have, as well. You arrived several days from the desert. Reports have been coming in for weeks, about some red glowing eyed man, fighting Black Muslim terrorist groups. Then, you and your people arrive and within a few days, this demon arrived. I suspect you know of this demon?"

"No sir. We heard of him. We saw him briefly in one engagement with Muslim terrorist teams. We were surprised as were you, when he showed up on this island. It is known, he fights evil and will defend those, that are in need of aid."

"Hmm," replied the ambassador.

Mike turned, seeing no reason to remain in the office longer. To remain, the ambassador will surely ask more questions, he did not want to answer. Outside, two Marine waited at the gates. They held their weapons to stop the young man from leaving. Mike had to insist they allow him to leave. The Top Sarge waved him through.

The gate opened with reluctance. Both Marine were sorely tempted to walk with Mike. Mike was swiftly grabbed by two mob members. One man slammed his rifle butt in his face. Mike saw the weapon coming, moving slightly to prevent any harm to himself. He feinted being knocked out. Both men dragged him off. Both Marines raised their rifles to fire. The ambassador shouted from his window to decease.

Upstairs, the ambassador quickly took Cheryl to the rooftop. Mike woke hearing the rotors of a copter approach the compound. He was tied to a beam, Sunlight shown through a window across from where he was tied. A man was slapping his face. His face was bloody from the slapping. Both feet dangled off the ground. His hands were tied by a rope to the beam. His shirt was ripped off? It was hard not to alert the men holding him captive, he was aware of everything done to him.

Two big men stood in front of Mike. One held a board; the other did the talking. Young man, I see you are no stranger to pain. You have many scars on your chest and back, heh?"

Mike remained silent.

"I see you are not ready to speak. We will see before the day has ended, if you still rather not talk. My boss has many questions for you, to answer. Beside me, is a man that is very good at making people talk. Oh, pardon me, let me introduce my friend. Heh, heh, you two will become very good acquaintances, I believe, heh, heh, heh. This is Georgio."

Mike looks at the big man across from him. The copter rotor blades had slowed down. It had landed on the rooftop. Georgio was fat, had a nasty grin on his face. His hair was oily and, in his hand, a large flat board.

"Hi, I see you stare at my friend. I call him Whacker. Here, let me introduce my friend, Whacker to you." Whack.

Mike grinned but did not say a word or yelled out. A rib was cracked by the impact from Whacker.

"See boss, I told you Whacker would enjoy our new friend. He bares his pain. Whacker loves to whack. He will last a long time, giving Whacker much joy."

"You were right, Georgio."

Boss man slaps Mike on his face. "Listen young man to what I am going to tell you. Each question you do not answer, Whacker will be pleased to whack you. The longer you desist, the more joy Whacker will have. Eventually, you will answer all my questions, heh, heh, heh."

Now for the first question. Who is this red face demon killing my men?"

Mike said nothing. He heard the copter begin to lift off the rooftop. Whack. The rib broke and one other rib was cracked on the same side.

"Still, reluctant to answer my question, heh? Georgio, take your knife and make a few cuts. Make your cuts on the other side of his chest. He appears lopsided with those that are there. He need balance in his life. Maybe, that is why he does not answer my questions? He is lopsided in his thinking, heh, heh, heh."

Many cuts sliced across Mike's chest. Soon, the floor was covered with blood. "Halt your slicing, Georgio. We don't want the young man to drain out of blood. Let me see, you were whacked and say nothing. Now you were cut and still say nothing. We have many methods yet" to try, my young friend. Maybe, we will learn which method is best, with the next one."

Mike was hurting bad. He did not want to give the boss satisfaction. The copter rotors were no longer heard outside the underground basement across from the compound. "Cheryl is safe," Mike thought.

Unbeknownst to Mike, Cheryl did not get on the helicopter. She ran and hid in a restroom. The door was solid. The Pilot asked the ambassador, "what he wanted him to do? If they remained longer, he feared a rocket would blow up the copter. I should leave. This is the only ride out of here. I will return when you call."

"Agreed, leave and I will contact you, when we get her out of the room. He had no choice and had to concede to the Pilots pleas.

"Halt your cuts, Georgio. We don't want him dead. Our employer will not be pleased. Well young man, I see you have a high threshold to pain. Turning to his friend sweating from his work, the Boss asks, "what would you like to try next, Georgio?"

Georgio was typical of many of the men on the island. He gained much weight over the years, living good from his work. He enjoyed eating as much as he enjoyed his work. His weight was taking a toll on his performance. He loved his work but tired of the long time it took to achieve the Boss's desire. Some of the pleasure was fading, he once had.

This man was making his job more difficult, with his reluctance to talk. The kid was tough. His first impression seeing the young man hanging on a hook was, "he was going to break his record."

"Georgio, make us fire, commanded the Boss. Maybe some heat in this cold basement, might make him feel better and want to talk. Being comfy sometimes loosen the tongue, heh, Georgio?"

Georgio lit a torch, then, slowly applied the flame to one toe. Boss man watched, waiting to hear the kid scream. No scream was forth coming from the kid. In fact, there was no reaction on his face.

"That toe doesn't seem to be a good spot, Georgio. Maybe I will have better success. Hmm, I wonder if this spot is the one, Georgio?" Boss man held a cigarette near Mike's bare back. He asked Georgio if the spot was a good one.

Georgio answered with a resounding, "yes. That is a good spot. I use that spot a lot, Boss, with Whacker. A searing pain followed with a stench, entering Mike nose. Which was the worse, the smell of his flesh burning or the pain on his toes?

Both men took turns testing areas on Mike's body. Each swore, their spot was the one to make the young man squeal. Neither were correct. Mike took that time to focus on the rope, he was dangling on a hook.

Each toe was burnt. Mike freed both hands after the last of the ten toes were blistered by the torch. Mike silently thanked Magic teaching him how to escape. While they thought, he was unconscious dragging him to the cellar, Mike secretly removed a razor blade from his belt. Once they lofted him off the floor tying his hands with a rope, he slowly began to cut his hands free. He dropped to the floor. The pain screamed from his feet, to his brain. Mike stayed focus. Mike yelled hitting the floor. Not from the pain, but to shock the two men.

"Hey Georgio, he screams. I won."

Georgio replied, "I figured he would, when you lit that last toe. That is my go-to-spot, when everything else fails, Boss."

Suddenly, both men spoke too soon. Each look with horror, seeing the young man standing before them. Before each had time to realize, the scream was not caused by their torch. The young man hopped up, making a back flip. One foot kicked Georgio in his face. The other foot did the same to the Boss man.

Mike landed on his feet. The torch went flying. Teeth in Georgio's mouth were flying from the kick, Mike delivered. A splatter of teeth was heard hitting the wall. Georgio would never enjoy any meal, after losing all his teeth. That and his tongue being ripped out through his gaping open mouth.

The Boss man had a different problem, lasting only seconds. The kick knocked him back against the wall with a loud splat. The stain from his body smeared on the wall, with blood, would be difficult to remove, later.

Georgio was alive and amazed at what he saw. "This kid shouldn't be able to walk, much less move. What he done, would break most men. Whacker never failed. He was astonished, the kid broke free of his bonds. That never happened?"

Mike stood in front of the big man. "Georgio, that was your name, isn't it?"

He nodded, sitting on the floor holding his mouth.

"Let me introduce you to my little friend, Georgio."

Mike locates his jacket, dons it, then, reaching down by Georgio, lifts the torch, and lowers the hood on his jacket. Both eyes lit with a red glow. After a long minute, Georgio mouth stopped bleeding. His face was melted into a blob. Later, he would recall the incident every day of his life. He would remember both eyes exploding, like over blown balloons from his face. His life would be forever in darkness and having to be fed by others. His mouth was a small hole for food to be shoved in. Georgio loss much weigh, quickly. Mike left Georgio alive, to relive his pain and hopefully what he done to others.

Mike tore Boss man shirt off his body smeared on the wall. He could barely walk. Both feet were struck by Whacker and each toe blistered from the torch. Two ribs were cracked, making it difficult to breathe.

Walking up the stairs, prove difficult. Each step, he labored to breathe. At the top of the stairs, he opened the door, hoping it led outside to freedom. He was wrong.

The door opened into a bar. The same bar, he entered earlier with Bone and Jamie. Five men sat across from the door, he was standing, at a table drinking beers. Mike wished the cold beers were the same nasty brew they drank earlier. It tasted like pig piss, than beer. Mike wondered if it was pig piss, thinking back?

All five men turned, hearing the door fly open. No one suspected what they saw coming through the door. Several men were sitting at the bar. A kid was standing wearing a bloody shirt. His face was swollen, they knew, he received Georgio's Whacker. They witnessed Georgio's work on other people. Seldom did anyone live or wanted to live from his methods of persuasion.

Each man swiftly kicked back their chairs. They hesitated, waiting to see if the Boss was coming up the stairs with Georgio. They didn't. Mike didn't wait for them to discover that. One man remarked as Mike took two steps from the door.

"Hey kid, where you think you are going?"

Mike was flying in the air heading to the man asking the question. A second man inquired, "where was the Boss." The first man went flying back. Mike landed softly, then swiftly did a spinning wheel kick to answer the second man's question.

A third man was looking at the stairs. "Hey, where is the big guy. The third man was attempting to lift a chair. He went spinning with the chair in his arm. Somehow, the second man was sitting in the chair after both stopped spinning.

The fourth man saw the ceiling. Mike dropped into a spinning sweep bringing him down hard on the floor. Mike stood up ramming his other foot in the fourth man's throat. A fifth man grabbed hold of Mike from behind. He was hipped thrown toward the stairs. Before he fell through the door, a sixth man made a move to get behind Mike.

Mike was weak from his torture. He spotted the sixth man attempts to out flank him. Mike stumbled toward the door, leaning against the wall near the basement. The fifth man had went flipping, head over heels down the stairs. He stopped his descent as Mike leaned on the wall. His neck was twisted in a distorted way.

Mike had no means to escape. He was too weak from blood loss. He bent down. The sixth man saw that the man was dropping. "He was done for. It was time to make a move on the lad," was his thinking.

Mike hoped his sudden attack would fill the men with fear. They would be paralyzed with fear. He could use that against them. He bent down to grab a chair leg. The sixth man charged at him. Later, the chair leg was located shoved down the throat of the sixth man by the stairs, by a medic.

For a long time, the police were puzzled over how the sixth man died. If was discovered by an ER tech, sitting the sixth man up. The chair leg poked out of his mouth.

The bar keeper watched with horror. It happened fast, he was trying hard to suck on a soda pop straw on a drink. He passed out turning blue. A bottle was rammed down his throat. Mike forgot to break off the bottom, for the bar keeper to breathe.

One man sitting at the bar, pushed away from the bar counter top. He wanted no part of the kid dropping the sixth man. That changed, when the kid shoved the beer bottle down the throat of the bar keeper. He grabbed the kid. It was like trying to take hold of a spinning greased pole. Mike spun within the grasp of the sitting man at the bar. He was hoped to keep the man from pulling him to the floor. Blood was coming from Mike's mouth. Her was becoming fussy. He knew, he was about to black out.

The last man was going to run out of the bar while his friend held on to the kid. His friend screamed to stop his fleeing. Turning, he rushed to his friend aid. He should have kept running to the front door.

Mike jerked the man squeezing him at the bar. Both men collided into a table then bounced off onto another table. His returning friend was met by both of them. He got whacked by Mike last ditch effort to throw off the man holding him. The man and him flew into his friend shoving all three into the bar. A section of the bar broke from the three impacting it. A splinter jabbed into the side of the friend, coming to the aid of his friend.

Mike jerked free of both men. He saw the splinter in the returning, man. He rammed into the two men again. This time, grabbing the long splintered, yanking it from the side of the returning friend. He screamed. Mike did a spinning wheel kick.

Mike raised the splinter. The first man saw the splinter coming down. He tried to block the wooden spike, with his free arm. He succeeded. The splinter shot through his arm, then forced down into his chest. He gasped for air. Mike reeled from his last effort. The returning man hit with a spinning wheel kick, was not out. Mike was startled, seeing the man standing.

"I must be weaker than I think?" Mike looked puzzled at returning man standing. The last thing he could muster, was yank the splinter from the man he poked in the chest. He threw the splinter like a dart, across the room at the returning man.

Mike was fading fast. He reached for any support. The dart sailed straight to its intended man. The Top sarge watched, stunned to see what just occurred inside the bar. He and a second Marine entered, with Cheryl seeing Mike ramming a chair leg down a man's throat. Both were stunned, watching a blur drop men left and right.

Mike was caught by Cheryl, to his surprise. Somehow, she escaped being put on the copter. The ambassador was by the door with both Marines from the gate. He held the Marines back with his arm realizing if they entered into the ongoing battle, the lad might mistake them, in his condition.

Mike was fighting on instinct without knowing who. It was plain to all watching. The Marines acted out of their training. They pushed against the ambassador's arm. Before they broke free, the fight ended. Each Marine went swiftly to aid Cheryl struggling to hold onto Mike.

Mike resisted at first both Marines helping him. He wasn't aware it was help. He quickly succumbed from his blood loss, to their hold.

"Damn kid, if I hadn't seen this with my own eyes, I would not have believed what, I was seeing," said one Marines. "Who in the hell taught you how to fight," he asked an semi-unconscious Mike?

"Hell Smithy, who else, a Marine," said the second Marine posed by the other Marine.

Both men, escorted Mike to the nearest chair. Cheryl ripped off his bloody shirt. She reeled back, seeing all the cuts crisscrossing his chest.

One of the Marine saw the bruising on Mike's side. "Ambassador, I think he has some broken ribs. He leans Mike forward, to examine his back. They burned his back. His back has small blisters from a cigarette, ambassador."

The other Marine looked down at Mike's feet. "Sir, he got more than cuts and broken ribs. Look here." All of Mike's toes were blister from fire.

"How can this kid walk, much less put up a fight, we just witnessed," inquired the ambassador?

Mike recovered from being passed out. He looked at Cheryl, "why aren't you on the chopper? Mike turned to look at the ambassador. He shrugged his shoulders.

"Son, believe me, I did my best to get her on that chopper. She broke loose and ran into a heavily fortified room. The chopper couldn't remain on the roof top. Once the copter lifted off the roof, she ran out of the room. My Marines had no time to react to stop her at the gates. We followed her to this bar. My Marines reported to me, before the copter arrived, you were taken across the street."

The ambassador stared at Mike with all the beatings, he received. He was amazed, the kid was alive, and more so, when Mike stood to walk.

Cheryl grabbed Mike helping him walk. One Marine spoke.

"Sir, this is a Marine. We ain't leaving no Marine behind."

"Nonsense, he is coming with us. Take the door, check to see if there are men outside with weapons, Sargent>"

"Yes Sir."

Outside were men coming down the street. Many left once Mike was taken to the bar. The mob dissipated. The police remained watching the gate. They left, once the men left.

"Get this man to the embassy, before they get here. I'll call a doctor."

"Excuse me sir, Cheryl said. The doctors will not come here."

One of the Marines quipped to the other, "that ain't happening. If any of those men get here, they gonna wished they hadn't pretty quick."

"I'm with you, spoke the second Marine slamming his slide back. Swiftly everyone left the bar scrambling across the street to the compound. The men coming up the street watched, stunned. Police were standing by the gate. The ambassador told them to move, politely. Both Marines held their weapons at both police. The Marines wanted to shoot, was written on their faces.

"Sorry ambassador, we have orders to not let you enter."

One Marine pushed passed the ambassador. "You want to repeat that again bub, poking his weapon between the eyes of one police officer. Both officers stepped aside. One officer reached for his side arm undetected by the Marines. Mike broke loose from Cheryl, kicking one police officer throwing him into the other officer, knocking both to the ground. One Marine held his weapon, pointing at both officers, while his people squeezed through the gate. A Marine followed locking the gate.

Both police officers quickly stood. Returning to the gate. The ambassador halted their advance.

"Take one more step or touch this fence, and my Marines will open up. You are on American soil. Neither of you have the authority to enter. My government will hold what happened here; you responsible. Do you want to start an international incident, today?"

Inside the compound building other Marines had rifle aimed at the gate. Both Officer turned, leaving without a word said. A crowd was beginning to form outside the gates, again. A chopper landed on the roof top of the compound. More Marines jumped from the chopper. More rifles were aimed at the growing crowd below.

Above, two chopper circled the streets below. Machine guns were pointing at the crowd. They continued to circle for a long time. More returned to continue their circling of the compound. The crowd soon dispersed. The choppers remained.

Within minutes, the ambassador was on the phone. Chopper answered the phone in the hospital. Before night fell, Susan was holding Cheryl in her arms. Mike was being treated by a doctor off the island at another embassy. All the bikers landed on the mainland driving directly to the embassy. Cho was by his side, along with all the others. Susan bent over to give Mike a kiss. Cheryl was crying, along with the other women. They looked at his feet and his bared chest.

"More wounds. More wounds."

The doctor interrupted the women wailing, wanting to coddle Mike in their arms. He administer a sedative to Mike. Of course, Mike declined the sedative.

He replied, "I need to focus off the pain." Cho understood, brushing the doctor away. The women stood agape to Mike's request, to not receive a pain killer for his burns or knife cuts, zig-zagging across his chest.

Susan sat across from Bell, holding Mike's hand. Both the doctor and ambassador stared at a kid, declining pain killers, watching bandages applied from head to toe. Not a word or whimper left his lips. The doctor commented, "moving him to apply bandages, is very painful."

Cheryl spoke with tears streaming down her face, "it is his way. He will never take any drugs."

Homeward

Before arriving at the hospital on the military base with all the bikers were waiting patiently, for Mike and Cheryl to arrive. Within minutes, two people loaded onto a helicopter. After a short hop, the copter landed at a military base. An ambulance was waiting. Mike was rolled into the ER and Cheryl sat patiently outside in the waiting room. Hours passes, no word was said. The ambassador came into the hospital. After talking to an officer, he went to see Cheryl.

"Mike is doing fine, miss." Cheryl looked up with tears dried on her face.

I spoke to Mr. Chopper about what happened. They all worried about you and Mike. Your mother was very happy to learn you were returning home. In fact, all were asking about you. You have many people caring a great deal about you."

"You mean Mike, sir."

"No, I said they were concerned about you. One man did seem concerned about the young man, in the ER. His name was Cho."

Mike laid in a bed while a doctor and his nurses tended to his ribs, then his cuts, and finally his blisters.

"Who ever done this to you, sir, intended to drag their fun out for a long time? The real damage here, are these cracked ribs. The cuts are superficial, not deep to scar. The same for your burns. There is a first, second, and third degree burns one can get. You have second degree. They will heal, but the pain will be severe. A little longer burning, the skin would have blacken resulting in nerve damaged. The healing process would take many months leaving scar tissue."

Mike nodded to the doctor's explanations. He motioned a nurse to administer a sedative. Mike stopped her.

"I need none of that, doctor. Tend to the wounds, please and allow me to deal with the pain."

"As you wish, son."

The doctor heard the story about what this young man had done. He was tortured, then fought off many men, alone. Getting to the compound, he assisted the Marines get into the compound, before him. On the rooftop, he told the Marines, he could walk to the waiting copter. Without their help. He was told, the kid could barely walk.

The ambassador confirmed what he heard. One Marine yelled to the kid walking to the copter; "You'll make one hell of a Marine," repeated the ambassador to the doctor. My Marines were impressed, with him. So was I."

"I heard them speaking while, the kid walked to the ramp to enter the copter. One Marine repeat a message I received by command, "a red glowing eye man was seen fighting many Black Muslin terrorists in the desert. He assisted soldiers getting ambushed. Later, freed many prisoners in a city, filled with soldiers. At a mountain, he took on an army of soldiers, by himself, armed only with a sword."

"I am sure, many tales have been rumored about this lad. I cannot say for sure; he is one and the same, the red glowing eyed demon in my reports. He most certainly is believed as one-in-the same, by my Marines. They gave him a salute, standing at attention, while entering the helicopter."

Three days passed, with Mike stay at the hospital. The ambassador checked on him and Cheryl daily. Cheryl would not leave his room. Two guards were issued to stand watch by his room. It was to keep Cheryl from attempting to bolt away. He was told, "if that occurred, he would have to answer for that." It was meant as a threat, the way the ambassador perceived the message, from higher ups.

Meanwhile, another plane was landing at a small airfield. It picked up many people at an airbase. It landed in Atlanta. Onlookers watched a short man walked alongside of a model. The other women, many with long flowing hair, wearing fancy night gowns. Men wearing tuxes and what appeared, leather jackets with words written on the back. They walked toward several cars on the tarmac. Four bikers were seated on bikes, wearing the same jackets, with the same words printed, Riders. The revving of the bikes, screamed louder than the plane's engines. Many onlookers held their ears. Four police officer waited to escort the cars and biker to their destination.

Razor, Chopper, Jack, and Bone walked over to the bikers. Each man was fully armed. The police stopped, once they saw all the weapons each Rider was toting. Each had a rifle, and a pistol, strapped to their bodies. The four men approaching the bikers were handed holsters with pistols and knives. The four officers decided to watch and not interfere, Their job was to provide escort, only.

Chopper received news from man runner up to him. The news came from the ambassador on the mainland. They left Mike with Cheryl on the military base. Mike was taken to another hospital equipped to handle his wounds. He reported news they already knew from meeting with the ambassador on the island. It was a courtesy call.

"Mike and Cheryl were attacked by the same group, your people encountered. These men wanted revenge. Mike was in a hospital at an airbase. He would be there for several days.

The ambassador went on to describe Mike's wounds. The lad was cut many times, then received second degree burns on his feet and backside. The worse damage was broken ribs. Then came words, he was being tortured.

Chopper reported that to Cho. Flames filled his eyes. "My son would never submit to being tortured. Chopper had to quickly explain how that was possible.

"He had no choice, Cho. The compound was surrounded. Few Marines were there to defend it. It was going to be over run. Mike made the decision with the guaranteed from the ambassador would get Cheryl to safety."

"Chery ran away. The chopper had to depart before it was shot down. She ran out of the compound to a bar across the street. Many of the revenge filled crowd had departed the area once they had captured Mike."

"My son was not captured, Chopper."

"Your correct, he surrendered to them. The ambassador with two Marines found Mike fighting off many men in a bar. They arrived too late to be of any assistance."

"He escaped as I knew he would., smile Cho hearing this part of the message."

"Yes Cho, Mike was severely tortured with a lot of blood loss. The Marines were freaked out, seeing this bloody kid take on a bar filled with men, twice his size. They found other men at the bottom of stairs leading to where they tied Mike and tortured him. Three men laid in a tangled mish mash at the foot of the stairs, dead. One other man was seen smashed into a wall like a picture hung to it. Later, the man had to be peeled off the wall, like tape had adhered to it."

"One man in the basement was alive. He was a big man. The ambassador said, "he knew of this man. He was Georgio, the man called to torture men for the big Boss." His face was melted. A torch laid by his hand. Neither of his eyes were present, just blacken holes, where they should have been. All his teeth were missing. My Marines carried him off to the hospital after Mike and Cheryl had flown off.

"Mike was in horrific condition, when we found him. It made me sick to look at that boy. All the blood and his back. No one could withstand that kind of torture. How he done, so is remarkable and beyond any reason of sanity," replied the mainland ambassador.

Finally, what Chopper and Cho were listening patiently from the ambassador to tell them. "Mike and Cheryl will be on a plane leaving to America by the end of the week."

Susan was the first to get the news about Cheryl and Mike returning home. She was clearly upset, learning Mike was tortured and happy that Cheryl was coming home.

"It was bitter sweet hearing the news," Susan said to Bell.

Magic met Chopper, Bone, and Razor at the clubhouse. Jack went home with his wife and daughter along with Pretty. Pretty seldom was far from Judy, after the fight at the hotel. Cho took Laura home. Penny went them.

Bell came into the bar with Miriam and Susan. All three went to the table where others were standing, listening to Magic's report. No beers were handed out.

"This is serious," Miriam quipped to Bell.

"Chopper, we got wind some men belonging to that group on the island have been notified on the hit to Mike and Cheryl. That hit on them, was extended to our club. I believe, we will have visitors in the not too future."

Before Chopper asked, Magic continues his briefing. "I have informed all the families about an impending attack. All precautions are being made. The wives and children will go to our shelter. Those that can assist, will be given places to man. A duty roster has been made and handed to all persons. Texas and LA have been informed."

Razor breaks in. "Chopper we cannot allow this fight to come here. We need to go after them."

"Your right, Razor." Cho walks in the bar. He left Laura at home with Penny to go to the meeting.

"Good," shouts Chopper seeing Cho present. Laura with Penny entered having decided they wanted go to go to the meeting. Both women realized that trouble was coming, after they were handed pistols at the airport. In fact, all expected trouble coming home.

"Cho, we got more trouble from that mob on the island it seems. The hit on Mike and Cheryl has been expanded. They are coming here, replied Chopper.

"No, we cannot allow that to happen. We need to return and finish this before they can get here."

"We all have been talking about that same thing. You with Jack will lead a seal team back. Take them all out. Leave a message behind that will deter any other actions. Be ready in a week."

"Why wait a week," demanded Razor?

"We got to prepare this place and gather intel, before we leave. Razor, you know this. Jack is going, because he has more experience than you. Cho, for obvious reasons."

"Bell interjects. Chopper, Cho just came back, he is to get married. How can you asked him to leave, again? Laura his recovering from her wounds."

Laura saw Cho's reaction to having to return to the island. He did not want to go. She was proud of her man. He had no choice. The wedding was going to be delayed, again. She wished Mike would be going. After Susan telling them of him being tortured, that looked improbable.

Bell had organized the women into care groups for Mike's return, the next day. She could feel Laura's hurt, hearing Cho was asked to return to the island, so soon after getting home. She felt awful for her.

Cho spoke, "Chopper, before we leave, I want our marriage to take place at our home."

Laura hearing Cho' demands got visibly upset. "Wait just one minute, mister. If you think, I am going to get marriage to you on a drop of a dime's notice, you got another thing coming to you. I and the women have been planning this event for months. We are not going to spoil all my plans, now."

Cho swiftly answered before all the women blew a casket. "Listen, I want this marriage for us. The wedding can still happen, when we get back. I promise."

All the women calmed down. Bell, especially was near an explosion, after hearing Cho wanting to cancel the wedding plans.

After beers were passed about, Susan left to go to the cabin. She and Penny with Bone drove to the front door. Entering through the open door, a message greeted them, written on the wall over Mike's bed. Boo barked.

Penny lifted Boo. He licked her face. The message read.," Mike is coming home".

Susan replied to Mister Casper's note. "Mike will arrive before the days end. He is badly hurt. Cheryl is fine. There is trouble brewing. We expect, men to come and attack our club."

A new message appeared over the bed. "Cheryl."

Susan was stunned. Mister Casper implied Cheryl was the cause. She could not deny it might be her fault. Still, seeing Mister Casper acknowledge her to blame, was too much. She walked to the table and sat in tears. Boo jumped from Penny's arms racing to be with Susan.

Penny finish explaining what was coming to attack them. "These are bad people. This place might be in harm's way, Mister Casper. If Mike gets back, he will need tending to. He is hurt. These people will come here to kill Mike and anyone with him."

"I know of Mike," replied words written on the wall.

Penny was amazed, "Mister Casper we just learned this moments ago. How?"

New words appeared on the wall, before Penny turn around looking at the others with astonishment.

"The dead talk."

It took a few seconds for Penny to make the connection. "The dead talk to other dead spirits. Then, Mister Casper knows everything," Penny said to all in the cabin. Susan stopped crying and looked up. Suddenly, all was clear to her, Mister Casper could help them.

After Penny fed Boo, Bone and Susan decided to return to the club house to inform the others of this new revelation. Inside the bar, Chopper and Razor were wrapping up the story of their fight with the mob.

Mike, Bone, Moss, with Susan, Penny, and Laura went to the container box to free Cheryl. Moss or One eyed saved them, throwing himself on the man holding a grenade. Cho with Razor and Jamie went to the airfield searching for Cheryl, unaware that she was in a container box. They all ran into each other on the road back to the city."

"Cheryl took off again, after being freed. Laura and Moss needed doctoring. At the hospital, Cho and Jamie remained behind to protect Laura and One Eye. The mob men came. Jamie was killed stopping a grenade."

Mike, with the rest of us defended the hotel from a full assault. Twenty maybe forty men advanced on the hotel. Jimmie and Razor caught a bullet inside the hotel. Mike went outside to defend the hotel. He ended the threat. Then, went to the hospital. He encountered another team prepping to make a second assault. He ended that threat temporarily. He blew a truck loaded with ammo and killed several men near the bar."

"At the hospital, Mike located Cho and the others, still alive. There was carnage everywhere inside the hospital. Many staff members were killed for being there and helping our folks. They came to the hotel, just before the second assault began."

"Mike devised a plan. Cho guarded the front while Mike went to the beach to cover the rear. What happened next, was pretty gory. The mob divided their men into two assault forces. Mike was correct, one came to the front, as a feint for a second team to enter through the rear entrance."

"Mike swam along the beach to where the men were gathering to divide up into their separate teams. Mike unsheathed his blade and began the gruesome task ahead of him. He lopped off their heads, poking them on posts along the beach. Cho did the same in front of the hotel. Jimmie defended the rear alone. He set several booby traps in the rear. Mike planned to make the mob men think, he was really a demon. Cho was to act the part, to create second demon. It worked better than expected."

Razor continued, while Chopper took a breather and a drink. You heard the stories coming back, about Mike making all them Black Terrorist think he was a red glowing eyed demon. Every death was marked with his sign, OZ. He continued that mark on each of the heads lopped off. The street ran red with blood."

Mike went to assist Jimmie. Many were killed attempting to charge the rear entrance. Cho ended his assault from the front, with the assist from snipers. Bell, Miriam, and Jack dropping men, Cho or Mike missed covering their rear. The women had set up a fortified position on the third story balconies, before Jack came to assist."

"When morning arrived, all the bodies without heads, were gone. That night, Chopper ordered all the hotel staff to load the trucks and dump the bodies far from the hotel. It was for their best interests. They assisted the Americans against the orders given to the city, by the mob. It was a death sentence for all of them, if one spoke."

"Morning came. The street was lined with dead heads, lining the boardwalk by the beach. Gossip spread throughout the city, like wildfire. OZ, a red glowing eyed demon devoured all the bodies.

Our team raced to the airport. Mike remained behind to search for Cheryl."

"He found Cheryl in a seedy hotel. She was drugged. After getting her back on her feet men, came to the hotel looking for Cheryl. Mike and Cheryl fled to the consulate. The island ambassador aided them. The compound was surrounded by an overwhelming force of armed men working for the Boss man. Mike surrendered to the mob outside the gate, to give the Ambassador time to ferret Cheryl off to safety. Mike was tortured. He endured the torture to give the ambassador time to get Cheryl off the island."

Cheryl did another run. She left the compound, running across the empty street to a bar, that we were in earlier. The ambassador followed with two Marines. They entered the bar, just as Mike was mopping up many men. He was bloody, burnt, and had broken ribs. The Marine marveled at our boy taking out all those men, alone. They wanted to make him an honorary Marine.

"Get that." Razor snickered at the others in the bar, not Marines.

"Hey Razor, you said that you went to the bar, earlier. Did you take some Seals and Green Berets with you?"

"No, ask Chopper and Jack, they were with me. Before us, Mike with Bone and Jamie were there first. Mike cleaned their slates, alone. When we got there, it was apparent, they been in a scuffle. We cleaned their slates a second timed. We learned later; our women went to the bar after us."

"Did they have a Marine escort with them, Ha, ha, ha," laughed several non-Marines.

Bell with Susan, Miriam stood up. "Care to repeat that remark, asshole?"

The joker shut up. Razor continued his report. "Bell, would you like to finish this part of the report?"

"No, you are doing just fine, Razor." Bell with the other two women gave a nasty stare at all the men at the bar. Many turned to take a drink.

"Well, out ladies were treated badly. That was corrected. Not one man was standing, when they finished their drinks. A shout rose up at the bar counter.

"Hooray for our girls. That will teach any men to keep a civil tongue. Better be glad, we were not there. We would return and make them rethink everything a second time, again," shouted one of the bikers at the bar.

One eye was mentioned, a second time. Boos went up at the bar. "Hold on a second men. One eyed helped us track down Cheryl. He nearly got killed losing an arm doing it."

Jimmie interrupter Razor, "prior to that, he helped Mike in the desert. He has done much to earn a fair trial." Razor continued making his report.

"We returned to the bar, before Mike and Bone with Moss's help, located Cheryl. At the bar, Chopper and Jack and Jimmie, our newest recruit, returned, we persuaded the barkeeper, or Jimmie did to tell us about the hit, the Boss man had plans to attack our people at the hotel. Jimmie is quite the persuader."

"Here, here," came shouts from the bar. Jimmie was handed a second beer.

"After shoving Boss man in the rear of our car, we drove to the hotel. In our room, he escaped while the rest of us were down stairs, after the battle ended and we were celebrating."

"We just learned, the mob has contracted a hit on our team, here at home.

Chopper breaks in on Razor. "Cho and a Seal team will be sent to settle this once and for all back on the island. If necessary, Jack will go to the mainland and terminate every last one of those sons of bitches."

A roar of applause erupted inside the bar.

A plane landed before night fell. Two people exited the plane. No one was waiting to drive them to the club house. Mike called Pilot to take them to the clubhouse. He mentioned not to say a word. Both Cheryl and Mike entered the bar when the roar erupted from what Chopper said. "To terminate every last one of those S.O.B.s."

Everyone stopped shouting turning to see two people, they were not expecting until the next day, standing just inside the door. Susan reacted first. She ran to Mike, hugging and kissing him. Then, to Cheryl hugging and kissing her.

Bell went to Mike. Chopper toted a beer. Cho watched his son carefully. Everyone was stunned, then, a roar of applauds went up. Everyone crowded around Mike and Cheryl. Cho broke through the crowd, escorting him to his table. Laura leaned over and kissed Mike.

"I am so proud of you, Michael." Whispered Laura into Mike's ear. She wanted to hug him but held back, after watching both women at the door squeeze him. He whence with pain, not making a sound. Everyone forgotten his wounds, seeing him suddenly appear in the door. Cho saw the same as Laura.

Bell sat beside Mike, putting her arm around Mike's shoulder. Laura quickly reminded her of his wounds. Bell was beside herself with embarrassment. Many of the ladies quickly gathered around Mike, like old biddy hens.

"My son, I see you act fine. But inside, I feel there is much harm."

"My father, I am better. I can go on another mission, now."

Mike knew about the hit on the club. The ambassador filled him in on what he relayed to Chopper. He knew his father was to be asked, to lead the return to the island. It only made sense, to stop the hit at its source. Cho had to go. Everyone believed him to be badly hurt. He was hurt, but Mike decided he was not going to let his father know, to what extent. He was getting married and did not need to be off on another mission, especially with Laura hurt.

Laura spotted bandages hanging from one arm's sleeve. Mike quickly tucked the bandage back up the sleeve. He saw Laura spotting the loose wrapping. Mike downed his first beer and a second, then a third. Many more were coming to the table. He stood.

"I want to get some rest from this long flight. I want to check on Boo. Please excuse me, guys."

Bell, Laura, Susan, and several ladies walked with Mike. He knew better to tell them; he did not need their help. Susan commanded Cheryl to stay in the bar. Bell saw Susan's concerned and told Cheryl to remain at the bar. The implication was plain. Susan wanted to make sure Cheryl, did not make another attempt to get away.

Many women followed Mike to the car. Laura drove the car crammed with helpers. Bell put the word out, Mike was severely wounded. Every woman eagerly volunteered. Each had Mike stay in their homes when he first arrived at the club and returning from Atlanta, badly injured. They grew to love this young handsome, brave child. Bell had to turn many away. She promised they would help later.

After Mike entered the bar, that all changed. Every woman's heart bled for their young hero. Mike never asked for any help. That made them want to do more for him. The men sat watching. They knew better to try and stop them. One man spoke up.

"Mike can deal with them. I am glad it is him and not me."

"Here, here cried several men. Drinks all around before the women return."

Mike wore a long sleeve shirt against the doctor's orders. In the car, the bandages were bleeding through the shirt sleeves. Susan saw the stains and took off her shirt over a tee shirt under it.

Mike couldn't help notice, both breasts giggled under her tee-shirt. She wasn't wearing a bra. Susan assisted Mike to take his shirt off in the crowded car. It was then, that they saw all the bandages he was concealing.

Laura watched the scene in the rear seat with Susan, Mike, and Miriam. The other women in the car sat up front. Laura quickly told them to not turn around.

At the cabin, their car swiftly unloaded. The cabin door was opening. Another car halted behind the first car. All the women entered the cabin. Laura with Susan escorted Mike to his bed, shielding all eyes watching with their bodies. A cover was laid over Mike. Penny watched Mike come in. She did not see the reason for such mothering. He looked fine to her.

At the mainland hospital, Penny with the other ladies on the island, witnessed his wounds. Mike acted as if he was not in pain. The doctor said, "the burns and cuts were not deep and would heal in no time." The way Mike acted, Penny assumed, he was better than, he really was.

All the women clamored about, finding anything to do, to help. One woman grabbed a broom sweeping the floor. Another, began wiping the only window, with a rag. Two bickered over straightening the three table chairs. It became clear to Laura and Susan; this was not going to work.

Before any of the women said a word, a message appeared over Mike's bed. "They must leave, now"! Many women never visited the cabin. They heard stories about Mister Casper, the ghost and him writing on the wall. Those that never came to the cabin were caught by surprise, seeing the words appear on the wall above the bed.

One woman left quick. Two were slowly backing out the door. Laura spoke, "I think Mister Casper does not want you here. He can be over protected of Boo and Mike. You need to leave, before he acts."

Mister Casper acted soon as Laura stopped talking. A new message appeared above the bed, "leave now." A strong breeze swept inside through the open door. Boo began barking. The other women ran from the room. The door slammed shut. All the women crammed into the second car, driving off.

"That was quick, retorted Penny. Why the tender loving reception for Mike?"

Susan attempted to answer Penny's question. "Mike showed up at the bar with Cheryl. He was as thin as a rail. He looked fine. Laura and I noticed he was not fine in the car. Mike wanted to come to the cabin, after they pumped him full with beer."

Laura took over when Mike tried to pulled the blanket off of himself.

Boo jumped on the bed, licking Mike. "Glad to be home, missed you, buddy." Mike hugged and petted Boo. Susan tried to push Mike to lie back down. Boo growled. Blood seeped through her shirt Mike was wearing. Her effort cause the cuts to open.

"Oh my, I'm so sorry Mike."

Quickly Susan began to unbutton her shirt on Mike. Penny watched, then reeled back seeing all the bandages and blood stains. Before Susan could do much more, Mike stood. Laura watched Susan trying to help Mike. Mike was in pain sitting on the bed. Laura could feel his pain and wanted to coddle him, like Susan was attempting to do.

Laura was startled Mike asking her how she was doing. "Laura, you look good. Will you be able to see from that one injured eye? We thought you might be blind, in it. It did look worse than it really was. You are as pretty as ever. Cho said, "you will be wedded tomorrow. I am so happy for the both of you. Have you plans for a honeymoon?"

Laura wanted to cry, hearing Mike being more concerned about her, than his own worries. "Yes, Cho insists before he leaves to go back to the island."

Laura realized to late, what slipped from her lips. Mike was not to be told about, the return to the island.

"Why is Cho returning? He should be on his honeymoon. I am perfectly fine to go back to the island. Who better than me? I just left and know what is happening on the island."

Laura tried to divert the conversation. "Mike, you better not miss this wedding. You are Cho's best man." Laura recalled words Cho said to her. "Do not talk about Mike's wounds or distract him. He must focus on keeping the pain at bay. He will need his full concentration. Mike was to accompany them, back to the island."

Laura stood, shocked listening to Cho tell her, "Mike was going to return with the Seal team and him, back to the island." She was visibly upset with Cho. "How could you expect him to return in his condition he is in?"

It took an hour for Cho to explain. "Listen Laura, his strength comes from his training. To take away his ability to overcome the pain, will make him weak. His strength comes from his Chi." Laura kept thinking Mike's Chi will help him overcome his pain. Seeing him wrapped up gave her doubts. Cho said, "Mike must build on his strength from every injury he receives."

Cho appeared at the door. Mike knew he was coming to the cabin. He felt his Chi knowing when Cho departed the bar.

"Father, glad you came here."

Magic came to the cabin earlier to inform Penny; Mike was coming home soon. Cho wanted Boo at the bar. Penny insisted Boo remain at the cabin. Mister Casper decided the argument. Magic returned to the bar telling Cho, what Mister Casper said, without Boo.

"Cho, Mister Casper insisted Boo remain at the cabin. He said, Mike would be coming there. Penny will stay until, then."

"My son, we are returning to the island. I want you to be with me."

"Father, that will not be necessary. You can remain here with Laura. I will go with the Seal team. Laura will need your attention. Besides, I know the island better than anyone. I am fine. All my wounds are minor. The doctor told me my cuts were shallow scratches. My burns were second degree or less. My rib is bruised, not broken."

"I see and feel your pain, my son."

"Then, you know I am capable to make a return trip, without your attendance. Do you doubt my training? Please allow me to go. Have trust in in me. If you go, then when will I ever feel, I am capable of holding this honor of a true master of our art."

Cho was trapped by his own words. His love had clouded his mind. Mike was correct. Still, this mission would test even him. He knew Jack and what he was thinking, seeing Mike enter the bar. He reminded Jack about the jungle. Still, Jack was concerned having Mike along would be a liability to the success of the mission. Now, Jack is going to learn, he was not going with his team. Mike would, alone.

Before the morning sun rose above the horizon, a plane was taxing on the runway. Jack and his men were at the airport, packed and ready. Mike arrived riding his bike. He stepped off the bike walking over to the Seal team. All watched Mike come over.

Jack did not see Cho. His team consisted of many of Mike's trainers at the club. Cowboy and Tall man stood out. Then, there was Pretty. The others, Mike knew from the bar. Beedie, Jojo, and Skipjack made up the rest of the team. Each had a special skill to bring to the team.

Each man greeted Mike with a handshake walking up the tail ramp into the plane. Jack was amazed, looking at Mike enter the plane. Cho would never allow Mike on this mission alone, unless, he had confidence the lad could get the mission done.

Every man said their goodbyes, before morning. Jack asked Pretty to stay behind. Judy requested her dad to make him remain behind. He said he would ask Pretty. The decision was his to make. Pretty was on the plane. Decision made.

Cho knew the mission came first. He asked Jack to put the mission off, until the wedding was over. He knew Jack's answer. He could not disagree. Mike would have to miss this event.

Many of the ladies arrived at the cabin. Mike was gone, the cabin was empty. Boo went home with Susan.

UNEXPECTED SHOT

Dawn swept across each house. The remaining shadow of the night ran from the morning sunlight. It could not escape the day. Many of the Seal team awoke early, with breakfast waiting. With a full belly, each kissed their loved ones before leaving the house. Those not married, planned for an early departure at the hotel they were staying at.

Cho awoke with Laura cradled in his arms. Both walked into the kitchen.

Laura turns to Cho," it's not too late to say, no."

"Never honey."

"Just giving you one more opportunity to change your mind, Cho. This is forever. Just so you know, don't you dare back out now. Honey, why didn't Mike stay the night with us?"

"Babe, he been away for a long time. He wanted to go home. He will be there for only this night. Susan remained the night at the cabin with him. She will take care of his needs, before morning."

Boo remained on Mike's lap the entire night. Susan slept next to Mike on his bed. Morning came early, seemingly to Mike. Susan was up making breakfast. Mike didn't feel much about eating. She insisted. Boo sat on his lap.

All through the night, Mike had difficulties trying to sleep, lying down. Mister Casper kept Mike company throughout the night. The word wall was worn from all the messages appearing on it. Mister Casper informed Mike of Susan discoveries. She learned about why, he was in the cabin.

Before morning, an eerie mist formed at the foot of the bed. It slowly took shape. Mike watched with intensity. A figure of a man appeared. Susan remained asleep. The image became sharper settling on the floor. A tiny, soft voice was heard by Mike emancipating from the image. He had to strain to hear what the voice was saying to him. After sometime, the words became clearer to Mike. Mister Casper was now capable of speech. Mike listened to his recanting of his life story.

Mike listened to Mister Casper tell how he died and about the man that killed him. Mister Casper's voice was a haunting ton. "My wife and son were killed by an intruder. He walked into a gruesome scene. Both were dead, bleeding out on the floor. The sight of blood made him sick. It was like that all his life. He passed out on the floor. The police arrived finding him and his wife and son lying on the floor. They thought him dead at first."

"The police never found the man. At a hearing, I recounted what I saw. My father-in-law doubted me story. For a year, he perused and watched him. My life was made a nightmare. Everywhere I went, my father-in-law was sneaking around, never once leaving me alone. He would tell everyone I was a coward and a murderer. I lost his job. Finally, I decided to leave my home, coming to this land and built this cabin. I lived in the woods for months, prior to coming here.

Mister Casper's tale reminded Mike of his adventure. They were brothers in that sense.

"My father-in-law located me, after searching for years. He came to this cabin to confront me. Once he realized I lived alone, he decided to even the score for the loss of his daughter and grandson. He knew then, I had not killed them. The police eventually found the killer. Still, he blamed me for not lifting a finger to prevent their deaths."

"We had a terrible fight. I was killed. My brother discovered the truth to my death. He had no evidence against my father-in-law. Shortly, after his discovery, my father-in-law died in a car accident. His brakes failed on his car plunging over a cliff. They found the cars after many days elapsed. He died in the car from his injuries and dehydration. It was possible, he might have lived, if the police discovered the car was driven over the cliff."

"Mister Casper, how can you know of your brother's involvement in his death?"

"Upon the death of my father-in-law, we met as spirits. He told me about his death. Everyone that dies and their spirits have not ascended, can communicate with other spirits."

"Then, you could learn where I was, all the time."

"Yes. There are some limitations. This is all I can tell you for now.""

Why haven't you ascended?"

Mister Casper did not answer Mike's last question. Morning was rising and Susan with the rays from the sun entering the one window. She could not feel Mike' body by her side. She looked at the table, he was sitting with Boo. She knew Mike had difficulties lying down. He must have awakened; she suspected he been sitting at the table throughout the night.

Mike marveled at Susan loveliness, sitting up in his bed. Standing, she walked to the table. Her bosom giggled with each step. Mike never saw Susan barely clad. Her figure was quite appealing. He was getting aroused.

Susan knew Mike was watching her. She hadn't mind. She made every effort to reveal her body to Mike's prying eyes. She bent over to put her shoes on. Her tee shirt was a vee neck. It opened wide, pushed from her large bosom. She was young and missed having companionship with a man. Mike was only a few years her junior. She learned that on the island.

Many within the club, thought Mike was ten years younger than her. She thought the same. That kept her feeling reined in. Learning he was a few years less than her age, made all her needs come rushing back. She found Mike more attractive with time. Soon, she realized, she was falling deeply in love with him.

Cheryl was alone at her home. Mom was at the cabin with Mike. As night fell, a knock came at her rear door. Bobby was standing at the door. She grabbed Jimmy, squeezing him hard. Kisses followed. Bobby entered holding Cheryl in his embrace. Both never made it to the bedroom. Morning came with both of them naked, embracing the other on the living room floor.

This love connection began as a ploy to get Bobby to help Cheryl get her drugs. Missing Mike and bobby here, their feeling re-ignited, again. Knowing Mom was in love with Mike, made her choice easy. She wanted Bobby more than ever. She begged Bobby's forgiveness, dragging him and the others into her drugs. She wished it never happened. Now, she and her friends would be faced with their families, learning the truth. She wanted the truth to be known. Mike said, "it will rid her of all her guilt. Take what comes and do good. This will help heal her," he said. She desperately wanted this terrible feeling to end.

"It was never too late to change, it is never too late to do good or help others," Mike said to her. She awoke feeling great. Bobby forgave her. All the others greeted her with hugs and kisses at the bar. She was going to be alright. Cheryl knew there was a price to pay for her misdeeds. That didn't matter, there was light ahead and that light, was love. They still loved her.

Mike left soon after eating breakfast Susan made for him. She made sure Mike kissed her, before he left. She wanted to tell him more, but held back. He needed to focus on the mission and not her needs.

Susan left the cabin with Boo. At her home, Bobby was there at the table. Cheryl was cooking her and him a meal. It was obvious Bobby was there, the whole night. Susan was tempted to say something. She held her tongue, Cheryl was of age and there was no need to begin to reprimand her soon after coming home. Besides, in one way, she was glad, she and Bobby were together. Mike was all hers, now.

Susan recalled Mike and her conversation in the cabin, after everyone left. Mike told her about finding Cheryl in a seedy hotel, drugged by the sex sellers.

Mike said, "he got her to take a bath and eat some food. Then, he had a long talk to her. She was afraid all her friends and family would hate her. That was why she ran, feeling they would hate her. He said, "he made her realized family was loving and forgiving. They would in time, forgive her. They loved her and came after her. That should prove how much they cared. They knew what she had done and still they came to take her home."

Susan was so proud of what Mike done with Cheryl. She was the luckiest woman in the world. He was more than any woman would desire, and he was hers. Mike asked her, "to trust Cheryl." It would take time, but she loved her. She knows Cheryl will have to answer for what she done. Cheryl wanted to face that by herself. It was important for her to stand on her own two feet.

"Mom, I love you, but this is my problem," replied Cheryl. She saw her mom staring at Bobby at the table and mom wanting to say something. She didn't. Cheryl realized mom accepted her as a young woman. She felt freed of her mom.

"Mom, Bobby, and I are going to check on our friends. I need to talk to them. We all must learn; we need to answer for what we done. This is my fault and my responsibility. I will return home, later." Susan said nothing, just nodded her head.

Mike said to her, "mistrust leads to anger. Anger can lead to hate. It is far better to trust now, than to come to regret, later. Allow Cheryl the opportunity to make the first moves. If she chooses wrong, then the hurt will come and go with little lingering for you. You will have a clear conscience. Cheryl was lost to you. You have been grieving for some time, thinking she was lost. Do not be quick to embrace her, until she has followed the correct way."

"Cheryl realizes her mistakes and is eager to prove, she will make atonement to ease her pain; that is normal. The sooner she faces those she has done wrong too, the sooner she can come to terms with her shame."

"Susan, Mike said, this is the time when you will be needed. She will come to see that her deeds, caused much harm. She will want to flee again. You must be her pillar of strength. Both of you will be challenged. Answers will be hard for the questions that will follow. They never are easy. We are not perfect creatures and seeing our imperfections for the first time, is daunting."

Susan revisited her memories at the cabin, prior to Mike's leaving. She sat at the table with Mike and Boo on his lap. Boo poked his head up under the table to get a nibble at Mike's bacon. Susan commented, "you are spoiling that dog."

"I know, but it has been a long time, since we have been together. I think we both deserve some spoiling." Susan leaned over the table. Both breasts pressed against the table top. Each fought to squeeze out of her tight-fitting vee-neck tee shirt. She looked at Mike, with a coquettish smile.

Mike's face reddened, when he was caught staring at her breasts. Look all you want, Susan said with an evil grin. You will have something to hurry you home with on your thoughts."

Mike, simple replied to her subjective remark," thank you, it helps take my mind off the pain."

"You are a devil, aren't you, Mike. Here, get a good look. Susan lifts her shirt up over her head, laying the shirt on the tabletop. Take off that stained shirt and put my shirt on. That will be a constant reminder of me rubbing your chest."

"Who is the devil, now? You are right. The look is a better sight. Ha, ha, ha;" both laughed.

"Before you put my shirt on, I need to change those bandages on your back. The doctor told Bell to do this daily." Susan stood, both breasts giggled.

"Hey, if you could learn to walk in rhythm evenly, both of your boobs could giggle together. People would pay plenty to watch them, do a dance."

"You are the funny guy. Now help me remove your shirt." Susan struggled to remove each sleeve off Mike's arm. His wounds looked bad. She held back her pain and tears. He did not need to see her like that, before leaving to go back to the island. She fretted with concern, whether he would return in his condition.

Once the shirt was removed, Susan began the task of pulling the bandages off. She was stunned to see all the cuts on one arm. Then, the other arms and on his legs. He stood to remove his pants. She had not realized cuts on his legs, until he dropped his pants.

Once all the bandages on both legs were removed, next, came the back she dreaded the most. Mike asked her to clean the wounds on his arms and legs, before removing the bandages on his back. Mike raised his pants. Susan was just standing putting her shirt on, when the door opened.

Outside, Mike heard a car approaching the cabin, he told Susan to get dressed. Bell with Penny entered. Mike was standing without a shirt on. Susan was standing from a kneel position. Both Penny and Bell saw Mike's backside. Penny reeled back out the door.

Bell walked close to Mike, facing the door. She saw the new bandages on his arm and legs. On his chest, the bandages had not been changed.

"Bell, you remove the bandages on his chest, please. I was just preparing to remove the bandage on his back."

Penny watched at the door. She could not bear to touch the bandages on Mike's body. Another car came to the cabin. Inside, was Cho and Laura.

Bell informed Susan to get Mike up early and she will come by to help change his bandages. Bell was stunned, seeing so many cuts on Mike's chest. Penny squealed, seeing the many cuts. Laura came inside the cabin. Immediately she went to Bell's side to help tend to the many cuts.

Susan slowly peeled the bandages off Mike's back. Cho saw the blisters. He knew the burns were not serious. Susan did not. She gasped with shock. Laura turned and went to help Susan. She gasped, but continued to remove the one bandage, still attacked to Mike's back.

Laura brought a balm Cho insisted would help heal his wounds quicker. Laura applied the balm slowly, not trying to open any blisters. Susan could not touch the burns. She feared, she would expose his skin, tearing the blisters. Susan went to the front of Mike to help Bell.

A display of all the cuts was before her eyes. Many cuts criss-crossed on Mike's chest. A sight, that would long remain with her. Every time to come later, she would expect to see those cuts, when Mike removed his shirt. They healed with little to no reminder. Many of the cuts were nearly healed. Still, a remembrance was seen with red lines marking where cuts were made for a much longer time.

Together, both Bell and Susan reapplied new bandages. Laura was still at work rubbing the balm on Mike's back. Bell assisted her, applying new bandages. Susan helped Mike put back her shirt on him. Laura and Bell noticed, he was wearing her shirt, saying nothing.

Cho watched Mike bear the pain on his backside. Each bandage being removed, caused Mike to whence silently in pain. He wanted to scream. Cho was proud his son could bare the pain. Susan stood holding the soiled bandages. She wanted to drop the bandages and run from the room. It made her sick. She had not wanted to let Mike see her get ill. She held it down.

Laura asked, if she was hurting him. Mike responding, not at all, Laura. I can hardly feel you removing the bandages. Outside, motor bikes were heard coming to the cabin. Four of the group, Cheryl and Bobby established, were driving up the road toward the cabin.

Skip, Lou, Macy, and Lydea got off their bikes. Skip spoke to all of them. "Cheryl and Bobby must be inside. Let me do the talking. Mike has company."

Inside, Lydea stopped, then screamed, then hid her eyes, then fainted. Cho caught the young girl, before she hit the floor. Laura turned, asking why they were at the cabin. Laura, also asked why they were here?

"We came to see Mike," replied Skip.

Lou looked around the cabin. Penny was watching. It was strange, the way all four seemed to want to check on Mike but were looking around to see if someone else was here.

Bobby and Cheryl were in the kitchen before breakfast, discussing their plans prior to her leaving over the ocean, to the island. Bobby would shoot Mike when he returned home. Cheryl had wanted Mike to die, for him and her mom being in love. She was a scorned woman and wanted revenge. Bobby often visualized that day; Mike coming home. He would go to the cabin, with Cheryl. Once Mike came to the door, he would fire his pistol. Mike would not be aware and evade the fatal shot, he explained to Cheryl before she left to the island for Mike's welcome back party from the desert.

Cheryl reminded Bobby; Mister Casper might prevent the fatal shot. If others were present, the bullet might strike one of them. She asked Bobby to not go ahead, with their plan to shoot, Mike. She forgave him and he saved her life. After a while; Bobby agreed. He was happy, Cheryl changed her mine.

Bobby visualized a wisp appearing before him at the cabin door. If Mike was shot, that wisp would come for him. A shiver ran up Bobby's backside. He imagined the ghost ripping his soul apart. The fear of burning in hell would follow. If not, the Rider club would surely make him pay. Cheryl or him never considered that, until now. They were high, before her leaving. He remained high, until Cheryl returned.

Bobby told Skip to take his pistol and do the hit on Mike, if he was not there. Skip held his hand tightly on the pistol, Mike could not live and tell the others what was happening. Bobby was supposed to be here, at the cabin. He went to see Cheryl. He never returned. It was up to him, to make the hit.

Mike sensed a threat. Cho was inside the cabin with the women. Mike was walking out with Susan. Skip removed the pistol. Cho dropped Lydea to the floor. Skip aimed. Mike twisted to avoid the shot. The bang was loud. The bullet flew passed Mike. It stopped, striking Susan. Mike lashed out at Skip. He ran before Mike could cover the distance. He jumped into the river. Emerging was a wisp forming around Skip's head.

Skip struggled to get to the opposite bank of the river. Each time he reached the top of the river's ledge, he was dragged back into the water. Finally, after swallowing a gallon of river water, he submitted to the wisp of smoke tugging, dragging him into the river. Cho was waiting at the other side of the river.

Mike went to Susan lying on the ground. A bullet pierced her chest. Bell pushed Mike away. Help me get her to the bed. Penny, get the doctor. Mike lifted Susan inside. Bell pulled her shirt back. A bullet hole was near her heart. It ran through missing any vital organ.

"Bell, am I going to die? Mike, Mike, where are you, Susan called out?" Mike took her hand. Bell looked at Susan. The bullet missed all the main organs. It went straight through. You will be bed ridden for a while, alive."

Cho returned to the cabin, dragging Skip inside. "Mister Casper stopped this kid from getting away."

Laura looked at the soaking wet child. "Why did you want to kill Mike?"

"He knows, he had to be stopped from telling everyone. Bobby told me, he was going to be here. He was going to shoot Mike. It was Cheryl and Bobby's plan. Mike knew about us selling drugs. I'm sorry. Please don't hurt me."

Susan stood in the kitchen at her home recalling that incident, watching Bobby and Chery walk out of the house. She knew the four kids were meeting somewhere. How could Cheryl do such a thing, after all Mike has done for her.

Cheryl and Bobby stopped at the cabin. The four kids were immediately sped away to the club house. Their parents sent for. Susan waited for Bell to enter the house. She asked Bell to remain outside, until Bobby and Cheryl left. Susan was shot but could walk. The doctor told Bell she made a slight mistake about the gunshot wound. The bullet hit a bone and ricochet back out. The hole was minor.

Mike left knowing, the bullet left little harm to Susan. He knew she had to face Cheryl about this revenge hit on him. He knew Cheryl was sorry and figured she would rectify her plans, returning home. The hit was unexpectant. Susan will learn the truth and tell him, when he returns.

On board the large cargo plane ladened with a Seal team, led by Jack were waiting for Cho and Mike to arrive. A lone biker drove up to the plane with a loud roar. One rider dismounted. It was not Master Cho. Mike placed his helmet on the seat, turned and walked to the plane's ramp. One comment came from Mike walking up the ramp getting greeted by the team members. Master Cho will be staying behind to tend to his wedding and care of his wife. Jack heard about the incident at the cabin from a phone call. He had not forwarded the message sent by Chopper and glad Mike said nothing. It was best no others knew. Tall' child was involved.

WEDDING BELLS

Soon after the ambulance departed the cabin, other Riders showed up. Cho met with Chopper, Razor, and Bone coming to the river. He was pulling Skip from the grasp of Mister Casper tugging at his legs. After several repeated dunking into the cold river, Skip was crying, pleading to Mister Casper to release him.

The three leaders watched a mist slowly fade around Skip getting out of the water. Cho took the young boy by the scruff of his shirt, lifting him onto his toes. Skip was coughing up river water standing by the three men.

"Hey Cho, why was Skip in the river and why was Mister Casper trying to drown the poor lad?"

"Chopper, this poor lad shot at Mike. He missed; the bullet struck Susan. She is inside the cabin. I don't know if she is alive or dead. Mike, Bell, Laura, and Penny are with her now."

"Penny, Bone cried, is my wife harmed. I'll kill that kid, if she is."

"Calm down big guy. Bobby was the main person sent to kill Mike. Skip couldn't wait for Bobby. Seems like, they wanted Mike dead before we learned about their nefarious activities."

"You mean them taking and selling drugs."

"Yes, that would seem so, Bone."

Skip looks at the men talking about drugs and them selling them. He attempted murder to hide that fact. That fact was already known to the club, Skip threw up.

"All this for nothing. I nearly killed two people. What will happen to me," Skip begged?

Razor turns to answer the foolish young man, standing, dripping wet, looking like he was innocent. "You should have thought of that, before you shot at Mike. What happens, is what you will deserve. Be content to know all those responsible, will also pay."

Bobby with Cheryl rode up to the cabin. They saw Skip dripping wet. Cho, Chopper, Bone, and Razor were by him. The leaders turned looking at the two stopping in front of the cabin. Each had a scorn look across their faces.

All the kids involved were at the cabin. They immediately cluttered around their two leaders, Bobby and Cheryl.

Lydea spoke in a soft voice to Bobby. "They know. Following her, was Macy.

"Skip tried to shoot Mike with your pistol, Bobby. He missed and your, your mom, Susan. They are in the cabin. We think Cheryl, your mom is dying."

Cheryl screamed, then hopped off the back of Bobby's bike running inside the cabin. Bone yelled at the kids, by the Bobby.

"Hold on there you four, we got a problem. Stay where you are."

Bobby was about to get off his bike, but reseated himself. A flashing thought quickly came and left to bolt off his bike. Where, replaced that temptation. Cho left the three men to deal with the group outside. Inside, Cheryl was by Susan's bed crying, begging for forgiveness.

"Me and Bobby left the house to find the others, to end their plan of killing Mike. We were too late. Cheryl feels a hand lay on her shoulder. It was Mike's.

"Cheryl, your mom is fine. The bullet fragmented. Only a small sliver did little damage, it passed through her body, out the rear with no harm done to any organs. It will heal quick. She will need some bed time and a person to be by her side. Can you take on this job? I would, but it seems we need to return to the island to clean up what we left behind. Cho will explain it to you."

Bell met with the three men outside the cabin. Chopper babe, these young murders came to the cabin under the pretense to welcome Mike back. They planned to murder Mike. Cheryl and Bobby cooked up this plan, before we left to the island. Mike learned of their drugs or they thought he hadn't. Their fear we would learn this secret, driving them to murder. Skip couldn't wait for Bobby to come and do the deed. He took the pistol and fired at Mike. He missed. The rest you know."

"Yes, Skip said as much. Bobby filled in the gaps. Him and Cheryl were looking for these four, to tell them the hit was off. We knew what they been doing. His main reason to do Cheryl's bidding was, because, he was in love with her. They been lovers, while Mike was off chasing One Eye in the desert. Bobby was jealous of Mike. He told Cheryl, why did he have to return? He is going to steal you away from him."

"So, it was not only for their drug taking and selling, but out of jealousness. God, what did we come back too, asked Bone?"

"Magic was right, calling me at the hospital. We got a mess, replied Chopper. Babe, I should have suspected this was going on. For weeks, I been hearing rumors about Bobby and Cheryl, while Mike was in the desert. Mainly, they been seen together, a lot. I thought that was only the tip of the iceberg"

"Yes, when the cat is away, the mice will play," commented Razor.

"Well, this adds up to one big mess. We return home, after fighting for our lives. Cheryl runs off. Mike going after her, then having to be tortured to get her away safely. Then, her running away before taken to a safe place. Mike tortured for nothing. Then One-eyed losing an arm, saving our women. Laura nearly lost an eye. We come home to be greeted with a murder attempt and five of our family taking and dealing drugs. Please, if there is anything I missed, someone tell me, cited Chopper."

"Boss, there is the wedding not happening, the hit on our club."

"Enough Bone, I was just being rhetoric."

"We got the wedding but not all the fixing that goes with it. That will be done after our team returns from this mission."

"Bell, you're an optimist, she right guys. Thank God for a silver lining in all this."

"Dang, the wedding, I plum forgot about the wedding," shouted Penny.

"Don't fret, we got plenty of time, Penny. Cho told me on the way here, it was going to take place before the plane departed."

"Yes, Chopper said, to wait until the wedding was over. Jack is coming back to the club house from the airport. I think he is a tad upset. You know him, when he gets ready, he wants to go."

"Well Razor, you and the rest need to get going, if you plan on being at the wedding in an hour."

Bell helped Susan home. "Mike will come home with us. Laura has everything ready for him," announced Cho.

Susan rode with Bell and Cheryl to her home. We will miss you at the wedding, Susan. Don't worry, I will get plenty of pictures."

"Won't need too, Bell. I intend to go."

"What. You just got shot!"

"It is only a minor wound. You heard what the doctor said?"

"Yeah, bed rest for a few days."

"I won't be moving much. Besides, it will be a short ceremony and afterwards, I will have all the time in the world to rest up."

"That and Mike leaving."

Susan did not reply. Cheryl was in the house. She feared her hearing that she wanted to say goodbye to Mike would open this wound that caused all this trouble.

"Mom it is fine. Mike and I, had a long talk. I told him all about Bobby and me. I told him, knowing you were in love with him, was okay. So, you don't need to treat me like a baby and avoid talking about the two of you."

Back at Cho and Laura's home, Laura was in a nice dress. "Babe, I am not going to wear my wedding dress, until we have the actual ceremony."

"You look great."

"I agree with Cho, Laura, you are beautiful in that dress."

"Good, glad you two approve. Cho, your suit is in the bedroom, Mike, yours is in the other room."

"Laura, I don't think I can wear my suit. I just got rebandaged by Bell, Penny, you, and Susan. Besides I changed into my battle gear. It seem tighter with the swelling. YI might need to have it peeled off me. Can I just wear the tux coat?"

"Nonsense, I will help you into your suit. You are not going to wear that hideous jacket and nasty pants to my wedding. Moments later in the other bedroom, Laura shows Mike his suit.

"Okay bub, off with the pants."

Mike slowly attempts to unbuckle his pants. Laura watches him tentatively try to pull his pants down. Mike looks up at Laura. Shh, don't say a word to Cho. If he knew, I was in much pain, he wouldn't let me go on this mission."

Laura understood, but still had a difficult time to decide whether to tell Cho. Cho said to her many times, "Mike needs to overcome pain in order to survive the missions he goes on." Seeing his legs and body covered with bandages made her realize, this was too much, even for Mike to bear."

Swiftly, Laura assisted Mike into his suit. Mike said not a word or feinted any signs of pain. Laura began to put his tie on, Mike asked if she would, fore go the tie.

"Laura, would you mind, this time I don't wear a tie. I promise to wear one for the ceremony?"

"Oh my, yes. You look good without one."

Now, sit down and I will put your shoes on. Laura slipped off Mike's boot. After loosening the shoestrings, she tugged on each boot. Next came the four-day old dirty socks. She held her nose, pulling each sock off by the tip. Only to discover a terrible sight.

"Oh my God." Mike had to cover her mouth, to keep Cho from hearing her almost screaming. Laura was shocked, seeing his toes were swollen, blue, and bleeding. The new clean bandages were stained with fresh blood.

Bell cleaned my feet and bandaged them. She got really mad at me, when I told her it wasn't necessary for her to do that. I told her, "I would change the bandages, they been done already."

"I can imagine what she said to you."

"Yeah, that won't take know imagination. She laid into me. Stop, stop, stop, she screamed at me. Never, do you ever, think that again. She said, do that for her and she might forgive me. You should have seen the look on her face. To be truthful to you Laura, I almost began to cry. I felt so bad about saying that to her. I know how much she loves me."

"Laura, do you know what she told me? She and Chopper thought of me as a son, just like Cho and you do. She said, "due to their ages, they might not be able to have children." She said, "when Cho adopted me and began calling me his son, it nearly broke her heart."

"I told Bell, I fell in love with her, the first day I saw her. She would always have my love. Her bringing me food, when I was frozen wet in the mountains, would always remain in my mind. Then, you up and marry Chopper, broke my heart. I found a new love, but she was my first. I told her all this, she does for me is out of her love and that I don't want to see her in pain, looking at my wounds. I don't want her to worry about me. I want her to be happy."

"That is some story you are telling me, Mike. I don't know what to say."

"Laura it is not my intentions to tell you this. I want you to know that Cho and you are just as much or more so, important to me. I told you this, because if this mission goes astray, I want you to know how much you mean to me. Cho knows my heart, you may not. Now, you know how much I care. I care for everyone in this club, but there are those that have a special place, reserved in my heart."

Laura hugged Mike. Mike held Laura tight in his arms. "Okay, think you can put these shoes on, Mike?"

At the club house bar, Chopper and Bell waited with all the others. Susan came in with Cheryl dressed just for Mike, in her blue night gown she wore at the hotel on the island.

Bone returned to Choppers side. "I got the kids in the back room. We can have a discussion after the wedding."

"Fine, say nothing to spoil this event for Cho and Laura. Shh, here they come."

Two doors are opened by a Rider as both Cho and Laura wait outside. Mike walks in and up the aisle. He was to be the ring bearer for the wedding. Chopper was the best man. Pretty was to be the best man for the ceremony. He was Cho's second in command and been with him ever since, he was invited to join the club. Every leader had his own small team. Chopper had Bone as his second, Razor had Cowboy, and Jack, Tall man. Since Tall man and Cowboy were Seals, they would be part of his team on missions, but, not on missions, each was assigned to a leader.

Cho walks in with Laura. Both looked great. Cho wearing a tux and Laura a beautiful long dress. Mike waited at the alter with the ring.

Cho noticed Susan was not here. "Why, he asked himself? She was one of the main persons involved with getting the wedding plans made. Could it be that her wound was worse than they were told? Bell said she was going to make the wedding. Now, she was nowhere to be seen."

Both Cho and Laura were met outside the bar by a cavalcade of bikes lined on both sides of the entrance leading inside the club-house bar. Both doors open. At the end of the aisle, was the preacher, Chopper, and Mike.

Bell was the bridesmaid. The music began, once the couple entered the bar. Chopper reminded Cho; he was to wait at the altar for the bride.

Cho replied, "I will walk with Laura up the aisle. When the ceremony begins, I will do what is the proper way." Thus, was it so, both held hands walking side by side down the aisle.

Bell stood by Laura and Chopper by Cho. Mike gave Cho the rings. He was glad to see his father was finally marrying Laura. He did not need to worry about him, while he was away. The wedding was perfect. Mike held out his arms to Cho.

"Do I get a kiss, Father? Cho chuckled at Mike's jest.

The only kissing anyone getting kissed, is Laura, my son." The whole crowd laughed. Laura gave Mike a kiss.

"Listen young man, that is the only kiss you are getting. Leave my man alone. Chuckled Laura." Everyone laughed again.

"I just thought with all this kissing, you might want to plant one on me, father?"

"I'll plant one on you later, my son."

"No need for that Father. I can live without that kiss."

"You better," replied Cho.

Bell walked to Mike's side. She watched him through the wedding ceremony. She saw the wet spot on the back of his coat. Cho took Laura outside the bar, to a car waiting. Cho turns to Mike, "I will see you soon. Be safe on this mission. Remember, you will need to be at the next ceremony." Laura kisses Mike one more time, then enters the waiting car.

The car drives off. Bell waited until they were out of sight, before hugging him. Mike's back was wet. She pulls her arms back, seeing a pinkest color to the wet coat on her sleeve. She waves to two biker ladies.

"Mike you are coming with me." Mike objected.

Bell, Jack, and the team are preparing to leave. This can wait."

"No, it can't," replied Bell.

Mike insisted, he did not need any attention. He left to go back to Cho and Laura's home. Chopper stopped Mike, before he went out the doors.

"You do as the women tell you to do, that's an order, Mike."

Mike turned and walked in the back room with Bell and the two women. A biker was sent to Cho's home to fetch Mike working clothes. Mainly, his jacket specially adapted. In the back room, the women had begun removing Mike's clothing. He stood there letting them peel his clothes off.

Once he was down to his shorts, one of the women let out a screech. She was not prepared for the sight standing before her. She told Bell, she was prepared for his many wounds. She wasn't. She was one of the many women that wanted to help tend to Mike.

The other lady fainted on the floor. Bell stepped out of the room, calling for Miriam and Penny. She returned, asking Mike how did this happen?

"Mike, I just finished dressing your wounds. How did they get opened?"

"I guess with all this hugging and kissing by all the women and some of the bikers, they were re-opened."

"Well, it is a good thing I brought some more bandages. You can't go on this mission, with open wounds." Chopper, Bone, Razor, and Rhonda entered the backroom.

Bell, Babe, Mike needs to be leaving. Jack is holding the plane for him."

"Chopper, he will be ready, once I am finish and no sooner."

"Yes madame, but hurry, please."

"Outside the room, once Bell was completed, Chopper met with her.

"Babe, all his wounds are minor cuts. Many have healed. His burns will heal soon. It has been a week, since he was tortured."

"Babe, how can you say that? All that blood doesn't come from small minor cuts."

Mike heard the bittering outside the room. He quickly tells everyone inside the room, he is fine. "I needed some rest. It has been a week, since I was cut. With all this tender caring by all you wonderful women, I am doing great."

Outside the room, Mike meets with Chopper and Bell. "He is right, Bell. I am feeling good. I am tender in some spots but nothing that will prevent me from going on this mission. I need a ride back to the cabin. I want to give Boo, the bad news, again."

At the cabin was Cheryl with Susan. Cheryl greeted Mike, before he went inside the cabin.

Mike, me, and Bobby been dating. I mentioned that to you. What I didn't say was, it was serious. He wants to marry me. I am pregnant. I told you about the others selling and taking drugs. I didn't want to tell you, we decided to have you killed. Bobby agreed to do it. That was before, we returned."

"I understand, Cheryl."

"I thought, I would never see you again."

"I understand, Cheryl."

"I, we felt bad. That is why we wanted to get them to come to the cabin, so we could tell them not to do the thing. I, we wanted to let you know. Everyone was to come here and tell you this. We couldn't get to them, to tell them."

"Cheryl, I understand. Cheryl, you did the right thing. It is not your fault, this happened. You attempted to rectify your mistakes. Your mom was hit by what you two planned. It failed, but the fact is, you two attempted to stop the wrong, you had done. Remember what I told you. I said, you will continue to make mistakes. One day, fewer mistakes, then fewer. You will learn from each mistake. Never doubt this, as long as you try to do the right thing."

"What Bobby done, was on him, not you. He did what you asked, but he could have just as easily, not done this. He chose to do so. He made his choice; it was not the right choice. To Bobby, that seemed the right way. People seem to look at their choices, as their only choice and justify it, with all sorts of excuses. Bobby will have to live with his choices as will you, and Skip."

"Remember what I said to you, we all make mistakes. To make them right is part of finding a cure for our wrongs. Good cures a lot of wrongs, we make. You will make mistakes again and again, just understand, faith will guide you, if you believe. The strength will come, with growing faith in doing good."

"I am going to break up with him."

"Why Cheryl, you just told me, you love him?"

"But, but, I."

"No, there you go with the excuses. Love is greater than that. Just because he made a mistake by trying to prove, how great his love is for you, now you use that as an excuse, to dump him. What must a man do, to show he loves you? Do you really love him? If you do, then commit to it. Don't try and say to me, you will dump him, to prove how much you regret what you set into motion. I told you; I have forgiven you. Quit doubting what I said to you. Accept my forgiveness."

"But."

"But nothing, Cheryl. Bobby needs you more than ever, now. If you love him, be there for him. I will be with you, to help guide you. Your journey will be mine, until that day comes, that it comes to an end."

"Now, tell me about Susan. Is she home in bed?"

"Ask her yourself, Mike. She is waiting in the cabin. I will remain out here with Bell and Chopper."

Mike quickly enters the cabin. Boo begins his yapping. Mike did not see the message written on the wall above his bed. He saw a beautiful woman in a blue nightgown, wearing a large blue sapphire and diamond necklace. Both embrace in the others arm. Susan kisses Mike hard. Boo stops his yapping. The door closes to the cabin.

THE APPOINTMENT

Every one of the leaders, except Jack, were present at the club house. Bone walked to where Mike usually sat. He recalled the hospital Mike went directly too. The staff parted like the Red Sea, seeing him walk down the corridor. Him arriving yesterday, was a shock to everyone. He was to remain at the hospital for many days.

He missed Mike coming home. He did manage to sit across from him at the meeting and again at the wedding. Penny made it nearly impossible for him to get to him, after Cho and Laura were wed. Then, Mike and Jack left. Jack went to the airport and Mike, back to the cabin with Chopper and Bell.

Bell was talking with the other women, about Susan staying at the cabin. They left her with Mike at the cabin, taking Cheryl home. Later, Bell returned taking Mike to the hospital, before going to the plane. He and Penny went along.

Bone recalled looking at Mike, sitting on the bed in the hospital on the military base before their return flight across the ocean. He was half clothed. Many slashes cut across his back and front sides. Then, there were all the cuts to both arms and legs. They really did a number on Mike.

Bell was in the room with him and Penny with the doctor tending to his wounds. He said, "Mike was lucky. Yeah, real lucky Bone thought with sarcasm to himself."

"The doctor went on explaining why many of the cuts and burns were not that bad. Many were shallow cuts, the burns, not deep killing the nerves. He said, "they may look serious but overall, were not. He would recover with time and rest. Keep the bandages changed," he said to Bell.

"When I think about his feet, Bone thought, how could my little buddy walk. Mike objected, going to the hospital by Bell. Susan went home thinking it might their last seeing each other, until he came home from the mission.

Mike said in an angry tone, "if he known they were up to this, he would have remained with Susan.

"Bell, you just changed my dressing, why do I need to see the doctor, before I leave?

Quickly, Bone changed the subject. "Hey, I bet your feet hurt a bit there, little buddy."

Mike chuckled, "yes it does a bit, big guy."

Two nurses enter the examination room. Mike was about to stand. Two massive hands pushed him back on his ass. "Hey, you said the doctor wanted to check me, not do some examination, Bell." Then Mike realized that this was planned. They waited until Cho and Laura went on their honeymoon.

"Yes, dear boy. We wanted to make sure you will be okay for this mission. We knew, you were not going to see any doctor. Susan was told. That was why she was at the cabin."

"Who else?"

"Well, Laura was told. She was concerned about you. She knew Cho was too but to damn hard headed to admit that you needed seeing too."

"He is correct, Bell. I need to endure my pain, to overcome it. It is the source of my Chi."

"Little buddy, we can do this the easy way or with my gentle helping."

"No thanks, big guy. I know all about your gentle helping hands. Okay, you three win. Let's get this over with."

Mike donned the robe handed to him by Bone, while the women waited outside the room. "Hey little buddy, you don't even see the bear claws on your chest. Kind of picturette. Gives you character. The girls will flock to you."

"Your just full of funny remarks today, aren't you?"

"Just trying to lighting the time, with humor."

Mike is escorted outside the room. Two nurses lead him with Bone, Bell, and Penny in tow. Penny remained outside the examination room. The doctor enters.

"Please remove your robe. Mike hesitated to strip in front of Bell. Then, recalled, she saw him unclothed several times. Once at the cabin, after returning from being chased through Atlanta by One Eye. The doctor inspected the burns first. He made a comment on the bandages. Bone thought Bell was going to explode in his face, if he said anything wrong about how she dressed Mike.

The doctor didn't say anything bad, in fact, he complimented Bell's job. Bone looked at Bell. She was readying to slap the shit out of the doctor. Later, Bell told me, she would slap his face twice. One for asking that stupid question and a second time, if he said anything was wrong with how she cleaned and dressed Mike's wounds.

The doctor looked up at Bell, "I want to congratulate the person, that did this bandaging, it was done expertly. Just wanted to tell that person," he cited.

That was swiftly followed by ripping off several bandages. Mike showed no sign of pain, nor flinching with each rip of a bandage. After examining several areas, he was content. He addressed the nurses to redress Mike's wounds.

Bone flinches every time the doctor probed Mike's cuts. He just knew they had to hurt. Mike never once showed it hurt. Bone thought to himself, "I 'll do all the winching for the kid." He did with every probe by the doctor digging into the cut wounds.

The doctor motioned Bell to one side. Whoever made those cuts did so intentionally? Each were shallow cuts. This man making the cuts, wanted this boy to feel a lot of pain. He will not need stitches. I wanted to tell you this in private, so the young man could hear."

"He can hear every word you said, Doctor.""

Nonsense, we are speaking softly and out of hearing range."

Bell kept quiet. No need trying to explain something, he wouldn't believe, anyways.

Both returned to talk to Mike. The doctor did the talking.

"Young man, you will not need stitches. Your wounds will heal quick. Those burns will take some time. Best to keep them clean and change these bandages often."

Mike could hear what was said. He already knew from the doctor at the airbase stopping at, leaving the island. Many of the Riders were not informed or if they were, it was not by him.

"Doc, what about Mike's feet," replied Bone with concern written on his face.

"Yes, I missed the feet. You did mentioned, he was burned on his toes?"

Bone heard the word, missed. That pissed him off. The doctor overlooked the feet to my little Buddy. What kind of a doctor was he?"

Bone began to count. When he made it to three, the doctor was going to have to deal with him alone. Bell asked Penny to keep Bone further from the examination. She heard Bone mutter, one. That meant only one thing. She knew, when Bone began to count, something was going to happen. The last time, was on main street in Mike's home town. Some truck driver smarted off to him, the police arrived to make them move their bikes off the road. The truck driver was thrown off the road before they came.

The doctor turns Mike's feet, then twisted, and finally tries to rotate the swollen foot. Bell had counted to six, now seven, eight, and nine. Bone was on two. He didn't count each twist, turned, or rotation as a separated offense.

"Yes, these feet show signs of being burnt. Ten, Bell made ten. No one knew Bell final count before she reacted, few wanted to know that fact. Bone was tempted to count three for that stupid assessment. He changed his mind after the doctor made another point.

"Both these feet have been severely beaten. One foot may have a fracture."

Bone quipped out, "you think doc. He couldn't help himself watching the doctor twist Mike's foot in contorted angles. If the foot is broken, it was the doctor doing all that contortion on Mike's feet thought Bone. Bell looks at Penny, she elbows Bone in a rib. He still made one last comment to the doctor.

"Hey, you think Mike needs an X-ray?"

"No, no, they are bruised and swollen. Keep him off his feet for a few days, until the swelling ceases."

The doc walks out of the room. Mike stood to walk back to his room, to change into his working attire. Bell went inside to assist Mike. Bone was told by Penny, to stay with her. She had a few words to say to him. Mike did not hear what was said, but could make a good guess.

The last recollection Bone had, was Susan telling Mike, Mister Casper shoved him out of the path of the bullet from Skip. Mike looked surprised. He thought, he side-stepped the bullet. So, it wasn't your fault that I got the bullet aimed at you. He saved your life, Susan told Mike."

Mike asked Chopper about the kids involved at the cabin. He said, "they were being detained in a safe place. They would listen to all the facts, later. Their parents are with them. It will be dealt with after he returns. I wanted to fill Mike in with more, but knew, I couldn't. "I did tell Mike; the police were being left out of this. It was a family matter."

"Now, here we are in the bar. Mike left with Jack on the plane over an hour ago. He was over the ocean when everyone met in the bar, to discuss the shooting."

THE TRIAL

Bobby sat by his parents. Skip by his, and Cheryl, sat alone. Both boys sat shaking. Bobby knew, Cheryl had forgiven him. They tried their best to prevent the act from occurring.

"Skip, Skip, if only he waited. All this would not have happened. He acted without approval. Bobby sat thinking, should he throw Skip under the bus or take the blame. It was easy to make him the fall guy."

Skip sat thinking, "I did it for Bobby. He was to do the shooting. Why didn't I wait and let him do his own killing? He is going to blame me for the shooting. I know he will. I going to be executed, by the Riders."

Cheryl was blaming herself. "Why did I make them do this? Why did I get jealous? Mike didn't want me. Bobby did. Why get mad at Mike, for not loving me? I had someone, before Mike ever came to the club. We were in loved. Now, I put our love in jeopardy. How can I fit this problem? Where is Mike, when I need him? He said he would be with me."

Cheryl wished she spoke to Bobby, before the trial. They had an explanation for the shooting. They concocted a story before Cheryl went to the island. It was to blame Mike, getting her pregnant. He raped her one night at the cabin, when they were alone. I would tell them that I was afraid to tell the leaders, about what happened. Mike was a powerful force. He was also, well respected. Who would believe her story?

Cheryl pondered on her next move. "In truth, Bobby was the father. If Mike found out, he would go after Bobby. That would help them say, they acted in self-defense. Now, all that changed. I pray, Bobby will not use our planned explanation.

Cheryl sat, watching Bobby tremble. "He is going to break and use their trumped-up charge. He was trying to remind me about the plan. Why didn't I take time to listen, when I got back?" Bobby was deep in thought. He did not look toward Cheryl.

"Should I use the explanation Cheryl and I planned after the shooting? I didn't make the shot. Skip did it, how can that explanation be used? They wouldn't believe our explanation, anyways. Mike comes home more the hero than he ever was. Not only that, he came home cut to pieces and burnt all over his body. What threat would he pose to us? Then, there is Cheryl. Mike finds her and brings her home. She quickly asks everyone to forgive her. Me, I'm looking like a fool. I'm only glad, we talked, before I went through it. Damn Skip. Besides that, Cheryl is a month into her pregnancy. Mike has been away for much longer. This plan, is going to pieces, really quick," thought Bobby. Skip sat near Bobby with his thoughts struggling to find any excuse to not be executed.

"How can I get out of this trouble, I am in? I got no excuse but to tell them, Bobby told me to hold the gun. It was my own doing to take a shot, at Mike. I don't want to die. Gee, I hope they won't hang me. Poison would be better. No no a bullet is faster. One between the eyes. Our club members are expert shots. It will be over quick, with a bullet. Yes, I'll tell them after I am found guilty, I want it by a firing squad." Skip smile knowing he will die fast with no pain with a shot between his eyes.

"How can I tell Mike, that I just learned, I am pregnant? Will he change his mind, if he knew? I am not going to know now; he left, before I could tell him. Maybe, if I confess everything to the leadership, they will go easy on my friends. It was Skip and not the others that took the shot. They came to the cabin, to back him up. No, no, that won't do. They were part of the plan. They are just as guilty. We all are. Mike was right, we need to face our wrongs and make amends."

"Mom and dad said that the leaders would go easy on the rest of us. Our taking drugs and selling them, will be worse to pay for. Dad said, "I would have to be restricted to the club area and be pulled out of school. He said that for Macy and Lou. Dad had to leave to go on the mission. Wish he was here, instead of leading that mission. Mom told me, it was more important than me. The whole club was in danger. She was right, when dad came and told me Mike was going too. If Mike went, then it was serious. He went on to tell me, those bad men on the island were coming here to kill everyone. Still, I am his daughter. Judy has Pretty. Oh, he went with dad. I guess, she wishes he stayed home with her," worried Lydea.

A door opens, Razor stood at the door waving all the parents to enter. Only the leadership was inside the bar sitting at a table. Bone, Chopper, Razor, Bell and two empty seats reserved for Jack and Cho. No beers on the table. That meant it was serious to Cheryl and Bobby. They been in the bar many times and never saw the tables, not have beer bottles littering the table.

Rhonda sat with Judy, with her was Bobby's mom and dad in a row of chairs spanning across the floor in front of the table. Every parent facing the leadership. Susan sat with Cheryl in the last seats

Once all were seated at the table, Chopper began to speak. "We have a problem. Some of you present are aware of some of the facts. I will endeavor to bring you all up to date."

Five, almost six months ago, we went after One Eye, to kill him. He was responsible for the ambush, killing several of our members months ago. He escaped on a plane with Mike on board. The plane was shot down over the desert. This much you knew. Also, Cho with Jamie and Pretty following them there. The search ended at the Twin Mountains with Cho and Mike wiping out two large, let's just say many soldiers."

"We planned a party for Mike and Cho, Pretty and Jamie at the island. Moss or One Eyed and a new man, Jimmie were with them. One Eye proved to be a great asset for our survival on the island. That will be another issue, we will deal with later."

"Mike remained behind, after the battle to continue a search for one of our own, Cheryl. Laura was injured. Moss loss his arm during this battle. We had to leave quick. Mike remained in a dangerous situation, alone. He located Cheryl, then gave himself up to the local mob, so she could be sent away to safety by the local ambassador.

Mike, knowing he would be tortured, surrendered to the mob. They cut, burned, and beat him."

A pause with dead silence, filled the room. Many knew little about Mike being tortured, especially the four kids at the cabin. Cheryl filled Bobby in on what transpired at her home. They attempted to prevent killing Mike, but was too late to stop Skip.

"Mike escaped and killed many men in the place, he was found. Two Marines and the ambassador came to his rescue. It wasn't required. They arrived to witness Mike ending the battle against many men. Mike was barely alive and still managed to finish off all those men single handedly."

"Cheryl ran away from the embassy to assist Mike with the Marines. They spent several days at an airbase treating Mike. He returned here after a week's stay. To what? Six people, he called friends conspiring to kill him. Why? It was to cover up their drug use. They thought he knew about them dealing drugs. They thought, without really knowing, if he knew."

Chopper turns to the kids sitting alone looking at him. "Mike never knew what was happening here. He found out when Cheryl told him. He did suspect Cheryl was using drugs. We all did. Not any of us, even suspected you were involved. You took that flimsy excuse not knowing if Mike knew, to kill one person that has done nothing, but help our club. He never asked for anything. He gave us wealth and security. Mike had stopped many of the dealers coming to our community by himself. Few knew and fewer thanked him."

Lydea began to sob. Lou and Macy started, after she begun. Cheryl grabbed Susan's hand squeezing it. Skip lowered his head in shame. Bobby wanted to scream; he was sorry. Chopper pounded the table with his gavel. All stopped what they were doing. The crying ceased. Bobby lowered his head. The rest followed Bobby's shame, lowering their heads.

All the kids realized how stupid they acted. Chopper was right. Mike did nothing wrong. He was their friend. How many times has he told us that, if for any reason, to come to him? He would listen and help, if he could. He said that their problems will be kept between them and him. He wouldn't have gone to the leadership.

Now all remembered what he said. They forgot, Mike never went behind their backs, to discuss anything they done to either their parents or the leaders. He kept their conversations and actions private.

"Bobby, and Skip stand, commanded Chopper. You two are accused of attempted murder. Cheryl, will you stand with them. Cheryl released Susan's hand and stood. Your actions resulted in another person being shot. Susan was innocent, a bystander. I want you to see, your actions involved others."

"When we do things, others will sometimes be harmed by those actions. We are not here to discuss what will happen to you all. We are here today to set the record straight. Now, everyone has the facts. No more lies will spare any of you. When we have a trial, the truth and only the truth, will be spoken."

Bobby quickly spoke. "Cheryl was raped by Mike." Silence came suddenly to the room, then a sudden eruption of chattered filled the room. Bell stood up.

"You are a liar, Bobby. How dare you accuse Mike of this hideous crime. He is not here to defend himself."

"He did it, when they were in the jungle. Cheryl told me all about it. We were in love, before Mike came here. When he went off on that plane, Cheryl and I got back together. That is when I was told. She told me, Mike raped her in a village."

Cheryl stood agape, listening to Bobby speak. "Some of what he was saying was part of our plan, to explain why Mike was shot. Now, Bobby is making up much of what he was telling everyone. Cheryl slightly recalled their plans. She remained doped, most of the time, when they were together. It was Bobby, he conceived of how the plan was to be executed. To me, it was just a dream. I met with Bobby and he reminded me of the plan. Both of us realized our mistake. Now, Bobby was too afraid to face the leadership with the truth. He decided to use their plan." Bobby stands up.

"I will admit that I wanted Mike shot. Skip took that pistol and did the job. Cheryl and I were coming to the cabin, to stop the killing. We got there too late."

Every leader sat stunned to this new revelation coming from Bobby. Bobby repeated the accusation of rape, Mike did. Bell wanted to ripped Bobby's tongue from his lying mouth. The room erupted in a loud chatter, again. Chopper slammed the gavel on the table a second time. Bobby continue his testimony.

"When Cheryl returned from the jungle, we got back together. She felt Mike deserted her. She confided in me. Later, she told me she was pregnant," plead Bobby.

"I know he was lying, now. I only learned of my pregnancy returning home. I told Bobby about it before coming to the cabin. I told him, he was the father." Susan was not aware of her pregnancy.

Susan sat looking at Cheryl, stunned that the man she loved, raped her daughter. Susan could not believe Mike had done this. She knew Bobby was lying. Mike was a good person. How is she going to convince others that he is lying? Cheryl had to tell the truth.

Bell took the lead in asking questions. "Why didn't you come to us, when you learned about the rape, Bobby? Why wait, until Mike returns from the island? Next and finally, why change your mind about killing Mike? He raped the woman you loved."

Bobby was ready for the question. It was what Cheryl and him expected they would ask. "We figured Mike would be treated like a hero, coming home. Who would believe what we were telling them? I couldn't allow Mike to get away with this crime."

The leaders sat quiet. Cheryl listened to Bobby telling them, "he couldn't allow Mike to get away with his crime. There it was. He confessed it was him, that wanted Mike dead. Bobby was taking the blame for the action, Skip took," Cheryl realized.

I told Bobby all about the island. I ran away, looking for drugs. I found a dealer. He offered to let me meet his boss, to get her off the island. They captured me, to sell into the sex trade. Mike with Bone and Laura, Penny, and mom came to my rescue. Laura got hurt. I ran away, again There was a huge battle at the hotel. Jamie was killed. Mike and Cho killed a lot of men. Mike remained behind to find me."

"Bobby had time to come up with another story. Did he know Skip was going to kill Mike? No, not possible, Cheryl pondered. Then, why is he lying and fabricating this lie?"

Bobby continued. "Mike surrendered to the mob on the island to seek forgiveness by Cheryl. He hoped his actions would show Cheryl, he was willing to sacrifice his life, to make amends to his crime."

Chopper asked a question to Bobby. It caught him by surprise. The truth was slowly squeezing through the wall of lies being told. "Bobby, if that is true, wouldn't he realize, returning home, his raping of Cheryl would be exposed? Cheryl would begin to show signs of her pregnancy."

Bobby looked stunned. He hesitated to respond.

Bell spoke up, "Bobby, Cheryl came home. She never said a thing about her rape. Mike said, she wanted to confess all that she had done. She told Susan everything, except her being pregnant. Why not tell her mom about the rape?"

"Bobby did any of your group know of this rape, asked Razor?"

"No sir."

"Why not?"

"Well, well, Cheryl and I, thought, maybe, but we thought, thought, it was a private thing. She didn't want anyone to know. We planned to have an abortion."

Cheryl had to sit down. "Never did I think of an abortion. I looked forward to having our baby. Bobby went too far." Everyone in the bar turned to look at Cheryl.

Susan stared at her daughter, with shock. Cheryl could feel their eyes look at her, as a pariah. Many women were pregnant, before they were wedded in the club. None ever desired an abortion. Life was precious, to everyone in the club. Death was all around them with their life style. A baby was a gift.

Bobby was slowly convincing many of the parents with kids on trial. None of the leaders believed a word. They knew Mike the best, he did not have the nature within him to do such a vile act.

Many believed Bobby's explanation about Mike coming after them. Some saw through his efforts to explain, why. Mike would still need to deal with the Rider's as a whole, even if he did go after Bobby out of revenge. Everything was falling apart, the more many listened.

Then, came the response by Bell that shook everyone, to see the lies Bobby was telling them. "Bobby, you said Cheryl and you went to seek out your friends to stop the killing. Now you expect us to believe that it was lie and both of you wanted to be present, when Mike was shot. You really intended to kill Mike."

"No, no, that not true. We did want to stop the shooting. I, I."

"Where did you get the gun Bobby," asked Razor?

"I, I, found it."

"Where?"

"I think I found it after, after, maybe later, I think it was when Mike, or Cheryl killed a dealer in the woods. Yes, that was when I found the gun."

"Bobby, you were never in the woods at that time. It was Lydea and." Bobby interrupted Razor.

"No, no, I learned from Lydea where the killing took place. I went there, to check it out."

"Bobby, a team was sent to clean the area soon after Mike reported the incident. All the guns were taken from the scene. Bobby's lying was evident to all. His pauses and stuttering revealed his story, had flaws in his story.

Bell stood, looked at Cheryl and spoke to Bobby." Did Cheryl know of the gun you found."

Bobby was in a pickle. If I said she knew of the gun, it would implicate Cheryl. She never knew about the gun. I told her, I would find a way to kill Mike. Cheryl assumed it was by a gun or that was what I wanted her to think. She knew about the plan, but not the where and when. She was told Mike was going to be shot. Skip was holding the pistol for me. If I said that them, Cheryl would hate me. That I could not bear."

Bobby sat quiet for a few minutes. Suddenly, he shouts out to the leaders and families present. No, Cheryl knew nothing of the cabin shooting, I planned that, before she came home. I tried to explain to her, what was going to happen, before we arrived at the cabin. She thought everyone was just going to the cabin to expose Mike about his raping Cheryl."

"So, Bobby, you are telling this leadership, Cheryl knew nothing of the shooting at the cabin? She thought it was to expose Mike raping her," inquired Bell?

"No, yes, I mean. I, I tried to talk to Cheryl returning home. Miss Susan kept a tight rein on her. It was only the morning before the shooting, I could talk to her about our plan."

Bone finally spoke, "Bobby is this all you have to say to this leadership. Do you want to repeal any of what you said? Before you answer, let me review your side to us."

"Bobby, you swore that Mike raped Cheryl. She is pregnant because of this rape. Cheryl and you devised a plan, to expose Mike on her return from the island. Cheryl knew nothing of the shooting. It was your plan. You found a gun at the place; Cheryl killed a dealer. The place was cleaned prior to you going there. Then, you say, you and Cheryl came to the cabin, to stop the shooting that Cheryl knew nothing about. You had a change of heart, on Cheryl the one you love the most being raped by Mike. Is that what you swear too?"

"Yes, yes, I guess so?"

"Hmm."

"Cheryl please stand, asked Chopper. Is what Bobby telling us the truth?"

Cheryl wanted to go along with Bobby's story. She knew he lied, but he was the father of their child. How could she speak against him? Then, Mike's conversation came roaring back into her head. "Be honest, admit to your crime. That is the first step to redeem yourself. Trust in the family. They love you."

"Mike said, he would make the journey back with me. He would endure my pain. He sacrificed himself to save me at the embassy. He gives always and never asks for anything. He said, my crimes are nowhere as his crimes. He killed many evil people. It could be easy to explain it was for the greater good. What I done was less than the burden, he had to live with."

"Mike said, Cho once told him, that killing and murder were two different things. God sanctioned killing, but not murder. To kill to protect others, to defend his family, to kill for food, was justified by the Lord. Murder was a sin of hate and desire. Killing was part of the natural laws, that govern life on Earth. God sent men to battle. Murder was not by God's decree, it was for the want of property, wealth, and desire."

"Bobby is using the lie, we prepared to tell. I was drugged and can't recall much of what was planned. I was mad at Mike. I wanted him hurt. Bobby loved me. I used his love to seek revenge on Mike. I don't recall us planning to kill him.

Cheryl paused looking at Bobby. Bobby listened, as she was exposing their plan. I told Mike about the plan on the island. I also said, that Bobby and me were lovers. Mike expressed he was happy for us. Even after I told him, we were having sex."

The room went quiet. Cheryl just said, she and Bobby were having sex. The unborn child Cheryl was carrying, took on another shocking fact. The child she was carrying, was Bobby's, and not Mike.

The next sentence Cheryl spoke, proved Bobby was lying.

"Mike never raped me. We never had sex. My mom asked Mike about his intentions, before leaving to his home town, after the battle in Atlanta. He told me, we were friends. He liked me a lot but not as a lover. I learned this later, after returning from the jungle. Mom saw how upset I was about Mike's away. Bobby was here for me."

"Mike, Mike, Cheryl began to cry. Mike said, he was happy for me. He wanted only my happiness with Bobby. Bobby and I planned on marrying, when I came home. On the island, all my feeling for Mike came roaring back. When I watched him and my mom dance together, well, I got mad. I got back with Bobby to get him to help me get drugs. Later, we had sex. We got; we fell in love again."

"Anything further Cheryl," asked Razor?

"We got the other kids to help us get drugs. At first, we kept them out of it. They wanted to know why we stay away from them? Once they learned, well, they wanted to belong. We got them on drugs to help keep them quiet, to keep them from telling their parents."

"Anything more," asked Bell?

"Mike knew about the kids on the island. He said, he would help me. He would stand beside me and endure my pain with me. We planned on returning and help the kids. Mike said, it was for me to confess to the leaders. I had to face my sins. He said, that was the one time that I would have to stand alone."

"Getting home, mom kept me inside for a time. Only when Bobby came by, did we meet and discussed the cabin plans. I was not aware of the shooting, Bobby was planning. He told me we had to rush to the cabin to stop what was going down. We both wanted to get there. Neither of us expected Skip to take the shot. He was to hold onto the gun for Bobby, to make the shot, That's all."

"Cheryl, whose child are you carrying?"

"Miss Bell, it is Bobby's."

"Then, why the blame Mike?"

"All I can say, is, I told Bobby the child was his, before we came to the cabin. The rape was just an excuse. I never knew I was truly pregnant until I returned home. I don't recall that part of the plan. If Bobby said I agreed to this story, then it was probably true. Like I said, I was in a daze most of the time. I know that is not an excuse and I stand by Bobby for this act."

Cheryl looks at Bobby, "I do love you, Bobby."

Bobby began to cry. Most of the family listening to both stories wished they didn't falter in their faith, about Mike. They felt a shame for doubting him. Now, they wanted to see Bobby get what he deserved. Not because of what he and Cheryl attempted but because, he showed them, for who they really were. Their only consolidation was, Mike wasn't here to see how they turned on him. They would make up for that, by demanding Bobby pay.

The front door opened. Jack ad Mike entered the bar. Chopper stood, when he spotted Jack come in. Bell stood, seeing Mike. Every one turned suddenly, frozen in their surprise, seeing Mike enter the bar.

"Chopper, the plane had a last-minute mechanical problem. We will leave late this evening. Pretty, with the other Seal team, stepped inside behind Jack. Judy went to him.

"Babe, they are having a hearing to find out what went down at the cabin."

Jack looked around, startled seeing all the families with their kids at the bar. His surprise was quenched, hearing Judy explain to Pretty what was happening.

Chopper spoke up. "She is correct. We have been listening to some amazing stories. Mike looks at Cheryl. She was crying. Cheryl lipped to Mike; she had told everything. Mike smiled at her. Susan went to Mike's arms.

"Mike, Cheryl confessed everything to the leadership. She did wonderful. I wished all this hadn't happened."

"I know Susan. Cheryl and I had a long talk. I explained that to you in the cabin. I am proud she spoke the truth."

"Mike will you please take the stand. This is not a trial but a hearing to hear all sides. There seems to be some false accusations toward you, by Bobby. He claims that you raped Cheryl and is the father of her yet born child. Cheryl has shed some light on what he accused you of."

Mike was stunned hearing he was a rapist. Cheryl never mentioned she was pregnant, nor about their plan to kill him, and explain their attempts on him raping her. Mike expressed little to anyone looking at him, for any signs he was accused o, either true or false. Mike kept his emotions in check, as Cho taught him.

Mike approached the table, where the leaders were sitting. Bell looked at Mike with her loving eyes. She knew, he was innocent. In fact, all the leader had the same feelings, he read from their bodies and eyes.

"Mike, Bobby claims you raped Cheryl in the jungle. Cheryl stood and began to cry out that it was a lie. Bone stopped her."

"Cheryl, sit down! You will have your turn to speak after Mike has heard all the accusations, he is blamed for."

Chopper continues, Mike, Bobby further stated that Cheryl and him were lovers. He was dealing in drugs. It has been shown, Cheryl brought Bobby into her drug habit, to get his aid. The other kids wanted in. They allowed the other kids to join, to keep them from telling their parents. Cheryl claims, she was not pregnant, when she left to go to the island. She only learned of this fact, returning home.

"On the other hand, Bobby said, they both knew she was with child, prior to the trip across the ocean. Magic has gone to fetch the doctor to confirm Cheryl's claim. If she went to see him. He would have told Cheryl about her condition."

Mike waited, till he could digest all of what he was accused of. "Chopper, I talked with Cheryl on the island. She confessed everything to me. There were some vague parts in her story. Never did she suggest that, they confided in killing me. She admitted to Bobby and her, being lovers. She said, she hoped she wasn't pregnant. I asked her, was it Bobby or some man on the island. She said Bobby was her first man she had sex with. She went on to say, he was persuaded to help her, obtain her drugs. Then, she admitted having the other kids aid in selling and taking drugs."

"Cheryl said, if she was pregnant, that an abortion might be required. I was shocked to hear her mention an abortion. I told Cheryl, wait, and see. Susan will need to know. Don't make a hasty decision, based on a maybe. Besides, if you were with child, Bobby and you would make wonderful parents. I begged for her to be patient."

"I told her, to give life was one thing, then turn around and take that life away was, another. That would be murder. Her sin, would be greater than any of my sins. I took life, to preserve others from being killed. Her life, she and Bobby will bring into this world was created, from an act of love. If you kill this life, then your love was false and your sin even greater."

"For the other kids. They felt left out of Bobby and Cheryl not hanging with them. Bobby and Cheryl said, they could join them or not hang around with them. These kids have been together for many years. They all had close ties."

"I see," retorted Chopper.

"Chopper, Cheryl truly wants to do the right thing and make atonement of all her wrongs. She returned with me, willingly. I gave her a choice to leave or return. She stands here before all of you. This was her choice. She is willing to accept her punishment. I will stand beside her."

Razor spoke. "Mike how do you feel about Bobby and Skip?"

"Razor, I have no bad feelings toward either of them. We are family and family to me, is forgiving our love ones. What they done, was wrong on many levels. Neither did they confide with their parents or this family as a whole. They acted on their own."

"Which of us has not done things, we wished we could take away? Our actions today, will decide whether this family, is truly a family or it is just words spoken, then cast away, when we make mistakes."

"If this is so, then I want no part of this family. I left a family once and thought, I found a new family, that will stand by me, whether I was right or wrong. I understand Bobby's feelings. Jealousy can be an ugly demon to excised from."

Mike looks at Bobby and Skip. "I am sorry, I led you to think, killing me was your only option. I hoped to teach some of the qualities Cho taught me. Sometimes, a lesson from a mistake is needed to drive that lesson home. After what is decided here. Never think that I condemned you two. Please forgive me and think of me as your family. I will never hold what you done this day, against you. Just take this as a horrible mistake and try your best to make amends to all. That will be your redemption, for what you done."

Bobby broke into tears. He stands, rushes to Mike and embraces him. Please, Mike, I am truly sorry. I only said what I said, to protect Cheryl. I love her so much. I deserve my punishment. I take full blame for all this. Skip is innocent. He was told by me to take the shot, if I wasn't there. He is young. It is all my fault."

"Bobby, it is not all your fault. Cheryl has accepted much of the blame. Both of you attempted to stop the shooting. In the end, both of you tried to atone for your mistake." Bobby couldn't look at Mike. He buried his face in shame into Mike's chest. Cheryl went to Bobby, holding him. Susan went to Mike and Cheryl and hugged all of them.

"Bobby, I forgive you. Mike has forgiven you. Why can't you forgive yourself," cited Susan to him?

Skip hearing how Bobby was taking all the blame, ran to his parents. They embraced him. He turns to Mike. "Mike, I am sorry. I, I."

Mike stops his feeble attempts to say anything. "Skip, I forgive you as well. I want you kids to know; I forgive each of you for your part in this incident. I do this, in hopes that the day I make a mistake, each and everyone here, will forgive me."

Inside his heart, "Mike realized that was only a hope. He saw firsthand how easy it was for people to change their attitudes. He recalled the cave people learning, he was the red glowing eyed demon. He brought food and power to them. He ended the threat of the army, coming after them. They shunned him."

Bobby went to both his parents. Cheryl stood by his side. "Mom, dad, I will accept my punishment. I am guilty. Both parents were glad, he confessed and Mike had forgiven him. They feared Mike would seek revenge. "Cheryl has agreed to marry me."

Mike turns to face the leaders. "I wish to plea for mercy, for all of these kids. It was me, they intended to kill. I do not wish for any to pay for their actions. Please dismiss this case."

Chopper stood to react to Mike's request. "Mike this is not for you to decide. Bobby and Skip, step forward. Understand this, Mike has asked us to dismiss this trail. I have said, this was not a trial but a hearing to get to the truth. Do you understand why Mike has asked this court of inquiry to dismiss what you have attempted?"

"Yes Sir, both said. Bobby spoke before Chopper had time to explain what will happen. "Mr. Chopper, I made a mistake and I accept my punishment. I expect no less, than that. I appreciate Mike asking for a dismissal. I did a great wrong, not only to him, but to the family. He might dismiss this act, but the family should see that this action will not be permitted, without consequences. I am to blame and will take full punishment for all involved."

Skip mumbled his acceptance to his punishment.

Bobby, I respect your willing to accept our ruling. This shows me and the other leaders, you are trying to atone for what transpired. We have rules. No one is free to go against the rules. You will receive punishment for your actions. That will be decided in a day or two. Meanwhile, both of you will remain in the back room of the clubhouse, under house arrest. Two guards will remain outside the room.

All are to be treated equally under the law, there is no exception, because of your ages.

Two bikers enter from outside the bar. Each were told to guard both young men, until a decision is made. Cheryl asked Chopper, what was to become of her? She was as much to blame for what happened as the two men."

"Cheryl, you, and Bobby will be another decision for us. Susan needs your help. Remain at home, until we call for you."

Both Bobby and Skip went to their parents to say goodbye. Cheryl waited at the rear backroom door for Bobby. Both hugged and kissed. Bobby entered his room with Skip. Everyone went to the bar for a drink. Few words were spoken. Chopper said all, that was needed saying. Mike went to sit with Susan, after he talked to the leaders. Jack went to be with his family, before they left. He had an hour to be with them.

Cheryl returned to the bar area and sat at a table alone. Mike spotted her sitting alone. Susan wanted to go sit with her. Mike held her hand. "Wait, she needs to come to us. If not, I will call her over here."

Cheryl come and join me at the counter.

Cheryl sat not wanting to face everyone after Bobby revealed their triste. She was ashamed of what she and he done. She could feel all the people stares on her.

Mike called Cheryl a second time. "Cheryl come over here. Be strong and not afraid." Cheryl stood walking over to the bar with down cast eyes.

"Stop that," Mike commanded. You made a mistake and then tried to fit it. You stood in front of all and confessed to them, what you did. That is not an act of shame, but of bravery. That took guts, to do what you done. Yes, it was wrong. Still, you made up with the truth. I for one, am proud of you. Now, please raise your eyes and allow me to see those pretty eyes, before I go."

Many heard Mike's words to Cheryl. They turned away, pretending that they could not hear what he told her. They felt ashamed.

Bone approached with Penny. "Them be fine words you spoke, Mike."

Bone slaps Mike on his back. Penny tugs at him. Bone did not get her meaning. Five beers had stunned his senses. Mike shrugged the pain away. Susan wanted to slug Bone.

"Here Cheryl, I got you a beer. Mike takes the beer from Bone. Hey Bone, you know better than to give booze to a pregnant woman."

"Oh, yeah. You drink it little buddy."

Penny drags her man to a table. Bell was next. We never believed any of what Bobby said, Mike. Chopper said, you would never do such an action."

"I am glad that you never believed that, I would. Thank you, Bell, for your faith in me. I never doubted that any leader believed Bobby's story. Mike kissed Bell and she hugged him. Not so tightly.

Mike turned raising a beer. Here to our club and family. An hour passed, with all at the bar drinking, except for the leadership. The leaders went to the rear of the bar. Soon, they came back to their table. Magic called for order.

Chopper stood waiting for all to seat. "We decided to come to an agreement, before Mike went off on his mission, with the Seal Team, led by Jack. The gavel silenced the room. A few hiccups and a belch followed, before Chopper spoke again.

Both Bobby and Skip were escorted back to the barroom. "Bobby you were found guilty by this leadership. Skip, you are an accessary to the crime. We hold Bobby the blame for your actions. We do not condone what you did. You will receive punishment for that act."

"Bobby, you committed a crime against one of the members in good standing. Your first offense, was your conspiring to commit murder. Then, have others involved in this action. The second, was the shooting. You gave a person, not old enough to have a gun. You made him think, he was responsible to commit this act, if you were not present. The third crime, was to lie and perjury yourself."

"Skip you committed the act. You nearly killed an innocent person. You were aware of your action and the results coming from that act."

"Bobby you are an adult, this hearing decided to punish you as an adult. We have considered your attempts in stop this act, from happening. We will show leniency for you. The other act of selling drugs, involving others in taking drugs, and selling them, will add to your offense. Therefore, we made our decision on both cases of drug and attempted murder."

"Both of you will receive lashes from the whip. Many men in this club had to endure similar lashes whippings for their crimes. So too, are you to bear the same, for your actions. Each of you will get ten lashes."

"Bobby you will receive another ten. After the lashings, you will be put on probation. You will serve the court at its leisure, for six months. Skip you will for three months."

"This decision has been given; the sentence will be given at dawn, the next morning. No parents or members of the club, will attend. Only leadership, as our code requires."

Bobby's mom cried. His dad felt the whip, years ago. He expected no less for his son. Skip's dad felt as Bobby's dad. His mom was of a different opinion. She later spoke up against, how unfair the leaders were toward her son. It was Bobby that made him do it, was her plea.

Many of the biker told her, she should be happy, he was not sentenced to death. If Susan died, he was going to lie next to her in a grave. Skips mom stopped her complaining.

Cheryl asked Susan, if she could visit Bobby. "I am not sure. I think you will have to get permission to see him," replied Susan.

"Mom, we were to get married."

"I think, the leaders will allow that to happen, since you are with child."

Bell walks over to Susan and Cheryl. "Cheryl, the court decided on you. You will work hard, doing many chores for everyone. Every need by any person will be on you, for a year or until you give birth. You standing, telling the truth weigh heavily on the leader's decision. That and Mike's pleas."

Morning came slowly for Skip and Bobby. Mike left with Jack early, before the punishment. All the leaders were present. Both young men, were escorted outside. Two bars were hanging. Each was tied to one. Their shirts were removed. A blind fold was wrapped around their eyes.

Magic passed a hat around the leaders. One that chose the black card, would administer the lashing. Morning arrived with the sun. One man stood apart from the rest.

THE PUNISHMENT

Night was coming swiftly at the bar. Mike asked to go to his cabin. Susan told Mike to come to her home. Bell insisted he did not. Cheryl was there. Penny spoke up. "Mike, come and spend the night with Bone and me. We will love to have you."

Mike sharply replied, "that is sweet, but I need to spend some time with Boo. We have so little time as it were."

"Nonsense, we will get him. Both of you will stay the night. This way, Bone can drive you to the airport early."

Outside the bar, Mike hugs Cheryl and Susan goodnight. Many bikes were still parked with their riders at the bar. Bone revs up his bike. Penny replied, "no way, Mike is riding in my car."

"Aw honey."

"Don't ahh to me, you drunken biker. He will surely end up in a ditch, the way you been downing beers this night."

"Mike ain't no baby."

Penny ignored Bone. Penny was leaving the parking lot, before Bone could resaddle his bike, after tipping it over. A car was speeding up the cabin dirt road. Not one pole lights along the lonely narrow winding road to the cabin. Penny been down the road so many times, she could drive there blindfolded.

The cabin door opened, when the car came to a stop in front. Boo ran to the car jumping into Mike's arm. Hearing the blare of a bike, Penny turned around to see Bone driving up. All three entered the car leaving Bone standing at the cabin door. It closed with a slam. He followed her to their home. Their home was a large ranch style as was many of the Rider's houses. It had a typical three bedroom, one and a half bath and a two-car garage.

One thing noticeable in Bone and Penny's yard, a lack of any yard plants. There were many bikers ruts parking in the yard. Penny began laying new sod down after several attempts to plants shrubs. Penny turned to Bone with a nasty frown written on her face.

"Now, you either park in the street or remained solely on the driveway. Pity the biker and his bike that strayed from the concrete driveway onto the lawn; being her last words said, to Bone."

Inside the house, Penny was swiftly making Mike's bed. Mike entered and quickly given marching orders, by Penny.

"Get a bath and then, into bed, you go."

Bone heard her commanding Mike and made a quip. "Hey kiddo, this is just the beginning." A quick retort came from a drunk Mike.

"Hey Bone, I got just this night, you got a lifetime of this. Ha, ha, ha." Mike expected Bone's usual slap on his back. Bone with-held his little tap, remembering the bandages.

Mike, on the other hand, realized, "hm, no slap is forth coming, "Bone is now, my prey." Bone had to endure all his taunts and couldn't give him a reminder, to watch what he could say. Mike was not limited by caution; he could unload on him. That, plus he was so drunk, he could use that as an excuse, too."

That was not the case. Once he was out of the bath, Penny did not wait to get him into bed. He laid there looking at Bone's silly grin.

"Hey little buddy, thought you could get away with some trash talk, heh?"

Mike laid there, nodding with a snicker.

"Yeah, I thought as much, when you knew I couldn't slap your back. There are other ways of reminding you, Heh."

"Yeah, big guy, you best remember that, yourself, heh, heh, heh." Came entered the room seeing her husband standing vigilance over Mike.

"Ah, that is so sweet, dear husband, watching you tend to your little buddy." Penny leaned over pulling the blanket up. It was the worse timing she could have done.

Bone smiled and waited for her to leave the room. Heh, heh, heh; hey little buddy, what you think the men will say, when I tell them, Penny had to tucky-wuckied you, into bed, like a little baby Oh I woke you in the morning and you were sucking your thumb, wa, wa." Bone turned quickly exiting the room before Mike could make a comment.

Mike watched, "I know Bone is going to tell all the Riders or use this as a leverage, later. I'll never live this down." Boo hopped on the bed snuggling up to Mike. Thank God, for my Boo. You never would slight me, will you?" Boo licked Mike on his hand.

Morning came with the aroma of bacon being cooked. Mike sat next to Bone at the table. He grinned his devilish smirk. Boo jumped on Mike's lap. Penny placed a large plate of bacon on the table, near another plate of biscuits. She returned with another plate filled with a dozen fried eggs. Mike knew, he better grab his eggs first. Bone would clean the plate.

To Mike's surprise, Bone allowed Mike to take all he wanted. Then, the same with the biscuits and bacon. Another dish was filled with eggs and bacon chopped up, prepared by Penny, for Boo.

Bone had eaten, before Mike sat at the table. Mike, Babe, I got to go. Mike wanted to asked where he was heading, so early in the morning. "He was going to leave soon. Jack was to come over and pick you up." Nothing more was said.

Two bright yellow orbs of light lit the road, going to the club house. Thick fog made the light spread out, increasing the aura of the beams. The fog parted, as the orbs passed through, revealing a car's headlights. Behind the first car, were bikes. The car came to a halt in front of the bar. Each bike was parked in a neat row, beside the car.

Exiting the car was Bell and Chopper. Behind them, was Razor, Magic, and Bone coming up the rear. Two other bikers, Jimmie and Mandy completed the six.

Jimmie was the newest member of the Rider's club. He was the one man, that picked the black card. It hadn't matter, that he just became a member, it was part of membership.

Two young men were escorted from the bar. Each was taken to a pole. Neither wore a shirt. Both hands were tied to a rope attached to the pole. Chopper waited, until they were secured before speaking. It was customary to wear a mask.

No other persons were allowed to attend the punishment. This kept the punisher from getting payback, from others. Jimmie was handed the cat of nine tails whip. It was a whipped used in the Navy, when such punishments were allowed. It had a tail, with tiny metal studs on the ends. This whip had the metal studs removed. Both the individuals were young.

Jimmie, not being a navy man asked, "what is a cat of nine tails was?" He learned about that and another way, a sailor was punished on board a ship at sea. Keel hauling, a term long passed been forgotten. Once, it was one of many punishments on board a sailing ship. A main might be confined to the brig with bread and water for a long stay or abandon on a deserted isle. Finally, walking the plank in shark filled waters. Jimmie was thankful he was not in the Navy back when.

Keel hauling, as explained to him, was a sailor having both hands or feet tied with a rope. The rope was lowered over the side and run, under the keel of the ship to the other side. The sailor was tossed over the side into the water. The other end of the rope was pulled, dragging the sailor under the ship across the keel, and up on the other side. Sometimes, he was pulled back across the keel to the other side. He rarely survived a second, dragging.

Chopper asked both young men, "are you ready." A wooden dowel was placed in each of their mouths. Bobby was given a reason for the dowel not wanting to take the dowel in his mouth. "The dowel was to bite down on. It kept you from biting the tongue," retorted Chopper.

"Bobby, the whipping will begin and continue, until you receive your full required number. It you pass out, the whipping will continue, until the number has been dealt out." Bobby signaled his understanding, with a nod.

Chopper began the count. Jimmie pulled the whip back to release the tails. "One," the whip lashed out marking Bobby's skin with a red whelp. The first five did little cutting, into his skin. By ten; the blood began to dribble from lashes that whipped onto others.

Chopper watched Jimmie tenderly apply the whip. "Mister, either do the job correctly or I will have another to assume your duty." The next five lashes, left Bobby hanging by his wrist.

Bell walked over to Bobby, feeling his wrist for a pulse. "He is fine, calling to Chopper. Bobby was awake and exhausted. His face was ashen in color. Bell said, "he needs to lie down, he is going into shock."

Chopper responded;" he will finish the count. Jimmie waited until Bell stepped away. "Begin, Chopper commanded. Nineteen, twenty. Untie him," commanded Chopper.

Quickly, Bobby was untied and taken back into the bar. Bell turned to look at Chopper. She could see written on his face, how much he hated having to meter out punishment. For days, he would sleep uneasy and awake, fretting about each time, this was done.

Back at the bar, prior to the verdict, several of the members hearing the verdict and the punishment to be held in private, argued that all the kids should be required to watch. They were voted down. This was the first time Chopper allowed the punishment to be done in private.

Bobby awoke in a bed, in the back room. He looked up at Bell. She was gently rolling him over on his belly.

"Bell, I am sorry. I hope, I am forgiven, now."

Razor standing beside Bobby spoke, "Bobby in time, this will be in forgotten. Do the right thing, all things will heal in time." Razor walks out of the backroom.

Outside, Skip was waiting for his punishment. He listened to the crack of the whip. He cringed with each snap of the whip. Chopper began the count. Skip was crying, before the first of ten touched his back. Chopper signaled Jimmie, to make the count faster. Skip passed out, on the second lash. He was untied and taken to the same room, Bobby was lying in. Bell had completed Bobby's dressing to his wounds and was waiting for Skip. He was laid face down, still out. That is good he is out cold," replied Razor.

"Yes, this will hurt," replied Bell.

Mike with Jack, were entering the waiting plane. All members were at the plane, walking up the tail ramp into the cargo plane.

Cowboy, Pretty, Tallman, Jojo, Beedie, Skip Jack, followed by Jack and finally, Mike, bringing up the rear. Bobby was receiving his last of twenty lashes, as they boarded the plane. Skip finished his ten, when the plane was in the air.

Jimmie entered the bar, to check on the two young men, he punished with the whip. Each boy was moaning or crying. Jimmie looked at both and silently commented, "they ain't no OZ." Both cried out, when Bell re-applied ointment to their wounds. Jimmie recalled seeing Mike's whip scars. "These two men had less degree of a whipping. Little blood came from the lash marks. Jimmie looked at the shallow cuts. They will heal, with no scarring."

Chopper entered the room. Both young men were awake and moaning from their punishment. "Listen up, tomorrow you will begin the second part of your sentences. We have many jobs, requiring attention. You will work to make repairs to many of our places. Once all that is completed, you will be farmed out to do any task, required by any member. You will work and work your butts off. Your pain, will quickly be forgotten from all the work, we have planned for each of you. This bar will require cleaning, mopping, head cleaning, dish washing, etc., daily."

Skip spoke, "can we see our family and friends, Mr. Chopper?"

You are not to see or speak to anyone, except bikers you work for. No other kids. You will not attend school. Your schooling will, be here. We will allow your parents to see you, in a week. Do not try to attempt to speak to them. They have been, will be informed on your conditions daily, by one of the guards."

Outside the room, Jimmie asked Chopper, "why the guards."

"Jimmie, the guards play two parts, one; to keep them from bolting, secondly; to make them do their chores."

"Has anyone attempted to bolt, before?"

"Yes, we learned, they say, they want forgiveness, but given the chance, they will run. When that happens, we will find them and make them complete their sentences. After that, they will be turned away from the club. Any one not honoring their punishment, are not needed in our club. If they remain, they become a security problem, in time."

Suddenly, a loud explosion was felt inside the bar. It was the second time; the bar was bombed. Everyone was unharmed. Many were in the back room, away from the front, where the blast originated. Pieces flew everywhere. Windows, new, were destroyed. Bar was intact. Everything else was blasted into pieces or thrown into a pile at one end of the bar. Small fires were everywhere. Smoke filled the bar. Bikers came pouring down the dirt road from many places. Little was to be done. Bobby looked at Skip, "don't need to guess what we are going to be doing for a while, was both their thinking."

It was a message. Razor came back to the club house later that day, to report to Chopper. "We got a hit from the island mob. They made the first strike. We need to prepare for others. The word was sent to all the Riders. Family members were preparing to leave to safe areas, destinated for them."

A called was sent to the plane. It made a turn back to the airport. Bone went to the airport to wait for the plane to land. Mike exited the plane with Jack while the other men unloaded the plane. They left their gear at the hangar, with Pilot. The plane was commanded to leave.

Mike left with Bone. Jack remained behind to finish, then left with his men back to the club houses. Mike was greeted by Chopper at the burning club house.

"Mike, no one was injured. We got hit by the mob from the island. I called the team back, because Cho is not here. We will need you, if you are up to the task."

"Chopper, I left on the plane, to deal with this, on the island."

"Yes Mike, you had time to do some more healing, before you got there, replied Bell.

"Bell fear not, I am up to this. This fight, is more mine, than yours. I may not be in top conditions, but dealing with these men on the island has taught me, they are not worth much of my effort, to take care of."

"That might not be the same case Mike, replied Razor. This hit was or may have been done by locals, hired by the mob from the island. They may be better trained. This bomb was planted, without our knowledge."

Bell asks Mike to allow her to examine his feet. Mike removes his boots. Surprisingly, Mike's feet looked much better than she recalled. You are healing very quick, Mike."

"Yes Bell, Cho has taught me many ways, to help heal my body using herbs and acupuncture. Just another day and I will be nearly healed."

Bell nods to Chopper.

Cheryl was seen standing, away from the bar. She was watching Bobby, along with many bikers cleaning up the debris. Before the day ended, lumber trucks were coming to the blast site.

Chopper discussed, with the other leaders, after the first blast on the bar, to stockpile lumber. Inside the bar was cleaned, before sun set. Susan, with other ladies came with meals for the men. A short lunch break was called. Mike went to see Susan. She was shocked seeing, he had not left.

"Mike, Mike, I, you left, before I could say anything. Mike looked at Susan with a curious stare. He did not expect her to say anything, as he was leaving. What was there to say?"

"Mike, I wanted to tell you, living with Stephen had prepared me and Cheryl, to our life style. I am a strong woman. I don't need you pampering me. I will deal with what comes. I will cry and moan, but my life will still go on. I want you to know, I love you."

Mike was stunned hearing Susan openly express her love, with so many nearby. Bell and the other ladies heard her confess her love to Mike. Now, it was in the open. Mike looked at Susan, "I love you, too."

WAR COMES

All bikers were at the bar waiting to hear, the news. One day, since the bomb blast. Bobby and Skip had done a great job cleaning up the debris. Both proved to be good workers. Construction began shortly, that same day. Carpenters from the local town, were called in to begin rebuilding the clubhouse. Bobby and Skip assisted them. Many of the bikers usually would be doing most of the reconstruction, but now, that changed with the new threat.

The next day, when the bikers arrived, all the framing was up inside the bar and some new additions added to the rear of the bar to increase the size. Chopper scanned all his men, waiting to hear the report. He especially stared at the married men, among his Riders.

"All married men, will remain by your families. Get them to the safe places destinated. Others will be assigned to provide extra guards. For those that are single, you will receive your orders from Razor."

"First, get this area secured. Everyone knows the drill. Jack, sorry to tell you this, get ready to take off. I was in contact with the Director. We got a local mob getting their orders from the island. Get to the island and take them out."

"Will do. Just waiting for Mike. He told me, he had some things to attend too. He is going to get a surprise, hearing we are taking off again."

Bone, beside Mike rode to his cabin. Everything was changing fast. The cabin door was opened, when Mike arrived. Mike had decided to get Penny to watch over Boo. He wanted to ask Susan but decided, she will be busy with Cheryl and did not want to burden her with extra chores.

"Mister Casper, I am sorry, we are under a new attack. I need to take Boo to Penny's home, for care and safety. Many of the persons that came to care for him, will be elsewhere, protected by the bikers in safe places."

A note appeared over Mike's bed. "He will be safe at the cabin. Penny and Susan should come and stay here. All will be under my protection. I am aware of the dangers coming."

Mike understood the meaning, Mister Casper implied. He spoke about, him speaking with the other deceased spirits. He knew where Mike was at all times. After what Mister Casper did with intruders in the past, Mike felt, he was quite capable.

"Bone, I think that is a great plan. Penny, Susan, and Boo will be far better protected by Mister Casper, than anywhere else, they are."

Bone pondered on what Mike was proposing. I ain't as sure as little buddy about Mister Casper's keeping them safe? A ghost protecting my wife is a bit hard to swallow for me."

"No hard feelings Mister Casper, but I will feel better, if she was with other bikers and their families," replied Bone to a blank wall.

Mike heard the sound of a car approaching outside the cabin. Bone and Mike stepped out. The car stopped by their bike. Penny, along with Susan, and Cheryl stepped out of the car.

"Well, didn't expect to see you here, Mike. Last I saw of you, was you leaving to catch a plane."

"Oh, Chopper had the plane return after the bar got blasted. Now, we are off again. The mob had hired locals to do their biddings. Chopper wants us to get back in the air. We are to take out the command on the island and continue to the mainland. He wants nothing to fear, later. Intel from some man, he called the Director, filled him in on the details."

"Why are you here, then," asked Susan?

"I came back, to take Boo over to Penny's home."

"Why, he has always been staying at our house?"

"I figured, you and Cheryl might have a lot to fix between you and her. Boo, might be in the way. That has changed." Susan and Penny were about to make a comment before Mike could finish. He held his hand to halt their attempts to make this into a contest. Both halted what they wanted to say.

"Mister Casper and I have had a long conversation, when I returned from the desert. He asked me, to keep Boo in the cabin. He also requested that you, Cheryl, and Penny remain in the cabin. Before you came here, he asked that all the ladies, with their children of the leadership come and stay at the cabin. We were just leaving to inform Bell, Miriam, and Rhonda, and her children; Mister Casper invited them to stay in the cabin. Before you decide, let me say, I think this will be a great idea. Mister Casper has informed me, about many things. You are aware of past events, he interceded, saving my life and yours Susan and Cheryl."

After a pause, Mike continues. "Mister Casper has told me much about the spirit connections, he has. You will be far safer here, than any other place."

Susan readily accepted the invite from Mister Casper. Penny looked at Bone. "Baby, I will remain here with her." Bone said nothing. Mike informed many things, Mister Casper said to him, to Bone.

"Susan, I must leave. Return home and get your things. Please stop at the club and inform Bell and Chopper of Mister Casper's invite. Bone is remaining, as a guard at the cabin."

Both Skip and Bobby were assigned a duty within the club for the coming battle. Each, knew how to use weapons. Training was required for all kids, above the age of twelve.

Cheryl stayed at the bar hoping to see Bobby, while Penny and Susan left to collect their belongings, after they spoke to Chopper. Chopper had his doubts, until Susan mentioned to him, Mister Casper demanded them to come. He sensed their safety was at the cabin, instead of a safe house. Susan mentioned, he spoke to other spirits.

Susan was feeling a tab down, after leaving the cabin. Bone, Cheryl, and Penny walked inside the cabin, to give Mike some alone time with Susan. Mike bent down near the car door. Susan sat waiting to listen to what, he wanted to say. It came to a surprise, to her, it wasn't what she thought he was going to tell her.

Susan looked concerned watching Mike's eyes. "Susan, I am needed again. Cho, being on his honeymoon. It was our plan to wait, until he came home and I was in better shape. This attack, changed all that. The club and families are in grave danger from this island mob. This time, it comes from locals paid by the island mobsters."

Mike held back, what he wanted to tell Susan. She had been through much, Cheryl running off, Laura hurt, the battle on the island, him being tortured. Bobby and Skip plan to kill him. Skip missed and shot her, then, the trial and revelation that Cheryl was pregnant, followed by the bar being blown up.

Susan listened, hiding her feelings from Mike. She knew Mike had senses, superior to many. Cho training developed his senses, to be a tuned to others thoughts and their feelings. Mike could see Susan's poor attempts, to shield what she was feeling from him.

Mike looked at Susan. She was concerned. Mike spoke softly, "Look Susan, I talked to Cheryl about, why it is difficult for me to have a relationship with any woman. Cho spent years, trying to avoid a relationship. He said to me, "it was because it would require an exceptional kind of woman to endure the constant dangers, he would be exposed too. He found a woman, he just wedded, Laura."

"I hoped to be as fortunate with my choice. It took many years for him to find happiness. Mike hesitated saying, Susan was the one, he was referring too. Instead, he said, "you will be on my thoughts constantly. I will be thinking of you, on this trip. Please stay safe. Mister Casper has the ability to know much about where I am and my condition. If you have a need to learn about me, ask him, in private. The others are not to be told."

Susan remained in the car sitting, Mike stood walking over to Bone's bike. Bone kissed Penny bye and both got on the bike. Susan yelled at Mike. The bike's engine roar was loud. They rode off with Susan screaming, "I loved you." Mike did not hear her cries.

Susan realized to late, Mike was trying to alert her, he might not return from this trip. Stephen had often said, the same to her. Penny came outside seeing Susan standing with her head bent down.

"What is wrong, Susan? Penny saw her tears wrapping her arms around Susan. Oh my, you really love Mike. Have faith in him, Susan."

Susan looked up to Penny, "I do have faith in him. This time, I think he has little faith in me. This is why, I am crying."

"Nonsense. Mike loves you. He knows, you love him. Bone said this much to me. So quit this crying, he is coming back."

At the airfield, Jack was waiting for Mike. Get the lead out and board the plane, oh great and powerful, OZ. Mike scuffles swiftly to the plane. Bone slaps Jack on his back. Kids always late, huh, Jack?"

"That's gonna change, before this trip is over, Bone."

"Hey kid, glad to see you could make it back. Thought you chickened out, heh, heh," snapped Cowboy.

"Shh, elbowed Beedie into Cowboy's side. Mike will get his feelings hurt."

"What you talking about, he going to whine like a baby, all the way there." "No way Magic, didn't you here, Mike is going to show us how to deal with these bad ass island mobsters."

"Yeah, I heard Jack, Razor, and some of the women, how he took on the whole island, single handedly. All we be doing, is sitting, drinking cold beers, on this trip."

Jack walks on board. "Cut the kidding with Mike. He shouldn't be coming on this trip, in his condition. Just in case you haven't heard, he was tortured on the island. He been home, just under a week. We learned of this two days ago. I have seen some of what they done to him. Every one of you S.O.B.s would be in bed. If Cho wasn't on his honeymoon, Mike wouldn't be allowed to come. Mike, for your information, insisted on coming on this trip. Give him some rest time. We are going to be damn glad, he came, before this is over."

"Hell Jack, we are just joshing him, like we do all the newbies. Mike knows this." Cowboy turns to Mike. Mike responds before Cowboy speaks.

"Sure, I do, Jack; it is just them, releasing their pent-up fears. They need someone to show how brave, they are."

"See Jack, he understands, wait, what did you just say buckeroo," asked Cowboy?

"Cowboy, Mike just said, you were scared. Can't you take some joshing, spoke Pretty, ha, ha, ha. Mike, I am damn glad to have you on the team."

"Thanks Pretty. You coming along, makes two snipers on this trip."

"Wrong Mike, retorted Tallman. All of us are snipers. If we count you, that makes seven. I saw how good you can shoot. I, also heard, you are not up to snuff. I guess, we will be doing all the hard work now, all the men laughed?"

Mike took the chiding in good nature. All the members of the Seal team saw Mike and Cho in action, in Mexico, and prior to that, at the mansion. And again, in the jungles chasing pirates. Many cited to Jack, they were dam glad, he was on their side, seeing him do what he did to all the pirates, alone. That was when Cheryl drafted his new call name, OZ.

On the plane, Jack went over the plan. He went over the plan again and again, before the plane reached its destination. The loud roar of the engines made hearing him, difficult.

"Listen up, you all know, we are heading to the island. Mike, this is your second trip. I will count on your knowledge about the places, we need to focus on. Once we take out every one of those S.O.B.s; we are heading to the mainland. Our intel has located the main man, living in a huge villa."

"Mike, you familiar with those types of mansions. You and Cho went in plenty of them, of late." Heh. Mike nods. The team giggles. One man, Beedie commented.

"Mike is good, at cleaning homes. Maybe, we should have brought him a broom and dust pan, Jack." More laughter followed, ha, ha, ha. Jack said nothing. Beedie was their morale man. There was always one man joking. He helped eased the fears and tensions in the team.

"Okay, allow me to finish. We got the state department blessing on this hit. Hell, we doing their jobs for them. They can't touch these people. Politics as usual. We can clean house and they, blame all that on a mob gang fight. Both sides get a win."

"Mike and Pretty will scout out the island. We will set up a perimeter on those spots, Mike will point out to me on my map. Both of you, will do nothing, until we are ready. Got that!" Jack looked at Mike saying that to his men. Mike got the meaning.

"Mike, this ain't no lone wolf mission. We will work as a team. We have only ourselves on this barren rock. If things go sour, we need to work as a whole, to survive. One thing, we want these S.O.B.s to learn, is we are not anything, they ever want to meet again. They will learn what they are up against."

Beedie blurts out, "Yeah, us hell spawns, bringing them all fire and brimstone. Oh yes, and no cold water." Everyone burst into laughter. Jack couldn't hold back, he laughed.

Once the laughter quelled, Mike spoke. "I understand that meaning well, Jack. In the desert, I spread fear of a demon coming from hell. They knew what fear was. It was two letters written on every door, wall, and foreheads of dead men. OZ. That is what we will do, on this island again. Every man on the team heard the report from Chopper, of the island attack. They learned of the horrors committed by Cho and Mike.

"Mike, you will return as the red glowing eyed demon, once again. This time, you will have help. Every man will leave the OZ etched or painted on every door, wall, sign post, window, and dead men. We will paint this town in those bloody letters."

"Chopper, Razor, Cho, and me went over how to best use fear, as a weapon. Cho came up with this idea. Cho is not with us, men. Jack turns to Mike. Mike, you are going to do the job of two, of you, without Cho here. Think you are up to the task?"

"Yes sir; But if you want them to think there is more than one red glowing eyed demon, I think, more hoods will be required with red lights."

"Got that covered. Cho thought of everything. Men, look inside your back packs." Each man opens his pack. On top, was a hood.

"Don then on. A switch is near the flap." Each man flipped the switch. The whole of the cargo plane lit up with red lights.

"Listen, while on the island, those hoods will remain on at all times. We never know who might spot us. One person can spill the beans. So, keep them on. Yes Beedie, even while taking a dump or eating," snapped Chopper?

Beedie lowered his hooded head. Jack took his steam. One of the men patted him on his back. "Can't say all the good stuff."

"Jack, one thing I should tell each of you. If you get separated or shot, ditch the hood. Don't let them capture you with the hood."

"Good point, Mike. You heard Mike, ditch the hood, if you are dying or about to get captured. We need the mystique and fear factor for any hope of success, on this mission."

Cowboy hands Mike a back pack. It was heavy, ladened with supplies. Mike declines the pack. "Thanks, I travel light. I can forage for any food I need. It will slow me down."

"Mike, take the phone, I must insist on that one gear, ordered jack's second. I want you to keep in contact, always. Whatever else you need, take."

Many of the Seal team members fiddled with a chore. Pretty kept cleaning his rifle sights. Cowboy organizing his pack. The others, had their own routines to past the time. Mike sat quiet. Jack thought, he was in some kind of mediated state. Cho did the same on missions, he was on with him."

Unknown to many on the Seal team, Mike could hear every word spoken and every movement done by each man.

Back home, Susan and Cheryl arrived at the cabin, with their belongings. Each had a weapon. Penny arrived, soon after they did. Bone stayed outside, with other bikers setting up a perimeter of mines and sniper positions. Two manned teams, set up a cross fire. Once he was happy with the outside perimeter security, Bone went inside the cabin.

Bone entered the cabin half expecting it to be changed into some woman's chambers, with drapes and dollies and all other girlie things. He didn't want to be around, when Mike returned, seeing all the girlie stuff inside his home. That wasn't the case.

"Well, I can see you ladies will be comfortable staying here," balked Bone seeing a Cabin unchanged.

"Funny, mister Bone, cited Penny. I hope you don't think we are planning to remain in this cabin like it is?" Susan, Bell, and Cheryl began to pulled items from their bags.

"Mike may want to live in this place, like a hermit, but we prefer a homy atmosphere," snipped Cheryl.

"Did any of you, asked the current owner, if he desired all this change?"

"Mister Casper has nothing to say. He asked us to come and he better well be happy for any changes, we make to this cabin. Boo barked. See, now it is unanimous."

Bell arrives with Miriam. Rhonda with her children, went to another spot. There was only so much room, in the small cabin. Miriam came to wish them the best. Her and Bell could not remain.

"Susan, Penny, I got to go with the other leaders. I will return, later. Chopper wants we to prepare the cabin for an attack. Bone has done a great job. I will be back in an hour. Here, take my bag. I got plenty of things inside for the cabin."

Miriam tells each lady; she is going to be with Bell. Chopper did not want all the leadership wives in the same place. He has confidence in Mister Casper, but precaution dictates to him, not to put all his eggs in the same basket. After some hugs, Bell and Miriam departed.

Bone was outside preparing his campsite, near the cabin. This was his area to defend. Penny made it clear; "he is to remain outside the cabin with the other men, guarding. This was lady's night out."

"Listen, my big bruiser, us sweet, young, helpless, weak women are grateful for you big strong, fearless warriors protecting us from them nasty bad guys, outside the cabin. Inside, we can deal with what you don't stop. Oh, don't you dare get yourself shot." Penny reaches up planting a kiss on Bone mouth.

Bone exits the cabin. Penny turns to face Susan and Cheryl. "See Cheryl, it is good to exert our woman power once in a while. It allows us to keep control over our men."

At a local diner, three dark men walked in. One man ordered for the others. He had a thick accent to his speech. A police officer walked inside the diner. He made this early morning trip every day, to fetch his morning cup of joe. He over-heard the stranger speak, with an accent.

A government man was assigned at the police station. The chief introduced the agent. Chopper had one of his men remain at the station, once he was informed of the agent's coming. Every officer was to report any strangers coming to town. One officer walked inside the station carrying a mug, with coffee.

Chopper got the news within seconds. His men rode directly to the bar. Men were planted at every conceivable area, for a good ambush.

Some men were sent out to scout for men attempting to enter the killing field, prepared for any enemy. Chopper had his men, stretched out thin, attempting to guard the subdivision and their homes. He wished; Cho was back.

At the police station, the Chief was readying his men to return to the diner, where three strangers are sitting. He was informed to hold back, by the agent.

"Not yet. Let us see where they are going. They may lead us to the main assault group," responding to the Chiefs call to his deputies."

The three men stood, paid their bill, and walked out of the diner into a car. The car drove south, away from the subdivision. A biker was waiting at each entry and exit coming and going into the small town. The four-door black sedan drove passed a biker. He waited, until they were out of sight, then followed.

Not long after the black sedan left the diner, two more cars left town. One went east, another west. North of the town was parked a truck. The black sedan halted in front of the truck. Men were mulling about the outside of the truck. Other men were in the rear. The biker counted ten men, he assumed, there were more in the rear of the truck. The biker viewing the truck, knew the area. It was a large open farm field laying north of the club house. The last explosion prior to this latest on clubhouse, Chopper had the field peppered with mines.

"Those men, if they intended to enter from the rear going to the club house, will meet a most unpleasant surprise waiting for them," snickered Chopper learning about the truck.

On the dirt road leading to the club house was never paved. One reason Chopper cited to Mike, "the dust kicked up by any vehicle would signal the watchers."

The first blast heard at the bar, was by a lone man coming through the farm field. The group coming the same way, might figure, the bikers would suspect their party to follow. They didn't. Snipers were posted along the field.

Chopper orders said, "allow all the men, to penetrate deep into the field. Wait until, the mines done their business."

Two cars roared down the dirt road leading to the club house. Another two cars came by a river. Men left their cars, following the river. They passed by a cave, under a waterfall. None noticed, the cave. They walked along stealthily, following the river upstream.

Everything was coming to a head, quickly. A three-pronged attack was their plan. Chopper figured there was only two good ways to the club house. The third was difficult to find by the river. He gave Bone by the river, the cabin to set up for an ambush.

Dust rose high into the air above the trees. A signal was sent. Chopper readied himself and his men for the coming battle. Both cars sped onto the dirt road racing to the clubhouse. They were to make the first attempt, drawing the biker's fire. The other two approaches would proceed to surprise their quarry.

The first explosion ended any surprise for the assault teams coming up the dirt road. None heard the explosion in their cars. Chopper had trees planted thick along the road, to hide their club house. Behind the hedge rows, was a ten-foot concrete wall. Behind that, was a fence with barb wire. Three barriers waited the team advancing from the road. They drove fast, not slowing down into the club house drive. They sped past the camp grounds, Mike once set camp. Chopper stood alone in the center of the parking lot, holding a machine gun.

Inside the underground control room, two men monitored the fields. Electronic lights and sensors layered the whole area. Chopper didn't want any kid from entering and get blown to smithereens. Cameras lined the walls viewing every angle of the field. Not one animal could crawl passed the monitors, without being spotted. A switch controlled the mines. One finger on the switch would turn the field into a deadly kill zone. It was flipped.

A second explosion was heard, then a third and fourth. Every man in the team advancing on the club house quickly realized, they were dead men standing. They entered a mined field. There must be snipers, readied to drop each of them, entered every mind of the men advancing soldiers.

The snipers began their deadly assault on the team. One man standing next to another, never heard the shot blowing the brains out of the man beside him. He watched the man hit the ground. He joined him, shortly. Each sniper had a silencer. Another explosion and two more shots, rang out. Ten men in less than a minute, were dropped by a bullet. Five by a mine. Those that remained, sat down on the ground. Their weapons thrown into the tall grass.

Below ground, the switch was flipped off. Chopper heard the gun shots standing in the parking lot. Both cars came to a screeching halt, short of slamming into this fool holding a rifle, alone. Each car emptied, swiftly. Every man pointed his rifle at the lone man. Chopper stood silently, not moving with his rifle held to his side.

Rifle bolts were pulled back. Bullets were chambered into each soldier's rifle. One man, approached Chopper. He looked at this middle-aged man, sporting a beard with a beer barrel. He said a few words to Chopper.

"Is this all your men? Did they run and hide, leaving you to fight us alone? We have seen this many times, in the past. Many men will be brave, until they face real men, carrying weapons. They scat like rats in a sinking ship, until the metal meets the petal, they will scurry and hide in fear."

Chopper looks at this man wearing a black hood. All his men wore hoods. In the field, mines killed men, wearing black hoods. "I see how brave, you are. You attack us, hiding your faces. Who is afraid? Me, standing in the open without a hood on or is it you? This debate has ended."

Choppers eyes went to the sky. The leader thought, he was accepting the bullet, he was going to get without lifting one finger.

"I have one question to ask you. Which way would you prefer to fall? Face down, in the dirt or face up, looking at the sky? The leader looked oddly at this beer barreled man about to get his brain spewed out, with curiosity.

Chopper repeated the question. Chopper stood stoic never moving one finger. His lips spoke, revealing little, to the leader standing before him. The leader's face exploded. Blood spewed in Chopper's face. The shot was silent. The leader fell forward, face down in the dirt. He did not decide.

"I figured; you didn't care which way you dropped. Face in the dirt, was my first choice, for you, Chopper spoke, wiping the blood from his face lifting his rifle.

Bang, bang, bang, three men slid to the ground. All three shots rang out simultaneously from three different snipers. The whole of the parking lot was ringed with snipers. Then, came the roar of rapid fire into the car. The driver fell back, his blood covered the windshield. One man, not all the way out of the car, dropped with one leg still inside the car.

Bell was one of the snipers. She dropped, the leader man. Bell watched Chopper unflinchingly stand stoically, in face of death. She was never prouder of her man, than at this time.

One man was dropped, but not killed. Chopper had ordered, to leave one man alive. He walked toward the lone wounded man; a whoof, whoof was heard overhead. He looked up into the sky. This was one thing, he had not expected. A copter was flying closed to the tree tops. It made a circle toward Chopper standing, watching the copter circling.

A machine gun, 30 mm. rapid fire, lit the area surrounding Chopper and the car. It was apparent to Chopper, the pilot was not yet aware, the men were all dead. The ground around him was litter with bullet holes.

Bell jumped up, running to her man. Teddy Bear grabbed her, before she revealed her presence to the pilot. He slammed her hard on the ground. She screamed to him.

"Let me go."

"Be quiet, Bell. We got this covered." Again, the copter gunner opened with rapid fire. Bullets circled Chopper on the ground. Miraculously, not one piece of hot lead came near, where he stood unmoving.

The tree tops lit up, like Christmas lights. Ever sniper poured every ounce of lead at the circling copter. Ping, ping, ping, little sparks flickered on every inch of the copter's hide, flashing from bullets popping on it. The gunner squeezed his trigger without aiming. Many of the rounds went toward Chopper on the ground.

One sniper's bullet, finally hit the pilot. The whirly bird began to spin, in the air. Smoke came out of the burning engines. It came down near Chopper. Still, he never moved an inch from where he stood. The copter tipped over on one side. The rotor hit the ground shattering. One piece went toward Chopper. Still, he remained still. A rotor blade hit the dirt, flipping up and over Chopper into a tree. Smoke quickly filled the sky.

Along the river, many of the black hooded men were nearing the cabin. Bone and his men were looking at the climbing column of smoke, above the trees away from the river.

Mister Casper was acutely aware of men, coming from the river. A note was written on the wall. Bell had not returned to the cabin. Susan read the note. A chill creeped up her spine.

"Men are coming. Bone is not aware of them. Be not afraid."

Quickly, Susan grabbed two rifles, one for herself and another given to Penny. Cheryl was watching from the window, at Bone. The front door opened. Five men she spotted advancing toward the cabin, from the river. Susan aimed, then, fired a short burst at the five men.

Bone stopped looking at the cloud of smoke. Turning, he saw five men racing toward the cabin. They opened up with a blazing lead storm at the cabin. Inside, Cheryl stopped looking at Bone. She turned, seeing men racing to the cabin.

Mister Casper slammed the door shut, before any of the men was withing reach of entering. Now, five men stood in the open, without cover, having women in the cabin, shooting at them. All scrambled for any cover. One man felled, before he could scramble. Another man made the turn, kept firing at any opening in the cabin. Bullets splattered inside through the window. Cheryl ducked, in time.

Penny shot missed, shot again, missed again. Susan took aim dropping her man. Penny looked at Susan.

"I am a better shot than this. Sorry."

"Just nerves Penny, calm yourself, the next man will drop from your weapon."

Bone saw the gunfire at the cabin. Foolishly, he dashed toward the cabin. His snipers were unaware of the danger at the cabin. They kept watching the column of smoke.

The only thought in Bone's mind was, "why did I listen to Mister Casper. Penny she is going to get killed."

Bone reached the road to the cabin. He saw two men firing at the cabin with dread. One soldier spotted Bone racing up the road. He took aim. The cabin door burst open. A mist, flew out from the inside. It went straight at the man taking aim, at Bone. Two men held their weapons, not firing, stunned seeing a spirit-like thing exit, the cabin. Quickly, the spirit wrapped around the man, aiming at Bone. A coil of smoke circled the man's throat. He gagged, desperately trying to remove the wisp of smoke from around his neck. He dropped his weapon. Bone closed the distance between the man aiming his gun, at him.

A giant appeared from nowhere, lifting the unarmed aimer high over his towering head. Bone brought the man down. Two pieces separated, like a wishbone. Both shooters stood. One was dropped by a bullet. One sniper turned in time to spot one of the two men, stunned, seeing a giant racing up the road.

Penny got the second man with her first shot. Both laid out on the ground dead. Bone turned toward the cabin. He saw Penny smiling holding her rifle. He knew it was her bullet, dropping the second man. Bone spotted the fifth man running to the cabin. He went inside.

"Oh my God," shouted Bone.

Penny was just at the window holding her rifle. The man ran inside with them. Bone ran toward the cabin. The door slammed shut, before he walked in. What the hell, he screamed. Inside the cabin, Bone heard screams.

"My God, he is killing the women. Let me inside Mister Casper," screamed Bone. Still, the door would not open.

Two snipers ran to the cabin, where Bone was screaming. "Let me inside, damn you."

Suddenly, the door opened. Bone walked inside. The cabin was empty. A man laid on the floor. He was as white as a sheet. Alive, but frozen, scared silly, lying in a fetal position. Penny, Susan, and Cheryl were not inside the cabin. Bone was about to scream.

"Bone, where are the women," asked one of the snipers peeping inside the empty cabin.

"I was just about to ask Mister Casper, that same question?

"Who, who is Mister Casper? We were told, only the three women were in the cabin."

"He's the ghost, that lives here."

"A what?"

"Ghost, where you two been living? Everyone knows about Mister Casper, the friendly ghost. Shh, quiet."

"What."

"Shh, quiet you two. I hear something coming from outside the cabin." Both snipers scrambled to the window. Bone peeks out the door. Three women came walking up from the river's edge.

"Where, how did you, you were just in the cabin, a moment ago," queried Bone?

Penny was the first to answer his question. "Mister Casper revealed a hidden door, on the floor. There is an escape tunnel leading to the cave, under the waterfalls."

"What, why then, did you not take the tunnel, when these blokes came shooting at the cabin?"

"Silly, we were too busy shooting back, to see the tunnel, he exposed. When you came running up the road exposing yourself, Mister Casper reacted to save your silly butt. If not for what he done, I would be a widow. I ought to rip into you for such a dumb action. I won't. Just promise me, you will not do anything, like that ever again. I love you." All three women entered the cabin. The door slammed shut, before Bone entered. He tried to open the door, with no success.

"What the hell, he screamed. Let me inside, you stupid ghost. I'll rip you into tiny little puffs of smoke," screamed Bone.

A note was written on the wall. Penny read the note.

"Honey, Mister Casper said, "you cannot enter."

"Huh, why?"

A new message was written, Cheryl read the words. "Penny, Mister Casper says, "Bone owes him an apology."

Penny yells outside to Bone. "He says, "you owe him an apology."

"What, you're kidding, like hell I will."

"Then babe, he will not let you inside."

Bone was pissed, because Penny was in danger. He forgot what Mister Casper told him. He said, "not to worry. They would be safe with him." Suddenly, Bone recalled Mister Casper's words.

"He's right. I owe him an apology. I doubted him. I am truly sorry for my doubts and bad manners, Mister Casper."

The door opened. No sooner, than Bone entered the cabin, a roar was heard coming up the cabin road. Boo barked. Bone went back outside. Chopper with Bell, and some bikers, were coming to the cabin. Bell dismounted first. She quickly went to the cabin. Chopper looked around, spotting four men lying dead on the ground. Bone spoke.

"We got one alive. Thanks goes to Mister Casper. He caught the rascal inside the cabin. He's still there, lying in a fetal position, scared out of his wits."

"You did good, Bone."

"Don't just thank me boss, the women did more, than I did. Mister Casper kept his promise. He kept the women safe. We know now, the cabin has a secret tunnel under the floor. All three women left the cabin, when this bloke, ran inside. Mister Casper got us a prisoner. How he knew you wanted some prisoners, Chopper?"

"I can't begin to fathom that, Bone. Mike might know."

"Inside the cabin, Penny will show you the hidden tunnel. She said, "it leads to the cave, under the waterfalls," Chopper.

Before night, the police arrived at the club house. Chopper and Razor waited for their arrival. The chief knew better, than to ask many questions. He wanted too, but with the feds here, it wasn't going to happen. He was glad to have been kept in the loop.

Inside, the partly rebuilt bar, the counter had bottles lined to the wall. Everyone was given drinks, on the house. The police had a few. It was a courtesy from the bikers. This was the first time; the police were allowed into the club house. Not even a search warrant, would get them inside. No police man wanted to serve the warrant.

Susan and Cheryl, with Boo went to the clubhouse. A medium-raw burger was his meal, served to him, at the club house. Boo was given a water-downed beer. Over time, he was known as a real booze hound, by many at the club. For obvious reasons, that fact was never spoken to Mike. Over time, Boo acquired the taste for the frothy brew. Susan, Cheryl, and Boo left the bar. Boo was carried inside. He was drunk. After all that went down this day, Cheryl quipped, the poor dog needed a stiff drink.

TO MANY RED GLOWING FACES

The war back home ended, no sooner than it got started, but not so on the island. The plane, carrying eight deadly men, landed in the dead of night. Eight men walked off carrying large bags to a waiting truck, parked at one end of the airfield. A key was left under the truck seat, on the passenger side. One man went alone on foot into the city.

A man drove the truck, with its passengers through the town. A town, that experienced a terrific battle. In many places, the lights were off. Approaching the dark shadow of a town, was an eerie sight. Passing through the town, many streets had little activity. It was not so dark weeks prior to the battle. Every bar was lit and of men drinking and whoring. Now, quiet with fear permeated the whole of the town.

Mike chose their headquarters. The truck stopped at one end of the island few residents ventured. It was for good reasons. Reports from the embassy stated, many people believed, rightly so, that many dead, headless, bodies were dumped in the waters. That report was discovered to be accurate, when a local girl went swimming with her boyfriend soon after, the battle at the hotel ended. Bodies were washing up on the beach.

Soon after the discovery of the headless bodies washing ashore, many of the island people began to imagine evil spirits of the dead men, would bring misfortune. Anyone going there, meant their deaths. That seemed to fit what happened later, to the boyfriend and girl swimming. Both were found dead.

The embassy figured, the two deaths was caused by the mob, to quiet all the fears mounting on the island. Visitors with money were quickly rerouting their vacations spots, to other, less dangerous islands. The lack of tourism was causing money to go elsewhere, with jobs leaving too.

Once at the camp site Mike established, Jack sent Pretty and Cowboy into the city. Mike was to locate the mob bosses. He knew where two lived. The other, was not readily known to him.

Meanwhile, Jack was glad Mike was with them. He was a valuable asset to the team. He pointed out all the hot spots. What to expect and where not to go. Time was important for the operation to succeed. The local church was the meeting place, if things went sour. Everyone alive was to be there, once a red flare was spotted over the city.

Mike was behind the bar, where he, Bone, and Jamie met the boss man. There was a small building with lights on, inside. Mike peeked in to learn why. Two men sat at a radio. Messages were heard coming in. Mike realized; the messages were from the mainland. This small shack was radio central for the mob bosses.

Cowboy was to meet Mike, at the bar. He spotted the tall antenna across from the bar. He radioed Jack. Pretty set up a sniper position above the bar. He could see the shack behind the bar and many other sites, of interest. Mike was correct about the spot.

Cowboy went swiftly to the rear of the bar, spotting the only alley that seemed to lead to the shack. Mike was outside the front, looking in. Cowboy saw Mike raise his hand to signal, slowly approach the front. Filth was every place Cowboy stepped. The smell was worse. The darkness helped. Cowboy was afraid to know what could cause such a stink.

"Cowboy, you speak the. Inside the dark bar, many men sat, drinking beers in darkness, talking Italian. Remain here and listen. Pretty has this area sniped in. He will have your back. I am going to watch the front, for the three bosses, across the street.

Mike sat across the bar for an hour, counting heads entering. The count was fifteen men entering, two men walking out, and one man thrown out.

Somewhere between one o'clock and two o'clock AM; Mike spotted one of the three bosses enter the bar. He was the barkeep, he met and later visited. He was the same man, the team put into the rear of the car. At the hotel, dragged up to Bell's room. He escaped, after the fighting ended and everyone was down stairs celebrating.

The barkeeper left the bar, thirty minutes after going inside. He hadn't changed much. He sported a beard, longer than before. He walked with a limp. Mike waited until he was several blocks away, before he followed. Mike was trained to see in the dark with all his senses.

The boss man stopped at a tall building, then walked up some stairs. He removed a key from his pocket, entered inside, relocked the door. A light flickered on the third floor. It was the only light on, in the building. Before the boss man reached the floor, Mike had scaled the front walls, peeping inside a room, lit.

The front door opened. A short dumpy woman, with oily-slicked-black-hair greeted the boss man. He gave her a kiss, then walked to a table. Food was prepared, waiting for a diner.

"One down," Mike thought. Mike crawled down the wall to the street. He was about to return to the bar, to wait for number two boss. He knew where number three lived. Mike decided to go to that home, before returning to the bar. At the home of number three boss man, a car just came to a stop. Inside, a driver stepped out, walked to the other side, then opened the passenger door.

It came to a surprise to Mike's eyes, seeing number two boss man, exit the car. The driver handed him a sack. The driver escorted the boss man to the building. Both, went inside. Mike swiftly went to the front door. It had a glass panel. He watched; the two men walk up a flight of stairs.

Mike saw the car earlier, before the first boss man left the bar. He entered after the first boss left, the bar. A driver stepped out. He came back shortly after, entering the bar. He was carrying a sack. Now, Mike realized the car was ferrying the third boss man. Why, was his next question?

Again, Mike scaled the brick wall of a building. It was a taller building. On top of the roof, he looked down the face of the building. Two lights were on. Mike slowly crawled upside down, on the side of the wall, to one of the lit windows below the roof. He hung there, like a bat listening to talk from inside the room.

It was a moonless night. No street lights revealing anything below or above. Mike was a dark shadow on the wall, to anyone looking up. Climbing up the walls to the roof was much easier, than his descent from the roof. Many bricks were loose. He jabbed his fingers into some of the old crumbly bricks, to keep from sliding down the walls. Finally, he halted at the lit window.

Mike reflected on Cho and Stephen teaching. "They did good. Stephen made me understand, how, light and darkness could be used to my advantage. Cho made me strong and taught me many skills, I put to use this night. Use the darkness to blend in. Make little movement and little sound, to a minimum. Above all, control your breathing."

Memories flashed in Mike's thoughts of the swamp. "I laid in a tree, listening to all the noises. Below were wild pigs, snorting. Every sound I heard, I tried to put a name to what made it. It kept me alert, the whole night."

The window was ajar. Light shined out of the window. Mike knew all inside would not see his presence, with the light shining out. Still, he remained cautious, keeping near but not in front of the window. The room acted like an amplifier and the opening, the speaker. It was not difficult to hear anyone talking.

A knock was heard, at the door. The second boss, opened the door. Both bosses went to a table, sitting down. The driver was told, remain at the car.

On the table, a sack was opened. A bottle of red wine was uncorked. Wine was poured into two glasses. The third boss did most of the talking, as the second boss took a gulp of red wine.

"I tell you this, with much fear in my heart. Not one of our men, will be returning home. Those men, took them all out. Not one of the Americans were killed. From all our reports, none even received any wounds."

The second leader sat quiet, sipping his wine, listening to the report. He was a short, pudgy, balding man with years of mob fighting, under his belt. Nothing seemed to faze him coming from the report, of the third man.

"I tell you, the plan was perfect. It went as expected."

"Hmm, apparently not," snipped the second man speaking without barely moving his thin lips.

"The plan was to attack, from three points. One, from the road leading to their club house. It was a seedy looking bar, out in some wooded area. Two cars drove down the road, into the parking space. This was a detraction for the other two assaults."

"The second, Team advanced from a corn cornfield. Tall stalks were a great blind, to hid their approach. Our men made their way through the field, to the rear of the building."

"The last point of the attack, the third team traveled along a river, it led along the west side of the club house. A cabin was the target. After they rid the cabin of any people, they would make for the clubhouse."

"Why this cabin?"

"This is the place, we learned, was a home of one of those demon men."

"If they were demons, why would they live in a cabin?"

"We don't think, they were demons. We learned from sources, a young American boy in the desert, was using the same red eye disguise, to put fear in the Muslim terrorists."

"Hmm."

"Our man watching the events unfold, spotted several snipers in and around the clubhouse. We prepared for such an event. A gun ship with men, were to fly in along with the two cars, to level the house, the distraction, the first part of our plan."

"Both cars came to a stop in the parking lot. One man stood in the center, holding a rifle. They got out of their cars. Then, each man was dropped by those snipers, before any of them raised their weapons. The copter flew in. They unloaded their guns, on that one man. Not one round hit that SOB. The copter was downed."

"The men coming up the cornfield, ran into a mine field. Those that survived were shot down, by men hiding around the field.

Somehow, they knew of our plans. Everyman in the cornfield, was mowed down, like the club house."

"The river route team faired less, than all the other teams. Women and children were in the cabin. They, took out that team."

"Alone, women did that?"

"Well, the report did say, a ghost aided them."

"A what?"

"Ghost, spirit, it attacked our men at the river."

"Demons, ghosts, any other crap to report?"

"No."

"Our first reports confirmed, all was loss. This new report came in to me. This is why, I came late this night. The report was in error. Several men were captured. They know, who was responsible for the attack. They are coming after us. We got to get off this island."

"First, you need to calm yourself, here, have a drink."

"I tell you this, our men were seen crying like babies. One man, from the cabin, was screaming mad. He kept shouting, a ghost attacked him. They know who we are. They are coming here. Hell, they might be on the island, now. A plane landed at the airfield."

"Calm down. Where did this plane come from? Were men spotted, leaving the plane?"

"No, it was an American military plane. It was spotted parked, near the end of the tarmac. No one was spotted leaving. Why did this plane land, without any body on it?"

"Calm down. The plane, was more likely there, to refuel. We have plenty of time to prepare, for these so-called demons coming back."

"Did you not remember, what they said to us?"

"Yes, and since then, I am convinced, these demons were men. We will not run, like scared children, this time."

"You think our men will believe that? Many recalled that night. Some are still in hiding, fearing the return of those demons with red glowing eyes. I think."

"That's right, you think. These men, come from the mainland. Every one of them were informed about these, so-called demons with red eyes."

"You can stay here, me, I'm leaving this island."

"You will and die my friend."

"You saw and felt what that demon can do. Dead is dead, whether it is by this demon or our bosses. I rather die from the hands of our bosses, than that demon from hell."

"Yes, this is so. But how you die, does matter. Pain can be inflicted, while you are kept alive for a long time. Once you die, the pains will go away. Your dead. That is forever, my friend."

"Yeah, where you go after death, matters to me."

Mike heard enough. "These men were responsible for the attack on the clubhouse. The team will be pleased, with this intel, Mike thought. It would be so easy to end these men lives, right now. I promised Jack, to wait for his command. I hope this opportunity, to take them out, is not wasted, because I held back."

Mike scaled back up the walls, upside down to the roof top. He spotted Cowboy, with his binoculars on top of another building, near the bar. He sent a message.

"Meet me on the beach."

Within minutes, both men met. Mike quickly informed Cowboy; he knew where all three bosses were hold up. He quickly asked for permission, to take them out. Jack contacted Cowboy, on the rooftop.

He told him, "to tell Mike, he was in position and to begin, whenever he wanted to."

Mike listened the report wishing, he knew that earlier. Cowboy, If I knew that, all three bosses would be dead, right now. This is why, I prefer to work alone."

"Look Mike, Jack is a good leader. He knows what he is doing. This is to go down as wc planned, got that. We need to keep in mind, the larger picture."

Mike conceded to Cowboy's reprimand. "He was right. The reason for the raid, was to make sure, there was not to be another raid, to come after this one."

"That is great news, Mike. Knowing these are the men responsible for the attack, is a relief. If we got it wrong, then another attack would follow. Taking these men out, will end this war quickly."

Cowboy was thinking about his wife and kids, listening to Mike's report. He relayed the news to Jack. Jack wanted to have a meet up, on the beach before any attacks went down. He deployed his men. To recall them for a get-together, would be harmful to the success of the mission.

Prior to the plane landing, Jack made Mike get his bandages changed. "This might be the last time, for some time, before we can change them. Bell, made me promise to make constant changes, to your bandages. I said, I would, to keep her off my back. Now, I can honestly tell her, we did change your bandages, Mike."

Some of the bandages had blood on them. Mike could feel blood on the bandages. He opened a few wounds, climbing up and down the wall on that building. "Jack was correct, they might not have time to change them, again."

Hearing Jack give the okay for me to do my thing, is good to hear. "My first impulse, is to visit my old friend, the boss man at the bar. Bar keep, will see me first. Let's see if he still feels the same way, as he did on our first meeting," Mike chuckled.

Jack was at the side of Tallman and Beedie. Everyone was given, the go. Red lights flipped on. The night became spooky, with red hues coming from around the bar. One Seal team member received a signal, step inside, to check out the contents. By the front door, every eye was watching all around the outside of the darkened bar. The Seal, stepped through the door and back out. No one inside saw or heard anything. It was not unusual, for the door to open and close, with someone deciding to not go any further. It was a known place for mob men, to hang out.

Suddenly, the front door was slammed opened with a loud bang. Two grenades flew inside, rolling on the floor. One man, noticed the grenade rolling on the floor, not suspecting the sound was a grenade. Every man inside, remained sitting at their tables or standing at the bar. The blast ended the party. No one finished their beers.

Three men rushed inside the bar. Red eyed glowing from each man. Those that survived the blast, wished they died from the blast. Anything that moved, got hit with multiple bullets. Those that ran, swiftly met with a beeline to death, by a shower of bullets. Within seconds, everyone inside the bar was downed. Blood splattered on every walls.

In the rear building, a man sat. His head, suddenly exploded. The man next to him, looked. He saw nothing. Both eyes, were blown from his face by a second shot.

Behind the bar counter-top, the barkeeper for this night. He alone survived the hail of lead. One of the red-glowing-eyed-demons reached over the countertop, snatching the frighten man by his shirt collar. He stood, looking into the darkness, staring at three sets of red-glowing-eyes. All the lights were shot out. It wasn't necessary. Pretty shot the power box, outside the bar, before he dropped the men in the rear shack. The man could barely see what was holding him up. The lights were out across the whole town. It was training. Take out the power source.

One demon spoke. His words would never be forgotten. It was a haunting tone, emancipating from the mouth of that demon. The barkeep did not go unscathed, from the gunfight. The explosion smeared his face with shrapnel. Blood dripped into his eyes. He saw the eerie apparition speaking, as a red glow.

"Where are your leaders? I will not ask a second time."

The barkeeper began to tremble. The rear door was heard opening. Another red-glowing-eyed-demon appeared, carrying a book.

"This is their code book."

The barkeeper plead to Jack. "Please, I will do good."

Jack pondered his words, "why would he do good, when he has been doing bad things, all this time?"

"Listen, you had many chances to do good and what was your answer? You are still here; in this den of evil, we have come to. You will pay the price, for all, if what you have allowed, come pass. Do yourself a favor, make peace with God. Do the right thing."

"I know all the names in that book. I know where they live and phone numbers, to all their clients. I can help you. Please, allow me to live. I will repent, please."

Jack listened to the man, squeal like a pig. "He had a good point. It would take time to figure out the codes, especially in another language. Okay, we will allow you to live. Sit and begin to write everything down, inside this book. I will leave. Have this done within the hour or you will certainly see hell, before the sun rises."

Jack watched the names, unfold on paper. He knew many of the names. "This is much too big, for us to release, to the government. Many government agencies, often used many names, written down. A leak was bound to occur, to protect their vested interests."

Jack decided," it was best to leave them in the dark. The family was more important, than these foul government groups, with little interest in America. Many of them, were self-imbued with other interests, to profit for themselves. Corruption, was in every aspect of American politics."

Jack contacted Chopper. Both agreed, to what he proposed. The government wasn't going to be informed, about the code book. Chopper said one thing, Jack did not want to hear.

"We have only one contact to check in with. Some of our intel, will be sent to them, after the mission has ended, Jack."

Mike was climbing down the walls, a second time, on the building, he witnessed the bosses. The short stout, oily, haired woman, opened the door for the boss leaving the room. The driver was standing by the waiting car, on the street. Gun firing was heard coming from the bar. They left.

Mike turned, saws flashing along with bursts of gunfire. He scrambles down the wall, to the street into the building and begins racing up the stairway, to the third floor.

Mike looked at both bosses. One man, was face down on the table. The other heard the knock on the door. He stood, staggering toward the door. Mike eased through the window partly opened. Swiftly, went to the door, that the stout woman moments ago, walked through. He quietly shuts the door. The second boss was at the front door unaware that the red glowing eyed demon was in the room, just an arm length from certain death. The door seemed to close by itself. The driver was standing, waiting to enter, when the door closed.

"Who is it?"

"Boss, there is gunfire at the bar."

"Get the car ready. I will get your boss down."

The driver rushes down the stairway. The second boss turns seeing two red glowing eyes, peering into his soul. He froze in place.

Mike escorted the frozen second boss to his seat, at the table. The lights were turned off, in the room. Mike stood in a corner, blending in with the shadows. With a flip of a cork, Mike waited for the third boss to arouse from his slumber. The cork smacked the third boss on his face. It left a red dent on his face. The sting, from the impact, quickly aroused the third boss.

The third boss, was staring at the corner Mike stood in. He rubbed his eyes, and stared harder. He sat, half-conscious looking at a dark figure looming in the corner, before him. He reached across the table, tapping the arm of the second boss.

"Hey, look in the corner. I think I see something? Turn the lights back on. Hey, turn on the lights. Wake up."

Mike raised his head. Two bright red, glowing eyes appeared looking at the third boss.

"Wake up, wake up, damn you. It's here. Wake up."

Before the third boss could prepare, standing up, Mike was on him. The third boss looked at the second boss. He was not moving. His eyes were opened. It dawned on the third boss; the second boss was frozen, with fear. The demon had given him, the touch.

It was too late to contemplate, "how he wanted to die. It now mattered, seeing the red, glowing eyes return to the island, as it promised. He said, "his return would be bring about a most terrible death. One that will endure for a year. Pain, so horrific, every day, he would pray to die."

The third boss reacted, falling on to the table. Then tumbled over the table, spilling what was left of a second bottle of wine, on the floor. He rolled to his feet. The red, glowing, cyed demon was on top of him. He released his urine on the floor. It mingled with the second boss's urine. A large puddle was forming near the table.

The third boss scramble to his feet, dashing to the front door. Mike had a machete out. With a snap, the blade went flying at the door. A hand reached for the lock. The blade sliced the hand in half, between the third finger and index. The boss screamed, pulling his split hand from the lock. With his good hand, he attempts to grab the sword blade. It was to no avail. The sword went deep into the wall. The stout woman, locked in the room, near the door heard the screams of the third boss. She began beating on the door.

The boss man held his hand tight, to stop the bleeding. The woman screamed," open this door!" The boss went to the table, snatching the linen off . Then, swiftly flings the linen around his hand. Bang, bang, the door pounded, "let me in."

Mike waited, until the boss man wrapped his hand, before giving him his tap. Both men, one sitting and the other standing near the sitting boss were frozen, in a state of fear and pain.

Boss man sitting was amazed, at the speed of red, glowing, eyed demon had made from the door, to his table. His partner, stood stiff as a board. "I know, he too, was in pain. Any move me make, increased the pain and our torment, tenfold."

The Boss man sat staring at the two red glowing eyes, praying. Fear crept up his spine, sitting, waiting, waiting, and waiting for this demon, to do his next thing. Then, it happened, a cold icy grip clutched his shoulder. Pain went from there, throughout his body. More pain with this touch, he received.

"God, how I want to scream. Breathing made my pain worst. If I screamed, God only knows, how bad it would become, he pondered."

A warm air, was felt near one of his ears. Slowly, words came. "To his hearing, the sound of the voice, was a deadly horse, guttural sound. Boss man sitting attempted to stand. Neither foot, responded to his command. He had not felt the touch from this demon, before this night. Reports about the pain, came to his attention, describing it. He joked at others for their silly fears and figured they were over exaggerating, to cover up their fear. Now, he feels that pain. What could be worst," he thought?

"You say, "dying is quick." Your pain will end, when you die. You say, "not to fear dying," to this man, standing beside you. His pain is short lived, then it is over. You looked at him with contempt. "He tells you, what about when you die, what happens to us?" More came words into his ear, from the red glowing eyed demon. Words continued to come.

"You had not given him, an answer. I have come to answer that question, for both of you, this night. You are correct, about the pain. It will last as long as you live. How long, you live, can make a difference? Let say, you survive for an hour. Not much to regret asking God, for forgiveness. Even a week of this pain might not make you bend a knee, for forgiveness. You think, any man can endure a week, of pain. Then, you think, you can escape the pain, if it lasts longer, by killing yourself. Yes, the pain will end, if you kill yourself."

Mike kept talking to sitting boss man. Boss man could not answer his words with, "I understand, now."

"His point was, when you die, where do you go? If you believe in an after-life, the question become a valid point, to contemplate. Is there a heaven and a hell? This day, if I choose to end your torment, you will certainly go to hell. The master has spoken, there are places reserved in hell, for the unbelievers. You are one of those special people, we welcome with open arms. This pain can last, as long, as I deem it to last. A day, a week, a month, a year, or until you die. I can enhance your body, to live for many years, so you can enjoy my gift, longer. I can plant in your mind, a command, to not kill yourself. I can make it impossible for others, to do your bidding to, kill you. I plant words in your mouth, to speak this to your men. None will attempt to free you. I will leave a message behind, to give all a warning, if they try and kill you. They too, will die."

"My friends, have a special pact with me. You attack them, I will attack you. Just that simple. Even if you do not give the orders, you will be held accountable. All who work for this cabal, will answer to my vengeance."

"Look at your friend, beside you." Mike taps the second boss. His head was free to move. "Look down at his feet. Your pee, mingles with his. He was warned if I returned, he would rue the day. You have not. Since, I have not warned you, you will be allowed to live. Your friend has chosen, his path."

"Before I leave you and your friend, remember this; God can forgive you of your sins. You can atone for them and pass through the golden Gates. On the other hand, my lord does not forgive sinners. He welcomes them, to his home."

Mike releases the second boss from his frozen state. He could move, but the pain remained. "The pain will last for some time. If you attempt to find relief, the pain will grow stronger. There is no cure, to this pain. Please try and seek a cure. Now, for your friend."

Mike looks at the standing man, beside the sitting boss man. "You have went against, what I said to you. Your pain will increase tenfold. Your life will not end. There is no escape. If others try to free you, they will suffer your pain."

Mike touched the standing boss. He dropped to the floor, wrenching in agony. Mike reaches down, clasping both arms. Like a pully bone in a turkey breast, he ripped the shoulders apart. Both arms fell to the side, limply.

Mike turns, leaving both men alive, in pain. Before, he disappears, he throws a knife at the door, where the old woman was behind. The knob fell off the door. The door opened into a dark room. Two red glowing lights abruptly vanished. The old woman flips the lights switch. The room lit up. Two men, to her amazement were alive. One, on the floor wrenching in pain, the other, sitting, his face contorted in pain.

The old woman turned seeing a dark figure leap out of her window. It was a three-story drop to the street below. Swiftly, she went to the window looking out. Nothing was seen below on the street, accept a car and a driver.

Mike caught the ledge of the window sill, allowing him to flip up, above the open window. He watched the old woman poke her head out the window looking down at the road. All she needed doing was, look up, if she desired to locate where he went. She did not desire to look up. Mike eased back onto the rooftop.

On the roof, Mike remained for a time. He listened to the old woman bark orders to the two bosses inside the room. The third boss cried holding his split hand to the old woman.

"He sliced my hand in half."

"Quiet you big baby, momma will tend to it. Momma always has to tend to your business. One day, you will miss your momma. Why did you two grown men sit allowing this man to treat you like he did? Stop your wrenching. What is wrong with you? Are you hurting," asked Momma?

"Yes, he touched me. We told you about this red, glowing eyed demon. We are in great pain. There is no cure."

"Nonscience. I got remedies to cure any ailments."

"Momma, he told us not to attempt to fix our pain. It would make it worst."

"Nonsense. You listen to your momma, boys. I know what is best. I only pray the mainland boss, doesn't get word of this."

The old woman reaches into her dress pocket pulling out a revolver. "I don't know why I shouldn't do it for the mainland boss. I would, if it weren't that you are my boys. What were you doing while this pathetic brother was getting his hand slice in two?"

"Momma, I was sitting, frozen to this chair. I couldn't move."

"Scared silly is more like it."

"He didn't do a thing to help me, momma," cried the third boss wrenching on the floor.

"Oh, he did something, you can smell his piss on the floor. Why were you running to the door?"

"Momma, I was, I was, going to get my man. He is by the car."

"Oh, I see. Leave your brother here to face this demon alone. Damn the both of you."

Momma raises her pistol, both boys sink to the floor. Mike heard enough. Quickly, he climbs back to the open window. While momma was focus on shooting her two boys, he flung his blade at the switch. Sparks erupted from the wall, before the lights went out again.

Mike knew the mother had no choice. "Damn that old woman, she will shoot those two cowards and spare the third son or allow these two to live, and hope the boss would not know about their cowardness. I have to act. The plan for the future relied on these men, living. Any man that replaced them, would not know of the red glowing eyed demon threat without further demonstrations and more attacks against the club."

Mike slipped into the room, to the same corner. Darkness shielded him from their eyes, in the dark room. Two red lights flicked on. Mike made a snap with his fingers. All three persons turned toward the sound. Each saw the two red glowing orbs staring at them. Momma raised her pistol to shoot. Mike held firm motionless, not moving.

Bang, bang, two bullets hit the wall by the two red glowing orbs. Neither hit the demon. Mike snapped his fingers, a second time. He was standing in the opposite corner of the room. "Momma snipped, that is impossible. No one can move that fast;" swiftly swinging her revolver to the opposite corner in the room. Bang, bang, two bullets hit the wall and not the red eyed demon. Again, Mike moves across to the opposite corner. One pull on the trigger followed, momma's shot and miss. One bullet remained. Mike stood into the light. Momma raised her gun. Number three boss stepped in her path, to stop her. He loved his momma. She would be killed, if she continued shooting at the demon. It was the only way. The gun fired. The bullet never hit Mike. Mike remained motionless. The bullet went into the belly of number three boss. He bent over, dropping to the floor. Momma cursed at him.

"Why you get in my path. I had the demon dead to right. She kicks her son lying on the floor, with a bullet in his guts. Then, she kicks him again. Damn you, I had him. Look what you made me do. This is not my fault. I would never hurt one of my babies."

"That is one mean momma the boss man had," thought Mike. Mike looked down at number three boss man lying on the floor. The second kick snapped his neck.

Mike spoke to the stout woman holding her pistol pulling the trigger many times, with no results. The pistol was empty.

"You do not believe in me? You think your boys lied. That is good. I prefer one, with no fear. It would please me, to see how long it will take for you to find this fear."

Mike slowly advances toward the short stout woman. Her hair was black and oily. It hung down her head, like a wet mop. She wore a black dress. She was in mourning, a widow. Sweat was pouring down her face. What make-up she wore was dying her face black has her oily hair.

Number two son could only watch his mom retreat from the demon. His pain was too great, to aid her. A blur, then his mother spun on her heels like a top. After several complete rotations, she suddenly stopped with a jerk. A jerk so hard, her spine separated. She would live but never walk again.

Momma went limp. Mike grabbed the old woman before she fell to the floor. He snatched a chair with his leg sitting momma in it. She screamed with pain. A blur was seen dashing across the room to a corner. A voice spoke to each of them.

"Madame, know this, you will never walk again. Before I leave, you will feel my touch, as have both of your sons. Your pain will be worse. Your crime was killing a man sacrificing himself to save you, from me. He died, not from his bullet wound but from the kick in his face. You killed your son, snapping his neck. I have told your second son, he has some forgiveness to make to God, if he seeks forgiveness. This is his only hope for salvation."

Mike tossed a bottle at the opposite wall. Both people turned to look. Mike swiftly removed his blade from the wall and was out the window, before they turned back to his corner.

Outside the window, Mike listened to the second son reproached his momma. "See, what we told you was true." Momma wanted to address his rebuttal but could not speak. The pain was terrible. Her mouth brought more pain with the slightest movement. She was sorry to disbelieve her sons.

"Momma, there is his mark, on your forehead. Second son reached for his head. Blood was dripping down. He felt the letters etched into his skin. The demon marked both him and his mom with the letters, OZ. The same marking on all the headless men found, perched on post along the beach boardwalk. He reeled back from the mark rushing to the nearest mirror. Horror filled his mind. Many will see this mark and know. He is to be shunned, like a pariah by all. He prayed to God."

Below on the street, the driver was waiting inside the running car for his boss. Mike spotted the driver entering the car from the roof top. The driver was asleep, waiting for his boss. One tap on the temple and the driver remained asleep. Mike reached inside lowering the window.

"After a few days, the reek of a dead man would draw someone to come and look inside the car. One more boss man I need to make a visit to," thought Mike.

The night was ever darker, as Mike passed through many allies and back streets. The third brother or boss man lived further away, than either brother at momma's home, he left. A large house with a cast iron metal gate stood before him. Only two guards at the gate in the shadows.

Mike watched, pondering whether to end their watch. He leaped over the metal fence away from the gate and guards. Once over the wall, he spotted the owner's car near the front.

"Good, Mike thought, he was home." Several yards to the house, Mike halted in his tracks. A wire was sensed ahead on the ground and in trees. "Ah ha, you made some changes, I see, since my last visit."

Mike scanned the area for any other devices. Cameras was mounted on every corner of the large house. Mike smelled the odor of a kennel somewhere on the grounds.

"Funny, why are the dogs not roaming the grounds freely. He has dogs in cages. Silly, foolish man, Mike silently chuckled to himself."

Swiftly, Mike avoided the cameras. Many cameras were ill placed, leaving many empty spots, the cameras were not overlapping. This left voided areas he could easily maneuver within, to the house.

Mike learned to move silently and swiftly in the darkness. If not for all the trees near the house, the flood lights would give him little to conceal his movement. He was at the window. Sensors were attached to each pane. It was apparent, he could not enter undetected. So, he decided to use his appearance as a weapon.

Two red lights shined out from the under his hood. His face was red from the lights. Mike stepped from the shadows into the view of a camera. Inside the mansion, a man sat looking at many screens. All screens were empty of any moving activities. Suddenly, from nowhere, one screen lit up with a red glowing glare. The monitor was watching many screens. Unexpectedly, he spotted the one screen with a red glowing face staring into the camera's lens.

Orders were given to look for this demon, with red glowing eyes. Stories were going around the town of him and many others. They called him, a demon. He froze, staring at the screen. Next, a chilling cold fill the room. His hand slammed down on the panic button. Red lights and siren went off inside the home. Guards were alerted. Dogs released in the yard. More flood lights lit the yard up. Nowhere, any signs of this demon seen in the lit enclosed yard surrounding the mansion.

Mike cared little about the yard and dogs. He was inside the home. A man was awoken, in a bedroom on the second floor. He knew at once why the sirens were blaring a loud scream.

"I have prepared for such an event. This time, this so-called demon wasn't going to be so scary. I am ready with more men better armed, dogs, and a safe place to hide in my house."

Not dressing, boss man jumps from his bed dashing to his safe room. Inside, was food, water, and a monitoring screen. He slid a shelf on the wall. Behind it was a button. Mike was at the window, outside the third boss man bedroom watching.

He was too late, to grab him. The boss man was entering the room. He watched the safe room door slowly closing. There was only one option left for Mike, he could dash into the safe room with the boss man.

The vault was not lit, when opened. Once the door closed, the vault lights would automatically turn on. Inside the room, the boss felt safe, once the door closed. Lights lit the room. He turned to switch the monitor on. Standing by the monitor was the red glowing eyed demon, he thought he evaded.

Boss man froze with fear and shock. He looked at all the wealth clinging to the wall shelves. Jewelry, bricks of gold, stocks, and bonds, then many shelves laden with money. Much was American green, some in other currencies. He realized this demon cared little, for money. A haunting, eerie, sinister sound spoke.

"You were given a warning. You did not heed it. I have a pact with these men, you attempted to kill. I must honor my pact."

"Yes, I am truly sorry, Mr. OZ."

"I see, you remembered my name. Is it because of my mark, that you answer me with my name or is it out of respect, no, maybe fear? Yes, fear is why you speak my name. You say you are sorry, why hide within this room?"

"I am not hiding from you. It was my alarm. I hide from my enemies."

"So, it is from me, you seek shelter?"

"No, no, you are not my enemy. I have not gone back on my agreement."

"Really, then, why did you send men to kill my friends in America?"

"It was not my doing. I swear to you. God be my witness. It was my brother's doings. See, behind you is a button. Let me press the button. The vault door will open." Slowly the boss man moves to the button.

Mike spoke as the button was pressed. The door began too slowly open. "How dare you speak of God, in my presence. Lord below forgive me. I spoke of God, in your presence. His names coming from my mouth, is blasphemy." Mike looked downward to imply, he was speaking to Satan. The boss man got the meaning.

"Please, I opened my vault to let you know, I had no plans to trap you within this vault."

"Did you really think, this vault could retain one, such as me?"

The door was opened enough for the boss man to make a quick dash out of the vault. Mike sensed men outside the vault with weapons, before the door was fully opened. He knew once the door was opened, the men would fill the room with a ton of hot lead.

Outside, the boss man cowered behind three men holding machine guns at the ready. More men were running to the mansion from outside.

Mike realized he was trapped within the safe room. He knew dashing inside would trap him. He had little options, once the door opened. "I need to make a feint, dash out of the room drawing their fire. Then, I can leap out, roll, and jump to the opposite wall, swinging out the window I came through. My other option is to cling to the ceiling and allow the men outside the vault, to peppered the vault with hot lead, hopefully avoiding the ceiling." Mike shattered the overhead light inside the vault.

Outside the room, a ruckus took place. Gunfire was heard. The three men in the room with him in the vault, turned to look at the bedroom door. Mike made his move while they turned away from the safe room door. More rapid firing was getting louder, outside the room. Then, just as sudden as the gun fire began, it ceased. The three guards turned to aim at the vault. Bullets filled the vault. Jewelry, money, bonds and stock were shredded with a hail of hot lead.

Mike was at the window watching the scene unfold. Outside the room, He heard sounds he recognized. It was men of the Seal team. Then, it dawned on Mike, the radio, he was toting, was being tracked. They located him through the radio, that, and Beedie being told by Jack, to keep near Mike.

Beedie had trouble following Mike at a distance Jack made him keep. Jack knew Mike would sense someone following him. Beedie saw Mike enter into the mansion, just as the lights lit the whole place up. A radio call followed minutes later, Jack and the Seal team quickly arriving at the mansion.

Mike lowered himself behind the cowering boss man, behind the three men emptying their machine guns into the vault. Boss man felt the warm air near his ear. A soft, gurgling, rasping voice spoke into one ear.

"Why are they shooting into an empty vault? You said, this was not a trap, to contain me inside. Is this what you meant, instead?"

A cold touch froze Boss man kneeling behind three men attempting to reload their weapons. The door blasted open, before any could reload. It was too late for the three men. Mike, with one swift stroke, severed all three heads with his machetes. Blood rained down on the boss man frozen behind the three headless men.

Jack entered the room. All his men stood behind him with their hooded red glowing eyes looking in the room. All the boss man could do, was watch his men lose their heads and pee. He felt the warm pee flowing down his leg making a puddle, where he knelt. Blood on the floor mingled with the pee. All three heads laid in front of him, looking up.

All the Seals scurried to a corner of the room. The boss man saw many red glowing eyes in the room.

"There is more than one demon," he thought.

Mike held a finger to his lips, motioning Jack to meet with him outside the room, before they could speak. Outside the room, Jack expected Mike to asked how he and the team were so quick to fine him?

Mike spoke first, "Oz not Mike, we need to talked to each of ourselves, as the same person. You are OZ, as am I, Jack. Jack shouts to his Seal team inside the room," OZ brothers, keep quiet." Jack waited for the question he knew Mike was going to ask. He was prepared for it.

"OZ, said Mike to Jack, you were quick to arrive here."

"That is because, we found the radio station behind the bar. A code book was found. One of the radio operators was very helpful in decoding, the book. He was also helpful, telling us where the three bosses lived. We found the driver in the car. Funny thing, a hole in the window was about the same size as the hole in the driver's head. I sent Cowboy upstairs. He found a room; the door opened. Pretty spotted you entering the building, from his perch. He watched you enter through the window and exit it, two times. Cowboy made a few inquiries with one man, left alive. The other was shot. An old woman was sitting in a chair. Her back was broken. Both were in severe pain. Only the man could speak. The little man told us where you went."

"The man in the car, help guide your tag, Beedie following to this mansion."

"I figured he was lost. I walked slow, to give Beedie time to keep up."

"Oh, you know about Beedie tailing you?"

"Yes, and the radio."

"Look Mike."

"Stop Jack, no need to explain. You are in charge of this team. It was your call to have me, followed. I hope, I have garnered your trust, now?"

"Okay Mike. About the dead boss man with the bullet hole."

"Oh. I did not kill him."

"I know, the little man never stopped yapping to Cowboy. Cowboy asked him all polite like, to talk. He did not talk. Cowboy said, he would get his brother OZ to come back and asked him questions. He couldn't get the little man to stop his yapping. He kept mentioning a dark lord or Satan. Is there something you have not told us, Mike?"

"No, he implied, I was a demon, so, I implied back, the dark Lord would meet him at death. He assumed I was from hell, maybe, I misled the poor man. That's all."

"He said his brother got shot by his momma. She was the real boss. He went on to say, she kicked him, breaking his brother's neck. What I want to know, should we kill the rest of them? Rid this whole island of every last one of these S.O.B.s. The only way now, is to rid this town of all the rats, and all the want-a-be rats. By the way, I noticed all the art in town on the walls."

"You liked that. OZ in blood red letters does give the town a modern art deco look."

"It does match, all the red roof tiles. Mike, I think that cargo container you located on the beach, will be an ideal place to stow the three remaining bosses. We can't leave them lying around, until we mop up the island. Others may get word to the mainland."

Outside the mansion, two people were tied to the iron gate. Jack's men dragged the third brother from his house. Mike walked toward the town.

"Hey kid, where you off too? We still got some work to finish up with."

"Got to make a call on someone, catch up soon, Jack."

MAINLAND

Outside the mansion, Mike left his Seal Team walking alone down a dark street heading to the hospital. He recalled, not asking Chopper nor Cho of the where-abouts of Moss. No one back, ever mentioned his name. At the time, to many things were happening at the club, to quick. Bobby's attempted assignation of Mike, resulting in Susan getting shot. Then, the bombing at the clubhouse and battle of the mob, sent to destroy their club members and families.

Moss redeemed himself several times over since arriving at the island with the club. Mike began to list in his thoughts the first redeeming act. "He was aiding me in the desert against the Muslim attacking the twin mountains people, they named the cave people. Again, on the island sacrificing his life, to save the three women at the container. He told Moss, he would help him get back home."

"Moss had little to return back home too. His gang was wiped out. He would be alone in the city without support, when he did return. Then, the fact he lost one arm, making him a handicapped man. Things looked bleak for this once most hated foe of Mike and the bikers," pondered Mike.

"At the hospital, I left him during the battle at the hotel. I hoped, he was taken care of. The bikers left the next day, on a plane in a hurry. Moss was forgotten. The ambassador wanted the bikers off the island, ASAP."

Mike remained behind to located Cheryl. For a second time, Mike was occupied by the mob, coming after him and Cheryl. Moss was forgotten. Mike was in bad condition from his tortures. This ate at Mike for the second time, he broke his word to help Moss.

Mike walked into the hospital. Things were clean but the damages were still present. Many windows were broken, the receptions desk was riddled with bullet holes. Blast damage was evident down one wing. The other wings were getting repairs. Patients were heard moaning. One woman was at the reception desk. Mike approached the desk, surprised to see the same nurse in the room with the doctor and Cho after the violent attack. They came with him and Cho to the hotel. The nurse quietly waved Mike to one side. She recognized him, right off.

"You shouldn't be here. The big boss on the island has put the word out for anyone spotting you or any of your friends, to report immediately to the mob. You got the mark of death on this island."

"I wouldn't worry about the big boss for a long time to come. What is your name?"

"Ceta, please, the big boss will have you killed."

"Ceta, Mike takes hold of her hands looking deep into her eyes. She was a beautiful, dark-haired woman. Her age beguiling the way she looked. The violence and constant threat of danger, made her appear older. She hated the mob. Mike was reminded how a beautiful person could change, with hate in their hearts. That inner beauty was wiped away, as was her joy taken from her. Mike spoke staring into her eyes.

"Ceta, the boss, and all his minions, are dead or wished they were, dead."

"Dead, no. How, we heard or not seen men coming to the hospital?"

"The fighting ended moments ago. Many of the soldiers are dead. Others are being sought, out as we speak. All three bosses are out of business. Before night comes, the island will be rid of this scourge for a long time. I leave, to go to the mainland, to end the threat at the source, Ceta"

Ceta looked hard at Mike, listening to the words, she prayed for, so long. Tears formed in her eyes. Ceta replied, "for years, I tended to many young men brought to the hospital, caused by conflicts with the mob men. One of those young men was my brother, entering the doors of the hospital." Memories flooded her mind.

"I always feared for her brother's life. He was young and filled with vinegar. He often had run ins with mob men. One day, he did not walk away from a fight. He entered into the hospital, dead, with his throat cut. It was on a day, when my brother and girlfriend walked to the beach. They were confronted by several mob men. His girlfriend, was a beautiful, young girl, both were in love. One mob man stopped them. He placed his arm on her, then whispered a foul remark into her ear. The snide remark, made my brother challenge the man. "Keep your filthy hands off my girlfriend, you dirty scum." Before he completed his sentence, the man pulled a knife. It was quick. The girlfriend was never seen, after that day."

Mike listened, then hesitated to asked Ceta, about Moss, after she told, her story. Ceta looked at Mike, knowing he came to the hospital for a reason.

"Please, my story is not uncommon. I should not have spoken of my problems, with a friend that saved my life. Please, tell me what you came to ask about?"

"He is the man, we brought into the hospital, before the violence erupted in the city. His arm was nearly blown off. Is he alive? Do you know where he is?"

After Mike gave a short description of a tall black man, with one eye, Ceta asked Mike to follower her to the front desk. At the desk, Ceta fanned through the check in and check out book.

"I recalled the black man coming in the hospital, but had not been involved in his case. Here is a man, fitting your description. A tall black man was admitted, then checked out one week ago. The American Ambassador aide came here. He left with him, in a car."

"Was he wearing an uniform?"

"Yes, a green uniform. I believe he was a Marine. I wasn't present at the desk. I do recall seeing him, being escorted out the door with a Marine."

Mike thanks Ceta, saying goodbye, turns and walks out of the hospital. Jack was waiting outside.

"Well Mike, did you find out, what you needed to know?"

"No Jack."

"Mike, it's is none of my business, and you can tell me to take a trip, but is it One Eye, you seek?"

Mike paused before answering Jack inquiry. "Yes."

"Mike, One Eye was flown back to the States. Two days after we left this island, Chopper requested him, be airlifted to the states. He is in a hospital. Chopper told me; we owed him for many things he done to help us. I thought you knew?"

"Thank God. Thank you, guys. What's the plan, now, Jack?"

"We are waiting for our boat ride across this sea, to the mainland. In other words, we got a long boat ride."

"Is everything wrapped up on the island?"

"Pretty much. Most of the mob is dead or if alive, in hiding. Are you ready to make introductions with the main man, off this rock? Once we made our introductions, we will go and deliver the package. This should end, any of our troubles with this mob."

Before the sun reached its pinnacle in the sky, a boat was waiting for several armed men. Along with the Seal Team, four other persons were assisted on the boat. One was a woman, dressed in black, pushed in a wheelchair. Two others alive, not able to talk, and a dead man in a body bag.

The small boat skipped over the breaking waves into calm, deeper waters, to a ship, anchored. The ship anchored, was a large transport, Jack told Mike. The small boat entered into its belly, via a rear ramp lowered into the water. Mike, marveled at the size of the ship. Opening a ramp and letting water inside the boat, seemed puzzling to him.

"What is keeping the ship afloat, he pondered?"

The bay door closed and water swiftly, drained. All the Seals Team and guests were inside the ship, as the crew secured the small boat. An officer was standing by a ladder, waiting for the team to arrive. He greeted Jack with a salute. Jack returned the gesture. All the gear was left on the boat. The officer led the team and three living mob leaders to several rooms.

Jack was led away, to another room. Inside the room, the Seal Team spotted hot coffee, donuts, and other snacks to eat. Many of the team had not ate for two days. This fare was a welcome sight, to all.

Jack returned, after his meeting with the Commander to his men in a room chowing downs donuts. On the wall, was a large map.

Mike was looking at the map, when Jack and Commander entered the room. Everyone turned, to attention. Mike remained looking at the map.

Every member of the Seal team was familiar with military protocol, except Mike. Mike felt like a fish out of water, once he turned to face the team at attention. The men were told to stand at ease, by Jack. Mike found a corner to sit in. Cowboys noticed him shying from the team. He came over, sitting next to Mike.

"Mike, don't let all this military crap get to you. Everyone in this room, feels the same as you do. You got quite the reputation, it seems. So, get over it. Here's a cup of coffee and a donut."

"Thanks Cowboy. I did feel a bit overwhelmed."

"Men, this is Commander Piper. He is going to give us the low down on where, we are heading."

"Welcome aboard men. I am Commander Piper. I will be taking and picking you up, once the mission is completed. You have made quite the impression on the island. Reports have been pouring in from your last foray. Is this, the young man, the ambassador speaks well about?" Commander Piper walks over to Mike extending his hand. Mike stands, to shake his hand.

"Welcome aboard my ship. I must say, to look at you, I have a difficult time believing all the fantastic stories, rumored from the locals?"

"Commander Piper, I can assure you, those are not stories to scare children, Pretty said."

"Huh, didn't mean to speak ill of the young man, just have a hard time, seeing him, doing all the things reported."

"You wouldn't say that, if you saw him in action. We are mighty glad to have him with us on this mission, snapped Cowboy."

"Well, as I was informing you, last night, gun fire erupted in town. Twenty or more men are reported, dead. A bar was shot to hell and back. Those people, you brought to my ship, are the heads of the local mob. The doctor on board is stumped, to what ails them.

Mike speaks up, "Err, Commander, I would advise you, try nothing to aid their condition. Anything you attempt, will only make the pain increase exponentially."

"My doctor is more than able to."

"Sir, Mike is trying to tell you, if you attempt to help them, the problem will grow worse. There is no cure, to what is ailing to them. I would ask Mike to demonstrate this condition on you, so you will have a better understanding. He is the only one, besides his father Master Cho, you know of him, from our reports."

Mike stands, walks over to the Commander.

"No, no that is not necessary, Jack."

"No, I insist Mike make you understand."

"You are on board my ship and I make the decisions." Before he could step away, Mike was on the Commander in a blink of an eye. Pain shot down and all through his body. No sooner than the pain froze him, Mike touched him a second time. The pain disappeared, just as swiftly as it came.

The Commander unfroze, staggered back a few feet. He turned looking at the young man moving so fast, he seemed a blur. Then, startlingly came the ungodly pain coursing through his body.

"I see what, what you mean." The commander steps farther from Mike, toward the map board.

"The hospital, it, it has been overwhelmed from all the dead arriving. Many were killed, without a bullet wound. The local police were curious. Many questions are asked. We are denying all involvement. This ship, is only providing transportation to your team, to the mainland. To any that ask, we are transporting tourists, off the island. Air travel has been denied, to all incoming and outgoing planes. We have no connection to your team."

Cowboy nudges Mike, "that is his polite way of telling us, we are on our own. There will be no back-up, provided. We get caught, well, that is on us. He will be waiting some miles off shore, to pick us up, when the mission is completed." Commander Piper interrupts Cowboy, talking to Mike.

"These persons on board my ship, are wanted by the local police. They have gone missing, it seems. We will provide them assistance, in so much is our authority given to us. They will be secured in a room, blind folded and guarded twenty-four hours. Your destination, is this naval port. The Commander points his wand at a speck on the map.

Jack had requested a small boat, to depart before we make port. It is being prepped now. This little trip, will take three hours."

Jack stands, "listen men. Mike, Pretty, and Beedie will depart, in a small boat to a destinated spot on the mainland. They will make for a large villa, near the water. Caves are everywhere. Mike will take leave from Pretty and Beedie to scout the villa. Pretty and Beedie will set up sniper positions overlooking the villa. Before any of you ask, the rest of us will obtain transportation. We will arrive at the villa, in a truck. Our job, is to secure the villa from any unwanted guest, coming and going."

"Huh, what about the guest on board Jack, asked Pretty?"

"Oh, I thought you understood, they go with your team. Mike will deliver them, to their boss, at the villa. If there are no questions, then get some rest. Mike, report to the corpsman. Those bandages require changing. That comes directly from Susan and Bell."

After meandering through many passageways to get sickbay, Mike was reminded of the day, his father was dead and a ceremony was conducted on board his ship. He was seven years old. A sailor carried him through the passageways. He cried, seeing the tall ladders going down and up on deck, to arrive at the ceremony being held. Mom and his sisters sat in the front row, listening to the Captain, eulogizing his dad.

The sun was near setting; a small boat, approached the shore on a deserted beach. Beedie leaped from the boat, to tie it off. Mike left the boat. Beedie and Pretty escorted the blindfolded mob leaders off the boat, into the waves, crashing on the beach. Beedie was unlucky, having to carry the short, stout woman to the small shack up the beach. Beedie was not happy toting the stinky stout woman, reaping of stale wine and not having a bath for many days or weeks.

"Why does it always have to be me, getting the bad ends of assignments, Beedie thought?"

A gentle breeze was welcomed by Beedie and Pretty keeping watch, on the three mob leaders. The dead man, was left outside the shack, some distance away, up wind. Mike walked the beach, like a tourist.

Beedie carped to Pretty, "damn lucky, SOB. We gots to stay here, smelling this sot."

"Beedie, you might want to talk privately, when you talk about Mike. I for one, will not hear any bad words coming from you. Also, you might not know this, that SOB, can here you from a long distance, even if you are whispering. If you don't believe me, ask him what you just called him, when he gets back?"

"Just talking, don't mean no harm, Pretty. I just hate having to be tending to these people."

"Me too, but I rather have Mike watching out there, than either of us. He can detect anyone coming, well before we know it."

Late, after sun set. Jack arrives in three cars. Pretty, met him.

"I thought, you were getting a truck."

"Three cars looked better. We got to deliver the packages. No need to take a truck. We might need a get-away. Three cars provided a better way to evade pursuers, if we need to. Inside the cars are supplies and ammo. Grab your hoods for this mission. Take your passports and money, along with your weapons."

Soon, three cars were winding through the narrow roads toward the villa. One car left the road, then another, before the villa was in sight. The third car, Mike drove with the three mob leaders and one dead man in the trunk with Jojo and Skip Jack.

Pretty with Beedie set up a sniper's position, overlooking the villa. Jack with Cowboy and Tall, guarded the road. Jojo and Skip Jack left the third car near the villa. They were to make their way into the camp, once Mike was allowed to enter the guarded gate.

Jack told Mike, his exploits in the desert, was known to the mainland boss. The hoodie jackets will strike fear in the mainland boss's men. Maybe, when they realized this demon, with red eyes has come to their villa, many will shiver in fear? Making our job, easier."

Mike recalls Sun Tzu lesson, about leaders. "Many of these mob bosses led from the rear. They had little real time intel on the battles. As recalled from Sun Tzu, leaders providing instructions far from the battlefield, are ignorant on how subordinates should attack, they lack knowledge. That lack of real time knowledge can lead to indecisiveness, by their subordinate's actions. Waiting for orders, can lead to doubt and wrong decisions. This was the case on the island and at the clubhouse. Their men attacked, not knowing they were walking into an ambush. They never adjusted to the new circumstances."

Arriving on the mainland, required stealth. The mob boss was expecting his people to kill the intruders. He most certainly got wind of the attack within a day. Jack hoped they got to the mainland, before the news was reported back to the mainland boss. Jack realized to be prudent, would put his team in jeopardy. He had to act swiftly.

Mike understood the plan and what was required by him. He realized, for all of them to get home alive, the attack had to be swift and decisive. He was aware of Jack's team and their abilities. He needed and wanted an edge to make sure of success. He decided a swift, deadly recourse, was best. Once inside the compound, he was not going to wait. He would attack swift. No one will have time to prepare. By the time they realized an attack, Jack and his men will drop those, he wasn't able to get to.

Jack knew Mike better, than Mike expected. He knew, once Mike entered the villa walls, he would attack. There was no need to counsel Mike into not doing, that. Instead, he planned for Mike to do, just that. All the team was in place, before Mike was near the gates. He realized, to attack in a large force, would bring more casualties to his men. It was better to strike in small, concentrated pockets. This would make for high confusion among the mob men. This plan worked well for Mike and Cho in the desert. Mike successfully entered a city, freed prisoners, and escaped, taking out many of the defenders in the city and outside following him.

Mike wished, he was more forceful in his attempts to get Jack, to make the red glowing face OZ, appear sporadically throughout the mainland. He figured, the boss would send many of his soldiers out, to find this OZ demon. Jack insisted, this boss had heard the stories of OZ and would fortify his villa, keeping his men close to home. Both points were valid. Jack was the leader and his decision prevailed.

Jack reminded Mike, their fear for families, knowing that this OZ demon was coming to the villa, would make them fight harder. They will be united, protecting their families from this demon.

Beedie and Pretty were dropped off near the hilltop, overlooking the villa. They spotted the lone car, approaching the villa gates. Jack with Cowboy and Tall had all entries to the villa secured. Skip Jack and Jojo departed the car, before Mike stopped.

Pretty spotted a large swimming pool, in the rear of the villa. Several women and men were enjoying a dip. Two men stood watch; one man sat in a chair, drinking with a woman sitting next to him. She was topless, as were the other women swimming in the pool.

At the gate, two guards waved the car off. "Well, that went that plan," Mike thought, turning his car around. Jojo and Skip Jack watched the car turn back. Mike signaled to them, hold off the attack, until he ditched the car.

Mike left the car along the road, making his way up a hilltop. JoJo followed the car, to see what Mike was going to attempt. Mike told JoJo, "drive the car to the gate, after I signaled Skip Jack."

Mike spotted numerous cameras and sensors everywhere. Bushes offered Mike good concealment, from the cameras. The sensors were a different thing. The sensors signaled the cameras. Mike recalled a similar incident following several kids, going to his campsite by the clubhouse bar.

"Cheryl never knew, he was following them. Each time she looked back, was me tossing a stone, to get her to turn from where I was moving. I watched them trash my camp."

Mike tossed a stone near one camera. Sure enough, the camera turned to where the stone was thrown. Quickly, Mike scaled down the hillside to the base of a tall brick wall. It was taking longer, than expected to get down to the wall. Every path, was made to lure a person, like a snare for a rabbit.

"They used every trick in the book. I have to act, before my team was found out. It would be better, if I triggered the alert, than the others, thought Mike."

Skip Jack spotted Mike's signal, JoJo was to drive the car, to the gate. JoJo driving the car, approached the gate. Both guards knew it to be the same car, returning. Mike made a leap on top of the wall. Both guards were watching the car stop. Neither heard, the sudden drop of a man onto their back. Both went face down on the ground. Mike opened the gate, then, quickly ran off into the villa grounds.

Skip Jack and Jojo left the car at the gate, then went to set charges around the villa. Cowboy was lower on the hill, than Pretty lying in his sniper position. He spotted several men approaching Skip Jack and Jojo. Pretty watched from the top of the hill. He had no shot. It was up to Cowboy, to drop the men. Mike Was at the villa.

Men were posted every hundred yards, carrying machine guns. Mike spotted the chink in the guards positions. Once they turned away from the other guard walking, they would be blind to each other. That short time, was all he needed. One guard dropped. His neck was twisted. Number two and three, met with the same neck arrangement. Each was dragged under bushes. Now, all Mike needed doing, was enter the villa.

Mike had planned to set a grenade snare at the gates. Once the gate guards allow him inside, he would set a timed explosive, to blow the gates. That would be his diversion, to enter the villa undetected. That was then, now it fell on the shoulders of Jojo and Skip Jack's. Mike entered the villa, through the front door. No one was there. Mike found the guard near the hallway, watching the half-naked women swimming in the pool. He snook up behind the guard. Two hands grabbed his shoulders. With a jerk downward, both knees of the guard gave way. He hit the floor with a thug. The impact drove his spine up into his skull.

Mike attached a grenade, with a trip wire to the front door knob. Outside, he climbed a tree to the third-floor balcony. None of the windows were locked. He entered the large bedroom with the biggest bed, he ever saw.

"Why would anyone, ever need a bed this big, Mike pondered?" On the ceiling was many framed mirrors. Five minutes had passed. Mike knew Jack was about to come down the road. At the gate, a timer was set to blow. Jojo and Skip Jack should have completed setting other explosive devices and waiting for the truck to arrive at the gate. Two minutes and all hell, was going to enter the villa. Mike had yet to locate, the boss man.

Beedie dropped two guards approaching the gates. His silencer performed has it should. Pretty scoped the two guard by the pool. He waited until the gates were to blow.

Mike walked out of the bedroom making his way along the third floor, checking each room. All rooms were emptied. Next, was either the second floor or the fourth floor. Time was running out. A car was nearing the gates. Thirty seconds and the grenade would blow. Mike went to the fourth floor speedily. At the first room, the door suddenly opened. A fat man, wearing a blue silk robe stood in the doorway. He spotted two red glowing eyes looking at him.

Mike grabbed the fat man by his head ready to snap his neck, until he realized, the fat man was the boss he was seeking. He shoved the man back into the room. Another man was sitting up in a large bed. He was naked. Before the second naked man could understand the intrusion, Mike was at the bed. One finger stab stopped the man from reacting. Another jab was made to the boss.

Mike froze both men, then ran from the room, to the hallway. He grabbed a large urn on his way to the stairs. At the stairwell, he tossed the urn at the front door. The grenade wire jerked, pulling the pin. The door shattered into thousands of splinters into a pillow of smoke.

Outside, other explosions were beginning a deadly barrage of carnage. Pretty dropped both guards, standing at the pool. One woman screamed. Another man in the pool, dipped under the water, a stream of red blood seeping from his missing head. The clear waters swiftly turned red. All the naked women scrambled to the side of the pools, to get out. The man sitting, stood. He sat back down with a hole in his chest.

Mike looked out the windows toward the pool. Pretty was dropping as many men, as fast as he could pull the trigger. Beedie was trying to take aim at men scrambling for cover inside the walls. He could not get a shot before the man was out of sight, making to the villa.

Jack arrived at the gates, with Cowboy and Tallman. Beedie met up with them, entering through the gates. He had no trouble dropping any man he spotted, now. Four men were marching to the villa. Not one guard turned to look behind them. It was easier than, shooting ducks in a shooting gallery at the park. Many of the soldiers twisted, falling down, while racing to the villa. Their bodies riddled with machine gun fire from four men with red glowing eyes. Red letters decorated the outside walls of the villa. All the soldiers knew what the letters meant. Mike made sure to leave his calling card, before entering the villa. Several men halted, seeing the red letters. They turned to see many red glowing eyes staring at them. They died, before they could pee in their pants.

Mike went to the second floor. He hid in a dark corner, while men raced up from the main floor, to the top floor. He stepped from the shadows when the men came to the top of the stairs. Two red glowing eyes, met them. It was swift. Both men went flying back down the stairs. Many soldiers were coming inside the villa. They spotted the two men, hitting the floor. They looked up to where they fell from. Two red glowing eyes were watching them. A hail of bullets filled the second floor, peppering all the walls.

Mike was on the third floor watching soldiers begin racing up the stairs. Four men entered the villa at that point. Ten, maybe fifteen men were shot with red hot lead, by Jack and his Seals. Those soldiers racing up the stairs met, the red glowing demon. Some turned, to run down the stairs. They saw many red glowing eyes staring up at them.

Mike went through the first three men nearest to him. One was struck in the neck by his index finger. A second man, in the chest received a kick. The breast plated armored vest caved in. He flew backwards into the men attempting to race down the stairs. A third man, had his rifle readied to fire. He watched his hand get torn, from his arm. The rifle was handed back, barrel end. It stuck from his face, like a flag pole.

The red glowing faces on the first floor, showed no mercy, for the men racing down the stairs. Some fired, at the red glowing eyed demons, below. They might had hit some, if not for a man colliding into them, from above.

Suddenly, a man ran from a room, Mike was standing nearby. He leaped over the railing. He would have made it to the floor below, if not for his foot not clearing the rail. Mike watched the man hitting the floor. His neck was snapped. His head was splattered on the floor. The body was contorted. He was definitely dead.

"That was a first, never had a man commit suicide, to avoid me, before," chuckled Mike.

Gun fire had ceased, outside the villa. Skip Jack and Jojo were told to bring in their guest, from the car. Jack waited patiently by Mike, at the bedroom door, where the boss and his playmate were kept. Mike departed, to return and enter the room from the window, once Jack took the prisoners in the room. Mike and Jack agreed, they wanted the boss man to see, there were more than one demon.

Three people were escorted inside the room. Both, the boss man and his playmate stepped away from the door upon seeing a red glowing eye demon entering. Behind him, was two more demons, toting three of his island bosses. Each was placed at their feet. The playmate screamed, jumping onto the unmade bed.

The boss man looked at the two men frozen alive, unable to move. The old woman, he knew right off. She was wheeled inside. She was motionless just like the other two men. The last man to come in the room, was a corpse. His body was twisted and contorted in an ungodly manner.

Jack motioned the two demons out of the room, before he spoke." These are the bosses that manufactured an attack, on our friends. This is how they will live, the remainder of their lives." Jack walked over to the main boss, to spit in his face. The boss was scared walking backwards from the red eyed demon, coming at him.

Boss man tripped, falling on the bed with his playmate wrapping his arms around him. Once he spit on the man, Jack turned, walking from the room. In came Mike, through the window balcony watching Jack spit on the man.

The boss man and his playmate felt a breeze, coming from the balcony. Turning, they spotted another demon entering their bedroom.

"How many are there of you," he screamed?

"I am many. I come with few. They kill, using your weapons. I kill, with but a word and a touch. My friends suffered at your orders.

Your friends suffer from my words. You have not suffered for your actions, against my friends. These men feared me but revenge, was a stronger motive. They now, see their folly in their thinking."

Mike continued; "I will wipe away my spit, off your face. That spit would bring death to you. I wish no death, as yet. You will suffer for some time. Lest you have me return. End this revenge now and live. If I should return, you will be as your friends are now, and forever. I came in peace. You welcomed me in violence. I was turned away from your home. I came back, to demonstrate your mistake in doing so. You will join in my feast, when I return."

"These people, will be a reminder to you, of my power and my Lord. Mike looks down to symbolized he came from a dark burning place." The boss man got the meaning. In his mind, a thought arose. This is some kind of charades. Does this man, expect me to be a fool and believe in his silly act?"

Mike released the three people from their frozen state. Screams, came crying from each mouth. The boss man and playmate shrunk into the bed. Mike left the room. Not one person saw him leave. They sat with the covers up to their chins, peeking over the rim of the blanket, watching three people scream.

Outside, Jack was loading the truck with his men. Mike joined the team, before the truck drove out of the shattered remanent gate. Down the road, many trucks and cars were flooding the road, leading to the villa.

Inside, the men jumped, unloaded their vehicles, only to discover a terrible reality. Inside the villa gated walls laid twenty dead, headless men scattered. On every wall; two letters were written in blood. Some men knew the meaning of the two letters. OZ, the demon letters reported, coming to the mainland from the island.

Men entering the villa, found more dead, headless men on the floor. One man, with his head, still attached. He died from a fall. The leader of the group, entering the home, raced up the stairs to the third floor. He expected to see his boss, without a head.

A door was opened. It was the room of the boss man. The team leader walked inside. Immediately, he spotted three people sitting on the floor. One dead man, laid near them. On the bed, were two men hiding behind a sheet. One was the boss man, cowering, hearing the ruckus outside his room. He feared it was the demon, returning.

Below on the main floor and outside the home, men were whispering. One man spoke out, sympathizing what many were thinking. This red glowing eyed demon came here. He left his calling card. Any man that attempted to slay it, will be dead and headless. The boss man was warned by a demon from hell. They were working for a man, warned by one of Satan's disciples.

A lone truck came to a halt, at the foot of a hill. One man walked toward the truck. It was Pretty, returning from his sniper position. Jack turned off the road, once he spotted many vehicles driving toward the villa. He expected men to arrive, once the gunfire began. The side road, hid his truck. To drive down the road, would have been suicidal. Jack prepared for such an event. He had an escape plan.

On the road, came an endless parade of trucks, in groups of three. The first group was at the villa. A second, was nearing where they hid. Swiftly Jack ordered the team to hide near the road. Mike suggested a plan. They were to stop the trucks, jump inside with their hoods and red lights on. It was to further instill fear to all of the boss's men.

All three trucks came to a halt at a road blocked. The blockage was the red glowing eyed demon, standing in the middle of the road. Suddenly, he leaped into the air onto the engine hood, and from there, over the cab onto the canvas canopy. The canvas was torn open. Mike landed within the rear of the truck, among sitting armed men. He turned to let all see his red glowing eyes. One man did not react, the way the others had done. He stood, raising his weapon.

No sooner than the rifle was raised, a head fell to the floor of the truck. Mike withdrew his blade, made a slice and dice swoop, a head was severed and lying on the floor. The man stood next to the man, raising his rifle. He was readying to fire at Mike. The blade returned to its sheath, before an eye could blink. The smell of urine filled the rear of the truck. Mike leaped from the truck before the head landed on the floor. No one saw him depart. He came suddenly, killed a man, then disappeared.

Every truck reported back at the villa, a red glowing eyed demon, called OZ was inside their truck. He gave them a dire warning. It was the same warning the boss man related to the leader of the men, entering his bedroom.

"I come in peace and will leave in peace. It you choose to fight, then you will join in my feast."

The meaning made little sense to the leader, entering the Boss's bedroom. It did later, when he was at the gate, hearing the same words spoken from the men inside the trucks. One man was left for dead, headless. He alone, raised his weapon against the red glowing eyed demon, known as OZ.

A Hole in the Escape Plan

Looking up the road, was the villa of the boss man. The gate was no more. Smoke rose over the villa from the fires. The screams and wails from crying women, subsided. Many men laid dead around the inside of the villa. Many trucks were stopped near the main gates. There were many soldiers exiting the trucks. Jack and his Seal Team watched from their vantage point, overlooking the villa. He spotted the soldier's leader inspecting the trucks. Beside him, was the boss man. Suddenly, the boss man turned away from one of the trucks. Mike giggled.

"What so funny Mike, asked Pretty?"

"Oh. I had one man in a truck raise his weapon against me. He lost his head. Every man pissed in their panties."

"I saw the boss man turned away from the truck with the headless man. He got a wisp of the piss inside the truck and maybe the head lying on the floor. He is a weak man. He has men do his bidding for him."

All the Seal members laughed. Jack, also laughed, hearing Mike explain what happened. Jack halted his laughing, when the trucks loaded with men, began to exit the villa.

"Mike, that boss man didn't get the message. He has those trucks coming after us. There is one or two ways out of this hole, we are locked inside. Neither are good. With all them trucks coming after us, we have only one way to get away? The beach."

In several minutes, a single truck was driving on the beach. Mike, with the Seal team members drove on loose sands toward a small boat, by the sea. It was to be a last-ditch attempt to flee, if things went wrong. Things went wrong.

On the beach, was a small boat prepped for their escape. The boat was not destroyed. How and why didn't matter. It was a clear sign; the boat was not where it should have been.

Several men spotted a truck come to a sudden halt on the beach. The Seal team swiftly exited their truck. Those soldiers on the beach were out manned and out gunned. Quickly, they halted digging by the cliffs. It was clear to Jack; they would put up a fight.

With men chasing Jack's team from the road and these men dug on the beach, Jack realized, his team would be surrounded. Swiftly spotting a dark area, above the cliffs. Jack ordered all to start climbing. The dug in, out-numbered soldiers watched not attempting to halt Jack's team. They laid in sand holes watching men climb the ridge.

Skip Jack, was the best climber, leading the way. He reached an outcrop dropping a line for the others to use. Once all the men reached the outcrop, Skip Jack neared another outcrop. Below, trucks were pouring soldiers onto the beach. All the men dug in on the beach stood, watching the men climb the cliff walls. Many men emptied out from the trucks.

Skip Jack spotted a cave. He entered. All the Seal Team members followed. Jack was the last to slide into the shadows before, any eyes were turned toward the cliff face. Mike was holding back, keeping an eye on the beach. He swiftly climbed the cliffs without any rope. Jack and his team watched from the cave's shadows. Each was stunned, watching Mike ascend the cliffs effortlessly, unaided.

Skip Jack remarked to Jack, "that kid is part monkey. Look, how he swings from each ledge, like he was clinging to a vine. He flies from one ledge to another with little hesitation. "He has a two-hundred-foot drop, if he misses," quipped Skip Jack to his team.

After the third swing, Mike was at the mouth of the cave flying inside, landing between the men. Below, on the beach, Jack feared the soldiers spotted Mike swinging from rock to rock to the cave. He was wrong. The men, from the trucks, ran to the boat. Many of the men looked confused, finding no one. Even the men dug-in seemed puzzled, seeing soldiers dash toward the boat.

Most of the soldiers on the beach worked at digging holes. Finally, the first group leader waited patiently for news explaining why, they were digging holes near a boat? He stands, walking over to the men with his rifle. One dug-in soldier turned, spotting soldiers advancing to their entrenchments, fired at the soldiers.

Next thing that happened, stunned Jack watching from his perch on the cliff. Both teams of mob soldiers were shooting it out. Why, didn't matter much. He was glad, they were killing each other. No sooner than the gun fire began, it ended. The first team was all dead.

Jack began to suspect, one party was sent ahead, to look for a get-away site. The other team, was unaware of that fact. They thought, the men shooting were the same men attacking the villa. Jack turns to his team asking," did any of you talked, to anybody about this mission." None responded to his inquiry. Mike pondered what Jack asked. He spoke to a nurse, on the island.

"Jack, I spoke to a nurse, at the hospital. I told her all the boss's men were killed on the island."

"Hmm, nothing more than that?"

She said, "bodies were washing up on beaches, many were brought to the hospital. She and the doctors were shocked, learning all the mob people were killed on the island."

Jack pondered on that thought for a minute. "It seems, we have a greater problem, now. The only person to know of our plan was the ambassador at the embassy."

After a long pause, Jack sniped out orders. Men, we need to check this cave out. We can't go down the beach. They looked to be posted there for a long time. From my experience, many caves usually have several entrances, that means exits. Skip Jack had begun foraging through the cave, once the first Seal entered the cave. He returned, just after the gun fire on the beach ceased from his excursion, deep into the cave.

Jack, this cave goes deep. I think it has an out, further into the cave. I spotted many people trash, dumped into this cave. It led further inside the cave.

Nearly two hours expired, before Jack or any man spoke. Mike interrupted Jack, before he spoke.

"Jack, look at this shiny streak etched on the wall." As they walked, another streak, then another appeared.

"That is a marker to follow," Cried Cowboy.

"It would seem that way," answered Jack. The team continued down a narrow winding corridor. After wading through knee high water, the cave enlarged. Skip Jack was standing near a spot that was recently dug. Fresh soft cave dirt was piled in a small hill. He was digging at it, when the team emerged from the water.

"Jack, come quick. Look at what I dug up."

Jack, with the team stood, looking at a large chest. Jack fumbled at the lock. Tall slams the butt end of his rifle on the rusty lock. Cowboy pushes ahead of Skip Jack opening the lip to the chest. Inside, filling the large chest, was old gold coins, goblets, necklaces with gems or pearls.

"It looks like a hidden pirate's treasure, shouted JoJo. Oh my God," quipped Jojo. He grabbed hold to a hand full of pearl necklaces. Pretty grabbed a ring with a large diamond. Beedie sat down. Talk was looking at the gold coins. He examined several, before speaking.

"Hey Jack, these are not old, but modern coins. I think this is loot, someone stole and hid here. It is not pirate loot."

"We gonna take this with us, Jack," squealed Cowboy like a girl?

"No, but we will find a new hiding place to stashed this chest. We can come back later, to reclaim it. Right now, we can't afford to tug this with us. Lest you men have forgotten, we got soldiers on our tails."

Before anyone could respond, Mike spoke up. "We got problems, Jack. I hear men coming."

Jack never questioned Mike's abilities, this time, he was glad for his hearing. "Quick, grab the chest, fill the hole, and let's get out of here."

After a long thirty minutes, the team came to another fork in the corridor. Jack instructed two men, to dig into the side of the cave wall. He had sent Mike back down the cave, to track where the soldiers were. The chest was placed into the cave wall.

"Cowboy, you, and Tall chip at the ceiling. Make a cave-in near covering the hole in the wall, to conceal the chest."

Mike returned spotting a large pile of cave wall debris, nearly filling the entrance to the second shaft they came too. Skip Jack came back just as Mike arrived from his scouting.

"Jack, they are twenty minutes behind us. This stop, provided time to catch up."

"Jack, I got good news. There is an exit about a two hundred yard in front."

"Great, thanks Skip. Let's get the hell out of here."

Jack hands Mike, a handful of gold coins. That is what each man took from the chest. We will come back to get the chest later, when this cools down. Skip Jack received a similar sack of gold coins.

Many of the Seal members wanted to ditch their extra ammo, to fill their pockets with loot. Jack recalled what the Commander said to him. If they are discovered, he could not come to pick them up. He ordered his team to grab only a small handful of coins. "We will be needing our ammo, if we are stranded here."

Mike pondered on the words spoken by Jack. He required no ammo or weapon. He relied on his hands and feet, plus both swords. Jack was correct, if this venture went sour. It did, and all their ammo might be needed, before the day ended. They were trapped inside a cave, with men advancing to them. His abilities would offer little assistance in the tight quarters of the cave. Men in the team would have no place to seek cover, once fighting ensued.

"Men, ahead lies an exit, to this cave. We might have company, waiting for us. We can't turn around and walk back where we came in. I believe at the time, no one spotted us entering this cave. I was wrong, soldiers have entered the cave. I believe, they knew about this cave. I expect, they are trying to trap us between them and men waiting at the exit," explained Jack.

"Mike, can you scout ahead before we get to the exit," asked Jack.

"On it." Mike dashed ahead. He meandered through the narrow corridor leading to an exit. A cool breeze greeted him, after ten minutes. This running reminded Mike, about Cho making him run back home. Every day, Cho required me to run with a fifty-pound sack on my back, plus lead weights on both arms and legs. Every quarter mile, I had to drop and count off fifty pushups. Then one hundred punches with squats, followed with a kick. Mike giggled, that was in the morning, after I awoke and before breakfast."

"Practice, practice, practice was every second of the day and night. One exercise, was my daily punching a board, six inches away. I only stopped punching for the day, when a new board was replaced by Cho. That ended soon. Too many times, I snapped the boards. I was made to practice hitting on a tree. It was worse, using finger strikes. It got so bad my fingers could not bend. Cho showed me a cure. Oh yeah, what was that old adage, how did it go? "The cure was worse than the pain;" Cho definitely proved that saying was correct."

Mike spotted a light in front of him. There was hope, until coming to a rock slide, where the shimmer of light found a path through the debris.

Mike began to toss rocks from the pile. Soon, the light grew larger. A hole was large enough for him to squeeze through. With some wiggling and determination, Mike's head peeked from the opening, into fresh air. Then, it happened.

The ceiling came tumbling down on him. He was trapped. Pain coursed through his arm. It was a rock falling, trapping his arm. The arm wasn't broken but serious hurt. Mike struggled, to get free his arm. After many minutes he squeezed from the hole onto the open ground. His backside was burning. Salty rocks entered into his open wounds from attempting to squeeze himself from the cave-in debris. Most of the bandages were torn off his back. Mike slowly stood up. Then, quickly dropped back to the ground. Men were heard talking below near the cave exit.

Mike peeked over the ridge of the hill, he emerged from. Below, were many soldiers. "Jack was correct. The soldiers inside the cave, were to force the men from the exit, into the waiting arms of these men." Then a realization occurred to Mike.

"The soldiers were standing around another opening to the cave. My opening was a result of a cave in. If I had proceeded down the cave to the original opening, I would have walked into all those soldiers waiting to ambush me. Thank God, for my luck," whispered Mike.

There were two choices for Mike to decide upon; one, should he deal with these men and maybe alerting others to come, or return back to his team, to alert them. A fire fight would ensue. If he could persuade Jack, to sneak out of this cave, they might get away clean. Mike made his mind up, once another truck and car arrived. The decision was made mute after Mike spotted the leader exit his car.

"Boss, our men have entered the cave, at the beach. They are forcing the men to come this way. There is only one way out. We got the hole surrounded."

"Good, hold your fire, until we can get all of them. Not one man better live?"

Mike, hearing the boss speak, realized, if any of the Seal team are caught, their ruse would be exposed. Mike could hear gunfire outside the cave, he was lying near too.

"The soldiers caught up with my teammates."

By the other exit, soldiers began entering attempting to trap his team between both groups. Ten men went into the cave before Mike decided, he had to act. He had an advantage, now. Two red glowing eyes appeared under the hood. Swiftly, he crawled toward the leader's Mercedes car. Two tires were poked with a finger jab. Air leaked from the tires.

Next, Mike made to the truck. Two finger jabs followed with two tires losing air. At the second truck, men were standing, smoking a cigarette. Most of the men, not entering the cave, gathered around the opening. His two men leaned on the truck, watching. Neither heard the air leaking from their truck. A cigarette butt was flipped to the ground by a guard. It landed near Mike's hand. The guard looked down, before Mike could pull his hand from the soldier's sight.

The soldier stared at the hand, thinking, why is there a hand at the tire. He couldn't recall a third man at his truck. It didn't matter, two red glowing eyes began to rise from the ground.

The guard was correct, it wasn't a third man. It was a body of a man, with red glowing eyes, standing in front of him. The hand belonged to him. Damn, he wished, he thought of that sooner. It was his last thoughts.

Oz slammed a palm heel thrust, on the chest of the man, looking down. He saw two red glowing eyes as the sky, turned dark. The second smoking man never saw the spinning arm, snapping his neck. He thought he saw a blurry figure. Both men slid softly to a sitting position, still leaning against the truck.

Mike had to act quick, before any of the men around the cave exit could react. Every man was glued to the entrance to the cave. Gunfire was coming out the opening, in rapid bursts. It was getting louder by the second.

One man spoke, "they are being pushed back by the other team. They should be running into our men soon?"

The boss, began to back away from the cave. He had a bandage wrapped across his shoulders. Mike waited, until he was nearly backed up to him. With a palm heel downward thrust, the palm slammed into a large bulge under the wrap. The ice bag splatter into tiny projectiles, everywhere. The boss dropped harder than a sack of oaks to his butt. A second touch to his shoulder, froze boss man on the ground.

"I guess, I should have told this boss man, no ice pack was going to stop the pain, given to him."

Mike hopped over the head of the downed boss, followed by a tumble coming off the ground, wielding both machetes in each hand. A simple song entered his mind, about the alphabet. It always amazed him going into battle, how he often recited some song or tune he once knew.

"Ah, this particular tune begins with, A, B, C, D, E, F, G. Now, how did it go? Yes, A is for apple; got no apple, will an arm do? I'll grab me an arm and whack it off. Thus, was it so, Mike swung both blades down simultaneously onto each shoulder. Both cut through the ball sockets of each shoulder severing the arm connections. Both arms dropped to the ground. Yep, A and two arms, not one, better, quipped Mike under his hood."

"B, is for banana. I have no bananas, today. Hmm bat. I got no bat. Then, it dawned on him. I got it; I'll use an arm like a bat. Bop went the bat on the head of the second man. Mike grinned. A homerun, I do believe, Mike whispered as the head went sailing over the trucks."

"C, C, C, nothing came to his mind. Then, oh yeah, C is for cat. No cat around. C, C what else starts with C, Mike ponders for a second? A flash came to him. C is for cannon. A pistol is called a cannon. Mike was happy, thinking of a solution to his dilemma, trying to match the letters to an object.

"Swiftly, I think I spotted a holster on the second man's waist." The second man was still standing, after losing his head. It happened really fast. Mike had time to yank the pistol from his belt, before the body dropped to the earth.

Turning back to number three-man, Mike taps him on his head with the pistol. Number three thinking, his comrade wanted something, turned to answer his question. He had no question to asked him. Mike showed the soldier the pistol. That resulted in him pondering why? He never saw the two red glowing eyes before an answer was given him. The pistol had a large barrel. Mike shoved the barrel into one of his eyes. It exited through the other end.

"Next was D. D is for dollar. Dollar bill or coin, which do I have. Well, after feeling inside my pocket, there is no coins. I will just pull a dollar bill from my pocket, swiftly rolled it tight between my two fingers I will place it."

Mike tapped number four; his back was turned. He would not turn to face him. Mike tapped again, on number four's back; this time, much harder. It appeared to Mike the fourth man was more interested in the gunfire coming out of the cave entrance, than being polite enough to answer his question. Finally, his not answering Mike, he tapped the man a third time. His rolled dollar bill found a soft spot between two vertebrates. The soldier went limp. The spine was severed.

"Oh shoot, Mike exclaimed. I guess you won't get no dollar from me, ever again," Mike said.

"Where was I; oh yes, the letter E. Dang, this is going to be a tough one. E is for echo. Hmm, echo is sound reflecting off a wall. I got it. I'll make a pipe from the dollar bill. Mike took the rolled dollar bill tapping the fifth man. He turned swiftly to shh Mike, from making any sound. He spotted the two red glowing eyes right off. Mike did not hesitate with his homemade pipe. It slid neatly into the soft spot on the soldier's throat. The new breathing tube, did little to help the soldier breathe. Mike slapped the man on his chest. The pipe went further down the soldier's throat. He hacked and hacked, but no air was to be had. He turned a pretty blue. Both eyes bulge out of their sockets. He grasped at his throat, with no avail.

Number five fell against number six. He turned, mad at the soldier for knocking into him. He turned to slug the S.O.B. A fist was raised to flatten his comrade. Mike forgot what letter he was on. It occurred to him, just as he dropped number six.

"F, that's it. F is for your fucked buddy." Two palms slammed against both ears of the soldiers. Six men down was as far as Mike got, with the alphabet song.

The other three men, were trying to squeeze through the cave entrance. Two other men were a tad farther away from Mike. They happened to be looking away from the cave entrance, when number six fell to the ground. It didn't go nicely, when number six soldier fell, shoving dirt into the hole. One man in the hole cursed at the fool, throwing dirt down his back. All three men turned. They all noticed the red glowing eyes of the demon OZ staring at them.

Two men farther from the hole, spotted six men, lying on the ground. One man raised his rifle, expecting to shoot at the red glowing eyed Oz, they heard about. Mike knew they spotted the six men. he had to act quick, before the two soldiers turned toward the exit hole. He was faster. He leaped over the entrance with a flying side kick, landing by the second soldier as the first man went flying off, down the hillside.

"Damn, Mike thought. I flew across the entrance, kicking number seven to the moon. F, I could have used F, for flying. Dang bad luck. My song is ruined, now. G. What's the point, Mike thought as he dropped the second man by the entrance. Oh yea, G is for the ground. He dropped to the ground. Okay now, I can continue with my song." Mike felt renewed with happiness.

The man in the hole, slid swiftly underground into the cave, before Mike could reach him. That was okay by Mike.

"Next letter, H. H is for hollow. Number eight was in the hollow of the cave."

The gunfire ended. Silence made the darkness of the cave eerie, for the two soldiers, that just entered. That eerie feeling went away, when another soldier shoved into them. They turned, both men saw two red glowing eyes follow the soldier shoving them. It wasn't necessary to ask, why the other soldier shoved them?

Both soldiers heard the gunfire cease, assuming their men killed the men attacking the villa. Their assumption was quickly misplaced. Jack, with his team intact, came into the light in front of the three soldiers. They were trapped between many red glowing eyes coming from the depth of the cave, and one set of red glowing eyes, behind them. The answer was simple. One was less dangerous, than many.

It was the wrong answer. One was more dangerous, than many. Mike was the real, red glowing eyed demon, OZ. Behind them, was a Seal team of the most dangerous kind. Jack set mines along the cave corridor. When the soldiers coming from the beach reached the mines, the walls caved in from the explosion. Many were killed, right off. The rapid gunfire heard from the other end, was Jack's men killing those that were alive.

The boss man sat frozen, watching all his men killed within seconds, in a most hideous way. He wished, he done, like the demon told him to do. He wished; he could run. He wished, he would be forgiven, for this one stupid mistake. He wished for many things, until the red glowing eyes re-appeared from the cave entrance.

Mike stood, walking slowly toward the sitting boss man. He could sense his fear and regret. "Should I allow this man to live, was on Mike's mind? The answer and only answer was a no, to that question. This fool, sent all these men to die for his petty revenge. They may have had family. He didn't give a hoot. His pride was blemished. He wanted his pound of flesh. So be it," Mike said to himself.

The boss man sat looking at the eyes of death walk toward him. Thinking quietly to himself, "I hoped to be spared, what my men suffered. All hoped is vanished, seeing the two red glowing eyes, meant my death. I hope for a fast death, like my men. That too, is my hoping to be. Mike picked up two severed heads. A mark was etched on their foreheads. All the heads were laid around the boss man. The last head was placed between, the boss man's legs. This demon is going to kill me."

Mike stood above the frighten sitting boss man. He stared down at the fool. "You were warned," these were the only words spoken to the boss man. He recalled the warning of the red glowing eyed demon OZ, "ten-fold the pain would be."

"What can be worse, than what I am suffering now, thought the boss man watching the finger, of the demon descend? Pain ran through the boss, like shit through a goose. The jolt made his teeth clench. Some teeth broke off. His eyes budged in their sockets. Sweat, nearly drowned him, pouring down his face. His stomach wrenched; it made him want to heave. Every bone in his body, seemed to have snapped once the finger touched him. He knew now, what ten-fold meant." He prayed for a quick death. It did not come."

It took several days, before any person found the bodies by the cave, on a hilltop, miles from the road. It was the terrible smell of rotting human bodies bringing people to investigate. The boss man was alive sitting in his 'sown feces. Heads surrounded his body. He was unable to speak or move. Two letters were written on all the heads and on the boss man brow. The newspaper reported his villa was burning and many men found dead and headless. There were strange writings written in blood everywhere. The letters OZ, were repeated on every wall, door, and vehicle. No one knew, the meaning of the letters.

Once the soldiers were taken out of action, Jack commanded the team to return to the beach. It was clear, the cave corridors were blocked from the explosions. It would take time to clear the debris or to return to the beach through the cave. Many of the team wanted to return and collect their chest filled with jewels, gold coins, and other items.

"Listen men, I want to go back to collect that treasure, but there is little time. We, still are not sure, how many men are coming here. Our boat is waiting off shore. If we stay to dig out the treasure, we might not be able to leave this place, alive. We need to return another time with a plan, to remove it. It will still be there. No one will want to enter this cave after they learn of the explosions and all the men dead, inside."

"Jack is correct men. We need to get away from here. We got some of the treasure on ourselves." Pretty was holding onto the ring he was going to give Judy, when he asked her for her hand in marriage. Besides, Jack would be his father-law. Wasn't no need to start off making him an enemy, by not agreeing with his command," thought Pretty.

"Load up," shouted Cowboy to the team.

All the trucks had flat tires, thanks to Mike's finger poking them. After twenty minutes, tires were removed from one truck and put on the other. The truck traveled along the shore, shying away from any town. Night was upon the lone truck within the hour. Sirens, with flashing lights sped past on the road above the beach where the truck traveling. Jack realized, they had to ditch the truck soon.

On foot, the small band of brothers walked on the beach hugging the cliffs. Mike was asked to forage for food. He left the party of men after the truck was ditched. Within a few hours, he returned, the team was setting up a make shift camp.

He was ordered not to go to any homes or towns. That meant, look for any food along the beach. He found a pool of water. After some time passed, he caught several fishes and collected many clams toting back to the camp.

Jack was dumbfounded, looking in the back pack at the bounty Mike returned with. He half expected him to steal food from some homes, nothing like what he caught on the beach.

"Mike, I thought you did not know how to hunt and fish. When we first met you in that bar in the mountains, you were near starvation.

"Yes Jack, you were correct. I was wet, cold, and hungry. I know how to hunt and fish,, pretty good. Knowing how is not the same has having the opportunity to catch food, if there is none to hunt for. At my cabin, I done a ton of fishing. I had little choice. I didn't have any money to buy supplies."

"I thought, our wives kept you fed?"

"They did, but not all the time. I went without meals many times. Once, they learned, I hunting for my meals, and Bell insistence, I was starving, living under the table at the picnic area, that changed. Still, there were times when holidays came, or something arose, and the meals stopped coming."

"Why didn't you go to the club house, for a meal?"

"I guess my pride was the problem, Jack. Besides, I went fishing and set snares for wild game."

"Still, there was all that money, we got from the mansion and the Cartel fortress raids."

"I know, but I needed to keep up with my skills of foraging and hunting. You know, just in case."

"In case of what, Mike?"

"I might not be in the club, or be on a mission. Like in the jungle and the desert, I had to get food. There were no stores to buy food."

"Good point," Mike.

Skip Jack, chomping on a fish, asked Jack, "isn't this the day, we need to get out of here, to meet up with that Captain's boat?"

"No, once we fill our bellies, we need to locate a boat for our agreed rendezvous time. We got until tomorrow night, to meet our ride."

Morning came quick. A guard was replaced every four hours, to keep a watch for any of the boss's soldiers coming. Jack made it clear, "when Mike said, the boss was still alive at the cave exit, men will be looking for them. He was the main boss, but that didn't mean, there were no other seconds in reserve, to step in to his shoes."

Jack was correct, again. Morning came with the sun rising off the waters. A loud noise came from the road above the beach. Trucks, filled with soldiers, were looking for them. Mike woke at night when the first of many trucks were heard by him. He went to the road, to assess the noise. He discovered the trucks were filled with soldiers and no other things.

Mike reported this news to Jack. He woke him from a sleep. "Jack, there are trucks on the road, filled with soldiers."

"Damn, after all the men we killed, you think there weren't any left to search for us. My wife told me, I better come home or she would kill me, Ha, ha, ha." Jack woke all his men from sleep.

"Listen, Mike just informed me, there are many trucks on the road, filled with soldiers looking for us. We got to find a boat, before morning. It was two hours, before they came to a fishing village. Boats were lying on the beach. Jack did not have to tell his men, what to do. Everyone was tugging at one of the boats. The boat was quickly floating on the crashing waves.

Men jumped into the boat. Those in the boat, grabbed gear from the other members. Soon, the boat was rowing over the waves, into deeper waters. The small village got smaller and smaller with each minute. The sun rose, bringing a grey cloudy sky.

Tall quipped, "Jack, I do believe, we are going to run into a storm."

"He's right, spoke Skip Jack, him being a sailor. I've seen many storms at sea. There is a storm brewing, quick. I think, we are not going to meet up with our Captain," Jack.

Jack immediately ordered the sail to be hoisted, once the small boat was out of sight of the small village. The sail filled quick, from the strong winds whipping against the boat. Waves grew higher, each minute. The sky was black, with no sun shining. Rain began slowly dropping. Then came, a sudden shower, with sheets of rain, pouring down on the tiny craft. It was about to sink, from all the rain filling the boat, plus, water coming from the waves, splashing across the hull.

Every man began to heave water over the side. It did little good, without buckets. Soon, the boat was level to the water, filled with the sea. Every man was tire from fighting for two days, with little to no sleep. Exhaustion was evident to Jack, looking at his team. Mike seemed unaffected. Jack order half his men to sleep. Night was coming. We will need all our strength, to keep this boat afloat.

FOREST SCREAMS

Three kids, not yet in their teens, were playing ball in the park, behind Susan's home. One kid, was swinging at a ball. Two were in the field attempting to catch the ball, after it was hit. The kid, swinging the bat, was doing a poor job at hitting any ball. He missed twice as many times as he hit a ball. Suddenly, he got lucky, the bat cracked from the sound of a ball getting whacked, hard. The ball sailed over the two kids in the field, across the street, into the forest.

Both kids were stunned from the hit, as the ball sailed over their heads. Most of the balls, barely rolled close to where they stood. This time, the ball flew over Susan's house continuing across the street, flying to the woods. It finally arced downward, just at the edge of the tree line.

Both boys darted across the street into the tall uncut grass at the edge of the trees. Each boy scratched for the missing ball. One boy shouted to his friend," I think the ball went into the trees".

The parents living in the subdivision, made it clear to all their children, never enter the forest, on the other side of the road. The reasons given to their children, was the usual kinds of warning. Wild animals inhabited the forest. There never was seen any animals in the forest, by anyone living by the wooded site. In fact, the forest was quiet. No animals screams or sightings was every known to have come from the forest.

The lack of any sounds or sighting helped spread rumors, by the local people. Some said, "the forest was dead. No living creature could live within it. It was old and dark. To enter, was to quickly get lost. Many tales talked of people entering and never coming out. Search parties went in, looking for missing people. Some of them, never came out. Talk of demons living in the woods were constantly being blamed for all the missing people. Soon, the stories were accepted, as truth.

The forest was a constant subject, at town meetings. Many propose a fence be erected around the forest. It never got anywhere. Money, to expensive was the town council's reasons for not erecting a fence. Young boys seldom listened to their parents. For some reason, that often-enticed young boys to enter the forest. Erecting a fence, probably wasn't going to keep them out of the forest, cited the council members. Not one council member

Both boys split up continuing their search for the missing ball. The shortest of the two boys, was called Stinky. It was a good name for him. He rarely bathed. His parent believed, a boy needs his freedom, without too many rules. Taking a bath, was not a rule enforced in his home. He didn't like baths, so he seldom took one. In his home, both parents argued on how to raise a child. Stinky was their first and only child. Both became experts, once the baby came. No one could tell them anything about raising a child. They ignored friends and family offering to give advice.

Both parents had good jobs. They were well educated. Education, they were still paying for. Both parents came from families, with strict parental discipline opposed on them. Needless to say, they felt discipline was not the correct method, to applied to their child's upbringing. To make a child toe the line, would limit his or her-self-esteem and creativity, was their credo.

Their parents, desired them to seek a goal. Be successful. Strick, strong, sense of self was required. This kept their child on the proper course, for success. Each of their parent believed, give a child what it needs and not what the child wants. It was tough love." That kind of up bringing, was not for stinky, both parents had this one agreement, neither disagreed with.

Stinky's parents gave him everything, he asked for. The mom, wanted to be his best friend. She hated to see him unhappy. She worked most of the day, like her spouse. That made her feel, she was neglecting her son. To say Stinky was spoiled, was an understatement. He was a likeable child, once you got pass his odor.

Once across the street, the two boys soon separated. Stinky went into the forbidden woods quickly. The other boy, walked near the edge but just out from the tree line. After minutes past, he turned to Stinky to say, "we lost the ball". He didn't want to quit looking for their last ball. The whole week they played ball. Five balls went into the trees. They never dared, to enter the trees looking for their balls. This time, the last ball ended playing catch, until they could ask their parents to buy another ball.

Stinky was gone. So was the ball. The other boy ran, screaming Stinky's name out. No Stinky was seen. Stinky was deep inside the trees and couldn't hear his name called.

The other boy spotted the ball by a tree. He stopped yelling picking up the ball. Then, he resumed calling for Stinky. "I found the ball. Come out of the trees. We can play ball, now".

Stinky never heard anything. He kept looking for a lost ball. The kid with the bat, ran across the street, hearing Stinky's name being shouted. Both boys begun screaming Stinky's name.

One parent, then another, heard the screams, calling for Stinky. Susan heard the screams and came outside, to see what it was all about. Her neighbor, Karen was outside looking. Two parents were walking across the street, going to one of the boys, shouting. It was near supper time. Most parents shouted out the doors to inform their children to come in for supper. Many kids knew to go home for supper time. Some, needed a reminder.

Susan first instincts hearing Stinky's name called out, was his mom telling him to come home for supper. She kept shouting, "My child is lost. We are looking for him. His friend said, "he entered the woods. I told Petey to never go into the forest. He just wouldn't do that."

Susan walked to where the two women were standing. One woman was holding the sobbing mother. Susan approached the sobbing mother, then an odor met her nose.

"My God, what is that smell? Susan couldn't help saying that remark, aloud. Both women acted as if they never heard her comment. That was good, thinking Susan. I surely didn't want the mother more upset from my comment about her stench."

Karen met with Susan, just before they got closer to both women. Karen asked the other boy with the bat, how long Stinky, AKA Petey was missing. Stick replied.

"Maybe fifteen minutes. Could have been longer. I got no watch."

Karen turned to Susan. "You think, we better call the police, or walk in the woods to look a little while. He might be coming back out, before the police arrive.""

Karen turns back to Stick with the bat. "Why are you told not to enter the woods? My child has been walking through the forest, many times. Most of our family children play there."

"My mom told us; the place is haunted. Other kids have been lost in the forest. Some people went looking for them and never came out," replied Stick.

"I never heard of this," replied Karen.

Susan listened to Sticks response, with a puzzled looked. None of the Riders families ever heard of any stories, concerning missing children, in the woods. Karen knew Stick. Her own boy played with him before the Riders ended all their dealing with the subdivision families not in their club. They never informed them, about men selling drugs and now, this story. After the party, tensions eased between the two groups, the wall of silence, still was prevalent between them.

"Mom told us, we can talk but keep our distance from the biker kids. That kid gone missing, happened years ago, commented Stick without Karen asking.

That distance grew swiftly among the two groups. Neither side's children had anything to do with the other. One group would sit on benches, another in the swings. It was that way more and more. Soon, neither group went to the park, if they spotted the other there.

The woman holding onto the sobbing mom, spoke. "I guess you people were not living here, when all that occurred." The meaning was not lost on Karen or Susan, it was a clear, but an unintentional snide remark, still there. A line was drawn in the sand, not to be crossed, between the two groups living in the subdivision.

Other mothers came walking up the street, toward the four women. One mother was Stick's. She saw Karen asking him questions. She grabbed hold of Stick's arm, pulling him away from Karen. That said volumes to Karen, on where they stood among the other families.

Susan couldn't help herself. "I take it, you do not want us asking Stick questions, to aid in finding Petey. You grabbed your son, like we were poison ivy. We came out to help find the missing boy. We are sorry to have made that mistake. Hope you find the child." Susan and Karen turned to walk away.

"No, no, you got that wrong, cried the mom of the missing boy. Please stay. I fear my boy is lost forever."

Stick's mom saw her mistake grabbing her son. "I'm sorry, I thought my son was scared and your questionings was not helping him. I was comforting him. There was no meaning inferred, other than that."

Stick's mom was a typical short, and dumpy mom. She wore a dress keeping her hair rolled up in curlers. She wore glasses and a lot of makeup, unlike the biker women. Many of them wore jeans or shorts, with blouses. Some had a bandana, holding their hair up in a bun. Susan was not the typical biker woman. Her and a few bikers women wore nice fitting clothes. Mainly, due to Laura styling. She was a model and dressed to the hilt, every time she went out. Some of the biker women began to emulate her way of dressing.

Mrs. Parker, Stick's mother, stepped back, after telling Karen and Susan. She saw the look in their eyes anticipating either to make another snide remark. She was glad none came.

Susan paused, calming herself. "Please calm down Mrs. Petey, we will help you find your boy. Karen, call the club house, inform them about the missing boy. You lady, call the police. No, never mind. Cheryl walked up. Cheryl, call the police. You are nearest our house to make the call."

"Oh, thank you, replied the other mother. My name is Parker, Mrs. Parker fumbling with how to present herself, to the two friendly biker women. I came outside to help Petey's mom. Our sons are friends. I heard her screams." Mrs. Parker waited to hear what either biker woman's response would be. None came, she continue with her tail.

"Years ago, children often played in the woods. They ventured only a little way into the forest. There is a cabin. A man was killed in that cabin. Many thought it was a bad omen for the woods. Soon after the man was killed, a child went missing in the woods. These same woods, we are near. Just yesterday, it was said, three children went into that same cabin They were found locked inside. Rumors say, a ghost was the reason, why they were lured to the cabin and locked inside."

Karen looked at Susan. Both thought the same thing. It was their ghost, but the children went in to find drugs, that was reason they were locked inside. That and hitting Boo with a can.

Both Karen and Susan appeared amazed hearing the tale about their cabin. The story was told, to make people keep away from the cabin. It worked.

Then, Mrs. Parker, Stick, her son, made a comment chilling both women to the bone. "That cabin needs to be burnt to the ground."

Susan spoke quick. "That cabin is on our property. If any burning is to be done, it will be by our people. The cabin is locked and a sign posted to keep out."

"Oh, I thought some kid was living in the cabin. Why any parent would allow their child to live in that filthy cabin, without any electricity or bathroom conveniences, is beyond me. I heard, he goes hungry and hunts small animals for food. My son told me, he was as skinny as a rail. He looked half starved."

"No, no, we know about the kid. He was living in the cabin, as part of his training. We use the cabin, for our training."

"Oh, what kind of training is that?"

"Oh, learning to fight, kill, survival, and weapon practicing. The usual kind of training required for all our members and their families."

Mrs. Stick was dumb struck, from Susan's remark. Then realized, she was making fun of her after Susan smiled. "Oh, I see." Secretly Mrs. Stick thought some of what Susan said, might harbor some truth.

Mrs. Parker continued talking about the events years pass, of the first reported missing child. This child went into the woods, he never came out. The police were called. A search lasted for days, finding nothing. They did find a torn shirt, with blood on it. I was there, when it happened. I ventured into this forest a short way. My dress was torn to shreds. I gave up and walked out of these terrible woods. I found burrs all over my clothes and ticks on me. I won't ever go back in that forest. It has all kinds of nasty things, living there."

Karen thought to herself; "Mrs. Parker wasn't going to be much help."

"Oh my," an awful screaming came out of the woods, for weeks. It was a terrible scream. Many think it was no animal, they knew about, making the screams. When I heard them, I knew it wasn't nothing of this world. I am going home with my boy; I advise you, to do the same. The boy is gone, like the others before him."

Mrs. Parker takes Stick by the arm, dragging him homeward. Susan with Karen walks over to Stinky's mom. She was tempted to hold her nose from the reeking odor.

"How in God's name, can her friend hold on to that woman with that smell," snipped Karen to Susan in a whisper?

Susan's reply almost caused a laugher to burst out from Karen. "I know, I almost passed out, when I caught wind of her stink. Karen, if that story is true and whatever took the children returned, we better get help, fast? I wish Mike or Cho were here."

"Me too, cited Karen. Susan, it just occurred to me, Mike lives within this forest and our children go to the cabin to train."

"Your right, but we have Mister Casper. He would let us know of any evil spirits in the forest. I think, we need to get the word to the other families in the sub. The way that Mrs. Parker reeks with stink and Petey's mom, I think they talk to very few people."

"Yep, I was thinking the same thing, Susan."

THE DEAL

The morning sun had yet, to dry the dew from the leaves, when a terrible truth was revealed about the mob on the mainland. Chopper, along with Razor and Bone were sitting at the club eating breakfast. Cho was returning from his honeymoon, their wives were preparing for their welcome home ceremony, hence, the breakfast at the club house.

Miriam, Penny, Susan, and Bell were to plan the surprise party for the two newlyweds, Cho and Laura. Susan did not show up at the Cho' home.

A phone rang at the bar. The biker tending the bar, answered the phone. It was for Chopper.

Chopper answered with a bellicose, "hello." The voice at the other end of the line was the ambassador on the island, where the Seal team disembarked, to leave to the mainland. News came early that week of the success, of the team. Chopper expected the same message, when the ambassador answered.

"Mister Chopper, my call concerns the team sent to the mainland. Many people were killed at a villa. Some strange letters were reported in the news, appearing on all of the victims. My office was contacted by the local police. We learned, another attack was forth coming, hours after the villa massacre. Many men were found dead near a cave entrance. Inside, the cave had collapsed. Bodies were presumed to be trapped inside. Another entrance was located nearby. They found more dead soldiers. No bodies were found, other than the mob's men. The police believe, the people responsible were one in the same attacking the villa. No news from our source whether, the killers got away. A storm abruptly arose by the mainland. We sent a ship to offer aid to victims caught in the raging seas. Many boats were sunk. No survivors have been reported, found."

Chopper heard something other than what the ambassador said. "Both attacks went off successfully. His men got safely away in a boat. The next part of the message was disturbing to him. A storm at sea, with many boats sunk. No survivors. His men left the mainland in a boat, the implication meant the Seal Team's boat was sunk in the storm."

Chopper expected his men to evade detection from the local police. There was no need to galvanize a new team, to search for his men. It was typical for evading detection, but now that changed.

The message continued; "Many ships are assisting the mainland search and rescue teams. Other small fishing boats were scanning the seas. The waters are too rough for many searching in their small boats. Once the sea settles, many boats will be out searching for any survivors from the storm."

The party was Miriam's doings. She took command of all the necessities. Bell and the other women, followed her directions. This was Miriam's element she strived in. Any party to be had, go get Miriam to organize it, was, the battle cry within the club.

Miriam's first decision was, where to have the party. Many felt Cho and Laura's home was, the obvious place. Miriam immediately disagreed. Her reasons were, their home was too small. The club house or Chopper's home. Chopper said, "no."

The second decision was, the theme for the party. Miriam disagreed with the majority of women, again. "No, definitely not a wedding theme, there will be one, when they remarry. It is Fall, the leaves are changing, our club is changing, we will have a Fall party to celebrate the change." Again, Miriam was right. The theme was brilliant.

Quickly, Miriam began barking out assignments to each woman. "Bell, you are in charge of the getting the flowers. Penny, you, and Susan are the best cooks, besides Laura. Where is Susan? Tell her, when she arrives, Penny, we will need a big cake. Rhonda and Judy take charge of the dinnerware. Now, for the main course, I think turkey. No, not turkey, maybe ham, no, not ham. Ah ha,

Roast. I have decided! Yes, roast will do, quite well. Turkey we will save for Thanksgiving."

Once the decision was reached by Miriam, every woman, at the meeting was on the phone talking to the other biker women. Rita and Cindy, to help with cooking diner, Susan can be in charge of that team. Penny enlisted her closest friends to aid in making the cake. Miriam barked orders like Chopper. Chaos swiftly turned to order. It wasn't long after that, Chopper was asked to leave his home. He went to the club for breakfast. There, he met Razor and Bone with the same problem confronting them, wives.

After the club house, all agreed to go to Darby's bar in town. They realized, the women would come a calling, when all settled down. They figured; Darby's would keep them safe from their wives' constant demands.

It was a good plan, until the phone call came. Chopper had to decide, whether to inform the club of the missing Seal team or keep quiet. He kept quiet until, he had more to go on. They were Seals and could survive any storm at sea.

The watering hole at Darby's was not the best place to hang out, when the Riders first came to this town. They were met with patrons, not so happy about some rowdy bikers coming into their town. A few local boys tried to persuade the bikers to leave. After a fight, drinks paid by the bikers, thereafter, when any bikers came to the bar, the locals became more friendly.

Bikers were now welcome in the bar. Drink ran free and plentiful. Smiling face and drunk patrons were plentiful, too. Bone never had any trouble in bars. He would walk into any bar, and immediately any disharmony ceased. It was far better to play nicey-nice with the big guy. It didn't hurt their pride much, when he bought rounds of never-ending drinks.

Darby even spent some of his money for a hitching post, for their bikes. It was reserved for only the Riders, no other bikes. Often bikers came to the bar, ripe for meanness. It was due to their wives kicking them out of their homes. They took out all their frustration out, in the bar. Darby was not happy but the money made up for it.

Inside the bar, Bone was first to notice two strange men wearing suits at the counter, drinking glasses of wine. "Hell no, was his first thoughts. We ain't going to have some dandies come and ruin our watering hole." He marched straight to the bar, slamming his fist hard on the countertop.

Darby heard the slam. He knew it was Bone. He knew, when he slammed his fist on the countertop, there was going to be trouble.

One man was tall, thin, with horn rimmed glasses, wearing a pinned striped suit. On top of his head was a black derby. A cane was lapped over one arm, it had a golden crown for the grip. The other man was taller, stouter, had muscles, wearing a suit, ill-fitting for his size. His suit was black, no cane, and no hat.

Chopper spotted the man; Bone was sizing up. He ignored the dandy. Chopper noticed the big man, to be a chauffeur. The large limo he spotted before entering the bar, made his assessment valid. Chopper attempted to stop Bone from going to the counter. The chauffeur was a large man. Not a sound was heard in the bar seeing Bone enter, wearing a scowl written across his face.

Bone neared the driver. A beer was quickly sat on the countertop. A huge hand raised not to take the beer but tapped the man on his shoulder. The chauffeur did not answer the tap, from Bone. He continued to drink his glass of wine. A second tap was required. Mike often said, "a tap from Bone was like a hammer hitting a nail."

The driver turned to face a man bigger, larger, and meaner, than himself. He gulped his wine down, seeing a man shoulders and not his eyes or the top of a man's head was startling. He never saw a man as big or bigger than himself. The thin man hired him as a chauffeur, mainly for his large, intimidating size.

The thin man remembered the last a quaintest he had, with these bikers in a small town. "I went to see a young boy making an incredible walk across the country, to find his family. The boy believed his mom was killed exiting a bar, drunk to the point, she couldn't walk. The first car knocked her down running over her. The second car, just ran over her. The third car stopped, after the first wheels ran over her. Then, backed up. Mike attempted to reach for his mom. A bar maid stopped him, before the third car stopped."

"I went to that town, the boy lived, to have the young man sign a movie contract. I met that abdominal Master Cho. One touch, that's all. I sat on the bike holding onto that behemoth; wet with my own urine. That dark, bumpy road; to the house, we were reconstructing for our next movie. Some gangsters arrived at the house. They went to kill everyone with Mike. Mike was injured, saving his friends. After that adventure, and my meeting with Master Cho, it was necessary to get a man equal to the task, to protect me. My man, never met Bone."

The driver was issued two revolvers and a set of brass knuckles. Seeing this huge man before him, the chauffeur quietly slid one hand into his coat pocket. It had not gone unnoticed, by Bone. Before his fingers slid in to the brass knuckles, Bone being in many bar fights, reacted.

The chauffeur spoke, just as his last finger entered the knuckles ring. "Err, Mr. Peabody, this man has a question to ask you."

Peabody turned around. Two words were uttered from his mouth. "That's him."

Bone saw the face of Peabody. He met him briefly, at the theater. Bone had an eye for faces. He never forgot, once he took sight of a man. Peabody was that sight.

"Oh, it is you, Pee in your Pants Body, wasn't that we called you?"

People at the bar watched Bone approach the two men. They expected some trouble. They got a good laugh, instead. They heard Bone call the dandy, Pee in your Pants Body and roared.

Bone recalled how Mr. Peabody peed in his pants. "He never could keep his mouth, in check. Even with Cho's first, second, and third touch, the man just couldn't learn his lesson. What are you doing here Mr. Pee in your Pants Body?"

"How dare you."

"Before you say another word, you might tell this driver, to slowly peel his fingers from that brass knuckles in his coat pocket, and remove the limo from our reserved parking space."

"What spot? I did not observe a private parking spot in front of this seedy, run down, slop bar for pigs, to drink at."

"Well mister, you seem to enjoy drinking, at this slop bowl of ours. Don't make me ask a second time, Mr. Pee in your Pants Body."

"Well, my big man, you seem to not observed standing by me, is my man. He is quite capable of rendering any of your feeble attempts, to intimidate myself. You might reconsider those choice words you spoke, with unfit grammar usage. Oh, the name is Peabody. That is spoken with a mister, in front of the name."

Chopper listened to the fool. "He never learned his lessons. You would think, any normal man, would think twice, before speaking to a man, the size of Bone," thinking to himself.

Peabody nudged his driver. "Be so kind, to tell this oaf, we will move our car, when we prepare to leave, not a second sooner." Peabody turned away from his driver, to take a sip of wine. The driver pulls his hand from his pocket releasing the brass knucklers.

"You heard the boss, back off bozo." That was the driver's first mistake. The second mistake came, when he jabbed a finger into Bone's chest.

"Big, big mistake," Chopper thought watching.

Razor sat down to watch. He ordered beers for the them. The patrons knew Bone and felt his tempers, many times. The bar went stone-dead quiet. Not a word was heard. Razor and Chopper gasped, seeing the big man jab Bone, with his finger. It was apparent, the driver was very stupid, blind, or mistakenly believed, he was the baddest man on Earth. That was until, he met our Bone. Two titans were going to clash. They and all the patrons had a ring-side seat. Stories will be told, for years to come, were subtle whispers, roaming Darby's bar.

The chauffeur made the first swing at Bone. Bone stood waiting for the hit. Wop on the jaw. Bone made little motion from the hit. He did feel a slight tingle in his fingers. The chauffeur stared at the big man.

"That hit, I gave him, should have dropped ten men or an elephant."

Bone shook his head and smiled at the driver. The chauffeur peed in his pants. Bone commented to Pee in your Pants Body, "does all your people pee in their pants." Peabody turned to look. He heard the dribble of urine tapping on the floor. He smelled the pee. Swiftly, Mr. Peabody removed a hanky putting it over his nose. The smell, offended him.

"Hey, that was not a bad shot, there, Mr. Chauffeur. I been hit with better."

The driver's mouth gaped open. That was the third mistake the driver made. He should have kept his mouth shut. Bone lowered the boom from above. He was known for his hammer fist strike to the top of the head. Few men survived the earthquake, that followed the blow. The driver stood motionless. The whole bar gasped with unbelievability, he was still standing and breathing.

Both eyes glazed over, the driver. His breathing slowed., Then, came a wobble. One to the left and one back to the right. Then came a twirl, followed by two knees giving way. He stopped, once the knees hit the floor. He remained kneeling, not awake and not dead. Some teeth fell from his mouth. Blood oozed over his lips. He bit his tongue, from the downward blow given him by Bone. Chopper walked over, to check his vitals.

"He is alive, Bone. Peabody, what in the hell are you doing, in this town, cited Chopper looking up from checking the driver's pulse?

Bone grabbed Pee in his Pants Body by his skinny, long neck. "You heard my boss. You need to answer him." Blood was limited to his brain, from the tight grip Bone had around Pee in his Pants Body's neck. His faced turned blue.

Chopper grabbed hold of Bone's hand. "Ease up big fellow. He can't answer questions." After some hacking, Pea in his Pants Body spoke. He looked at the giant man with fear.

"Not again, this can't be happening to me, again. I got the best, the biggest man around."

Bone tightened his grip. "Hack, hack, I came to talk to Mike. Please stop choking me," begged Pee in his Pants Body. On the floor, was a puddle of urine dripping down Mr. Pee in his Pants Body's legs, mingling with the driver's pee. The patrons roared with laughter.

Chopper spoke, "let the fool down, Bone. You can play with him later, if he forgets to respect us."

Bone turned sad. "There came an ooohhh emancipating from the patrons, looking at Bone's sad face. They felt bad for him. He couldn't play with his new toys. Daddy made him quit," all thought, but only one man dared to whisper out loud.

"Mr. Pabody, see what you did, you made Bone sad. I hope you have good news. I surely don't want my man, to be unhappy. I think that is best for you, too. Please try hard to make him smile, again."

"That was not a polite, how do you do. You have your driver attack my man. See, bad manners are not welcomed here. You respect me and I will respect you. Easy peasy, replied Chopper.

"Yes, easy peasy, as you say. I apologize for my bad manners. I came here to speak with Mike. Cho made a deal with us, on the boy's behalf." Bone squeezed Peabody's neck. "Sorry, sorry, I mean Mike, not boy," replied Peabody. Bone eased off his squeeze.

"I am sorry to tell you, Mike is not here. Cho was married and on his honeymoon. He is expected to return, in a few days."

"I was do hoping to finish this today. I could remain until Mr. Cho returns. Can you direct me to a good hotel, Mr. Chopper?"

"Nonsense. You will stay at the club house, until Cho returns. Mike will be away for some time, I'm afraid." Peabody was about to replied to his invitation to lodge at some run-down biker club house. He kept that to himself.

"It will please me to lodge at your club house, until Mr. Cho came back from his honeymoon."

Chopper couldn't wait to see Peabody drive that beautiful limo down his pot holed dirt road, to the club house bar. Bobby was in the bar backroom for the time being. He was working off his sentence, for his attempt at killing Mike. Chopper decided to wait, until the limo drove to the bar, before he filled him in on staying at the cabin.

"Oh, Mr. Pee in your Pants Body, that limo is parked in our reserved space. Do you want me to move the car, for you?" Bone, grinned from ear to ear. He hoped he would say yes.

Chopper followed Bones request, he made to Peabody. Bone will be more than happy to move your limo. See, he is smiling. You want to keep him smiling, don't you?"

"No, no, I will move the car."

Peabody was abhorred to put his hand into the pocket of his driver, to fetch the keys. Either that or let the big oaf make hash out of the car. With a snickered grin on his face, Peabody slid his hand into the driver's pocket. To his bad luck, it was the wrong pocket. He pulled his hand quickly from the pocket and moved to the other pocket. He wanted to heave touching the driver's pockets, a second time. This time, he found the keys. He walked out of the bar and moved the car.

Peabody retuned inside. Razor waved him over to their table. He removed his hanky, wiping the seat, before sitting. The bar keeper brought a glass of beer. Froth from the mug of beer splattered on impact to the table. Foam landed on Peabody's silk, suit coat. Razor and Bone smiled.

Razor spit a wad of tobaccy in a spittoon, by Peabody's feet. It made Mister Peabody want to heave, again. The beer, he drank, reluctantly. He developed a love of fine wines. This swill turned his stomach. The second beer was no better. Before they left the bar, he downed five beers. His driver was awake, groggy but awake.

Razor found amusement spitting tobaccy in the spittoon. After six beers, his aimed was off. Most of any wad landed on Peabody's suede shoes. He could care less, after the fifth beer. He still had a habit of cleaning his clothes every time, he got dust on them. He held back from wiping the tobaccy off his shoe, when he looked at Razor staring at him.

LOST AT SEA

Six men crowded in a small boat riding on a turbulence sea, of high rolling waves, with hurricane winds buffeting their small craft. It was not lost on any of them, they might join a long list of men, lost at sea. Before the sun settled on the horizon, the wave grew in size proportionally with the blowing winds. The sky was black and made blacker as night approached.

"Quick men, tie everything down," shouted Jack. Many worked on the sea but lacked any real knowledge of seafaring skills. The storm came to men lacking the abilities to cope with it.

Mike recalled the last storm, he was in. It was a hurricane. "I wasn't at sea, instead, I was locked inside a make shift tent made from sticks and grasses for shelter. Rain poured inside my flimsy shelter. It held against the strong winds constant buffeting. I left, when the rain eased up. I learned a lesson on that day."

"I was in the eye of the storm. It was calm. Soon, that calm was replaced with winds blowing from the opposite direction. I fought the winds and rains to a barn. I was sick and fainted in the straw. Then, I awoke with an old man tying my hands to a post. I can still feel the sting, of that whip tearing at my flesh. It ended when his wife screamed, release that child."

I ran from the barn, until I couldn't run no more. I fell just outside a farm house. The family took me in caring for me. I had pneumonia. I awoke trying to leave the home, unnoticed. I was glad to get caught. Jack and Ellie were good to me. Jack taught me how to forge. His son, Beau, how to noodle for fish." Mike grabbed the knife on his belt. "It was still there."

"I need to go back and see them, Mike thought bouncing up and down in the small boat. I sent them money, before coming to live at the club. I hoped they didn't think, I owed them anything. They made that clear, before I left them. They needed the money and never once made it known to me."

Each wave was followed by a ceaseless crashing of other waves. Each wave grew in size. Every man was bounce around the small boat. One Seal was thrown overboard by the mast ripping from its tie down. The mast slammed him hard, kicking him from the boat. It took some effort getting him back inside, the safety of the boat.

The waves seemed to swallow the boat. Up and down, rode their boat on the waves. Water flowed into the boat. More water, than one bucket could handle. Soon, the boat was filled with water.

Jack yells to his men. "If the boat sinks, stay with it. Don't get separated. It is better than trying to thread water, hang on to the boat."

Night was upon them. The storm remained the same, winds made the winds colder. Being wet, made it worse. A crack was heard.

Beedie yelled, "the mast."

All hands scrambled to save the mast from the winds. The mast went with the winds. Each man watched the sail spin across the boat, into the churning waters. It floated away, into the darkness quickly.

Morning came. The sun, never was seen rising. The sky was still black as sage cloth. Winds kept up a steady howling. Everyone was soaked through and through. Some began to shiver. The rain halted for some hours. It was a glad tiding to all of them. The sun was still blinded, by the dark clouds.

Night came again, to quick. Before the night, Mike looked at the sky. "What was that old adage, "red skies in the morning, a sailor's delight and red skies at night, sailor's beware, or was it the other way," Mike pondered?

Jack became bellowing out a constant stream of orders. "Mike, check the mast, see if there is a leak, where it once was. Cowboy check our water. Pretty drop the anchor. It will keep us steady. JoJo, look for damage to our boat. Help JoJo plug any holes, Tall."

Beedie didn't answer Jack's call. "Skip Jack, check Beedie." Beedie had not moved since the mast flew off, into the raging waters.

It was dark, when it happened. Beedie was lying over the rail of the boat. No one noticed, he had not moved for a long time.

Cowboy was the first to get to him. He rolled him over. He looked back at Jack. "He's dead, Jack."

"What, how," asked Jack?

Cowboy saw the splinter, sticking out of his chest. The spar broke. It, it splintered. One splinter stabbed him in the heart."

Silence came over the boat. None could speak. Then, Jack spoke, it broke the spell of Beedie's loss. "We will wrap his body in what remains of the sail and give him a proper burial at sea."

Mike was agape hearing Jack say, "bury Beedie at sea. I thought you said, we leave no man behind, Jack?"

Jack wasn't in the mood to explain to Mike, his reasons. "Beedie was the second man he lost, on a mission. Mike was there, on both missions."

Cowboy pulled Mike to one side. "Mike, we can't allow his body to stay on board. It will begin to smell. Then, there are other reasons I am not ready to discuss, with you. This is not easy for Jack or the rest of us. We are Navy men. We welcome a burial at sea. Wasn't your father, in the Navy?"

"Yes. I see your point. I 'll tell this to Jack. Mike thought about his dad's death. He had a ceremony on board his ship. In reality, his body was never recovered from the plane crash over the ocean. Mike stared at all the Seal members on board. Strange, he never noticed the beards sprouting on their faces. He felt his chin, no hair grew there."

By the beginning of the third day, the storm was abating. Jack spoke to his crew.

"Men, this storm has twisted us in many ways. I have no idea, where land may be. The sun has not shown through the thick cloud cover. Three days, this boat tossed and turned. The night sky and day, gave little to guide me. I fear, we are lost at sea. But there is hope. Look at Mike. He can't grow a beard."

Everyone laughed. Spirits soared for a while. Food was gone, water was two caps for each man, daily. Five days at best, was Jack's best guess.

Mike spoke up. "Hey, I nearly forgot. I got some food stashed away in my pack, also, I have fishing line and hooks. There should be baits. I never travel without some means to get food. I got a large sheet of clear plastic. It can heat water, to make steam condensate for drinking, when the sun comes out of its hiding. It's not much, but will keep us hydrated."

"I knew there was good reason to bring you along, Mike," sniped Pretty.

"Ha, ha, those candy bars I got in my pack; you better be nice, if you want a piece, Pretty?"

"Ha, ha, to you. Jack's in charge. He will give me a piece."

"I don't know about that, Pretty? They are Mike's after all."

"Quit your kidding, you two. Okay. Okay, I was just funning. Gee, can't anyone take a joke anymore?"

Jack pondered on Mike's remark. "He was becoming more of an asset, every day."

Jack, was soon to learn just how much Mike would prove to be an asset, in the coming days. The storm began again. They were in the eye of the storm, when the calm came.

EPILOGUE

Book 7
The Tranquil Forest

Jack and his small band of Seals were entering, the second half of the storm. Beedie was killed, by a splinter off the mast. Would their luck hold. A new threat was to challenge the team, the boat broke in half. Mike was separated from the team. He was injured, afloat, alone in the sea.

Back home, a new problem came to plague the Riders and the subdivision families. A child went missing. The cause was too terrible, to consider. The community was more divided than ever before. Living deep in the Tranquil Forest, was a mansion hiding a secret. What escaped from the mansion, would destroy the town, if not stopped.

Cheryl learned; love can be difficult. Many of her friends, hated her. She was ostracized from their group. Peabody arrives and quickly finds himself embroiled in the new dangers the bikers were to face alone. What help came from the community, was too little and useless. Cho returns with his bride. He learns the fate of the Seal team. He has little time, to deal with the pompous Mr. Peacock.

Mike had new troubles. He found himself was on an island, inhabited by pirates. His thoughts worried for his companions lost at sea. A terrible game was played on the island. Back home another more dire game of life and death was coming. A terrible, ferocious mythical creature is released.

BOOKS TO READ, NOT YET IN PUBLICATION

HOPEFULLY SOON

<u>BOOKS</u>

1. Book 1 One fine Adventure in print and e-book
2. Book 2 Rama Rowdies in print and e-book
3. Book 3 Battle in Atlanta waiting publ.
4. Book 4 Rumble in the Jungle waiting publ.
5. Book 5 Desert Storm waiting publ.
6. Book 6 Wicked City waiting publ.

<u>BOOKS</u> written, not yet in publ.

7. Book 7 Tranquil Forest
8. Book 8 Ghost of Past
9. Book 9 The Gift
10. Book 10 Voodoo Queen
11. Book 11 Alien Agenda
12. Book 12 Sensei's dilemma
13. Book 13 Wisp of the Willow
14. Book 14 Time Loop
15. Book 15 Invisible Assassins